MARIUS'

D0505510

SANDS OF EGYPT

BY S. J. A. TURNEY

1ST EDITION

"Marius' Mules: nickname acquired by the legions after the general Marius made it standard practice for the soldier to carry all of his kit about his person."

For Sarah and Alistair

Also by S. J. A. Turney:

Continuing the Marius' Mules Series

Marius' Mules I: The Invasion of Gaul (2009)
Marius' Mules II: The Belgae (2010)
Marius' Mules III: Gallia Invicta (2011)
Marius' Mules IV: Conspiracy of Eagles (2012)
Marius' Mules V: Hades' Gate (2013)
Marius' Mules VI: Caesar's Vow (2014)
Marius' Mules: Prelude to War (2014)
Marius' Mules VII: The Great Revolt (2014)
Marius' Mules VIII: Sons of Taranis (2015)
Marius' Mules IX: Pax Gallica (2016)
Marius' Mules X: Fields of Mars (2017)
Marius' Mules XI: Tides of War (2018)

The Praetorian Series

The Great Game (2015)
The Price of Treason (2015)
Eagles of Dacia (2017)
Lions of Rome (2019)

The Damned Emperors Series

Caligula (2018)
Commodus (2019)

The Knights Templar Series

Daughter of War (2018)
The Last Emir (2018)
City of God (2019)
The Winter Knight (Winter 2019)

The Ottoman Cycle

The Thief's Tale (2013)

The Priest's Tale (2013)
The Assassin's Tale (2014)
The Pasha's Tale (2015)

Tales of the Empire

Interregnum (2009)
Ironroot (2010)
Dark Empress (2011)
Insurgency (2016)
Invasion (2017)
Jade Empire (2017)

Roman Adventures (Children's Roman fiction with Dave Slaney)

Crocodile Legion (2016)
Pirate Legion (Summer 2017)

Short story compilations & contributions:

Tales of Ancient Rome vol. 1 - S.J.A. Turney (2011)
Tortured Hearts vol 1 - Various (2012)
Tortured Hearts vol 2 - Various (2012)
Temporal Tales - Various (2013)
A Year of Ravens - Various (2015)
A Song of War – Various (Oct 2016)

For more information visit http://www.sjaturney.co.uk/
or http://www.facebook.com/SJATurney
or follow Simon on Twitter @SJATurney

PREFACE

It is not my habit to add a preface to the start of the Marius' Mules books, yet I have elected to do so here solely to give the reader a valuable word of advice. Due to the nature of the story in these pages, and of the story originally told by Aulus Hirtius in Caesar's name, the action of this, the Alexandrian War, is very tight, non-stop and extremely convoluted. The action largely takes place within the city, and the geography of ancient Alexandria is already troublesome before throwing into it new Greek terms like 'Heptastadion', and trying to make clear which of the three harbours is being described at any time. As such, I have added a map to the opening pages of this book, which is also available on my website and on my Facebook page. I strongly urge you to familiarise yourself thoroughly with the map before you begin, as this will make reading a great deal easier going forward. For maximum ease, print off a copy of the map and keep it to hand, at least until you are as familiar with the geography as I now am.

Happy reading and cartographising!

Simon

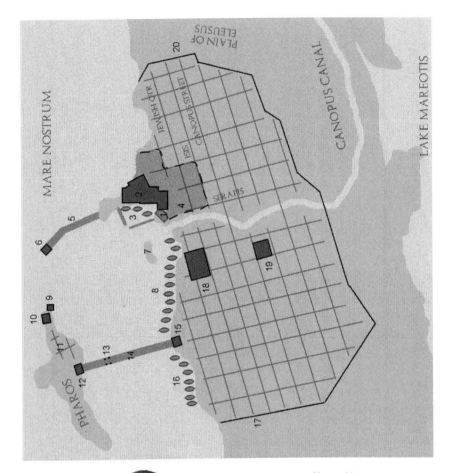

ALEXANDRIA

IN THE TIME OF CLEOPATRA VII

1   Theatre
2   Palace
3   Palace Harbour
4   Palace redoubt
5   Diabathra mole
6   Diabathra fort
7   Antirrhodos Island
8   Great Harbour
9   Pharos fort
10 Great Lighthouse
11 Pharos town
12 N. Heptastadion Fort
13 Arched bridge
14 Heptastadion
15 S. Heptastadion Fort
16 Commercial Harbour
17 Walls
18 Great Library
19 Paneum
20 Canopian Gate

MARE NOSTRUM

PLAIN OF ELEUSUS

CANOPUS CANAL

LAKE MAREOTIS

JEWISH QTR

CANOPUS STREET

ISIS

SERAPIS

PHAROS

He came towards me as I stood
And I placed myself next to him
Every heart was burning for me
Women and men pounding
Every mind was willing me on,
'is there any hero that can fight against him?'
And then his shield, his dagger, his armour, his holder of spears
fell,
As I approached his weapons
I made my face dodge
And his weapons were wasted as nothing
Each piled on the next
Then he made his charge against me
He imagined he would strike my arm
As he moved over me, I shot him,
My arrow lodged in his neck,
He cried out, and fell on his nose,
I felled him with his dagger
I uttered my war-cry on his back,
Every Asiatic lowing
I gave praise to Mont
As his servants mourned for him

From "The Story of Sinuhe", anonymous Egyptian author c.
1875 BC

In announcing the swiftness and fierceness of this battle to one of his friends at Rome, Amantius, Caesar wrote these words: 'I came; I saw, I conquered.'

Plutarch: "The life of Julius Caesar"

CHAPTER ONE

Royal palace, Alexandria, November 48 BC

'Why would they risk putting into port here, with us in control?'

Fronto drummed his fingers on the windowsill, peering out across the wide harbour. The main stretch with its numerous jetties and wharves was almost empty, barring a few intrepid merchants. The ships that had brought Caesar's army to Aegyptus wallowed in the private Palace Harbour, which they failed to fill despite its smaller dimensions. Gulls wheeled overhead and the city steamed. Fronto would never get used to this perpetual heat, even in late autumn. The Alexandrians claimed that the sea breeze kept it cool. If this was their idea of cool, then he'd hate to experience Aegyptus *away* from the coast.

The queen looked up from her hastily-drawn maps, glancing at the legate in the window.

'Achillas has my brother's army marching through the delta, and we know they are less than a day away. At this point, there is no reasonable position on the coast to anchor a fleet that size and board an army in such numbers. And while there are navigable channels, moving warships of that size and number presents many challenges. Achillas knows your numbers are few, and therefore so will his commanders. They will feel safe putting into the city and meeting with the army when they arrive. They cannot comprehend, I am certain, how any force as small as yours could present a threat to them.'

Caesar smiled. 'Then they underestimate us at their peril. This cannot be more than half of the Aegyptian fleet, but securing it will both make our own supremacy possible and halve the seaborne threat. Fronto, the port is yours. Take a cohort of the Sixth away from preparations and secure me the harbour. All other infantry are to continue their work until the last moment.'

Fronto nodded. Every man upon whom Caesar could call, and every slave available, were working on the defences. The Aegyptian general Achillas, leading the king's army even without him, were mere hours from the city, and the fight would be a hard one when they arrived, for they outnumbered the Romans by a large margin.

The city walls could never be held against them. That had been the first notion of theirs the queen had quashed. The circuit was simply too long for the number of men at Caesar's command. They would be too stretched and inevitably leave weak spots. Instead, the queen had worked with Caesar over a hastily-drawn map and viewed the city from the palace roof, pointing out the narrow kill points in the streets nearby and those alleys that could be readily sealed.

Working together, the general and the queen had created a perimeter that could be swiftly put in place in the streets around the palace, enclosing that complex, a theatre, and the royal harbour. They could not hope to hold the city, but they could hold an acropolis, as the queen insisted on calling it, a redoubt formed around the palace. Walls had been constructed with fighting platforms, all by the few legionaries at the general's command.

Now, they were relatively secure, but were working on further defences, with the queen's unparalleled knowledge of the city. Four different concentric systems had been drawn around the palace, with this strong redoubt as the last. Each would slow the enemy and cause many casualties before the true siege began.

Leaving the shrewd ruler and the general, with a respectful bow of his head, Fronto ducked out of the room and hurried along the corridor. Down a wide, decorative staircase he encountered Salvius Cursor and his brother, the pair arguing with gesticulations. It seemed the natural state for the brothers. They were unable to speak without argument, yet it seemed to produce results and so no one intervened.

'Where is Decimus Carfulenus?'

Cursor looked up, hushing his brother to narrow eyes with a finger.

'In the square, shouting at someone.'

Fronto nodded. 'How go the defences?'

'We'll be ready for Achillas. He's going to pay a high price to reach the palace.'

'Good.' Ignoring them as they went back to their arguing, Fronto hurried on through the monumental complex, all lotus flower capitals, animal statues and bright colours, and through the door between two of Caesar's bodyguard.

In short order he reached the square and found Centurion Carfulenus berating a junior officer. The senior centurion of the Sixth was young for a man in such a position, not quite the regulation thirty years of age for even a junior centurion, and more possessed of wit and speed than of strength and inherent violence. What he lacked in the usual physical bulk of his type, though, he more than made up for in controlled force. When Fronto found the man, he was busy berating a legionary for the state of his armour, which showed numerous rust patches, a common problem in the salty, warm conditions of the Aegyptian coast.

'Centurion?'

Carfulenus turned and bowed his head.

'Legate.'

'Perhaps half the Aegyptian fleet is inbound for the harbour. I presume you've heard?'

The centurion nodded. 'Good,' Fronto went on. 'It is believed that the ships are manned only by a nautical crew with no marines or military, all their manpower currently bolstering Achillas' force. If this is the case, they should be a relatively easy target. We cannot afford to let the fleet combine with the army. The First Cohort are to come with me. Our remit is to secure the harbour and overcome the fleet, keeping control of it and not allowing it to fall into Achillas' hands. Are your men up to the job?'

Carfulenus gave a strange, hoarse laugh.

'Easily, Legate. In anticipation, I have three centuries at the harbour already, creating a perimeter and fortifying the approaches.'

'Good man. Gather your soldiers. It is my intention to secure the harbour but keep the men out of sight until the vessels have largely docked. Then we rush them. Any earlier and we run the risk of them fleeing and putting out to sea again.'

The centurion nodded once more and began to bark out orders. Fronto wiped the sweat, which formed rapidly out here in the blistering sun, from his brow and then hurried off to the room in the palace where he now resided. There, one of the palace slaves helped him into his armour. Suitably attired and as hot as he had ever been, he stepped out into the bright gold light once more and found four centuries of the Sixth formed up with Carfulenus, waiting for him.

'The rest?'

'Already on the way with instructions, Legate.'

'Excellent.'

The centurion gave the order to move out, and the cohort marched off through the streets, heading down to the dockside. The Great Harbour of Alexandria consisted of an enormous enclosure with only two exits, one the narrow approach between the Pharos lighthouse and the mole known as the Diabathra. The other was a man made arch in the long Heptastadion mole that linked the city to the Pharos Island and formed the western edge of the enclosure. The Palace Harbour was a separate, smaller affair leading off the main harbour, below the walls of the palace. The main problem they would have was that the main harbour was outside their defensive cordon, as they'd not counted upon a fleet there to protect.

They passed a narrow gate still being completed by soldiers and slaves working side by side, and crossed the bridge across the Canopus Canal that emptied into the harbour here, forming part of their defences. He smiled at the sight. Even a really good commander would lose huge numbers trying to storm that bridge and gate. He had to hand it to the queen, she knew her city and seemed to have a surprisingly acute strategic mind.

By the time they reached the harbour's dockside, he could see the small units, half a century each, blockading the streets that led to it from the city. Barely, however, had he reached the waterfront than a strange horn that resembled a bovine with some sort of digestion issue booed out over the roofs, and the men on watch in the high tower at the dock's far end waved frantically.

In practised response, the men of the Sixth melted away into doors, alleys and alcoves, disappearing from view. Fronto chewed his lip. Something was wrong in this plan. It looked too good.

He turned to the centurion. 'Get two centuries spread out along the harbour side, in units of sixteen. Have them look ready for a fight.'

'Shouldn't be hard, sir. They *are* ready for a fight. But why?'

'The fleet know they're not invisible. If no one comes to challenge them they're going to suspect something's up. We need enough men out there to look like we mean business, but not enough to scare them off.'

Carfulenus smiled viciously. 'Got you, sir.' Turning, he gave the orders, and men fell in along the harbour edge. Fronto stepped back into the shade of an awning, the centurion alongside him, and peered out into the glare, hand shielding his eyes as he squinted.

Past the small island of Antirrhodus that lay in the midst of the harbour with typical Greek carelessness of planning, he could see shapes now approaching the harbour entrance. He watched them slip between the Diabathra and the Pharos and found himself musing. If they wanted to properly control the harbour, they would need to garrison Pharos. Then, they could control all entry to the place. Still, that would be a consideration for later, probably when they had more men.

Two dozen ships, he reckoned. Two dozen vessels of roughly trireme size or thereabouts. There might be small boats too, but it was these big ships that they needed to control in particular. Scrabbling noises made him turn his head, and he realised that the Sixth were moving from alley to alley back out of sight of the dock, finding the best positions from which to race to the jetties.

He smiled. Achillas might be coming with a large army, but it would be Rome that struck the first blow, in the name of the king and queen, of course. After all, not only Cleopatra remained in the palace in close consort with Caesar, but her hated brother Ptolemy and the oily eunuch Potheinus both languished here too, officially opposed to the army led by a general in the king's name. Rome could legitimately claim the moral grounds here, even if it stretched a few points here or there.

Fronto's hand went to the blade at his side and he slowly slid it from the scabbard, steadying himself, breathing slowly. Carfulenus nodded and drew his own blade, steady and alert.

The enemy fleet closed now, sweeping through the harbour, splitting into two groups to skirt Antirrhodus and head for the jetties. Chiding himself for poor estimation, Fronto adjusted his count upwards. Near three dozen big ships, in fact, and several smaller vessels among them. Most were of native Aegyptian design, which was to say basically Greek. Not quite indistinguishable from Roman ships, but very similar, if smaller and more given to speed than power.

He couldn't make out the occupants yet, and chewed on his lip again. If their intelligence was incorrect and those ships were packed with marines, then this was going to be a very short and unpleasant fight.

Slowly, they cut through the water towards the jetties. He realised now that they were slowing more than usual, eyeing the land carefully to see what awaited them. Likely they had timed their arrival to coincide with the approach of Achillas' army so they could link up, but had instead appeared ahead by some hours. They could not know what was awaiting them and were wary. Fronto hoped his estimate had been right.

They watched in silence, the sound of sea slapping against stone and the wheeling cries of gulls overriding both the ambient noise of the city and the rhythmic sound of oars approaching in their hundreds.

Five. Four. Three. Two. One.

He heaved a sigh of relief. He was no sailor – *hated* the sea, in fact – but had been around ships, and men like Brutus, enough now to know how they worked. They had just passed their point of no return. There was no longer sufficient room for a fleet that size to comfortably turn and make for the open sea once more. They were committed now to backwatering, slowing the ships as they glided into position at the jetties.

Squinting, he looked at the small figures on the ships' prows as they neared. For a horrible moment he thought they had indeed been wrong and the ships were packed with soldiers. In fact all they proved to be, as they came closer and the view cleared, was a small unit of sailors armed with swords and shields.

He breathed a sigh of relief. Their numbers would be more or less equal, discounting the oarsmen, who would be unskilled natives, all men of fighting ability having been recruited into the armies of either Cleopatra or Ptolemy. And somehow, the few armed sailors, no matter how experienced they were, he couldn't imagine standing up well against the Sixth.

'Ready the trap, Carfulenus. Whistles at the ready?'

The centurion nodded slightly, sword held in white knuckles, eyes locked on the men at the prows of those ships. Fronto smiled as he watched the vessels move in perfect formation, each lining up with those to either side, such that the entire fleet was putting in at the same time. From their commander's point of view, simultaneous docking would allow them to throw all the men they had against the soldiers on the dock. From Fronto's it meant they were all committed to the disaster with no reserves able to pull back.

Good.

He felt the centurion next to him tensing, waiting for the order, yet Fronto remained silent, watching as the ships came in to the jetties, bumping against timbers, sailors throwing out ropes. The soldiers on the quay began to clatter their swords against the rim of their shields in a rhythmic crash, threatening the approaching Aegyptians. The men on the ship prows waved their swords in the air and shouted imprecations at the waiting soldiers.

As soon as the first ropes were in place, those shipboard warriors left the prow, running across to jump from the ships to the jetties.

'Now?' the centurion said tensely.

Fronto held his hand up, indicating a further wait. He watched as the second line was tied off and the ramps run out. *Now* they were too committed. One rope could easily be cast off and a ship pushed away from a jetty. Two or more ropes and a ramp made it almost impossible to depart with any speed.

'Now,' he said, and Carfulenus lifted the whistle to his lips and blew three short bursts.

All along the dock, the units of the Sixth standing in small knots pulled into tight formation, stepping back as their fellows rushed out of the shadows at the rear and fell in alongside them. In a matter of six heartbeats, the force on the dock went from a smattering of less than two hundred men in disorganised groups to over two thousand in tight formation. Another three bursts from Carfulenus and the call was picked up with two blasts from each centurion.

Along a quarter mile of port, each century moved, their commander having marked their target as the ships slid into dock. It was beautifully orchestrated. Even as the twenty or so armed men leapt from the ships or ran down the ramps to face their laughably small enemy, that enemy increased tenfold and ran for them in formation, boots pounding on the stone, whistles blowing and shouts issuing forth in Latin.

'Come on,' Fronto grinned at the centurion, and then fell in behind the nearest century, racing for the ship.

The song of battle filled him once more. No matter how creaky his joints became, and they were getting noticeably so these days, and no matter how grey his hair, Fronto knew his place in the world and it was generally at the grip-end of a blade amid men screaming their fury at an enemy.

Racing for the nearest ship, he realised as he looked up at the prow that it was the weirdest hybrid of Greece and Aegyptus. A vessel that would not have looked out of place at Salamis or Mytilene, shaped like a traditional Greek ship and with the same ram and the painted eyes, yet with the prow curved up and back, painted in garish colours and depicting some kind of plant life.

The soldiers were all on the jetty now, but the oarsmen to their credit, back up aboard the vessel, were hurrying to grab spars or clubs of some sort. Those in charge had now seen the increased danger and realised belatedly that they had fully committed. All they could do now was fight for control of the ships or try to flee under threat and with diminished numbers, some of their men fighting on the jetty.

The soldiers of the Sixth were good. One of Caesar's most established, veteran units, raised in Gaul and present at Alesia. Acquitting themselves well at Pharsalus they had become the core of the consul's army in the chase to pin down Pompey and were now his strongest unit in Aegyptus.

The century in front of him had closed on the men with swords and spears and had formed up, shields held forth, swords ready, left knee and left shoulder braced into the curved board and head down so that only the eyes showed above the rim. In that very protective formation they moved forwards at an inexorable pace. He watched two Aegyptians with spears throw them inexpertly and then draw swords. One of the cast missiles went wild, skittering across the jetty and disappearing into the water with a splash. Another struck a shield, and could easily have skewered the man behind it, had he not been watchful and prepared. In the end he lurched to the side, pushing his shield forward and out, angling it down even as the missile struck so that the shield might be useless now, but the spear punched only into the ground. The soldier, missing his shield, danced out of the formation to the side and jogged around to fall in at the rear, the next man taking his place.

Then they hit the enemy.

To give the sailors their due, they fought well for who they were and what they wielded. They wore only tunics, lacking armour and helmets. Some had shields and most swords, and they did their duty, fighting on. Three still had spears and were using them from a little further back, jabbing over or between their companions. As Fronto reached the unit and hurried around the side, dangerously close to toppling into the water from the jetty, he saw one of the Sixth fall, blood washing his face where a lucky spear thrust had slid between the cheek plates of his helmet.

After a couple more hairy moments of trying not to topple into the water below, where he risked getting crushed between ship hull and jetty even if his armour didn't pull him to his doom, Fronto reached the fighting. Constricted by the width of the jetty, and no one wanting to get too close to the edge, the fighting was concentrated on a narrow, six-man front, where they hacked and battered at one another. The sailors were fighting for all they were worth, knowing that there was no place to retreat, and they were doing damage, as was evidenced by the fact that when Fronto reached the fore, three of the legionaries lay dead or writhing on the timbers.

Grunting with the effort, he threw himself forwards at the edge of the fight and for a panicky moment thought there was not going to be sufficient room and that he would fall, but managed to right himself and thrust his blade home with some force. The sailor, who had been busy parrying one of the soldiers and had his arm too high, had presented an open armpit to Fronto, who had made the most of it. His blade bit deep into unprotected flesh and the man issued a scream that swiftly passed through a gurgle and into a sigh before he fell back, dead before he touched the timbers.

In truth there was no real need for senior officers to whet their blades here. Oh, there might have been, had reports been incorrect and these ships been crewed with appropriate marines, but they were under-staffed in terms of a fight, and the Sixth more than had their measure. Fronto had been stuck in this seething oven of a land for some time now, though, knowing that enemies were coming for them and they were trapped in the city, and the ability to take out his frustrations on a valid and visible enemy was too good a chance to miss.

One of the sailors, realising a new threat had edged down the flank, turned, covered by his mate, and came at Fronto, sword jabbing out swiftly and wildly, like a nervous man moistening his lips with his tongue. Fronto parried once, twice, three times with ease, but realised suddenly that the man was not simply a bad swordsman. In fact, he was not really trying to wound Fronto at all, but to drive him back, which he was succeeding in doing as Fronto's heel met only empty air and he was forced to lean forwards on his other foot to avoid tumbling from the jetty into the water. The man laughed and jabbed again.

Aware that he was delicately balanced and with little room to strike, Fronto parried one more blow and then struck in the only way he could think of that would help. His left hand shot out, grabbed his assailant by the belt, and heaved it towards himself even as he dived to his left. The swordsman, taken entirely by surprise, fell forwards with a jolt, lurching past Fronto and out into the open air, where he disappeared with a terrified cry.

The sailor was unarmoured and the sucking depths of the harbour would not see an end to him, but the sound of heavy timbers colliding, combined with an unpleasant cracking noise and a brief bloodcurdling scream confirmed that he had been caught between the wallowing ship and the jetty, and had met his gods in that dreadful manner.

The fight would be over in short order, he realised as he righted himself and stabbed hard into the thigh of the nearest sailor, pushing him away as he shrieked.

A groaning noise made him frown, though, and he turned, a suspicion dawning on him.

Yes, the reason the ship had been moving enough to crush the unfortunate sailor was because its captain had decided that the jetty was lost and was pulling what men he could back to the benches ready to depart before the vessel was overrun. One of the ropes had already been released and the ramp was being lifted. There were still just about enough sailors aboard to get it out in the water.

Determination gripping him, Fronto looked back and forth between the ship and the melee on the jetty. He could slip past and get on board, but alone he could hardly take the ship. The Sixth were held back by the sailors, though. He had to end the fight quickly.

One of the enemy turned, realising that Fronto had all but flanked their number at the jetty's edge, and Fronto realised in that moment what he could do. *And* how stupidly dangerous it was, but that seemed of less import.

Sword down at his side he clenched his teeth, put all his weight into his right foot, and launched himself. He'd seen the wrestlers at the baths in Rome doing this sort of thing, and the principle was

11

simple enough, but they were almost universally a lot younger, heavier and more robust than Fronto.

He hit the man preparing to go for him straight in the torso. He felt a line of pain scarred across his thigh as the man's intended strike went wild in the sudden press. Fronto hit him as hard as he could, given the lack of momentum and with only three steps of space to run. Then, like those wrestlers at the baths, Fronto put all his weight into his shoulder and pushed, using his right leg as a brace, heaving and forcing his way forwards.

There were still quite a few of the enemy, but they were closely packed and busy with the melee, not expecting this weird new attack. He sweated and strained, teeth still clenched, pushing that man at the head of a wedge of sailors. The man tried desperately to fight back, to bring his sword to bear or find room for a punch, but Fronto was all over him and the pressure on his chest was immense, making it hard to breathe.

Fronto's shoulder suddenly dropped forwards into space and he wondered what had happened for the blink of an eye until he heard several cries of consternation, then splashes. He grinned and redoubled his efforts. Two steps forwards and he hit the man again, pushing, driving the whole damn lot of them across the jetty and into the water. The legionaries had seen what he was doing now and threw their support in. Some continued to stab at the sailors, keeping them distracted, while three more threw themselves bodily into the fray, helping push the panicked men across the timbers and over the edge.

As more and more sailors toppled, crying, into the water, the soldiers of the Sixth Legion rushed past Fronto to the ship. Men grabbed the ramp that was being lifted and hauled on it, pulling it back. Others grasped the ropes and pulled, hauling the ship back closer.

Fronto almost went into the harbour with the momentum as the last of the sailors plummeted into the green water. Wobbling and shaking, he straightened as more and more of the legionaries ran for the ship.

He turned and looked up.

His men were on the ship now. The sailors on board were surrendering in droves, unarmed and at the mercy of the Sixth. This ship – the Diomedes – was going nowhere at least. Looking along the dock, first one way then the other, he could see similar actions being played out. The vast majority of the ships had been stormed at the jetties. Four had managed to cut themselves free and were now racing for the harbour entrance and the hope of re-joining whatever ships remained of the fleet elsewhere.

He smiled. It had gone well. If only they'd commanded the Pharos, he could have sunk those ships attempting to flee too. That would have to be a priority in due course.

He closed his eyes and removed his helmet, wiping the sweat from his face with his scarf and shaking his head to watch the droplets spray from his hair. Gods, but he'd never been this hot.

Cleaning and sheathing his sword, he held his arms out like a crucified man, letting the sea's paltry breeze refresh his armpits and sides and listening to the strange decline in sound that occurred at the closing stages of a disparate and widespread fight. Gradually, the sounds of pockets of combat faded and the tapestry of seaside noises returned to overwhelm it.

As the sweat poured, Fronto stood and listened to the gulls and the waves…

…and the horns.

The horns.

He turned and looked back across the city, a somewhat futile act as from this angle all he could see was the nearest buildings. But it confirmed for him the source of the blasts. They were the signal from the lookouts across the city.

The warning was out.

The Aegyptian army was here.

CHAPTER TWO

Lucius Salvius Cursor stood above the Canopian Gate, and looked at the assembled force approaching across the plain of Eleusis, dust from the thousands of tramping feet shrouding the army enough to make judgement of numbers impossible. Many more than Caesar could call on, certainly. He couldn't see a lot of gleaming, which gave him hope, for that meant that few wore a full chest of armour. The odd glimmer of chain or scale showed through the dust, but mostly they were a riot of colour, muted with the tan-hued cloud, bearing oval shields of white.

Individually, he felt no nerves about facing them, but any experienced soldier knew that numbers counted in any engagement. The only way to beat a force so much larger than your own was to break their morale, and that seemed unlikely. Their general, Achillas, reputedly had them in the palm of his hand; this was their land, and they knew how small the Roman contingent was. Everything remained in their favour and their confidence would be high.

He looked back across the city to the northwest. The palace region beside the water was visible above the roofs of the city. That would be their last position. If the enemy reached the palace walls they were done for. With luck, Fronto had secured sufficient ships to allow them an escape route if they needed it. But Caesar and the queen both seemed to believe that the enemy could be held at the last redoubt until a solution could be forced, once Caesar received reinforcements.

Salvius hated playing a retreating game. It was no way to soldier. He had this nagging, irritating suspicion that this was why Fronto had placed him here instead of commanding himself, since he knew Fronto hated it just as much as he. He couldn't see all the lines of defence, but he knew them all well enough. He was permitted a ten per cent casualty rate at most before pulling back to the next line.

So his cohort of the Sixth – just short of five hundred men – holding this long stretch of wall would be down by fifty when they reached the first major cross street, where buildings had been pulled down to form a second barricade wall. There he could hold to four hundred men. Then back once more to the streets approaching the gymnasium complex, where the ground had been broken up with picks and mattocks to make movement slow and difficult, parts of the sewers and water channels opened to the air to cause hazards. There would begin the bombardment. Then, with only three hundred and fifty men remaining, he would fall back to the redoubt they called 'acropolis', and hold with the rest of the army, and any other forces that had fallen back across the city, for his five hundred strong contingent was only one of five. Five hundred men to hold a mile of walls. Laughable.

There was a pause as the enemy reached the first temple and split into two groups. The larger of the two picked up to a double pace, hurrying south and west, skirting the walls and crossing the canal on the Eleusis bridge to threaten the other stretches of city wall. As the dust began to settle, the men facing the city became clearer.

Salvius Cursor's lip twitched. No sign of the Gabiniani. They were probably at the rear, around the general himself. Instead, the colourful men with white shields that seemed to be the main force of Achillas' countrymen formed the centre of the enemy army. They were the most disparate group he'd ever seen on the field. Mercenaries mostly, he'd guess. Easterners with desert garb carried bows and spears, Levantines with swords and bronze over their white tunics, desert riders on small horses and with light javelins, lighter-skinned men with slings... all manner of soldiers and warriors, showing no real sign of formation. But what really caught his eye were the men with almost ebony skin atop the swaying forms of elephants.

Was Achillas clever, or stupid? A man who fielded elephants in battle was always one or the other. Deployed and handled well they could be a terrifying force, but the republic's history was replete with tales of how disastrous elephants could be if it went wrong, ploughing through their own lines in panic. Carthage had suffered dreadfully when they fielded elephants. Salvius had never fought the beasts, though he'd read about such engagements, but he suspected that Achillas knew what he was doing. The animals were at the rear of the force, where they could not easily be spooked and where if they fled the field they could not trample their own side. Of course, their value diminished with them there, but they were undoubtedly filled with archers.

The army began to move again, and Salvius knew then with the sinking stone of acceptance in the pit of his stomach that Achillas was at the least a competent general. His skirmishing riders peeled off to the flanks, out of the way at this stage, slingers and archers from half a dozen peoples moving into two groups, each supported by infantry with ladders. As they parted, the elephants moved into the centre, their archers nocking arrows already, forming in essence highly mobile siege towers.

The queen had been quite right about their inability to hold the ramparts, he realised. With twice or even three times as many soldiers, he'd likely still lose the walls. Achillas was prepared to take on Alexandria.

He looked left and right. Most of the men had pila, though only one each. Crunch time. Keep the pila to jab down from the wall, or use them early to take out the enemy? He sucked on his teeth, peered at the enemy and sighed, as he turned to his musician and standard bearer.

'Send the order. Cast all available pila. Target the elephants' drivers, missile unit officers or standard bearers, or men with ladders, but prioritise with the elephants. We want to break them if we can.'

17

What he'd give for a good unit of archers. Ah well.

A horn booed out among the enemy as the manoeuvres completed, and with a roar, they began to charge. Salvius braced himself. His men had been evenly spaced along the wall, some fifteen feet apart. Now, those at the periphery would be moving back towards the centre, knowing where the great danger lay, but it was a pitiful defence, for sure.

The enemy managed to keep pace, which was a neat trick for infantry and elephants together. As the entire front line slowed to a halt at bellowed commands, the archers nocked, stretched and released, slingers whirling their weapons with a 'whup whup' noise that was audible even over the din, the elephant archers almost on a level with the wall top.

Across the entire Roman line, centurions and optios blew whistles, and some three to four hundred pila arced out with varying levels of efficiency. Salvius watched, sword gripped tight. One particularly lucky strike against the elephants, among several good hits and a lot of fails. That pilum struck the elephant's mahout square in the chest, punching through him and pinning him to either the beast or some arrangement between he and it. Whatever the case, he screamed, transfixed, and died there, still in place, and the elephant began to panic. Unfortunately among a dozen or so elephants, one panicked animal was not enough. The beast tried to turn and flee, but there wasn't room, and so it remained in place, gradually calming as one of the archers leaned forwards and sought control. Other elephants had brushed off scratches from pila, and archers had been struck, but not enough to make much difference.

In all, the entire volley had been, to Achillas' army, little more than a gnat to a horse.

The enemy's initial assault, on the other hand, was a thing of horror. All along the line, archers and slingers released, from ground level or elephant back, and the cloud of missiles that struck the wall was like a hail storm, clattering, thudding, cracking and battering all along the wall top. Knowing what was coming, every man had ducked below wall level as soon as their pilum had been cast, and consequently most of the arrows and stones had whipped over their heads or struck the parapet. Still, here and there a man had been too slow and had been struck, or a lucky shot had ricocheted off a merlon and ploughed into a crouched legionary.

If this was a taste of things to come, Alexandria was a disaster in the making.

He forced himself to see it from the point of view of a general rather than a man on the wall. They had lost a few men, but had caused more than twice as many casualties among the enemy, perhaps even three times. And that was what this was about: doing as much damage as possible with every step back.

Salvius risked rising above the parapet, shield held up just in case.

The ladders were coming forward now, and he cursed. In the perfect world he would now order the men to rise and defend, but the hail of arrows and stones was almost constant. Even as he worried, two sling bullets cracked off his shield, one tearing some of the edging from it, and an arrow clacked against the stone a foot to his right. This was insane. He wasn't going to waste soldiers here. If his men rose to defend, he'd lose that ten percent in the first breath. No, he needed to fall back early. The wall was too wide to hold.

Cursing again, he turned to the musician and gave the order.

All along the wall, men hurried to the nearest stair and began to race back along the streets. The last to leave, apart from Salvius, were the gate crews, who set their traps ready before running. With a last look at the enemy, who were whooping triumphantly, he dropped from the wall, hurrying down to street level.

A quick glance at the gate as his men finished their jobs, gathered their gear and fell back, and he nodded with satisfaction. He'd done all he could here without losing men unnecessarily. He'd killed a hundred or so Aegyptians, he reckoned. Not good, but then *he'd* lost only about a score. And the second line would be easier to hold.

As they ran from the wall, he slowed. One of the optios from the gate frowned.

'Come on, sir.'

'Go. I'll be along.'

The soldier ran on, looking worried, leaving Salvius standing in the street, roughly half way between the city wall and their next line. He waited, watching. There was a strange silence now. His men were settling in at the second line, and the missile flurry had died off. The locals were either ensconced deep in their houses or fled to relative safety. Then it came.

The gate gave at the first blow. Achillas had more than one use for elephants, of course, and the city gate simply could not stand against a blow from such a great heavy beast. The traps began to kick in immediately.

The elephant pushed on through the splintering gate, and the cord that had been attached to the two gate leaves, and had been released when they parted, slipped up through two iron rings, letting go of the heavy wooden beam they had held up, little less than a stumpy tree trunk suspended high. The great log swung down. It had been intended to hit a group of infantry at chest height, of course, but the effect was perhaps better in the end, for instead it smashed into the legs of the elephant, breaking both and causing the animal to collapse in the gateway, bellowing, crushing several of its riders. It would take some time to shift that, and the effect on enemy morale would be pronounced.

The other small traps would kick in as they were encountered, but the first had worked well. Satisfied that the enemy would be more careful, slowed down from here, he ran on, careful of where he went, jogging from side to side appropriately until he reached the barricade.

The second line had been formed in every street by pulling down houses and using the rubble to block the way. Over the preceding days they had formed a barrier some ten feet high with a fighting platform. Wicker screens had been constructed, backed with layer upon layer of animal hide. A stack of long spears taken from the palace armoury stood to one side, and his men were already lining the makeshift wall. The centurion here was ahead of the game, for he had judged the number of men needed to hold the street, and sent the rest on. Of the better part of five hundred men, they had ten such streets to hold, and the lion's share of men had been assigned here to the main thoroughfare that ran from the gate into the heart of the city. Of the hundred men who'd run back here, forty had continued on, ready to man the next stage. Salvius fumed for a moment. He would like to involve himself and draw Aegyptian blood, but he was playing the role of commander here, and it was more important that he have a good idea of what was happening.

Greeting his men with enthusiastic comments, he clambered up and over the makeshift wall, careful not to dislodge anything critical, and at the far side entered the building to the left, climbing steps and a ladder, and emerging into the sun's scorching glare on the roof. There, he moved to the best vantage point. The enemy were succeeding in clearing the gate. In a short time, they managed to drag and push the dead beast from the arch. Salvius couldn't see the detail, but he could imagine the panic and pain as the men doing so triggered trap after trap, breaking legs, spiking flesh and causing trouble. Finally, he saw the light in the distant gateway as the animal was completely moved aside. Slowly, nervously, the enemy sent another elephant through the gate, riders ducking as they passed beneath the high arch. The rest held back, but as the beast cleared the gate area without triggering further traps, they brought the other elephants in. Satisfied that all was clear, that lead elephant began to move down the street, stirring up the scattered palm leaves and detritus as it came.

It managed some fifteen paces before it encountered the first *lilium*. Normally these pits were dug in turf and planted with a sharpened stake as an anti-personnel defence. Such was not possible in the city street, and there was precious little time to manufacture sufficient sharpened stakes anyway. However, with officials from the city detailing what lay beneath the streets, they had managed something similar. Men with picks had dug holes into sewers, water channels and other drains, cellars and tunnels, covering them with palm leaves that barely stirred in the lack of any great breeze.

The elephant encountered one such pit, front right leg plunging down into the hole, limb breaking as it fell forwards. It screamed, and the enemy roared in panic once more. A second elephant lost to enemy trickery. The beast rolled and writhed in the street, and no one could come close as it smeared what was left of the riders into the stone beneath it. Salvius watched with grim satisfaction as it took them more than a quarter of an hour to put the beast out of its misery and shift it enough to one side to allow passage.

He almost laughed as he watched the other elephants being guided back out of the gate, the beasts unsettled by the death cries of their brother. That was the great animals out of the fight, then. The cavalry similarly remained outside the walls, of little value in the streets. Now the infantry came on. They ran, presumably imagining the elephant's fate to be a single trap. They learned their lesson in moments as half a dozen men disappeared into the ground with shrieks, some entirely, others only far enough to break bones and cause pain.

Another pause for reorganisation, and the enemy formed up, white shields to the fore, and came on slowly, testing the ground with every other step, and reorganising to shuffle around any pit as they found it. As they neared the secondary blockade, they reformed once more. The infantry filtered into columns to allow archers to move to the fore. They paused some forty paces from the barricade and nocked their arrows. At the centurion's command below, his men grasped those great wicker frames.

The arrows came in a flurry and the frames were lifted simultaneously. The arrows thudded into the cunning defences, their momentum stolen enough by the wicker through which they passed for the layers of hide to halt most of them completely. Of several score missiles, a handful passed through the screen, only one striking a man, who cursed and threatened to 'rip the cock off the bastard who did that'. The men roared defiance, and the Aegyptians, perhaps uncertain as to their effectiveness, released a second volley.

Some clever sod had aimed high, and Salvius was forced to lean back and angle his shield to deflect an arrow meant for him. Once again the bulk of the arrows, though, caught in the screens, and some enemy officer put out a call. The archers dropped back and those white-shield soldiers, alongside several units of foreign infantry, bellowed and began to run at the makeshift wall.

More commands rang out from the centurion and the screens were discarded, the men instead grasping those long spears from the armoury and dropping into position. Half the men stood on the fighting platform with their swords and shields ready, the other half below with the spears. The enemy came on and as they neared to ten paces, the centurion gave his next order. The men at the barricade thrust the spears into the carefully positioned long, narrow holes in the makeshift rubble wall.

'Wait for it,' the centurion shouted, judging the speed of the enemy, and then, as they reached five paces: 'NOW!'

The effect was horrific. As the first wave of infantry hit the rubble barrier, feet finding purchase as they clambered up towards the top and the waiting legionaries, spear points suddenly burst from the wall front, and thirty points drove into the flesh of the climbing men from an unseen source. The chorus of screams was appalling, and without the need for further commands those spears were yanked back in. The nature of the rubble wall was so chaotic that it was extremely difficult to work out where the holes were without the spears poking from them.

A score of enemy infantry fell back, yelling, blood pouring from wounds, as the men behind them pushed past, uncertain of what had happened, but determined to reach the wall top. Without the need for the centurion's command, spears lanced out of the holes in the barricade again and skewered more and more of the enemy. Now they were working at their own leisure, jabbing again and again. The enemy dead began to build up, but the Aegyptian commander was not foxed by it and, rather than pulling back, committed greater and greater numbers, swamping the wall.

The spears started to lose their efficacy as some had their heads cut clear by enterprising infantry outside, others grabbed and hauled like a tug of war back through the wall to be disposed of.

Here, Salvius acknowledged, he was going to lose men. He would have to leave a rear-guard of doomed legionaries to hold the enemy. He watched carefully as the spears failed and the Aegyptians reached the top of the rubble wall and began to launch themselves at the Romans. Here, at least, the legionaries had a better chance than they had at the wall. There were no missiles, and it was a simple matter of sword against sword, in which the Romans quickly proved their superior training.

He continued to watch, tense, as his men fell gradually and the chances of holding the barricade decreased. Soon he would have to abandon it. The centurion made the decision, looking up and gesturing to Salvius, signalling his belief that they were about to lose control of the wall. Salvius nodded. They'd lost more than twenty men, maybe approaching thirty. Time to go.

He gestured at the centurion, holding both hands splayed, and then two fingers, indicating twelve in total. The centurion nodded and picked a dozen men to stay and hold. He spoke to each man quietly and individually, and Salvius was pleased at the fact that not one of the men argued or attempted to run. They had been commanded to sell their life to buy time for their comrades. Whatever the centurion had said to them had done the trick.

Moments later, the rest of the legionaries were running. Salvius paused only long enough to watch the centurion fight the urge to stay with his men, before he too ran, disappearing inside and taking the steps three at a time, emerging into the street and running. Behind him, he could hear a dozen legionaries bravely holding the enemy back, selling their lives dearly.

The second line had been successful. He couldn't imagine how many enemies they had dispatched there, but the number had been high, vastly so compared with Roman losses. It was partially about reducing their numbers as much as possible, but it was mostly about shattering their confidence and making them slower, warier and less prone to launch assaults. Caesar wanted them unwilling to commit to a full assault while he waited for his reinforcements.

The chalk marks on the road were clear, but only if you knew they were there. Salvius slowed, knowing he was at the edge of the third line of defence. He glanced over his shoulder. The fight way back along the street must be almost over now. In fact, even as he watched, he saw white shields passing across the parapet. They were slow, though. Having encountered the nightmares the Roman defenders had prepared time after time, they were now in no hurry to rush into the next one.

Satisfied, Salvius Cursor reached the last chalk mark and looked around. All windows and doors for the preceding and next ten houses had been blocked off, the only way out of the street the ladders that had been left leading up to the rooftops. All those ladders were gone now, pulled up onto the roofs, bar this one. With a deep breath, Salvius grasped the rungs and climbed. At the top, muscular arms reached out and helped him up onto the roof before whisking the ladder up and out of sight.

In moments the street was empty, no sign of defenders. Salvius dropped below the parapet, a low wall just two feet in height. He could see the rest of his men, every one lying out of sight, half this side of the road, half the other. Beside each man stood a small heap of rocks and tiles gathered from the demolitions. He smiled grimly. This one was nice and simple.

The enemy approached the next position slowly. Now, they were checking every foot of ground before moving along it, wary of traps. There was no need to ponder on what lay ahead as they passed those chalk marks, unaware of them, eyes locked on the street. There might be no Romans there, but they had torn up the surface and the only way on would be to slowly and carefully pick a way between the holes in the ground and the jagged lumps of rubble and stone jutting up in between. Slow, laborious and potentially painful, but at least no surprise.

Carefully, slowly, the white-shielded Aegyptians began to thread their way through the troublesome terrain. Salvius lay still, peering down through the small hole which allowed water to sluice off the roof and into the street at the bottom of the parapet, on the odd days when it did rain during the winter season. The centurion a little further along waved tightly at him, his face a question. Salvius peered down again. The enemy were committed. He nodded.

The centurion blew a whistle and suddenly legionaries were up at the parapet along both sides of the street. The Aegyptians, surprised by the whistle, looked this way and that in confusion, their gazes turning upwards only as the Romans began to cast their rubble down.

The effect was impressive. The enemy were forced to move slowly and carefully between obstacles, presenting the Romans with easy targets. Few of their missiles failed to find a home. Enemy soldiers were pulverised with boulders and tiles, limbs broken, skulls opened, faces mashed, blood everywhere. Screaming pervaded the street, and the men who remained below tried desperately to pick up speed, either running forwards or retreating, only to find that increased speed inevitably tipped them into deep holes or ruined shins, feet and ankles among the rubble, at which point they were once more pounded with stones.

Very few men made it out. Over more than a quarter of an hour the Romans cast everything they had. Every time the enemy tried something, they failed. Shields over heads only held off the inevitable, the boards gradually broken and ruined and then bricks finding their way through to break the men beneath.

Salvius Cursor sighed. If he'd known it was going to be this effective, he'd have stockpiled more stones. Perhaps they could have kept the enemy here indefinitely.

His musings shattered at a strange foreign cry as an Aegyptian suddenly burst through a hatch in the roof, out into the sunshine, wearing some ridiculous, ostentatious armour of crocodile skin. While they'd been held back, someone had found a weak point and managed to get into the buildings. Even as Salvius bellowed the order to fall back to the acropolis, another Aegyptian emerged from the trapdoor behind the first. Two soldiers rushed over even as Salvius ripped his sword free and ran for the man. One of them tackled the second Aegyptian while the other rushed to the trapdoor and slammed it shut, jumping on it to block access to the roof.

Salvius dipped left as he approached the man in the crocodile skin, whose sword was some strange curved cleaver of local design. As the man stepped to his right to meet Salvius, the wily tribune recovered from his feint, instead moving right and slashing out. He was impressed at the efficacy of the crocodile skin. He'd expected to cut through it, but it turned his blade as readily as any iron, and he managed only with some luck to draw blood on the arm in passing.

The man spun with difficulty in the bulky armour, his sword lashing out. Fortunately, despite his own armour and the oppressive heat, Salvius still had the advantage over the strange getup his opponent wore. He danced out of the way and lashed out twice in quick succession, the first blow slamming into the leather ties that held the front of the armour together and, as it flapped apart, the second thrust into the ribs and on through the body, cleaving the man's organs and robbing him of life. As he twisted the blade with difficulty and yanked it back out, Salvius heard more cries. Other trapdoors were opening, and men emerging. Even as he shouted at the two men with him to run, the one standing on the trapdoor stiffened as a spear rammed up through it, deep into his groin from an unseen assailant below.

Salvius looked around. Many of his men had gone. Some had been cut off by Aegyptians emerging from the houses below. The rooftops were lost. There was nothing he could do now but either sacrifice himself or run and get out alive.

Regretfully, and wondering if Fronto was having a deleterious effect on him, since a few years ago he'd probably have stayed and fought it out, he put boot leather to rooftop and pelted off to the north, racing for safety. Behind him the last tardy legionaries were overrun.

Breathing heavily, he reached the roof edge and without the luxury of a ladder trusted to luck, jumping from the parapet onto an awning below. The fabric tore with the force of the impact, but remained intact enough for him to roll, and then drop from there to the ground without injury. Looking up to see enemy warriors appear at the parapet, he wiped his sword on a piece of fallen awning, then sheathed it and ran.

At the count of sixty three racing heartbeats he turned the corner to see the redoubt of the acropolis awaiting, packed with legionaries and the last of his men racing through the new gate to safety. With a prayer to Mars he followed them, disappearing inside as the soldiers slammed the portal shut behind him and barred it, stacking beams and barrels against it.

'That's it then sir?' a centurion probed as he leaned over, hands on knees, to regain his breath.

'That's it. We're under siege. But they're going to be careful and slow now. We made them pay for getting this far. A good thousand enemy bodies line Canopus Street to the walls, and they won't consider committing their elephants again. Is this place secure?'

'As secure as we could make it, sir. We'll hold them here.'

'We have to. It's that or die. Unless Fronto's got us some ships.'

He turned and peered towards the harbour, though he couldn't see that far. He tried not to think what Fronto was going to do now if he'd secured the harbour and the fleet. They had expected to have time to consolidate their grip there or perhaps move the ships into the Palace Harbour, but in the end they'd run out of time. The legate and his men would be trapped in the harbour and cut off.

'Good luck, Fronto,' he breathed, as he listened to the sound of whooping Aegyptians moving slowly but relentlessly through the streets.

CHAPTER THREE

Galronus crouched in the manner of a hunter atop a strange edifice that appeared to be part-temple, part-gateway and all peculiar, covered in statues and carvings of men with animal heads. His position was deliberately chosen as hard to spot from any local ground level location, which was, in retrospect, a good thing, given the positions of the enemy.

Glancing this way and that at the last moment before he needed to move, he plotted every position he could see. Street fighting and sieges were not the field of choice for a horse warrior like Galronus, and he had willingly taken on the role of scout along with several of the more alert men of the Sixth and the Twenty Seventh. His role, to give warning primarily to the men at the harbour, was well-suited.

Away to his left – to the east – he could see that the last of the legionaries had pulled back to the redoubt line around the palace, the theatre and the Palace Harbour. There the strange, clever, queen and Caesar were content that they could hold an enemy for a protracted period, possibly indefinitely if they could open and maintain a supply route through the port.

Behind him, to the north, the harbour was under Fronto's control, with a thousand men of the Sixth to defend it. The rest of the legions had been sent back to the redoubt to help hold there. The problem was that while the redoubt was a solid fortification, having been carefully planned and executed over days, the harbour was almost impossible to fortify, being a wide front with many access points. All Fronto's men had been able to do since they'd taken control of the ships was tear down some shanty buildings and use the rubble to block the streets. A determined sheep could cross the defences there, let alone an enemy army, and Achillas' force outnumbered Fronto's by a margin too high to comfortably count. Moreover, there was no connection between the harbour and the redoubt. When attacked, Galronus' friend could not pull back to the safety of the others. And there was little doubt he was going to be attacked.

Again, Galronus peered intently at the streets off to the south. The army of Aegyptians was moving slowly, carefully, more like a tide coming in than a flash flood. The Roman defenders had made them pay so heavily for their initial advances that now, even though nothing really remained between them and the Roman centres, they were wary and sluggish.

He could see Aegyptian forces moving parallel along at least five streets. Some of them were moving towards the redoubt and the main Roman position, where Caesar and the queen commanded. Others, though, and a sizeable number of them, were closing on the harbour. Fronto was about to be hit and hit hard.

Time to move.

Galronus rose suddenly, red flag hanging limp from the top of the spear shaft as he lifted it from the rooftop. Three waves towards the palace, warning them that the enemy were just three streets away, then five waves back towards the harbour. Five streets. Not much.

Having given away his position in delivering the signals, Galronus became a target in an instant, archers and slingers among the units just a few dozen paces away in the street, nocking and swinging with sudden urgency. But by the time the first shot whipped through the air, Galronus was gone. Dropping from the rear of the roof, he landed on the head of the statue of a dog-faced man of ancient black stone. Plenty of handholds on this thing, and in a couple of heartbeats he was in the narrow alley behind the strange temple-thing at ground level.

The enemy would be close, but he felt confident they wouldn't hurry after him. They were moving nervously and slowly as an army, and he was only one man, not worth risking running into a trap for. Turning a corner, he entered a wider street and pelted along it. Ahead, he could see the barrier of rubble in the street, the red and silver shapes of Fronto's legionaries behind it. Beyond them, distantly, he could see a blue-grey haze scattered with masts. It did not look defensible.

Galronus gritted his teeth. His orders were to pull back to the redoubt, but he had no intention of doing so, and leaving Fronto fighting without him. Caesar would get over it. It wasn't as though this was the first time Galronus had blithely ignored his orders.

His feet clapping on the stones of the street, he closed on the rubble, calling the password as he neared, and the Sixth stepped to the sides, opening a path across the makeshift barrier for him. As Galronus scrabbled up the broken stones and mud bricks, he noted the defenders with dismay. Maybe fifty men. Enough to hold the blockade for only a very short time. The defences were so spread out with so many accesses that Fronto's men were too thinly distributed. There was, in Galronus' opinion, absolutely no chance of holding the harbour.

Nodding his thanks to the men, and warning them that the enemy would be on them at any moment, he asked where the legate was to be found.

'Ship three jetties along,' said one of the soldiers. 'The Diomedes.'

'Thank you.'

Running on, Galronus entered the harbour. Small pockets of legionaries were clustered along it, presumably reserves to plug gaps, as though they had any chance of holding this leaky sieve of a fortification for more than the blink of an eye.

As he pounded along the stone dock, making for the colourful trireme three jetties along, he frowned. No, the small pockets of men along the length of the harbour were not idle, waiting to help. They were standing at the ends of certain jetties while some of their number were clearly active aboard the vessels at those places. As he neared the *Diomedes*, Galronus watched with interest. They were more or less at the centre of the dock, and Fronto had split the fleet in two, with his command post on the ship at the centre. For some reason, he had the ships on the jetties to either side already on the move, crewed inexpertly by men of the Sixth.

31

As he ran, frowning, along the jetty for the ramp that led up to the Diomedes, Galronus watched the farcical sailing of the soldiers. The two warships that were pulling away from the jetties continually bashed against the timbers, moving slowly under oar power from a very small number of inexpert rowers, while a man with apparently no sense of direction steered at the rear. He clenched his teeth as the ship to the left crashed into the next one, the two scraping along each other with the groaning of tortured wood and the sound of oars smashing and splintering. He hoped fervently that there were no men at those oars, for if there were they would have almost certainly just died horrible deaths.

What were they doing? They were going to wreck both those ships, and any vessel they came into contact with. Two of the legionaries saluted him as he ran up the boarding plank and onto the deck, and he nodded at them as he angled towards Fronto, who was standing with a man in a senior officer's uniform at the highest part of the ship, looking this way and that and gesticulating.

'What is going on?' Galronus asked curtly as he came to a halt, breathing deeply.

Fronto turned in surprise.

'You're supposed to be safe at the palace.'

'What's going on?' he repeated, pointing at the ship that was still scraping along the side of another.

'Opening up a space around my command post,' Fronto grinned.

'They're wrecking the ships.'

'I expect so,' shrugged Fronto. 'Hardly matters.'

'You don't want to preserve them?'

Fronto shook his head. 'We can't. I went through every option in my head. Defending the ships is impossible. You saw our situation. We'll be overrun very quickly. I wondered whether we might manage to sail the ships, or at least as many as possible, into the Palace Harbour. In fact we've done that to a small extent.'

He pointed off to the east and Galronus peered past the other ships, through a tangle of masts and ropes, and could just see the shapes of several vessels disappearing into the protective arms of the Palace Harbour.

'That's many of the prisoners we took, under a small guard. More – the defiant ones who were not willing to comply – were just released into the streets as we can't afford the men to watch them. Others... well...' He swept a hand around the ship and Galronus looked around. Aegyptians sat at the oar benches of the Diomedes.

'You're going to sail away?'

Fronto nodded. 'With all the men I can preserve.'

Galronus heaved a sigh of relief. It was good to know that his friend at least had a plan.

'Sun's only a couple of hours from the horizon now, I reckon,' Fronto mused.

Galronus nodded.

'We're dragging it out as long as we can,' Fronto said. 'I want to leave the enemy with an evening in which they can't rest and recuperate.'

Galronus frowned again, and Fronto chuckled, tapping the side of his nose conspiratorially.

A noise rising from the city behind them indicated that Achillas' army had finally come into contact with Fronto's blockades. The sound seemed to arise from numerous places at once. They were being hit all along the harbour.

'How long will you hold?'

Fronto rubbed his hands together. 'Each position has orders to pull back only dependent upon the retreat of other units. It's all been orchestrated for the best possible defence. We need to hold them as long as possible while the men work.'

'What are you up to?'

Fronto simply tapped his nose in that infuriating manner again. 'Just watch and enjoy.'

Galronus did just that. Standing at the rear of the Diomedes, he looked this way and that. The two adjacent ships were now well clear of their jetties and had managed in a haphazard way to come around behind the other vessels, and there drifted to a halt. Frowning, he watched the men who had badly handled them into position throwing ropes and tying them to the nearest ships, then leaping from one to the other and hurrying back to the jetty and safety.

Barely had they made it that far before a signal blast arose from the far western end of the dock.

'The dance begins,' Fronto grinned.

A second signal answered that first from the eastern end of the dock, and in moments Galronus watched a small unit of legionaries, small indistinct figures at this distance, fall back from a street in tight formation. They moved slowly and carefully, backing towards the nearest ship. His head snapped the other way and confirmed that the same had happened at the far end. The men were falling back from the extremities first.

As the soldiers neared the two furthermost ships, Galronus narrowed his eyes. Men leapt from that ship and joined their comrades on the dock, retreating towards the next ship along. Simultaneously they blew whistles, which received whistled answers from the next blockaded street, and another unit slowly backed out to join them, the forces combining, growing, as men now leapt from the second ship to join them.

Why this was happening escaped Galronus until the third ship, and the addition of a third unit. At this point the enemy appeared at the ends of the harbour, advancing on the retreating Romans carefully and suspiciously, wondering what new trap awaited them. But it was not traps they had to look forward to. Galronus' eyes widened as the triremes at the far ends suddenly burst into flame, columns of roiling black smoke rising into the pristine blue afternoon sky.

'You're burning the ships?'

Fronto grinned. 'Good, eh?'

'*Burning* them?'

'We can't sail them away without the sailors to do it, we can't protect them as there aren't enough of us, and clearly we can't just let Achillas have them.'

'Caesar will be furious.'

Fronto shook his head. 'Caesar would have ordered it had he been here. He will ratify my decision when we meet him. He would no more want Achillas retrieving those ships than I do.'

Galronus stared left and then right as the second ship went up. As they burned, the procedure was being repeated along the dock. The units were falling back in careful order, working by a system of whistled signals, and as they passed the ships men leapt from them, having ignited the kindling they'd packed in at the last moment. By the time they were closing on the harbour centre, and the position of the Diomedes, the ends of the fleet were burning furiously. The enemy force that had spilled out onto the dock were panicked and confused, not knowing what to do. They were too late to save the ships already ablaze, no matter how many buckets they grabbed, and the ships that were still unburned were behind the retreating lines of the Sixth. Each ship and each blockaded street they passed they grew in number, and more and more vessels exploded into flame.

'Ready the lines, oarsmen do your thing,' Fronto shouted to the men on the ship somewhat inexpertly. He turned that grin on Galronus. 'I'm determined to enjoy this. Depriving the enemy of the fleet, saving the men. It's the best win I could hope for here, and even I should be able to make it as far as the Palace Harbour without being sick.'

Galronus shook his head. Fronto was enjoying this all too much. And it was neat. Something had to go wrong. He watched the legionaries now falling back and joining together at the end of the Diomedes' jetty. The enemy were closing, edging forwards nervously. The entire fleet was ablaze now. The sheer quantity of wood docked at the harbour side ensured that the fleet would burn for quite some time and would be entirely unsalvageable. Despite non-specific misgivings, Galronus had to admit that Fronto's plan seemed to be working well.

He felt the tension building. The Sixth were now falling back in neat formation along the jetty and up the ramp onto the Diomedes, the only ship now not burning, and separated from the nearest engulfed vessels by one empty jetty, saving it from the worst danger. Even so, sparks and flaming canvas, caught by the sea breezes, fluttered down onto the Diomedes, where men with buckets hurried to put them out.

The enemy were close enough now for Galronus to see the hunger on their faces, mixed with nerves at the idea of taking on the bloodthirsty Romans and the burning ships. As the last unit of legionaries retreated onto the wooden jetty they paused, some of them producing axes, and hewed at the timbers in four places. There was an unpleasant groan from the wooden walkway, a warning sound, and, shouldering their axes, the men of the Sixth Legion hurried to the ramp, sweeping up and onto the Diomedes.

Galronus watched expectantly. The enemy's leaders were shouting. Their language was peculiar to him, even the ones speaking Greek, but the tone made it clear. They were exhorting their men to take the Romans before they got away. These men had failed to secure Achillas his fleet, and he would be furious. Imagine how well those leaders would be received by their general if they also let the Romans escape.

Still their men were hesitant, all the more so now that the narrow jetty lay between them and their foe. The last of the Sixth reached the ship, and began to pull in the ramp even as other men untied the ropes and prepared to get underway.

Finally, driven by their frenzied, furious officers, the Aegyptians rushed forwards in a last effort to take the Diomedes before it left the dock, but they were doomed from the moment their boots touched the timbers. The retreating Romans had cut the wooden supports, not enough to sever them, but enough to weaken them. The weight of the approaching Aegyptians was too much. As perhaps a hundred of them pounded over the half-hewn section it gave, the whole jetty leaning precariously. Men cried out and grabbed at one another as they were tipped unceremoniously into the water. In a heartbeat it swung past the point of no return and with a groan and the deep cracking of ancient timbers the whole thing crashed to the water and lay there with screaming men bobbing around amid the broken wood.

Fronto was still grinning like an idiot as the ship pulled away from the ruined jetty, out into safe water.

'You're going peculiar in your old age, you know?' Galronus said, shaking his head.

Fronto turned and looked out the way they were heading now, instead of at the foiled and impotent enemy on the harbour side. He sucked on his teeth, his head switching back and forth between the Palace Harbour off to their right and the main exit to the harbour.

'You're not thinking of sailing out to sea?' Galronus said quietly.

Fronto snorted. 'Hardly, with *my* stomach. But...'

He turned to the centurion beside him. 'How adventurous are you feeling, Carfulenus?'

The officer frowned in confusion. 'Sir?'

'Feels like we're on a winning streak here. Do we test our luck?'

'Pharos?' Carfulenus asked quietly, looking in the same direction as Fronto.

'What's Pharos?' Galronus said, peering off ahead, where they appeared to be looking at the harbour entrance.

'*That's* Pharos,' Fronto grinned, pointing at the heavy, tall lighthouse standing at the eastern end of the island, beside the harbour entrance.

Galronus rolled his eyes. 'What about the redoubt at the palace?'

'We can get into the Palace Harbour at any time now, as long as we control the main harbour, and with the enemy fleet burning. But if we can secure the sea entrance too, that gives us an extra edge.'

At a nod from the centurion, Fronto turned and threw his hands up like an orator. 'Men of the Sixth Legion, have you had the fight knocked out of you yet?'

There was a strange pause, and then a smattering of negative grumbles.

'No? So you're up for a fight then? Not defending a pile of rubble this time, but a proper fight?'

This earned more of a surge of support.

'There's a small fort below the Pharos lighthouse, with artillery, which commands the entrance to the harbour. I have a mind to make sure that's ours. What do you say?'

This time there was a roar. He turned to Galronus and Carfulenus. 'It seems the men fancy a scuffle.'

The centurion laughed. 'Pharos it is, then.'

'You shouldn't encourage him,' Galronus advised Carfulenus.

The three men stood at the rail as the ship, having expertly back-oared away from the ruined jetty, turned gracefully and began to move forwards now, heading for the eastern tip of the island below the huge, iconic lighthouse. The oars rose and dipped with rhythmic splashes, and Galronus peered ahead as the small fort gradually became clearer and clearer. They swung wide round the low Antirrhodus Island and closed on their destination as the sun began its slide towards the horizon. It always surprised Galronus how this far south the afternoon slid into evening so much faster than it did at home. They should just have time to take Pharos and perhaps even sail back to the Palace Harbour before dark.

So long as Pharos held no surprises...

The ship cut closer and closer. He could finally make out the shapes of men on the walls of the small, squat, mud brick fort at the water's edge. It was far from a strong fortress, having clearly been constructed more for controlling the water, as part of the homogenous system of city defences, than for withstanding an attack in itself.

Square, and with ramparts little over two and a half times a man's height, the walls had a slight slope and, having been formed of mud brick, had suffered at the hands of the sea and its winds, becoming pitted and worn. It was not a lot longer in any side than the Diomedes, one corner supporting an offshoot wall that marched out down a flight of stairs to the water, forming a single dock as well as part of a sea wall. There were no towers, but each of the two eastern corners had been widened to create a stable artillery platform. On both stood some sort of ornate and arcane version of a ballista, angled out at the water, where they could cripple shipping attempting to enter the harbour, especially when added to the similar fortification at the far side, on the end of the mole that ran from the palace and was under Roman control already.

Galronus held his breath as they closed. Men were pointing their way, and no one seemed to be able to decide what to do. The

Diomedes was a local ship, stacked with legionaries resembling the Gabiniani, who had been stationed in Alexandria for years. These were under Caesar and the queen, of course, yet some would remember that the king was also in the palace now. The small garrison on the island would probably be somewhat confused over where their loyalties currently lay. Theoretically whether they supported Ptolemy or Cleopatra, both were in the palace and nominally free and safe, while the army attacking was led by the general Achillas. But Achillas claimed to be leading in the name of the king.

Someone in the fort seemed to make a decision that came down against Fronto whatever the case, for there was a flurry of activity around the weapon and in a count of sixteen heartbeats it was wound and released. The men there were trained on that very weapon, and their first shot was no ranging missile. Dead on target it tore through the lower corner of a sail, thudded into a man's shoulder blade and carried him, screaming, over the side and into the water where he was immediately beaten to death by the actions of a dozen oarsmen.

Galronus made the quickest of estimations and decided that they could probably get three shots off before the ship reached them, and the far weapon one or two. Tongues of orange flame bursting into life near the weapons suggested that they were preparing fire shots. As an anti-ship installation, it would naturally be capable of launching flaming missiles.

They closed. A second shot came, this one still unlit, and it impaled a second man, pinning him to the deck as he writhed and screamed, until a friend put him out of his misery. Galronus clenched his teeth, breathing shallow, as expert sailors now in Fronto's control angled the ship towards that projecting wall that doubled as a dock.

He watched the artillery carefully. Archers were now moving into position on the wall. Flickers of flame betrayed their plan. He turned to Fronto. 'Fire arrows.'

Fronto nodded and turned to the deck. 'Water buckets at the ready. Be prepared for fire arrows and ready to dock and disembark quickly. As soon as your units hit solid ground, run for the fort. The walls are low, sloped and poorly-maintained, so the stairs aren't the only way up. Don't work to careful strategy. Look for an open stretch of defences, get over them and subdue the inhabitants. Seize the artillery as soon as you can, and stop those archers. Bucket men and sixth and seventh centuries of cohort one, you remain on the ship. Make sure these oarsmen don't suddenly decide they're Achillas' men again and row away. Are you all ready?'

Before the men could reply there was a chorus of twangs and thuds from the fort and shouts of men with guttural Aegyptian accents. Galronus tensed as the missiles came in. Once more the large bolts were perfectly aimed, though this time they were coated with burning pitch, the sticky fire violent enough to keep them aflame even as they flew through the air.

The first caught a sail and tore a piece of rail from the ship's edge, carrying it out into the sea. The second thudded into an oar bench, pinning a man's thigh to it as it engulfed him in flame. The sail caught immediately, but men with buckets were moving straight away. Only a small part of the sail charred before the water extinguished the flames. Similarly, the burning man was immediately doused with water, though he was still swiftly dispatched, having been crippled and fated to bleed out within the hour anyway.

Fire arrows struck here and there with thuds and squawks of pain, but men were rushing everywhere with buckets, refilling them from one of the two water barrels on the deck. Galronus watched, tense, as they glided in alongside the dock-wall and men immediately leapt ashore with ropes. The vessel was hauled close and tied up, the ramp run out and oars all shipped in mere heartbeats, and then the fight was on, men running ashore in small unit groups but without much nod to formation.

'Shall we?' Fronto grinned at the other two officers.

'You've been in the sun too long,' grumbled Galronus. 'Come on, then.'

'You should stay and command the ship, sir,' the centurion said pointedly to Fronto. With a feral grin that rejected Carfulenus' suggestion, Fronto clapped his hand on the man's shoulder and, ripping his sword from its sheath, ran for the ramp. Shaking his head, Galronus followed suit.

'You know that when you take this place, you'll have to hold it?'

Fronto nodded. 'We'll leave ten centuries. And we can resupply and support them by ship. I want to control this harbour.'

Galronus, still shaking his head, ran on after his friend down the ramp. Glancing ahead he decided that despite his fears, this looked like a relatively easy fight. Getting close enough under arrow and bolt fire had been the main issue, and the enemy had wasted half their time trying to decide whether to shoot, and lighting their braziers. Now there were just poor-quality walls holding them back.

Somewhere amid the stream of legionaries, Fronto and Galronus ran alongside Centurion Carfulenus who wore a crest of green feathers and a cloak over his armour despite the heat.

'Doesn't it get hot in that?'

The centurion smiled. 'Stops the metal getting to finger-burning temperature, but it's mainly to stop the sea salt rusting the bloody thing to bits, sir.'

Fronto laughed, and the three of them ran on amid the men. Reaching the walls of the fort swiftly, where the projecting dock was the height of a man below the rest, connected by a staircase, they began to pound up the steps amid their men. The enemy had gathered at the top and were doing their best to hold back the Roman tide, but they were falling foul of one of the oldest strategic failures in the book. In committing the bulk of their force to hold the stair access, they had insufficient troops to man the rest of the walls. With a pronounced slope to them, and the spaces between the bricks widened and eroded with the weather, they were little more than one giant stepladder, and men were clambering up the walls themselves almost as fast as the stairs, though they'd had to discard their shields to give them a free hand for the climb.

The native garrison could not have numbered more than a hundred to Fronto's thousand legionaries, and by the time the stairs fell and Fronto and Galronus emerged onto the top, the fort was almost theirs, just a few small pockets of men left fighting.

Galronus had to roll his eyes again at Fronto, who displayed initially clear disappointment that he'd missed the fight, and then desperation to be involved in one of the last few struggles. Pulling men out of the way, Fronto pounded across to one of the artillery platforms where the defenders were making a last stand while their artillerists continued to pound the ship with blazing missiles.

With a cry of triumph, Fronto leapt into the fray, Sword coming back and then stabbing out, gutting one of the poorly-armoured defenders. Again and again his sword rose and fell, as he joined the men of the Sixth in dispatching the last of the Aegyptians from the fort. Galronus simply watched. The fort had fallen before they got here, and there had been no need for the two of them to become personally involved, other than Fronto's usual desire to pretend he was an ordinary soldier and not a member of Rome's aristocracy and military elite.

In moments the thuds of artillery had stopped.

Galronus hurried over to the parapet and peered down. The men on board the Diomedes had managed to keep any fire attack under control, and the ship remained unburned and intact at the dockside. At least they could get away, then. He didn't relish the idea of being trapped here for the night.

The sun was low now, and his gaze turned to the city back across the harbour as Fronto, wiping his blade with a cloth, fell in alongside him.

'I think your firing the fleet might have been a mistake,' Galronus said darkly, and pointed.

Fronto followed his gesture to where the wind had carried sparks from the burning ships to the dry, brittle buildings of Alexandria.

The port district was aflame.

'Damn it.'

CHAPTER FOUR

Fronto stood on the top tier of seating in the theatre attached to the edge of the palace, one of the best viewpoints to be had in the 'acropolis.' Galronus heaved a sigh beside him and handed him a wooden cup that sloshed. Fronto nodded his thanks and took it, peering out across the night.

The fire was being contained, though not as well as everyone would like. Fronto winced at the memory of that uncomfortable moment when they had returned to the palace from their successful assault on the Pharos Island fort.

They had left the majority of the First Cohort to garrison the fort, which, along with its twin on the mole, commanded the harbour entrance. There was still a way into the harbour, through the arch in the Heptastadion that connected Pharos to the mainland and formed the western border of the great port, but it was narrow and could admit but one ship at a time. There was now little danger of an enemy fleet sailing into the harbour again, and Caesar's ships would be able to depart in the morning to seek reinforcements and supplies, safe in the knowledge that they could return to port securely. It had been a victory, without doubt.

Fronto, Galronus and the centurion had sailed back to the Palace Harbour with four centuries of men, and the legate had immediately reported to Caesar.

The general had been standing at a window with some local administrator, discussing something while the queen, her expression black, had been at the table of maps. As Fronto had clomped into the room and bowed his head, Cleopatra the Seventh, disputed queen of Aegyptus, had looked up and riveted him to the wall with a glare.

'You are the one who burns my city?'

Fronto had been preparing to report with his usual manner, opening with the good news, putting the best spin he could on the bad, but had the rug somewhat pulled out from beneath him with this abrupt introduction.

'The fire is my doing, unintentionally, your Majesty.'

'Your unintentional fire rages through my capital, soldier. I entered into an alliance with the general here in order to restore Alexandria and the Black Land to control and peace, and to put down dangerous generals and idiot brothers. Of what value is securing a city that is little more than ash and bones. What have you to say for yourself?'

Fronto bridled. It was not the queen's right to interrogate him, yet the general seemed oblivious to the conversation, deep in discussion with his administrator. The legate cleared his throat.

'Your rebel general moves through the city like a plague, Majesty. His army is greatly superior in numbers. Since I had not the manpower to fight for control of the fleet, I was left with two choices: surrender them to the enemy, or destroy them. Because of what we did, we now have a safe supply route and the harbour is under our control. Had we left the ships for Achillas we would be entirely cut off and his forces would now have far increased freedom of movement. We did what we had to.'

'You have spent long enough in this kingdom to realise how dry and flammable things are, soldier. Fire is a killer in any city. I understand that Rome burns with unpleasant regularity, so you should know the dangers. Now *Alexandria* burns.'

Fronto shook his head. 'One thing Achillas does not want is the city destroyed, for all he confronts us. His men are dousing the flames and restricting the fire. It has not spread further than the port district and a small area of the city beyond. In the grand scheme of things, it could be far, far worse.'

'You should have scuttled the ships instead.'

'That would have taken hours longer, Majesty. We simply did not have time. The ships would have fallen to Achillas and my men would be dead.'

'Then you should have pushed them out to sea before igniting them, where they were safely away from the city.'

Fronto sighed. 'Again we had insufficient time. And I suspect you have less grasp of naval matters than even I if you think doing so would be a simple matter. I considered every possibility and when I discarded the impossible or the pointless, I was left only with the one I pursued.'

Cleopatra snarled.

'My library is burning, soldier. The repository of all learning in the civilised world. A place great philosophers, scientists, poets and inventors seek out from all over the world for the lettered treasures it holds, and now smoke pours from its roofs.'

Fronto winced. That was the thing he'd heard that he wasn't looking forward to apologising for. Luckily he was saved the need for it right then, as Caesar suddenly turned from the window, gesturing.

'My dear lady, please. Do not waste venom on Fronto here. Firstly, he is correct that Achillas has controlled the worst of the fire, which means that not only will it not spread, but it is keeping our enemy busy and causing him trouble. From what I understand much of the learning from the library is being saved, for the priests and scribes are carrying scrolls to safety by the armful. And above all, it is said plainly that the library long since lacked sufficient room, and that it is now only one of four buildings in the city that serve this purpose. What has happened is that a *part* of your fabled library has burned. It is infinitely regretful that it has happened, but it was also an accident, and in a time of war such things happen.'

'That is a platitude.'

'Yet true, nonetheless. You are shrewd, queen of Aegyptus, and clever, but your experience of war is extremely limited. I have fought Rome's enemies now for three decades, from the sands of the south to the misty isles north of Gaul. The collateral damage the world suffers is one of the saddest parts of soldiering, yet it is a necessary evil if war must be contemplated. Cicero, just a few years ago, addressed a trial with the words *"law falls silent in times of war".'*

The queen's eyes narrowed. 'Plato reminds us that if a city is good it will have a life of peace, but if evil, a life of war both within and without.'

Caesar chuckled. 'Plato goes on to say that all cities ought to practise war not in *times* of war, but while they are at peace. And every city should take the field at least for one day in every month. But enough of these playful banterings. If you must direct your venom, daughter of the Ptolemies, do so at me. I gave Fronto direct orders to do what he must to secure the fleet. By extension it is therefore my order that saw your city burning. I will not have my officers questioned for doing their duty in an exemplary fashion.'

Fronto felt a strange swell of pride. It was easy these days to paint Caesar the military autocrat – much of Rome did so after all – but it was moments like this, when his care for his people rose above even international treaty, that reminded him why he had served the general all these years. Why he had come back even when he'd retired.

The queen gave Caesar that evil glare, then, and finished matters with 'We will discuss this at length later.'

There had been something in their eyes as they remained locked that had carried an undercurrent that was most definitely not military, and Fronto had left the room wondering what the general's wife back in Rome would think of it. He snorted. Caesar had been so devoted to war and politics this past decade, Calpurnia probably only saw him at festivals in the winter anyway. He tried not to admit to himself that the latter was also largely true of Lucilia and his self.

Now, as Fronto stood on the theatre seats and watched the golden glow in parts of the city, he found himself nagged again by notions that the general was in the queen's chamber... 'cementing' their alliance.

He gave a childish guffaw that drew Galronus' frown.

'Something is funny?'

'No. Not really.'

They peered off instead over the stage and the scaenae at the dark harbour beyond and the blaze of the Pharos lighthouse. Lights twinkled in the fort, and one small beacon burned at the end of the wall-dock that jutted out into the water, a constant signal for the palace confirming that the Sixth were still in command of the fort. Ships had been back and forth in the dusk delivering supplies and changes of men, until the dark made spotting the lurking dangers beneath the harbour's northeast waters impossible to see and safely avoid.

They controlled the harbour, but the enemy had learned of their small victory and had already begun to move against it. They had seized control of the Heptastadion that led to the island and begun to deploy units there, threatening that fort. In response, the cohort had worked through the evening to strengthen the land-facing walls and to dig a trench and lilia pits before it. They intended to hold out. Sooner or later the Roman forces would be required to move out from there and secure the island. If they could take the whole of Pharos and then the Heptastadion, they would truly control the harbour, and the long pier would be easier to defend than one end of an island anyway.

Still, there was stalemate now. The enemy had tried assaulting the redoubt for an hour or so, but their losses had been grievous enough that their commanders had soon pulled them back. Now Achillas and his men sat glowering at the walls that contained their king and queen, while the rest of the army either secured the approach to Pharos or fought the fire in the city.

Peace would reign at least through the night. Very likely both sides would now settle into watching one another and sizing each other up while they waited for some change that gave them an advantage and broke the stalemate. Both sides would have a breather.

A clearing of throat made them both turn to see Salvius Cursor strolling around the seats towards them.

'Salvius, taking the night air?'

'A little smoke-filled for me,' the tribune replied with a trace of acid, but broke into an easy smile in the end. 'No, I thought I'd report in. Been touring the defences. From Isis to Serapis is being constantly upgraded, and I wouldn't fancy the chances of getting through there even with Roman engineers. From Serapis around to the port we're leaving for now, as the canal gives that section an extra layer of defence. And from Isis to the coast of the Jewish quarter the enemy have kept three streets back, so Cassius has been having parties sortie from the lines and pull down the closest buildings. They've created a two hundred pace kill zone now, and every missile weapon he can lay his hands on is being placed there. It's the acropolis' weakest spot, but now it's becoming a nasty proposition.'

Fronto nodded with satisfaction. Sometimes he forgot that Salvius had spent time in the city in his murky past under Pompey, and his easy familiarity with Alexandria was useful now.

'Cassius needs to be careful tearing down Alexandria. The queen might take offence.'

Salvius Cursor snorted. 'She has already made her feelings known. The tension between her and Cassius you could cut with a knife. Caesar is having his work cut out mediating.'

'He'll come down in favour of the queen,' Fronto said quietly.

'Because he's bedding her,' Salvius murmured.

Fronto blinked, turning his worried face again on the tribune. 'Careful with words like that, man.'

'It's hardly a secret. Half the palace slaves talk about it. His room is hardly ever slept in now.'

'I meant he will come down on the queen's side for political and military expediency.'

Salvius laughed. '*And* because he's bedding her.'

Fronto pictured Cassius' face if the general sided with the queen against him, and over a very similar situation to that in which he had supported Fronto against her. The man needed to be more careful there. Cassius had only recently been an enemy, avidly supporting Pompey. His move to Caesar's side was still fresh, and Fronto could quite imagine sufficient offence pushing him back. He resolved to speak to them both soon.

'So we are secure for now?'

'I believe so. Settle in for the long wait.'

* * *

In the event, the wait was not long. The following two days saw only more of the same, with both sides settling in, but on the kalends of November, the palace broke out in an uproar. By the time Fronto arrived at the hall Caesar and the queen used as their headquarters, a junior centurion was standing with his head hung low, hiding a sheepish look.

Roman officers stood around, including both Salvius Cursor and his brother, Cassius, Hirtius and Carfulenus. Fronto shuffled closer to Salvius Cursor who seemed to be permanently abreast of all news in Alexandria, but before he could enquire, Caesar called the room to silence.

'Report,' he demanded of the centurion, who straightened, trying to bolt an expression of contrition threaded with competence upon his face. It didn't quite work.

'General, it is my duty to report that the princess Arsinoë defected to the enemy force in the early hours of this morning.'

'Defected?' Caesar said, a dangerous edge to his tone.

'It is the opinion of one of her manservants, who was arrested thereafter, that the young princess believes her older siblings to be incapable of rule while they are at war and both locked here in the palace. It seems she sees the army of general Achillas as the tool of command and intends to claim the throne of Aegyptus over both the current king and queen by the simple expedient of controlling the army.'

'Gods, but these Aegyptian women,' grunted Cassius, casting a nasty look at the queen.

Cleopatra stepped to the fore directly before the centurion. 'I am led to believe that the Roman army, considered by some to be invincible, and who have held a force ten times their size at bay in this city, who have created an uncrossable fortification that even my elite units dare not assault, managed to leave a hole in their defences sizeable enough for my heifer of a sister to slip through, with an armed escort? Were your soldiers all asleep, Centurion?'

The officer winced. 'With respect, your Majesty, many of the ordinary soldiers are more than a little baffled by who are their allies and who their enemies. They often wonder why the royal army besieges the city when both the king and queen are in the palace with us. They don't know whether your royal brother is friend or foe. They cannot understand why Achillas is in command of the army yet claims Ptolemy's authority in it. And into this enters a third sibling of whom they know little. They had no idea that they were supposed to stop her. She simply demanded egress and, with her royal status, an entourage and a guard, it all seemed so official that my men saw no reason to stop her.'

Cleopatra's face changed colour a little, her eyes flashing. She turned sharply on Caesar.

'So now my sister betrays us all and lends legitimacy to Achillas. Your men are a joke, Consul.'

Caesar took the bile with surprising calm, shrugging. 'Answer me this, Queen of Aegyptus: are you saddened to lose your sister?'

'She could be boiled in a pot of asps for all I care.'

'And is she a tactical genius?'

'She has no experience of war at all. She is less than twenty summers old and has lived in the luxury of palaces all her life.'

'And will she bring any real value to Achillas?'

The queen's eyes narrowed, and Caesar smiled. 'Of course not,' he said quietly. 'She will bring nothing to our enemy. The army will likely not see her as a better patron than her brother, and the general already claims royal authority. All she will do is sow discord among our enemies. Had I known she planned this, I might well have *encouraged* her to go, in fact. She is of more use to us there than here.'

The queen continued to glower. 'This kind of thing cannot be repeated. I want this man executed for his failings.'

'If I executed every officer who was confused by the Aegyptian royalty this winter, we'd cull half the army, my Queen. Remember that much of great rule lies in appropriate clemency.' He turned to the centurion. 'Have you disciplined the men who did this without seeking the authority of a senior officer?'

The centurion nodded vigorously. 'Of course, General. The four men on gate duty have been flogged and demoted.'

'Then I think the matter should be drawn to a close.'

The queen was not calm yet though. 'I am growing tired of your men, Caesar. Men who burn my library, tear down my city and free my sister.'

Her gaze darted round the room, pinning Fronto, Cassius and the centurion, Fronto managed to maintain his calm, and the centurion kept his face lowered, but Cassius glared back at her, lip curling. Trouble was brewing in that quarter.

The queen turned, sweeping her flowing gown into her arm and making to exit as Apollodorus fell in at her shoulder, when the door opened and the king entered. Three men tried to hurry ahead and blast horns but they managed only a brief toot before the enraged young king stomped petulantly into the centre, throwing his sister an acidic look.

'Am I to understand that my sister – not this harpy, but the young and stupid one – has managed to slip through your lines and usurp me, suborning my army?'

Cleopatra paused on her way to the door to throw her brother – her *husband too*, Fronto remembered with a start – the most vicious look she could muster. 'Usurp *us*, dear brother.'

He sneered at her and then proceeded to ignore her further, turning back to Caesar.

'What have you to say for yourself, Roman?'

Caesar's brow altered just slightly. Fronto knew the look and was tempted to stand back. The general took three steps, hands clasped behind his back, until he was so close to Ptolemy that the king actually quivered and retreated a pace. His bodyguards hurried forwards but stopped as half a dozen Romans drew their blades threateningly.

'Ptolemy the Thirteenth, Theos Philopator, both of which I might dispute, and king of Aegyptus, welcome. I will remind you at the outset that your good health, and one might say even your continued existence, are owed solely to Rome's close ties with your father, and my great patience in attempting to reconcile your fractious land under a safe and peaceful rule. When the time comes that the difficulties you present outweigh both the value you bring to a potential peace and my strained patience, that health and, yes, existence, become much more questionable. Do I make myself clear?'

The general was tall and lean, given to military dress at the best of times, and his receding grey hair, combined with his prominent cheekbones and strong nose, gave him something of the look of a hunting eagle. The effect when he towered over the youthful and pampered king was profound. Fronto almost laughed as Ptolemy backed away nervously.

'What... what do you intend to do about Arsinoë?'

Caesar shrugged. 'Nothing whatsoever. I pray that she is little more than a painful boil on Achillas' backside, and I suspect I am close to the truth there. She stands about as much chance of rousing the Aegyptian army to greater threat and replacing Achillas as its commander as... well, as *you* do.'

The insult was cutting and hung in the air like an acrid smell.

Ptolemy trembled, though whether through anger or fear no one could tell. Both, Fronto suspected. After a long pause, Ptolemy subsided and stepped back again. 'When will you acknowledge my position and send me back to the army. If you did so, I would be able to end this.'

Caesar sighed. 'Releasing you to Achillas would almost certainly have one of two results. Either you would immediately renege on any oath made here and revive your conflict with your sister, dragging this entire thing out further, or Achillas would no longer be able to claim your authority, you would be an impediment to him, and he would remove you before continuing to make war in the hope of seizing control himself. You will remain here in the safety of the palace until we are in a strong enough position to impose a proper rule of law and remove Achillas from the equation. Now go. You are dismissed, your Majesty.'

Ptolemy's lip twitched but he backed from the room, his musicians giving a desultory tootle before following him and his bodyguards. It was only as he disappeared that Fronto realised the queen had also gone.

'Keeping the Aegyptian ruling bloodline so pure does have the unfortunate side effect of producing the odd runt,' Caesar said bitterly as the door closed. The majority of the officers laughed, but Cassius stepped forwards.

'Caesar, given that we are as alone now as we are likely to be, I must needs point out a few truths to you.'

'Oh?'

'I know that you favour the queen, and all the world can see why, but I fear you are becoming lax in your care here. Cleopatra might *seem* to support you, but that will only remain true as long as you are of use to her here. Do not underestimate her potential for duplicity. And her brother might be a young fool with more bravado than brains, but he is also bitter and ambitious. Add into that mix that both have servants and slaves loyal beyond even death in this palace, and you can picture a bubbling cauldron of peril. I would ask that you remember that your focus here is the will of Rome and your strongest support comes from we Roman officers.'

Caesar turned an irritated look on him.

'Is this because I would not support you tearing down buildings when the queen berated you, Cassius?'

Fronto winced. *Don't poke that bear, Caesar.*

Cassius bridled. 'I did what any sensible leader would, and would do it again. And any commander who was not under the perfumed spell of a witch queen would agree.'

Fronto clenched his teeth, waiting for Caesar to burst into a fury over that. Instead the general glared coldly at Cassius. 'Be careful, old friend. Men who served Pompey so avidly can rely upon my clemency and support only as long as they stand by my side.'

'I *do* stand by your side, Caesar,' snapped Cassius. 'That you cannot see it only makes my point for me. And my meaning is that you are a target for Aegyptian malevolence, and will only become more so as time goes on. Watch your back in this palace.' He swept an arm around the room. 'And that goes for all of us to a lesser extent. Watch your backs. Sleep with an eye open. Have someone taste your food. Be vigilant.'

With that he bowed his head curtly to Caesar and strode towards the exit.

When he left, shutting the door behind him, Caesar stood for a long moment, eyelid flickering, until Aulus Hirtius cleared his throat. 'Despite any personal issues there, I fear Cassius had a valid point about vigilance. We *have* become a little carefree, allowing powerful Aegyptians free run around us. Perhaps we can see to the tightening of Roman security in the palace?'

Caesar continued to hesitate for a long time, but finally nodded. 'There are clearly those in our midst who might wish us harm. I have men in place already, but I recommend that you all follow suit as Cassius advised.'

Fronto shivered, partially at the news that Caesar had already set up a secret private network of security, but more at the ambiguity of whom Caesar considered potentially harmful. It seemed more aimed at Cassius than the Aegyptians.

* * *

The days of November moved on with little change in either camp, but for the increasing tension in the palace. The king and queen avoided one another more than ever, and Cassius made sure to be in the general's presence only at meetings, when he was required.

Fronto did note, though, that the general's habits started to change. Never a man given to excess sleep or unnecessary relaxation, he began to remain awake late into the night, sleeping only in brief naps, and always with men of Aulus Ingenuus' bodyguard around. Food tasters checked every meal, though they did that for *all* Romans now, but Caesar had also employed someone to check his rooms for snakes and scorpions before he retired.

It was an evening two days after the Ides of November that found Fronto hurrying to the general's door with a report of activity among the enemy. The praetorians at the entrance checked with the general and then admitted Fronto at his behest, and the legate made his way into Caesar's room, the door clicking shut behind him.

'General, just a warning that we may be in for a fresh wave of attacks. Wood is in short supply hereabouts, but scouts have reported timber being brought in from the delta for Achillas' men, and he's had teams deforesting Pharos Island too. It is heavily suggestive of the construction of siege engines.'

Caesar nodded. 'We have known it would come. In a way, I prefer to face a fight, even a bad one, than to sit in this tension and wait, watching my back all the time.'

He rose and gestured to the room's corner. 'Speaking of which…'

Fronto glanced that way. He'd not noticed the man beforehand. A slave, one of several who travelled with the general's baggage, attending him in his quarters. His barber, Fronto thought he remembered. He frowned.

'Bulo here has been using his free time well, acting as my eyes and ears in the palace. One of several,' he added. 'This evening he has managed to intercept a communique that I find interesting.'

He held out two pieces of parchment. One was scribbled in the indecipherable local language, the other in good Latin. 'I had it translated just now,' Caesar explained.

Fronto read down, eyes widening. Whoever had penned the note sought the assurances of the general Achillas that both he and King Ptolemy would be preserved in the fighting to come, promising in return that Achillas would be honoured above all men and granted great lands and positions. It went on to request that the general dispose of the inconvenient Princess Arsinoë, in return for which the unknown author would ensure that the queen met her demise in the palace, along with the Roman consul. The writer believed that with the death of Caesar, Roman will would crumble and the other officers would flee Aegyptus. In a dark corner of his mind, Fronto suspected that latter might be unpleasantly true.

'So someone *is* plotting against you. Cassius was right. And against the queen, too. There are very few men who could have written this, of course.

'Potheinus,' Caesar said with definite finality. 'It was observed leaving his very hand into the care of a messenger who sadly never reached the acropolis boundary, for he met with my eyes and ears – and knives. His remains are in the harbour now. Which is what I am tempted to do with both Potheinus and Ptolemy.'

The general sighed and leaned back. 'I am tired, Fronto, and more than a little driven by anger at this particular time. You seem composed and sensible. Tell me, what should I do about this irritating eunuch and his juvenile king?'

Fronto shrugged. 'Not sure you can lay this at the king's feet, in fairness. He's an idiot, but too important a piece in the game to dispose of out of hand. Potheinus, on the other hand, can only be of further use irritating the other damned spirits in his afterlife. Build him a pyramid and drop it on him.'

Caesar chuckled. 'I had a feeling you might think that. I have no great wish to spend any more time in young Ptolemy's company, but perhaps you are right. Potheinus, though? Yes, and a grand gesture, I think.' He gave Fronto an odd look. 'Perhaps not a *whole* pyramid. These Aegyptians seem to be fans of beheading. Let's send Achillas the head of Potheinus, with the incriminating note stuck between his teeth. That should serve to make he and Princess Arsinoë argue for a while, and perhaps delay their next assault.'

Fronto nodded, wincing yet again. He wasn't keen on the idea of such grisly ostentation. Better to simply execute the rodent and dump him in the harbour. Still, dead was dead.

'I'll speak to Ingenuus and see that it's done.'

CHAPTER FIVE

Late November 48 BC

The officers gathered in the large room, open to the warm sun and the sea breeze by a colonnade of brightly painted, lotus-capitalled columns, the drumming of fingers and sucking of teeth abounding as they waited impatiently. Fronto looked around the assembled faces. Some he knew of old, some were more recent additions, but all were good. One thing about civil war, he mused bitterly, was that it weeded out the chaff. There was no room in any army now for weak leaders.

Aulus Hirtius, Caesar's secretary and a nobleman with a strong military career in his own right, standing twitchily like a crane, with his beaked nose and strangely avian gait. Cassius, a staunch, solidly-built man who had been both friend and foe to Caesar in his time, but had been a renowned military mind throughout. Decimus Junius Brutus, long-time friend and officer of Caesar's, famed naval commander and as loyal a man as could be found in the republic. Tiberius Nero, a hero of the pirate wars some decade earlier and ex officer of Pompey. Salvius Cursor, a man equally at home with the officers on the tribunal or with his blade out and bloody in the field. Titus Orfidius Bulla, tribune and commander of the present contingent of the Twenty Seventh. No Marcus Antonius, though, who had been dispatched early to Rome, before the landing in Aegyptus, there to maintain Caesar's interests. Staunch men, here, though. Ready to face the army of Achillas personally, let alone as commanders of the meagre troops available.

The door opened with a click, and Caesar strode in with the queen at his side, his watchful slave Bulo at his heel, and then several of Ingenuus' praetorian bodyguards.

'Gentlemen. Apologies for the slight delay.'

There was a mumbled chorus of platitudes as the officers waited on the latest news.

'The last of the ships has now left, and once more I must commend Fronto on his seizure of the Pharos fort. Control of the harbour's main entrance has proved invaluable.'

'What is the final tally, General?' Hirtius asked quietly.

The general nodded at Brutus, who had been placed in charge of the fleet in the Palace Harbour. The younger officer, eyes black-rimmed with exhaustion, frowned as he dredged his memory over several days of activity.

'One ship to Syria, seeking Calvinus, attempting to ascertain where he and his legions are. Those armies should be well on the way to Alexandria by now, so the ship will call at all coastal cities once it is past the delta, seeking news of the reinforcements. Then it will continue to Antioch and Tarsus seeking further support and tidings before calling back via Cyprus. Four ships for Cyrenaica and Crete to seek the support of the governor there and to request supplies and manpower from both island and mainland sources, including vital Cretan archers.'

He leaned back, stretching. 'Two ships to Sicilia. Two ships for Asia and Greece. Two ships have been dispatched, rather bravely I might add, up the Nilus, seeking support for the queen from the native governors inland. One ship to Cilicia, one to Rhodos, and not just for the excellent wine,' he gave a weary smile as the officers chuckled. 'The rest of the fleet remains here.'

Hirtius nodded with satisfaction, and Caesar huffed. 'I would have liked to send more ships for supplies, but between volatile political situations in the Armenian region, Achillas' control of much of Aegyptus, and Pompey's cronies still in charge of Africa, our sources are diminished. Still, we do what we must. Salvius Aper, who knows the region well, has taken a century of men, protecting a deputation, across the dangerous delta, seeking King Malchus of the Nabateans, for their cavalry would be valuable. I believe we have done all we can to secure men and supplies. We cannot move against Achillas until at the least Calvinus' legions arrive, for we are still greatly outnumbered. All we can hope is that the enemy have burned their fingers on the fire of our resistance sufficiently to hold off until we are better equipped to deal with them. What other preparations are underway?'

Salvius Cursor cleared his throat. 'Forays by brave men of our legions have secured a good stock of timber, ropes, tools and nails from the harbour dockyards. They have been brought in and are now being used to create weaponry and siege engines. The longer we are left alone, the better our armament becomes.'

Caesar nodded.

'Likewise, the defences themselves improve by the day,' Cassius announced. 'We have now sealed all entrances bar two and begun to increase the height of the walls, adding extra pits, bulwarks and all manner of defences along the line.' He threw a defiant look towards the queen. 'Fortunately many of the native structures are formed of very good, solid stone blocks that are perfect for repurposing as defensive lines.'

The queen hissed as she snapped an angry look at the man, the two of them remaining locked in a war of stares until Caesar stepped between them. 'Is it not sufficient that Pompey's former colleagues war against their own, and the Aegyptian royal house suffers internecine conflict? Must we war among ourselves even here?'

Fronto watched carefully. Every unspoken moment between Caesar and these two was of import now. There was a long pause as Cassius threw a look at the general that sought validation and support. Fronto almost groaned as Caesar turned with a nod to the queen. 'We will do what we can to limit the damage to your buildings.' Fronto could not miss the bitter anger that swept across Cassius at that. Fronto had not been willing to accept the notion that Caesar was somehow falling under the queen's spell, something that had become a strong current of rumour recently, but it was becoming hard to deny.

'I have sent out deputations,' the queen announced into the tense silence. 'Men I trust who can slip past Achillas' army, and who know both where and who to entreat for supplies of grain. Beyond the city to the south lies close fertile land, which can source a steady flow of supplies. I expect to see a response very fast. If they cannot bring the grain in by ship we may have to temporarily secure a passage through the enemy for them.'

Fronto cleared his throat, noting how little that notion appealed to the officers, and trying to divert the conversation before a fresh argument broke out. 'There are places where the walls simply cannot be strengthened adequately by adding stones. In these places we have put our best veterans and the most inventive engineers. They are working constantly to use hides, timbers, dug trenches and whatever they can lay their hands upon to plug gaps.'

'What of water supplies?' Hirtius queried.

'Our men were careful not to ruin the underground channels leading here when they prepared the road defences,' Cassius said, again firing an optical assault at the queen. 'As long as those channels remain undisturbed, we have sufficient water.'

'What of the enemy?'

Salvius Cursor and Orfidius Bulla shared a look, and the former cracked his knuckles. 'We have seen supplies coming in from both east and south, along the larger routes. Artillery and major siege equipment, weaponry and ammunition. It is telling and somewhat unfortunate to note that the sources of some of these supplies can only be inland Aegyptian Nomes that nominally support the queen. Their numbers swell, and I am sorry to report that it would appear that a significant portion of the queen's force that had remained at Pelusium seem to now be serving Achillas.'

Orfidius Bulla nodded. 'There is some suggestion that the queen's army has disintegrated, following various rumours of her captivity or death. Those who have not thrown in their lot with Achillas and now added to the enemy are said to have moved upriver to Memphis to support the youngest brother of the royal house, yet another Ptolemy.'

'The unpleasant reality suggested by all of this,' Salvius continued, 'is that Achillas has been sending bribes and demands and pulling to his cause anyone he can, including those upon whom we hoped to rely.'

Orfidius Bulla scratched his neck. 'Additionally, the activity we have noted from our best viewpoints suggests that Achillas is preparing for a major assault. Smoke pours out of buildings where it shouldn't, an indication that metallurgy is now carried out there. It is my belief that every available slave in the city has been put to work in factories and workshops manufacturing weapons and ammunition. I believe that the city's rich and influential, fearing to oppose Achillas, have turned their back on the queen and supplied the enemy with funds and goods.'

'Let them come,' Cassius snarled. 'Our defences are now triple walled in many places and up to forty feet in height. The Aegyptians might have a vast force, but their experience with sieges is sparse at best, while Rome is well-practised at the art. I fear not this Achillas.'

* * *

Days passed and, given what Fronto had heard in the meeting, he began to prowl the defences keeping an eye on the enemy, often with Galronus at his side. The reports of Orfidius Bulla and Salvius Cursor were clearly accurate. It became clear in the proceeding days that much of the city had been given over to the production of equipment and to preparations for war.

And whether the queen liked it or not, Cassius' work had helped secure the citadel. Houses and shops were gone by the dozen, but the engineers under the Roman officer had created a triple wall system that Fronto would hate to have to tackle, the inner wall as tall as four or five men. Moreover, they were formed of well-shaped stone, mortared into place as strong as any fortress Fronto had seen. What had been a maze of narrow alleys around the palace had become a fortress in less than a month.

Fronto passed the end of the Canopus Canal, where the wall was granted extra strength by the wide watery channel, and passed into the triple wall region. Climbing the ladder to the fighting platform, he felt a little dizzy at the height, and took a moment to settle as Galronus joined him.

'Cassius is thorough,' the Remi nobleman noted.

Fronto nodded. From this high position, he could see the defences in all their impressive glory. 'Would that we had more archers. When the ship returns from Crete, we will be better off.'

Galronus glanced down at the baskets of rocks and small caches of javelins and darts that had been gathered from all over the harbour, palace and Diabathra fort. 'The cavalry sit impotent and unhappy. City streets are no theatre of war for riders. Would that we could meet them in open ground.'

'Then we would be massacred,' Fronto sighed. 'Numbers.'

The two stood quiet for a long moment, listening to the distant sounds of construction and manufacture, the croaking of gulls, the splash of water, and the constant work of the Caesarian soldiers in consolidating their defences.

'Can you hear something?' Galronus said.

'Many things. Like what?'

'I'm not sure. New activity.'

They both fell silent again, listening carefully. Then Fronto heard it. From one of the nearby neighbourhoods, a little east of where they stood. The surge of voices some distance away. A rhythmic chanting.

'That cannot be good.'

'It's about three streets that way.'

The two men started to move fast along the wall top. As they passed the soldiers on duty, the general sense of alertness increased. Something was happening, and everyone was becoming aware of it. A signal horn blast went up not far ahead, close enough that they could see the musician with his cornu, puffing and blowing as men beside him pointed down the street.

Back inside the walls, men were now spilling out of the nearest buildings, all of which had been commandeered as barracks for the defenders, jamming helmets on their heads as they ran, doing up belts and slinging sword baldrics over their shoulders. Fronto and Galronus closed on the location. A centurion was now standing at the wall with the musician and a standard bearer, men rushing all about them.

'Attack?' Fronto asked as he neared the man.

The centurion turned. 'Yes, legate. Looks like they're about to test their new stuff.'

The two officers fell in at the parapet beside the centurion. Before them lay a wide open area, courtesy of Cassius' work at pulling down buildings for his defences and to create the killing zone. Beyond that lay a wide street, one of the grid that criss-crossed the city.

A mass of men were moving towards them from the distance, large shapes among them. Fronto squinted in the sunlight. They were light infantry, surrounding new constructions.

'Quite right,' he said. This is a probing attack. Achillas has committed only his most expendable men. We need to make them regret this. Every black eye we give them will make them more wary.'

'We're well prepared, sir,' the centurion said.

'Good.' Fronto stepped to the side to allow legionaries into place where the baskets of rocks and stooks of javelins stood. The enemy were moving slowly, chanting in time with their footsteps. A forty foot siege tower held pride of place towards the rear centre of the force. That would be of little use until they managed to get past the first two walls, of course. Long siege ladders were being carried among the men, and carts with timber and hide sides taller than a man rose among the mass. Long ramps, like those for boarding ships, moved among them on two wheels, guided and balanced by the men.

'Brace for a fight,' Fronto said. 'They mean business.'

'They'll get a bloody shock, sir,' grinned the centurion. 'Watch this.'

Fronto nodded, watching carefully. There was little he could do to help at this point. He would not be able to reach the enemy to fight until they had all but succeeded, reaching the top of the inner wall. He would be ready for that, but if they got that far with this small probing force, then the Roman defences were done for anyway. Until then it would be down to the ingenuity of the engineers and the skill of men with missiles, and Fronto was realistic enough to accept that there were sheep that could throw a missile more accurately than he.

As the mass approached the open area, the centurion blew a whistle and the signallers picked it up. The few ranged missiles upon which they could call began to loose. The legions had brought a few scorpion bolt throwers with them aboard the ships, and the legionaries had claimed four more in the city. These precious weapons had been positioned around the defences at the places that were most vulnerable and with the best arc of targeting, which meant that here two could train upon the enemy. Moreover, the few bows that had been found in the palace region had been distributed among the soldiers, granted to any man who could claim competence with the weapon, and these few archers now nocked arrows.

The second signal went up as the enemy flooded into the killing zone. Officers yelled out the command for shooting at will, and the men on the wall top marked their targets, trained the weapons carefully, and loosed. Missiles were in short enough supply that the defenders had been granted the right to loose slowly at their whim, in order to best achieve a kill. The result was not a cloud of stinging death falling like rain upon the force, but more carefully selected and almost surgical damage. Each of the men had marked someone they considered important, and Fronto had to concede that the archers had been well chosen for their skill.

All along the front few ranks of the enemy the missiles hit home, few failing to make their mark. Those that did strike had been very carefully selected. Enemy officers, marked out by their lavish equipment, fell with cries, as did standard bearers and musicians. All men who could direct and control an attack. Other missiles targeted those men carrying ladders or leading the carts or ramps, causing them to falter and jam the advance until other men stepped in to take their place.

'What's next?' Fronto asked the centurion.

'And spoil the surprise, sir?' the man chuckled, and Fronto rolled his eyes before turning them back to the advancing mob. Across a wide ground of rubble they moved, their carts and wheeled ramps encountering constant obstacles and requiring adjustment and aid, sometimes dozens of men flooding to them to help lift them across the worst hindrances. The first line of defence lay perhaps ten feet from the lowest outer wall – a heap of rubble and wooden beams and sticks gathered in a line around the defences. It would take some clearing for the vehicles, certainly.

'Is it in reach of missiles?' he mused. The centurion grinned.

Watching, tense, Fronto saw the first lines of men reaching the makeshift barrier. They slowed as they neared it.

'Give 'em shit, lads,' the centurion laughed.

Once more, the few archers and scorpion crews launched their missiles into those men, and soldiers along the wall carefully chose rocks, weighing them and moving to the parapet. As the enemy slowed to negotiate the barrier, the defenders let loose with a barrage of missiles, both crafted and makeshift. The enemy cried out as the rocks and arrows fell among them, and those men who now knew they were within range and in danger started to run forwards, clambering over the barrier as fast as they could.

Fronto almost laughed.

Whoever had set that barrier out had a wicked sense of humour. Far from being a gathered pile of rubble and sticks as it appeared, it was a much nastier idea in truth. The engineers had jammed sharpened stakes into the ground, angled alternately outwards, straight up, and inwards, and then carefully laid detritus atop them, disguising the wicked points as a simple rubble heap.

Men screamed and wailed, fell forwards and back as the sharpened timber points tore through shins, calves, feet and thighs, and when men fell they were impaled further on the spikes. The attack slowed in an instant, faltering, and a fresh wave of missiles fell upon them, accompanied by jeers from the wall top.

The attack might well have failed right there, the enemy pulling back out of danger. Certainly their morale collapsed, these troops the weakest among Achillas' army. Fronto had to hand it to the enemy officers. They might not have quite the discipline of the legions, but their control over their men was powerful, the bulk of the army seemingly more fearful of their own commanders than of the enemy. Words of anger and command poured from the

Aegyptian officers and the enemy force, after a brief falter, pressed on.

Men endured the hail of missiles as they worked to remove the barriers in sections wide enough to admit a dozen men, or the carts or ramps among them. In fact they had little to worry about, for the ammunition supplies on the wall top were not plentiful, and gradually the missiles thinned out to occasional releases. Soldiers were even now ferrying fresh supplies of rocks from the harbour in heavy baskets that were then raised to the wall walk on ropes.

Gradually, Fronto watched the tide overcome the rubble and spike obstacle. However, they no longer chanted, no longer rushing ahead with enthusiasm and the belief of an easy victory. Now they came on slowly, carefully, sullenly, only moving forwards because of the vicious officers in their midst, some of whom wielded whips or staves, using them to beat or lash any man who baulked at the advance.

Now, the mobile ramps were brought forward, and Fronto realised that they had been designed for this specific attack. This whole probe had been designed to overcome the triple walls. As the ramps were rolled forth by desperate men, he realised the ladders were just the size to pass the second wall, the tower tall enough for the inner, third rampart.

Some of those ramps failed at the start, the better shots on the wall picking off the men moving them into position with their few remaining arrows, waiting until other men took their place and then pulverising *their* heads with sea-smoothed cobbles in turn. Still, the ramps came on, wheeled up against the outer wall, which was perhaps eight feet high. The ramps were slammed against the upper edge of the wall, wedges jammed under the wheels to prevent them rolling back. The enemy bellowed triumphantly, though there was still enough uncertainty and nervousness that no one rushed up them until a number of ramps were in place.

Finally, content that there was sufficient access for a large number, Achillas' soldiers, exhorted by their vicious officers, clambered up the ramps and over the first wall, dropping into the eight foot gap between it and the second, waiting nervously well within missile range as their comrades brought forward the scaling ladders that would take them over the second wall.

'They will still have to dismantle a wide enough section of both walls to get the tower close,' Galronus noted.

'And all the time within missile range,' Fronto agreed.

'They might not get that far, sir,' the centurion noted, and blew four short blasts on his whistle. All along the wall, every fifteen paces or so, soldiers stepped forwards in pairs. As the enemy poured into that narrow space between the outer and middle walls, one of each pair hefted a pitch-soaked torch in a strong arm, while the other struck flints and sparked until the torches caught, all below the line of the walls, invisible to the enemy.

Fronto gritted his teeth, anticipating what was coming next. War or no war, this was no way for a man to die. Gradually the torches along the wall burst into life and still the centurion waited. Fronto peered down and watched with hushed anticipation as the enemy began to bring their ladders across the outer defence and into the central gap. The moment the officer thought they had the optimal enemy force in line, he blasted his whistle again and all along the rampart men cast blazing torches down into the gap between outer and middle wall.

Fronto winced. Here and there a thrower missed, but it mattered not. Days ago the entire length had been soaked in pitch. Fronto realised now that he'd been able to smell it as they approached, despite the fact that it had been covered with sawdust to dampen the tell-tale stench. Some of the enemy had swiftly realised the danger and had tried to flee, shouting warnings that went entirely unheard in the general din. They were trapped. A few managed to grasp the top of the eight foot wall and pull themselves up in an attempt to get out, but even fewer of them succeeded, many being pushed back in by the flood of men coming the other way.

All along the line the torches landed, instantly igniting the pitch-soaked and sawdust-covered ground. The land between the central and outer wall became a deadly fire pit in moments, roaring flames filling the entire trap, frying hundreds of men and burning their siege ladders. They panicked and screamed, floundering, desperate to escape but trapped by the eight foot wall they had already scaled.

The attack broke. Many of those driven officers had given up hope of further advance and were calling their men back, preserving their remaining carts and ladders, and that tower they had no hope of bringing close enough to be effective. Even had the officers maintained their aggressive pushing of their men, they would now have failed, for the spirit of the Aegyptians had been totally broken by the sounds of their compatriots burning to death in the tightly packed space between walls. The army fled back across the open space and up that wide street, accompanied by victorious cries from the wall.

Fronto laughed as the centurion bellowed invective at a legionary who had turned on the wall's parapet and bent over, baring his buttocks at the fleeing enemy.

Galronus looked down at the corpses strewn across that wide space, trying not to look too closely at the continually burning nightmare that lay between the walls, where few still lived, most already charring and twisting, blackened and roasted in the conflagration.

'That should make them think twice,' he said.

Fronto nodded. 'But only for a few days. You saw their officers. Achillas is determined, and that's driving his commanders to push their men. He will not allow too much delay. They will think on this and find new ways. The next attack will not be repulsed so readily. And I would be willing to wager that the palace's supplies of pitch are thin. Replacing that against a similar push might well be difficult. Every attack we drive back lowers our supply levels and reduces our capability to do so next time.'

'Your wife is right, you know,' Galronus snorted. 'No cup for you is ever half full is it?'

Fronto sighed.

'We had best pray that reinforcements and supplies are coming on those ships.'

* * *

Fronto watched Galronus depart as his friend turned and strolled off wearily towards the room in the palace set aside for the Remi nobleman. Continuing on to his own chamber, he was surprised to see the figure of Gaius Cassius Longinus leaning beside the door.

He'd not spent much time in Cassius' company since they had met at the Hellespont earlier that year, or at least not without the entire cadre of other staff officers being present. He eyed the man warily. As yet he remained unable to weigh Cassius up.

The man was from an old Roman family, as noble as Fronto's own. His mother-in-law had been rumoured to be a lover of Caesar's, though that had been years earlier. He had a reputation as a staunch republican and a hater of despotism, which had likely been part of the reason he had thrown in his lot with those senators opposing Caesar. He had been an enemy throughout this bitter civil war, and had only given his oath to Caesar recently, under duress and after the victory over Pompey at Pharsalus. There were voices in the staff that suggested he may not be trustworthy, and certainly he had no clear reason to support Caesar.

Yet he was also a man with a good, noble reputation. A clever and experienced military mind, Cassius had been the only senior officer to survive the field at Carrhae, which had seen the demise of Crassus and his army. His was a name spoken of with respect, and even awe in some circles.

To Fronto he represented the ultimate in inscrutability.

'Cassius?'

'Fronto. I've come to pick your brains, if I might.'

Fronto frowned, but opened his door and gestured inside. Cassius joined him and wandered over to the window with its beautiful view of the Palace Harbour and the theatre, allowing the fresh sea breeze into the stifling warmth of the room.

'You have served with Caesar most of your career,' he said. Fronto searched the tone for a hint of accusation, but found none. In the end, he shrugged.

'*Most* of it.'

'It is no secret that he's always been ambitious,' Cassius said quietly. 'Lucky, brave, clever and all sorts of things a Roman proconsul should be, but more ambitious than most. A Sulla in the making, some might say.'

Fronto sighed. He hated it when people started this sort of conversation. It was a subject that broke friendships more surely even than adultery. He and Balbus had often had to agree to avoid the subject.

'We live in an age of tyrants, and would-be tyrants, Cassius.'

'No, Fronto. We live in the great age of Rome's republic. It is simply endangered by despots.' He huffed and swept his hand around, as though brushing things from a table. 'But it is not despots and the danger Caesar poses to our government of which I wished to speak.'

Fronto heaved another sigh, this time of relief.

'Good. What is it then?'

'I understand that there have been times when you have walked away from the general because of your personal grievances, yet you came back. More than once, if I am not misinformed.'

Fronto nodded uneasily.

'I worry about him,' Cassius said quietly. 'I worry that Rome should be settling after all this war. That we should be defeating the last few who stand for Pompey's flag, or for preference negotiating with them and drawing them back into the fold. Only when that happens can the republic begin to mend. Then Caesar will have to put aside his imperium and become part of Rome's good.'

'I think we all agree that's what needs to happen,' Fronto agreed.

'Yet instead we are here, doing this.'

'Aegyptus needs to be settled before we move on.'

Cassius shook his head. 'That's blindness, Fronto. If the general simply wanted a settled Aegyptus so we could move on, he could confirm Ptolemy's authority on the throne, hand the queen to her enemies, and leave. Ptolemy would grant him almost any concession. Rome would prosper on it, the land would be settled, and we could move on. To me it is clear that we tarry against all sense. We endanger ourselves and face warfare every day entirely unnecessarily.'

Fronto remained silent. It was, at the bare bones, truth. Admittedly there were subtleties at play here. Rome's support of Cleopatra's father and the commitment of the senate to maintain their joint rule was at the nominal heart of what Caesar was doing, and on some levels it was clearly the right thing to do. Whether it was expedient, and whether the senate would see it as right was another thing entirely.

Cassius turned. 'I am sure we are doing the wrong thing here, Fronto. What I cannot decide is whether we are doing it because Caesar is under the spell of that harpy queen, or whether it is because of the general's deep-seated need to control, and his unwillingness to pass an opportunity to increase his imperium. Is this an effort to avoid finishing the war and laying down his power, Fronto?'

The older legate sighed and leaned back against the wall. 'I struggled long and hard, more than once, with what I think about Caesar. Did you know Pompey well?'

Cassius shook his head. 'I knew *Crassus* well, Pompey peripherally.'

'Then you probably still know enough. You know that Crassus was greed incarnate, that acquisition was at the heart of everything he did. You will know equally that anger and violence raged in Pompey's blood. Had he no war to fight he would have ended up tearing himself apart. I'm a practical man, Cassius. I would love to believe that the best the republic can hope for is still to come, but I see it half-mouldering in its tomb already. It started long before even Sulla and Marius, but they hastened things. If the republic has a hope of survival, Caesar is it. I have watched every other man of power rise and fall, and they all displayed cankers in their soul at the end. Caesar might be ambitious. Dangerous, even. But he does care about Rome, and he is the best of what the gods offer us. That is why I serve him, and that is why I keep coming back.'

'None of that answered my question, Fronto.'

'I know. I am becoming aware of the influence the queen has over him, but I'm confident it's temporary. The general attracts women like clients. Wives? Cornelia, Pompeia and Calpurnia. Lovers? Well, let's not talk about that, given his connection with your wife's mother. But none of them have lasted. Calpurnia too will surely end in divorce, and this queen will fall by the wayside like all the others. He might be influenced by her, but no woman will get between him and duty.'

'So power is all.'

'Certainly he will not want to leave Aegyptus until he has achieved all he set out to do. He wins often. He loses occasionally. But he never backs down.'

'And you think he will give up his power when this is over?'

'I hope so,' Fronto said. 'I will follow him into the maw of Cerberus, but the day he stands against the republic, I will turn my back on him. I think he knows that.'

Cassius nodded, an odd sparkle in his eye.

'You are a good man, Fronto. And one with principles, I think. When all this is over, I see you and I becoming fast friends.'

'For now, let's just hope we survive this long enough to test that.'

Cassius smiled, bowed his head and left, shutting the door behind him.

Fronto wandered over to the window, heaving the breeze deep into his lungs. He tried to ponder on what he had to do in the morning, but kept finding himself mentally drawn back to Cassius. To the man's worries about Caesar's addiction to power, and to the strange sparkle in his eyes.

Damn it, but Fronto wished this war would end so they could all go home.

CHAPTER SIX

The Paneum, central Alexandria, The Kalends of December 48 BC

Queen of the Black Land and daughter of the pharaoh Ptolemy Auletes, Arsinoë *"Horus who conquers"*, *"Watched over by the Two Ladies"*, *"Sun falcon"*, glared at the general.

'That is your final word?'

Achillas looked down at the queen, still nothing more than a princess in his eyes, with rising contempt. 'Your brother assumed the throne legally upon your father's death, and sanctified his reign with his marriage to his cursed sister, as the pharaoh had wished. I have no intention of bowing my head to that bitch queen who thinks herself a new Hatshepsut, but my sword belongs to the new pharaoh, your brother. We fight to oust the Roman interference in our affairs and consolidate his place as king of our land. You have no place in this matter but as a pretty little figurehead to bolster the morale of your brother's men.'

Arsinoë's eyebrow cocked a little, dangerously. At less than eighteen summers and slight of frame, the shortest member of her family, she might appear somehow less when standing beside the ageing general in all his military power, but she knew that she had in her veins the blood of the great Ptolemy, that famed general who had conquered the world with Alexander, while Achillas was but a nobody from Thebes.

'Your avowed noble task and the loyalty you profess would mean a great deal more if it were not for the common and most credible understanding that when you finish off the last Roman in the city, the bodies of my brother and sister will almost certainly be found in the wreckage, sadly caught in the killing and leaving you in sole power to found a new dynasty. Do not think for even a moment that your motives are unobserved.'

'Watch your mouth, tiny princess,' Achillas snarled, bunching his fists. 'I will fight for the king, and you are useful in goading the men into action, but the moment your difficulty outweighs your value, it will be the end of you, mark my words.'

Arsinoë stood still for some time, her glare boring holes into the general's skull. When finally she shifted her gaze, it fell first left and then right, taking in the other two officers present, who remained steadfast in Achillas' camp, each accompanied by their guards. She smiled unpleasantly.

'I wish you luck, then, Achillas sand-born, for you will most assuredly need it.'

Turning, she strode from the room, two half-naked slaves pulling open the doors for her, making the braziers gutter and flicker. As they closed behind her once more, she stopped in the corridor for a moment, composing herself. She had allowed that low-born fool to rile her. She should have kept calmer, made sure to give nothing away. Still, he was short-sighted enough not to recognise a threat. It was, she mused, a failing in men. They always thought themselves superior in both physique and mind. They were often wrong on one or both counts. Achillas was certainly strong, but Arsinoë was fast. Achillas was possessed of a good military mind, but Arsinoë was cleverer in every other respect. Just as her brother had underestimated Cleopatra, so Achillas was doing the same with the youngest daughter of Ptolemy Auletes.

She strode from the building, through the great pylon entrance, between the impressive statues, and stood on the top of the steps looking out over the city. A city divided; cut into defensive pieces like some great *senet* board with two players eyeing each other warily, for the next move could end the game. The calm was eerie, deceiving. Just like the enemy, the men of her army – *her* army, not that of the fool back in that room – were quiet, manning the defences. It was, to her mind, a mark of how foolish he was, or possibly how timid, that Achillas had set his men to fortifying their own position with a facsimile of the Roman lines, a hastily-assembled triple wall.

She shook her head, lip curling in a sneer. This army was not a force of builders like the Romans, but one of warriors. While the Romans had in mere days turned rubble into a fortress of strength and power, their own army had cobbled together a poor imitation of ill-fitting and badly-placed rocks. And what was the point anyway? They outnumbered the Romans by a vast margin, and Caesar was hardly going to lead his men forth in an assault against them. The only time the Roman consul might consider attacking would be when substantial reinforcements arrived, and if Arsinoë's army had not overcome them by then, no fortification would be of use.

No, Achillas was an idiot.

And her brother was the idiot who relied upon this idiot, thinking he was loyal and would come to free him from the clutches of the Romans. The idiot that had calmly ridden into the Roman camp on a mobile throne assuming he could order the consul and his men around. *Men.* They were all fools, and deserved everything they got. It was a shame about Cleopatra, though. Arsinoë was genuinely sorry that her sister had to suffer in all this. Cleopatra did not deserve to die, really. She was clever, as clever as Arsinoë even, and even had the right to rule, but she was also inconveniently in the way. Cleopatra had all but sold control of this land to Caesar and clambered into his bed. If she were allowed to remain on the throne, the Romans would become the de facto rulers, and that must not happen. So Ptolemy would die because he deserved it, and Cleopatra would die because she could not be suffered to live. Their youngest brother was pliable, and had no expectations as he languished in Memphis far from trouble, so he need not be touched for now. When Arsinoë was sole ruler, she would marry him and legitimise her claim completely.

Now, though, she needed to seize full control – the first of three steps to a secure throne. Then she had to cease these costly and futile attempts to take the Romans' walls. And then, at the last, she would find a way to end this swiftly before Rome sent her legions to Caesar's aid, and they became unbeatable.

Standing like some ancient statue, powerful, haughty and taciturn at only seventeen years, Arsinoë gave a single nod. A figure emerged from the shadows of the colonnade off to her left just as a cart rumbled into the open space before the steps, trundling to a halt with the snorting of beasts of burden and a creak of timber. The vehicle rode so low with weight that the wheels groaned and struggled.

The time had come.

In response to a second nod, a man in a Gabiniani officer's cuirass and high, bright horsehair crest in the old Macedonian style rose from the cart's bench beside his two companions. Soldiers from Arsinoë's retinue rattled and clanked in from the rear of the vehicle and lined up around it.

'Men of Kemet, the Black Land, and of the Gabinius Legion,' the officer intoned, his voice cutting across the still evening, 'rejoice. Her Majesty, Horus who conquers, Watched over by the Two Ladies, Sun falcon, Arsinoë, daughter of Ptolemy Auletes, recognises your sacrifice and your loyalty, and rewards you with gold.'

Men threw open chests on the wagon and started to cast small, heavy pouches to the nearest soldiers, who leapt forwards to grab them. In moments the army was flooding from the walls, hurrying to the cart to seize their share of the queen's largesse.

Men were so easily bought.

Turning her back on the securing of the army to her cause, she walked calmly towards that great pylon flanked by the statues of her predecessors standing, kilted, with one leg forward in the ancient manner, each three times the height of a person. Ahead of her, that figure who had emerged from the shadows was already moving through the vestibule ahead.

She smiled at the sight of Ganymedes. He was a man of immense value to her. First and foremost he was fanatically loyal, and that value was incalculable. Moreover, she knew just *how* loyal, for he had submitted without argument when they had made him a eunuch on her orders, accepting that his role had changed.

76

And that was another thing of value: he would be forever childless, which meant that he could remain her lover when she married her brother, without fear of siring offspring on her. And he was strong, too. Gods, but he was strong. Of a physique that would allow him to tie Achillas in knots if he so desired, and fast as an asp, besides. And perhaps best of all, he was intelligent.

He was her man, and he knew he was valued.

She watched as the razor-sharp gleaming blade hissed free of its sheath, catching the gleam of the lamps in the vestibule. Two slaves stood by the door to the room currently used as the army's headquarters. Two on this side of the door, two within. Symmetry. Arsinoë picked up her pace a little, for she needed to be part of this.

The slaves paled as the big eunuch closed on them, sword held out menacingly. They were coming close to panic, Arsinoë noted. Things might become difficult if they screamed, so she hurried ahead and closed on Ganymedes, holding out a soothing hand towards them as she reached him.

'Fear not,' she told them, and smiled easily.

They continued to look overly fearful, but neither cried out and Arsinoë maintained her encouraging smile as she motioned for them to open the doors. With worried looks the pair did as they were bade, pulling the doors outwards and almost using them as a shield, lurking behind them out of sight of the big eunuch with the sword and the frightening queen by his side.

'Achillas,' she announced with a steady voice as they entered, 'your usefulness is at an end. Submit to my command and I may yet spare you.'

The general turned, his face a picture moulded in equal parts of derision and disbelief. 'Princess Arsinoë?'

'*Queen* Arsinoë,' she replied archly.

'I warned you,' he snapped, 'not to test my patience. You may have tipped the balance of usefulness.'

'You *have* no patience, Achillas. Like most of your sort you rush at things like a bull, heedless of what goes on behind you. Blind to anything but your own ambitions and desires.'

Achillas frowned, and it was only as Arsinoë gave a meaningful nod to the room behind him that the general turned to look. Arsinoë could not see his expression as he faced away from her, but imagining what it looked like brought a smile to her own face.

Behind Achillas, those two senior officers who had been his anchors and staunchest followers were both being slowly garrotted by their own guards, hands grasping in terror at the narrow but strong chains being tightened around their throats at an almost languid pace. Neither had reached for their swords, but had they done so it would have been fruitless anyway, for their guards had slipped the weapons free and confiscated them even as the chain loops fell over their heads.

There was a series of horrible strangulated gasps, but that was the sum total of the sound of Achillas' allies perishing. The general turned to face the queen once more, his eyes gleaming darkly. He looked defiant and angry, but Arsinoë could also see the flicker of fear dancing behind that mask. He reached down to his belt for his sword hilt. In that instant, Ganymedes' head turned just slightly, enough for him to register his mistress' nod before he leapt.

Achillas' hand was coming up, the sword not quite free of the mouth of his scabbard, as the big eunuch struck. The blow had been astonishingly swift, swung wide and across at neck height. For a heart-stopping moment, Arsinoë feared he had failed, for there was no sign of a wound, and the general continued to pull his sword free, hefting it.

Her first clue, though, was in the general's eyes as they widened in horror. Even as he held his blade out to the side, ready to face Ganymedes, his head tipped back just a little, as though he were looking upwards, seeking the favour of the gods.

A wide, dark smile opened up across the general's throat from side to side, and blood gushed forth, pouring down his neck and chest into his white tunic and cuirass. Arsinoë was impressed. He was dying slowly, and deliberately so. Ganymedes had hit him with just the very tip of his razor-edged blade. Not enough to sever the neck, missing the important blood vessels to either side that would spray like fountains, but opening up the front, cutting through the air pipe and the food pipe together.

The blood slicked down Achillas' chest, and he took a hesitant step forwards, lifting his own sword, in defiance of the certain knowledge that he had already been dealt a fatal blow. A first step, and then a second.

Ganymedes took a step back himself now, and to the left, away from the general's sword arm. As Achillas, shock and rage combined in his face, and mouth bared in a silent snarl as the words hissed out breathily from the hole in his neck, stepped forwards again, clearly intent on taking the queen to the afterlife with him, the big eunuch struck once more.

Having stepped left, he swung low and back, his blade biting into the rear of Achillas' knee. The cords there snapped, severed by the sharp blade, and all the strength went out of the general's leg, which folded beneath him.

Achillas fell to the stone floor, leg twisted unnaturally and bleeding, a lake already forming under him from the terrible wound in his throat. He lay there for some time making rasping, wheezy sounds as he tried to curse her, pumping his life out onto the ground.

When he finally shuddered and lay still, Arsinoë looked up. The two officers were also dead now, lying on the ground with their faces swollen and discoloured, eyes full of blood. She nodded in a business-like manner and gestured to the slaves at the door.

'Remove these three. Have them taken beyond the city limits and cast into the wild for the scavenger beasts.'

The slaves hurried to do so, grateful simply to have cause to leave the scene. The two inside the door and the two outside gathered together, a pair of them lifting the blood-soaked corpse of Achillas and bundling it out, the other two each dragging the mess-free corpses of the strangled officers.

Almost mess-free, Arsinoë thought, wrinkling her nose as the bodies went past. Some messes at the end were involuntary and unavoidable, after all.

Stepping into the room, she walked carefully around the pool and spatters of blood, nodding her thanks to Ganymedes as the big man wiped his blade clean and slid it into his sheath once more, squaring his shoulders and straightening. She smiled as she approached the table at the room's centre.

'Escort them in,' she said loudly, seemingly to the empty air.

With the sound of numerous soft-booted feet, the main surviving officer corps of the army were brought in, escorted by Arsinoë's loyal soldiers. They looked sheepish to a man, but not one appeared remotely defiant, and no blades had been drawn. Gold had bought most of them, and when combined with fear it made a powerful driving force. As they filed into the room and stood in a small group, staring with distaste at the blood on the floor, Arsinoë smiled. They would have passed the three bodies being removed in the corridor outside. It was a statement that said more than any number of words.

'You are leaders of men, commanders in this army, whether you be sons of the Black Land from some distant nome, officers of the Gabiniani, or vassals from a valued neighbour. Your expertise and strength is appreciated and will continue to be so. Be assured that I do not intend to discipline anyone or impose an iron rule upon this army. You are the warriors of my family, and as such your loyalty is assumed, now that the traitor Achillas and his associates have been dealt with.'

She stepped back, so that she stood beside the towering form of Ganymedes.

'I do not pretend to possess the mind of a military tactician. I will *lead* this army, but I shall not *command* it. That task will fall to General Ganymedes.' She gestured to the big man, who stood impassive as a statue. There were a variety of looks evident on the assembled faces. Some were unhappy, some disbelieving, some worried, but none, once again, bore even a hint of defiance.

'This is a fact, not a request. You now answer to Ganymedes, who in turn answers only to me. You are no longer the army of the would-be pharaoh Achillas. Nor are you the army of the fool Ptolemy, who languishes in golden captivity with our enemy. The former king has failed his land and people by walking into the Romans' grasp when he should have been leading you against them. Nor are you the army of Cleopatra, who has sold her heritage for the bedsheets of Rome.'

She threw an angry pointed finger towards the doors and the embattled royal palace in the distance beyond it.

'My older siblings are now tools and prisoners of Rome, and with their foolish acts have encouraged the consul, Julius Caesar, to interfere in our kingdom. Rome has come to insinuate herself into our land. They came uninvited, and they do not intend to leave until their eagle stands above our temples and palaces. But they are vulnerable. At this time they are few, and we are many. They cannot call on vast support, for their republic tears itself in two around them. Here, now, in this campaign, is our one, our only opportunity to defy them and cast them out.'

She smiled inwardly at the effect of her words. Many of those worried, angry, doubting faces had cleared to expressions of resolution. She was right. She knew it, which was why she was so easily able to mould her words, but they knew it too. Rome had to be fought back out of the land before she decided she was here to stay.

'I see from your faces that I was right. That this army is all I hoped and expected. We will defeat Rome and her acquisitive consul in this city and deny them the Black Land forever.'

There was a chorus of agreement and assent, somewhat hesitant from the men of the Gabiniani who were, after all, Roman themselves, and Arsinoë folded her arms.

'However, in order to achieve that, our approach must change. Caesar's men are masters of this kind of warfare. I have seen what they have done from within, while they have done it. Their minds are naturally disposed to ramparts and traps and great weapons. We outnumber them, and we have the equipment and the skills, but what we do not have is their experience. We are not given to their ways of war, so we must find another way. Rome is stalwart and hardy, but we are subtle and cunning.'

There were more nods now. She smiled again. She'd discussed this with the remarkably clever Ganymedes, a giant whose martial brute appearance belied the shrewd mind within. It sounded as though *she* had come to these conclusions, and not the big general beside her.

'I am not disposed to wasting our forces,' she said quietly. 'Throwing wave after wave of men at their walls and watching them burn is pointless. This was the tactic of a fool,' she said, indicating the pool of blood at her feet. 'We must change. We must reassess and find a new way.'

She fell silent, and after a pause Ganymedes spoke, his tone as large and powerful as his body.

'We cannot waste time,' he said, 'as the queen suggests, throwing men wastefully at defences we now know will not be readily overcome. Unfortunately, we are also aware of the limited time we can enjoy. Sooner or later reinforcements will arrive to bolster Caesar. We know that two legions are on their way from Syria already. With two more legions we can still overcome them, but victory becomes far less certain. And when any more than that arrive, we may as well kiss their eagle and hand over our birthrights. So we need to do something different, something that changes the whole course of this war, and we need to do it soon.'

The big man smiled. 'A substantial gift of coin will be made to you all in recognition of your service and loyalty. The size of that gift can differ. Find me a way to break Rome and we will be yet more generous.'

There was a tense, somewhat avaricious pause as every officer digested this information and began to wrack their brains for an idea that might make them rich.

'Cut off their supplies,' one said.

Ganymedes sighed. 'A basic strategy and one we all know. But how?'

Another frowned. 'We have the numbers, and their defences are poor on Pharos. If we press on the island, push forwards, we may take the Pharos fort. If we do so we can prevent the Romans from receiving supplies and reinforcements by ship. With command of Pharos we could sink any incoming vessel.'

Ganymedes shared a look with the queen and nodded.

'This notion is of value, yes. It alone does not provide our answer, but as part of a grand plan it is worth noting. Good. This thinking is useful. Rather than throw men at their triple walls around the palace, we attack the old fort on Pharos, which will be harder to defend. Then we begin to strangle their food supplies. What else can we do?'

'We need to prevent them gaining any supplies from the south, outside the city,' another man said. 'It is only so much use cutting off their shipping if they are still somehow sneaking supplies in by land, and we are sure that is happening.'

Ganymedes nodded again. 'We are already doing what we can in that regard. The former queen has allies and contacts who seem able to slip supplies to her past our forces. We have many men, but the entirety of Alexandria is hard to keep patrolled sufficiently to prevent supplies leaking through. The simple fact is that with Cleopatra and Ptolemy both within that palace, many of the people will try to aid them, for they cannot abide the idea of starving the children of Ptolemy Auletes, even if that is what is required to remove the Romans.'

'Sow misinformation,' another man offered. 'Tell the people the Romans have already executed the king and queen.' He noted Arsinoë's expression, and quickly corrected himself. '*Former* king and queen.'

Again, Ganymedes nodded. 'There are already rumours that Cleopatra is gone. Her army at Pelusium has disintegrated. These rumours will not be hard to spread, and in doing so we can turn the people against the Romans all the more. Good. This all helps. Anything else?'

'Water,' said a figure near the back.

'Explain.'

The officer pushed his way to the front. 'As sons of the Black Land, we are all aware of the value of water. Men can eke out grain and make it last for a surprisingly long time, but without water a man thirsts swiftly. Water is the answer.'

Again, Ganymedes looked at the queen, who smiled.

That officer stepped forwards. 'I have looked at the places the Romans ripped up our streets, leaving sewers and cellars open to the air. There are certain areas they carefully left, where fresh water is channelled into the palace region along subterranean channels.'

'But we cannot cut off their water supply,' the general reminded him. 'The Canopus Canal runs right past them, which is fresh water from the delta, not salty water from the ocean.'

The officer shook his head. 'Much of that water is unhealthy, having eddied in marshy lands before reaching this far. Men do not drink from the waters of those channels for it brings with it disease and illness. If the Romans drink such waters, they will win our war for us by dropping dead of the bloody flux without a fight.'

Ganymedes laughed. 'How good to have such knowledge among us. Then we must cut those channels that feed the palace with fresh water and drive them all to rely upon poisons. This is a good plan. *This* is what will win us our war.'

Arsinoë cleared her throat. 'Better still, cut just *some* of those channels and narrow the sources upon which the Romans rely, and then ruin the rest.'

Slow realisation dawned on the general until he gave a malicious chuckle. 'Divert the sick-making waters into their drinking channels. This is excellent. We shall work slowly and carefully, trying not to waste troops, to take Pharos Island and to remove any source of grain from inland, and while we do that we will kill them with thirst and disease. I approve this plan. My queen?' he added, turning to Arsinoë.

She smiled. 'Let disease carry the Roman dogs away to their afterlife. See to it.'

CHAPTER SEVEN

Alexandria palace, 10th December 48 BC

Fronto followed Carfulenus down the short flight of stairs, his spirits sinking as they descended. He had no need to be told how bad things were for already, merely on the approach, he could hear the low murmur of myriad groans and moans, and the smell that washed back up from below was like the breath of a sewer demon.

'How many?'

'One hundred and eighteen suspected. Over a hundred confirmed. Of course there will always be a small margin of misdiagnosis and the requisite number of malingerers.'

Fronto nodded, pulling up his scarf to cover the lower part of his face and hold back the worst of the miasma. The smell of his own sweat was far preferable to the air here. He was finally grateful he'd continued to wear the scarf despite the heat, while many of the soldiers had discarded theirs. It had uses other than warmth, after all.

They reached the bottom of the stairs and turned a corner, dancing light from oil lamps illuminating the ancient corridor, its ceiling painted blue and gold and red with images of broad-winged birds and stylised kneeling men. As they rounded that corner, the fresh blast of stink almost floored Fronto.

'Minerva's bollocks, can't you get some fresh air down here somehow?'

The officer frowned. 'That *is* fresh air, sir. You should have smelled it when they were enclosed.'

Frowning his disbelief, Fronto followed the man to the end of the corridor. There a large door bore some arcane local text, over which a helpful legionary had painted a rough version of the *caduceus*, the winded serpent staff that denoted, among other things, medical professionals. The centurion rapped neatly on the door and now pulled his own scarf up over his nose as there was a click and the door swung inwards.

The smell that wafted from the open doorway hit Fronto between the eyes like a mallet, a solid wall of stench that nearly floored him. It was almost indescribable, but if Fronto had to try, it would include Cerberus' sphincter, a flood of shit the size of the Euxine Sea, a corpse drowned in fresh vomit, and the sickly-sweet smell of rotting matter.

He paused in the doorway, forced to wrench down his scarf and expose himself to the worst of it all for the simple expedient of not throwing up inside the material. He coughed and spat bile to the floor, which seemed to be half-coated in such matter anyway. Gagging and shuddering, he pulled his scarf back up, grateful for the smell of sick that drowned out what was far, far worse.

The man was right. This hastily-assembled quarantine section was open to the air. What must it have been like when they were in an enclosed room? This place seemed to be some sort of warehouse below the palace, a colonnade open to the air connecting it to the royal harbour. The meagre sea breeze wafting in and out of the columns did little to overcome the miasma, though, more stirring it around in eddies than actually clearing it.

Cots had been set up in neat rows, many of them occupied, and as he moved into the room, Fronto could now see that wide square vestibules connected this former warehouse to other rooms both left and right. Moans emanating from them suggested that those other two rooms were much the same as this.

'Gods, but this is bad,' he muttered, muffled in his scarf.

The centurion with him nodded and gestured for him to follow. As they threaded their way between the sick beds, Fronto tried to look encouraging and sympathetic at the figures in them – soldiers they had brought with them, their skin a pale olive colour now turned waxy and green-tinted, a sweating rubberiness to their faces.

Each man lay in a sodden mess of sheets, sweating and writhing, moaning and groaning. Most beds had a simple bowl next to them and a cheap wooden bucket. The bowl held water and a cloth, the bucket something unmentionable. It was clear as he walked past the invalids that some of the men had been too weak to rise from their bed and reach the bucket to release their latest foul explosion, whatever orifice it came from.

He gagged once more inside his scarf as Carfulenus finally led him to an Aegyptian in a white and gold robe with a strange, smooth white skull-cap, the odd cross-with-a-loop symbol Fronto kept seeing hanging on a thong around his neck.

'You're the medicus?' Fronto mumbled loudly into his scarf.

'I am the royal physician,' the man said in a haughty tone, his voice unhindered by material. How he managed to work without throwing up, Fronto could not imagine. He looked about. Numerous palace slaves dashed this way and that helping the sick, and among them moved the two capsarii, one from the Sixth and one from the Twenty Seventh.

The centurion gestured towards the colonnade and the physician nodded, leading them all from the ward and out into the air of the royal harbour's quayside. Fronto waited until they were safely away from the room before pulling down his scarf and heaving in lungs full of sea air, cleansing the stink from his body.

'Gods, I'd heard the situation was bad. but I'd not realised just *how* bad.'

The physician nodded. 'We are admitting new cases every hour.'

'And what's causing it? Is it a disease? Can we catch it by being in the room?' Fronto asked nervously, suddenly aware that he'd walked through the foul air all the way across the chamber.

The physician shook his head. 'The illness seems to be coming on in a matter of hours in all cases, and both my staff and your combat medics have been treating them for two days, three even, since the first case showed up. If it were contagious we would have caught it by now. No, this is ingested.'

'Food?' Fronto asked uncertainly. It seemed unlikely. Their food supplies were low, and mostly consisted of bread, fruit and a little salted meat, but nothing had been rotten as far as he was aware.

'No, cases like this are almost universally the fault of contaminated water.'

Fronto's frown returned. 'But we were fine for months, and now this all of a sudden?'

The physician nodded. 'I have questioned the men over their water intake and I cannot readily identify the source. Some of the soldiers, men you brought with you who have no clue as to the ways of the Black Land of course, had taken water from the Canopus Canal. This channel can cause dreadful illnesses as it is fed by waters that have passed through marshes and latrine outfalls. Locals, though, know better than to drink the water of the canal, and that includes the palace guards. They have been in this city long enough to know what is safe, and none of them have slaked their thirst from the canal, relying upon the sources we know are secure, yet they suffer similarly. As you see, it is a puzzle.'

Fronto nodded, cursing silently.

'I'll report to the general. Keep me updated.' With that he nodded to the centurion and decided to take a different route back despite the distance, walking the length of the harbour and climbing the staircase there. At least there he could breathe, though that did little to comfort him in the grand scheme of things. Ten days ago things had become more troublesome than ever in the redoubt of Alexandria.

Word had swiftly seeped in that there had been a coup in the enemy ranks and that Achillas was no longer in command. While a few of the officers had welcomed the news, and it had lifted spirits a little, Fronto, Caesar and a few of the others had been sceptical, an attitude that now seemed to be being borne out. Far from the army now having come under the command of a clueless girl as some expected, it seemed that it had been focused by the will of a sharp princess and the talent of her pet general. They had put an end to their costly forays, which could only mean they were putting a lot more thought into the campaign. And worst of all, with Arsinoë now leading them and claiming the throne in spite of her siblings, it meant that there was no longer the need for the fiction that they served the pharaoh currently lounging in an apartment in this palace. This made Ptolemy henceforth pointless as a bargaining tool.

Further bad news had come with the discovery of rumours circulating the city claiming that both royal siblings in the palace had been executed by their Roman 'captors'. This made securing the aid of any supposedly loyal locals in the region more and more difficult.

Then the new focus of the enemy plan had become apparent. Over the succeeding days, thirst began to present a distinct problem. There were four channels of good water coming into the palace area underground, all of which had remained untouched by the Roman engineers. Two were large, high-pressure conduits that filled fountains and basins, baths and pools, a third was a lesser channel that fed the kitchens of the palace and the slave quarters. A fourth, distinctly minor, channel fed a small bath house down near the palace theatre, apparently on a separate system to the rest and from a different source.

The first grand channel ran dry two days after Arsinoë's coup. The timing made it clear that it was no accident. Then, the next day, the other large channel dried up. Certain that it was the work of the enemy, Roman engineers had climbed down into the ancient conduits and crawled along them in search of a way to clear the blockages, but had only confirmed with dismal voices that the channels had been totally sealed with rubble which went for some distance and would be a massive job to clear, even if they could do so with ease, but since the channels ran through territory heavily manned by the princess' army, that would not be possible anyway.

Then the service channel had run dry and with the loss of the third source, panic had begun to manifest itself among the defenders. It seemed a boon that the small theatre bath channel was apparently unknown and remained untouched. Consequently, while the palace ran dry, men began to rely entirely on that one small source which was vastly inadequate for the number of people using it.

Alexandria began to thirst.

Fronto had to acknowledge the bright new approach to the war by the princess and her general. Achillas had not thought to do as much.

And as men began to grow weak and worried, the enemy began to increase their numbers on the Heptastadion, forging a bridgehead onto Pharos Island and apparently preparing for a major push there. The fort by the lighthouse was poorly-constructed, which was, of course, how they'd managed to take it so easily in the first place. Unfortunately that same weakness would make it an easy target for the enemy, and there simply were not the resources to seriously strengthen the defences, especially lying across the harbour as it did. The men there had done what they could, but it would only hold for so long. Moreover, the gradual weakening of the army over the last few days of increasing thirst threatened to deplete the force enough to leave the fort dangerously undermanned.

Whoever was planning the enemy's new campaign was worryingly bright.

Now, though, Fronto had fresh worries. Over and above the dearth of reinforcements, the lack of word from any of the dispatched vessels, the loss of local support, the devaluing of Ptolemy's value and all the rest, Fronto had a nagging feeling that the one boon to which they had all clung had in fact been a nightmare in disguise.

He had to confirm his suspicions before making them known, though.

Rather than climb to the top of the stairway and join the grand approach to the palace's main harbour entrance with its glorious columns and statuary, he slipped down a side alley, heading towards the theatre. The bath house beside the theatre was only a small example, and meant for functionaries and ordinary folk, not the rich and influential up in the palace. But despite its minor importance, it currently claimed the second strongest guard unit after the queen and the consul's headquarters. As the only source of fresh water now in the entire area it was of great value, and men were often caught and punished for desperately trying to break in and secure extra water.

As if there was any. The minor flow was little more than a trickle and was constantly at work filling barrels that could be moved around to help water the men and animals. There was no more to be had than was being distributed anyway.

But Fronto had a worrying notion.

Waving to the guards, he watched them step out of the way and leave the door open. Passing inside, he went into the third chamber, where the flow had been diverted into the barrels, a dozen men here waiting for it to fill so they could swap for an empty cask and send the full one to where it would be useful.

Nodding at them, he crossed the room, reached up to a shelf and grasped one of the jugs from it. Motioning the soldiers out of the way, he placed the jug under the flow, watching as the trickle slowly filled it. Once it was slopping at the brim, he thanked the men and then headed for the open air once more, moving down the alley to a place where the sun shone in. Frowning his worry, he pulled out his own water flask with the other hand, unstoppering it with some difficulty, and then lifted both vessels, one in each hand.

Trying to keep the flow even he tipped his hands, both falls of water close together and in the sunlight. He peered at them intently as he tipped, and felt his spirits sink. He had been right. The water in his own flask had to be clean, else he would have been down in that room, writhing in a bed in his own sweat like the rest of them. His own water was clear as crystal. The flow from the jug he'd filled in the baths had a slight green/brown tint. When directly compared, the difference was clear.

The water in the baths was tainted. They'd not noticed, as the colour was not dark enough to register unless one ran a direct comparison. Any man who'd noticed the tint would probably put it down to old pipes, or moss or some such. Now, though, the reason seemed clear.

With a sigh, he strode back to the bathhouse and gestured to the optio in command of the guards there.

'Cease distribution, soldier. No more of this water is to be given out.'

'Sir?'

'It's causing the illness that's dropping our men like flies. Not another drop leaves these baths until I give the order. Got it?'

'Yes, sir.'

'And send someone to stop any barrels currently in transit. Let's limit the damage as best we can.'

The optio saluted, unhappily. 'Yes, sir. Are you sure, sir?'

Fronto nodded. 'Sadly so.'

With that he took his half full jug and his own flask and hurried back to the stairs and up into the palace. Through corridors and halls he passed until he reached the door guarded by Ingenuus' praetorians, where he nodded his greeting and passed within.

Caesar, Brutus, Cassius and Hirtius stood in the room, along with the queen, the general wearing a look of thunder.

'...long overdue,' Caesar finished before snapping his head round to Fronto. 'I was busy cursing Calvinus. I cannot conduct a campaign blind, Fronto. Calvinus' legions should be here by now, supporting us and granting us sufficient numbers to turn the tide and take control. Instead, not only are they somewhere unknown, but news from Syria seems to be sparse at best. All we hear is vague rumblings about trouble, with no details. We do not even know who is causing the trouble or whether it involves Calvinus, though that seems likely given the delay. I cannot command while blind.'

Hissing irritably, the general stopped, brow creasing. 'Where have you been, Fronto, and why are you carrying wine?'

'Not wine, General. Water. And bad tidings.'

He turned to Cleopatra, who stood sultry and quiet near a window. 'Majesty, can you confirm something for me?'

'Go ahead, Legate.'

'What is the source of the water we have been consuming in the central palace?'

The queen shrugged. 'The cisterns, of course.'

'Cisterns?'

Cleopatra drummed her fingers on the table. 'There are two cisterns in the palace that are filled by the main conduits. The conduits have been cut, as you know, but the cisterns were appropriately full at the time. Their contents are diminishing rapidly, of course, but while they are there, we utilise them.'

Fronto nodded his miserable understanding.

'That is why the illness that stalks our men has yet to claim a senior officer or any noble or palace staff. The main conduits were clean, and therefore so are the cisterns. As long as we drink from those diminishing supplies we are safe. The enemy cut those channels, though, and removed our main source.

'But there is the lesser conduit they missed, down at the baths,' Brutus said. 'It's a low flow, but enough to get by on with care.'

'The wily enemy know that,' Fronto said. 'They did not miss the small flow. What they did was cut the others to ensure that we rely upon that one. Princess Arsinoë is as familiar with this palace as you, Majesty. She must have known about all four sources, and even if she did not, it would be an easy thing to establish. They didn't miss the fourth channel, they just made it critical to us, and then poisoned it.'

'What?'

Fronto walked over to the window and lifted his two vessels, tipping them in the bright sunlight. 'Palace cistern water left, nice and clear, conduit water right, slightly tainted.'

The room's occupants stared.

'How have they poisoned it?' Hirtius said, confused. 'To apply a poison to a constant flow would require vast effort.'

Fronto shook his head. 'Some of our more clueless lads have been slaking their thirst from the Canopus Canal, and they've contracted the same illness, or at least something very similar. That suggests that what the enemy have actually done is to divert the contaminated river water into our drinking channel somewhere way upstream. Simple and brilliant. The channel poisons itself outside our reach and we have been blissfully unaware of that, guzzling the water. No wonder the sick beds multiply by the hour.'

'Jove on high,' Caesar breathed. 'We must stop the channel.'

'I've already put a hold on it. But our problems are only just beginning. This means that once our cisterns run dry, we are out of water. It seems that the illness of our men will probably pass with few fatalities, but without a fresh supply of water, our lifespan could be measured in mere days.'

The queen gestured out of the window at the harbour. 'There lies your answer.'

'Majesty, sea water is poison in itself,' Hirtius reminded her.

The queen rolled her eyes. 'You have free access to the sea and you still have ships in port. There are sources of clean water elsewhere on the coast, both east and west. Send out ships full of barrels and good men and source water from outside.'

Fronto nodded. 'That's an idea.'

But Brutus was shaking his head. 'We are suffering strong easterlies at the moment. Ships will battle to move east along the coast, and when they head west, they will have trouble returning swiftly. It is a valid idea, but is reliant upon the winds. Many men will suffer from thirst before they can sufficiently fill our cisterns once more.'

Cleopatra nodded her agreement. 'This is true. It is a long-term solution, not a quick one.'

Caesar tapped his lip thoughtfully. 'Fronto, what did Pompey do when we cut his water at Dyrrachium?'

Fronto thought back, brow creased. 'From what I understand they dug wells.'

'Quite. Water is usually to be found in coastal regions with sufficient work.'

'Pompey's wells were not over-healthy if I remember hearing correctly.'

Caesar smiled. 'Pompey's wells were sunk into boggy lands. They were probably no better than the water Princess Arsinoë is sending us. Here, however, the water to be found underground is clear and safe, as is evidenced by several wells in the city. The men will have to dig for it, but the result should keep us going, especially added to any shiploads we can secure.'

'Good,' Fronto nodded. 'Can I make another suggestion? The soldiers are becoming panicky. The situation is getting to them. It is always better for the men to hear things from their commander, though. Visit your men, Caesar, and encourage them. Tell them the plan and explain it all.'

'And open up the palace cisterns to them, too,' Cassius added, earning a disapproving look from both consul and queen.

'There is precious little there, Cassius,' Caesar reminded him.

'But the men have *none*, Caesar. Put the officers and civilians in the same boat as the men. Let everyone share the peril, and then the troops will appreciate the value of their commanders. Better that than risk trouble from angry men who watch their superiors drinking clear water while they themselves die of thirst.'

Caesar nodded. 'Of course. The water from the palace will be rationed among all. Ships will be dispatched along the coast to secure supplies at whatever pace they can manage, and I shall personally exhort the men to dig wells. Thus will be confound the enemy.'

* * *

The first well bore fruit late that night. The men had been digging throughout the afternoon and evening, and even with Caesar's constant encouragement spirits had begun to flag once more. The exercise had seemed pointless and doomed, and the men were wearing themselves out, worsening their thirst with the work, sweating and complaining, digging and worrying.

Then, as the moon rose into the sky, a contubernium of the Sixth down near the Diabathra heard their pick hit with a splash instead of a crack. Hungrily, excitedly, the men worked feverishly and managed swiftly to open a well almost two feet across and eight feet down into the hard ground. The water gradually seeped in, filling the bottom.

Before they drank, just in case, their officer brought a sample to the palace, where it was compared with both the remnants from the cistern and the tainted water from the baths. To the relief of all, it was pronounced clean.

It was actually brackish, a little dirty and tasted uncomfortably salty, but it was not diseased, and while a little unpleasant, it was like the gods' own nectar to the thirsty men of Caesar's army. Word of the well's success spread and work redoubled across the redoubt. By the dawn four wells were yielding water.

In truth, it was far from enough, and twice as many wells had produced nothing, but even a small level of success felt like the greatest victory to the men, and they were heartened sufficiently that they continued to dig more and more wells. That morning two ships left full of empty barrels, hopeful soldiers, and a few locals from the palace with good geographical knowledge, one heading east and one west.

* * *

The east winds continued to blow, and no one expected to see those two vessels for days, which was why it came as a surprise when a ship was heralded as approaching that evening.

Fronto, along with the other officers, gathered in the hall, waiting for Caesar. Once the general put in an appearance, they left the palace and hurried down the steps towards the Palace Harbour. All around, soldiers were cheering their general as men sipped precious water from canteens filled from the wells. More were being opened up constantly, and it would take hundreds of them to supply sufficient water, but even these small quantities were deliciously welcome.

'Can it be a water ship?' Fronto muttered as they hurried towards the dock, praetorian soldiers clattering along to either side.

Brutus shook his head. 'No. A vessel the size of the ones we sent will be slow and heavy, especially full of water. Even under full oars it will take some time.'

Fronto nodded, fretting. If that was the case, then this ship had to be small and light, almost empty in fact, to successfully battle the coastal easterly. Who in Hades was it?'

They arrived on the harbour side just as the vessel cut between the arms of the harbour moles, slicing its way through the calm waters towards the dock. Relief and excitement began to wash through the assembled officers.

It was a Roman ship.

Barring the farfetched notion that it had come from Africa, then it was almost certainly an ally.

It was a liburnian, and without the usual ram, defences and other accoutrements. A courier or scout vessel. Small and fast, one of the swiftest ships to be found in the Roman fleet, and the perfect vessel to strike against the heavy easterly wind. Fronto watched, breath almost held, as the ship slid towards them, and gradually more details became discernible. It bore a full crew of oarsmen, and they were professional, dragging their vessel through the water at a tremendous pace, the steersman equally good, guiding it into place at one of the nearest free jetties.

It flew Roman pennants and its sail was plain white. Best of all was the sight of a small unit of legionaries surrounding an officer in gleaming bronze and a man with a small vexillum flag. The excitement continued to build as it closed, and even Fronto felt his usual pessimism slipping away to be replaced with unaccustomed hope.

Still, they were in no position to take things for granted, and even as the sailors threw out lines, Ingenuus sent a dozen of his best guards to the near end of the jetty, where they formed up under a decurion, just in case there was something underhand going on.

That decurion strode forwards as the ramp was run out and the small party descended, led by the gleaming officer. There was a brief conversation and what little tension remained in Fronto ebbed as the praetorian saluted, returned to his men and then reorganised them to line the jetty at either side like an honour guard.

Fronto could feel the expectation among the officers rising, and all around the harbour now, soldiers who had been hard at work, or digging new wells, or simply standing guard, hurried to the nearest viewpoint to look over at this new arrival.

Without the need for a command, every officer around Caesar straightened, adjusting their uniform and moving into position flanking the general.

The officer marched forwards across the dock, his men at his back, along with the praetorians, and stopped ten paces from Caesar, bowing from the waist. Fronto tried to identify the vexillum behind the man, but with the combination of salty air and insufficient breeze, it sagged lifeless and it was difficult to make out the legend upon it. Along with the rest of the officers, he turned his attention to the man. He wore the uniform of a narrow-stripe tribune, still awfully young and fresh.

'I bring greetings,' the officer intoned, 'to the consul and general Gaius Julius Caesar from his loyal legatus and governor of Syria, Gnaeus Domitius Calvinus. My name is Marcus Lucretius Fidus, and I have the honour of being a tribune in service of Uttedius Pollio, commander of the Thirty Seventh Legion.'

'Well met indeed, Lucretius Fidus,' Caesar smiled. 'What of your legion? We have eagerly awaited their arrival, and that of their sister legion from Syria.'

The young tribune, straight backed and formal, cleared his throat. 'Uttedius Pollio sends his apologies for not attending in person. Our ships made landfall some way along the coast, and the current unfavourable winds make reaching the city difficult at the least. It may take some time to battle the winds, and our senior trierarch is of the opinion that the legion will be trapped in place until the weather changes. We put ashore but a little scouting suggested sizeable enemy forces in the area, and with the lack of geographical knowledge, the legatus thought it wise to remain with the ships and wait for a westerly, rather than risk falling foul of unknown forces and being separated from yourselves by the enemy.'

Caesar nodded. 'He is wise. Yes, better a few days delay and put to port here than risk cutting across land and meeting the enemy army unexpectedly. And what news of your sister legion?'

A look of faint unease passed across Lucretius. 'I cannot say anything of the Thirty Sixth, Consul, other than that they had not left when we did. Their objective was to travel by land, while we embarked upon the ships, but the date of their departure had not been confirmed, as the governor was unhappy committing both legions to travel until he was more certain of the local situation.'

Caesar took a step forwards. 'I have heard vague rumour of troubles. Tell me.'

The tribune frowned as though it should be common knowledge.

'King Pharnaces of Bosporus, Consul? He invaded Pontus in the autumn, taking advantage of the current rifts in republican control. Domitius Calvinus has demanded that the king withdraw, but Pharnaces is defiant. Both gather forces and a military conflict appears inevitable, or at least it did when we last heard news at Cyprus.'

Caesar fretted. 'Then we cannot be certain the other legion is even coming. And if such troubles have arisen in Pontus, drawing men from Syria, then we cannot be sure upon how much support we can call from the east. I had hoped for reinforcements from Asia under Mithridates of Pergamon, though he may now have been drawn into local conflict instead. I fear that our numbers are not fated to grow to the figure upon which we had pinned our hopes.'

Cassius coughed meaningfully. 'With respect, Caesar, even the one legion will more than double our numbers. With them we do not need to fear easy defeat. The Thirty Seventh represents a chance of victory.'

'And increased thirst,' Fronto said suddenly, drawing all gazes. He shrugged, embarrassed at having spoken aloud what he had intended only to think. Sighing, he continued. 'Simply, we do not have sufficient water for our current force. More than doubling that number will only more than double the problem. I think we may need to step up the plans to bring in water from along the coast, Caesar.'

The general nodded. 'That concern is noted, Fronto. But for now let us rejoice. After so many days of uncertainty, finally our brothers have arrived.'

CHAPTER EIGHT

Alexandria Palace Harbour, 11th December 48 BC

Fronto stood at the ship's rail looking utterly miserable, face a greeny-grey.

'Why me?'

'Because you're a mine of unexpected ideas,' Salvius Cursor said, 'and Caesar needs that at the moment.'

Galronus shook his head. 'That's not it. Caesar thinks he's lucky. It's like carrying a phallus carving to rub.'

'In fact...' began Salvius, but Fronto snapped his angry face around.

'One hint of a comment about me being a giant knob and you'll be in the water looking for your teeth, Salvius.'

The tribune gave a malicious grin. 'In the water? The swirling, ebbing, eddying, flowing water?'

Fronto threw him a vicious glare and then gulped, holding down his food with difficulty as the ship wallowed this way and that.

'Everyone's aboard,' Salvius announced, pointing at the boarding ramp.

The sounds of departure echoed across the deck as the ship made ready to put to sea. Fronto's gaze rose from the horrible slapping waves and to the city. It was dangerous, taking out the entire fleet and leaving the garrison cut off once more, but Caesar had decided to take the gamble.

The idea of sailing ships along the coast to collect fresh water from known sources was good, they had all agreed upon that. And now that they knew the Thirty Seventh Legion waited just a short distance along the coast, Caesar had decided to combine his missions. He would take all the ships and just enough men to crew them. They would sail with the wind along the coast to where the legion waited, via one of the best local water sources. They would load up with fresh water and then move on to collect the legion and split them among all the ships. With the hugely increased quantity of vessels, the reduction in cargo weight would make them lighter and it would be easier to navigate their way into the troublesome winds. Moreover, with them they would take local sailors who knew the coast and the winds well and would be invaluable in bringing the ships back east.

Cassius had been left in charge of the Roman defences, with the queen doing her part. In fact, the anticipated friction between those two and the chance to miss it all was the only bright side of having been ordered to be part of the ships' command crews.

Fronto turned, a little too sharply for his stomach, and peered out across the harbour. At the head of the fleet, Caesar's flagship was already carving a path out to the open sea between the two forts controlled by loyal men. Fronto tried not to think about what the return journey could be like should the Pharos fort fall before then.

He continued to stand there, looking miserable, until the ship lurched suddenly out from the jetty and began its rolling, swaying journey out with the fleet.

Fronto threw up again.

* * *

It was mid-afternoon when they finally stopped. According to reports they were still some hours from the camping place of the Thirty Seventh, but here, the Aegyptian sailors said, was one of the better local sites for the acquisition of fresh water. The ships anchored a short way from the shore and sent small sloops out with barrels and sailors, finding the local water sources and filling the receptacles for return to Alexandria.

'Are you sure you want to go?'

Fronto turned to Salvius Cursor. 'For an opportunity to get off the ship, I would step into the jaws of Cerberus himself. Yes I want to go.'

And with that, still grey-faced, Fronto slipped from the rails and dropped into the small single-masted boat with its crew of half a dozen men and its cargo of four empty barrels. Galronus followed him down, leaving Salvius in command of the ship, and the two men settled in on the rough bench as the sailors began to row for land. Similar boats were in evidence like a swarm of ants all along the shore for a stretch of almost a mile, seeking the numerous seasonal wadis that carried plentiful fresh water in these winter months.

It was with a profound sense of relief that Fronto dropped from the boat onto the wet, giving sand of the shoreline. All around, other crews were beaching their vessels and unloading the barrels. He could see soldiers here and there among the sailors, but only rare and sporadically. Few men had come with the fleet, other than the sailors themselves, and most of those had stayed aboard the ships.

Two small villages stood on this stretch of coastline, and the fleet had more or less anchored between the two. Already, hopeful natives were rushing out with their local produce and trying to sell baskets and tunics and all manner of junk to the busy sailors, who waved them away, sweating and grunting as they carried the barrels inland towards the visible areas of vegetation that marked water sources.

Fronto and Galronus followed the half dozen men from their boat and stopped on a high sandy dune-ridge. Ahead, they could see a narrow and shallow valley running from the hinterland, with scrubby greenery along the edges. The watercourse changed as it reached the beach, no longer a defined stream, but rather a very shallow, wide fan of rivulets carving their way across the sand to the sea. No one could gather water there, and the six men carried their barrel over towards the greenery, where they could lower it into the flow and fill it, topping it up using the skins each man carried. They would only half fill it, despite the need for water, since carrying a full barrel of water would be beyond even six burly men.

The two officers sank to the high sandy ridge with a sigh of relief. Fronto gave Galronus an ironic smile as his friend offered him a swig from a skin containing part of the dwindling store of water from the city cistern. He took a small gulp and sighed as they watched the men at work. Other crews were at this stream now, while further groups gathered at other wadis awaiting their turn. Already a few had filled their first barrel and were swearing and groaning as they manhandled the heavy weight back to their boat, knowing this would be only the first of four trips.

'I'll be more comfortable when we've got the legion with us,' Galronus said.

'Ten years ago, stomping around Gaul and chasing the Helvetii, worrying about troublesome German kings, I would never have thought to hear a Gaul say such a thing.'

Galronus snorted. 'I'm Belgae, of the Remi, not a Gaul, you cock. And some of us were allies from the start, you know.'

'Only your tribe, if I remember correctly. I think every other tribe in the whole land fought us at one time or another. Your lot were our only permanent allies. But you know what I mean.'

'I do. The world is becoming Roman. There is no room for tribes now. Tribe becomes region, regions form provinces, provinces make the republic. How long, I wonder, before Aegyptus is too important to allow them their freedom? Before Caesar finds a reason to march in here.'

Now it was Fronto's turn to snort. 'To an extent that's what already happened. Don't forget the Gabiniani have been here for years. But as long as they have pretty, scheming little queens who can play a consul like a musician on a harp, they'll get exactly what they want.'

Galronus chuckled. 'The general certainly has a...'

He tailed off into silence and Fronto frowned, turning to him.

'A what? An eye for a shapely bosom? A desire to sow his seed among foreign royalty?'

But Galronus was staring off into the distance, brow knit tight.

'What is it?'

'Saw something. I think, anyway. Maybe I imagined it.' He shook his head as though clearing a fog. 'Yes, the general and women are…'

Again he fell silent for a moment, then spoke under his breath. 'There *is* something.'

'What?'

'Movement inland. I saw shapes twice, up beyond the rise, in the distance.'

'Probably more villagers trying to sell us new underwear.'

Galronus made an unconvinced grunting sound and rose to a crouch, hand coming round to shade his eyes from the afternoon sun. The seriousness of his friend had Fronto on the alert now, and he rose similarly. At first he could see nothing. Then, between distant scrubby bushes on the left high bank of the stream where their men were currently righting their first barrel to bring back, he saw a shape, briefly, passing from cover to cover.

'That was a rider.'

Galronus nodded. 'Horsemen. More than one, as well.'

'If they're just nomads or desert raiders, or even scouts from Arsinoë's army, they'll be too few to deal with this lot. Our men might just be sailors, and many unarmed, but there are hundreds of them along the beach.'

'And if it's a proper cavalry unit?'

'Then we're in the shit.' Fronto peered into the sunshine, squinting. Another figure, mounted, briefly showed. It was possible he was the same one, but Fronto didn't think so.

'Did he look closer to you?'

'I think they're coming closer all the time.'

'They might just be interested locals, coming for a look?'

'And they might be Castor and Pollux on their divine steeds come to wish us good fortune,' Galronus replied archly. 'But I would wager they are Aegyptians from Arsinoë's army.'

Fronto nodded distractedly. 'There are more.'

'More every heartbeat. I think trouble is coming.'

'Galronus, get back to the boats. Find one that's near ready to go and row for the fleet at speed. Deliver the warning. I think all the boats will be coming back to the fleet in moments.'

'And you?'

'I'm going to confirm our suspicions and get the men moving.'

'Don't do anything stupid.'

'When do I ever...' Fronto started, then broke off with a sheepish grin and pointed back towards the ships. Galronus nodded and rose to his feet, jogging away down the slope back towards the sea. Fronto went the other way, intercepting the men from his boat, struggling along with their barrel of water. 'Forget about the rest. Get that to the boat and then push off for the ship.'

The men gave him a perplexed look but nodded and grunted their assent beneath their heavy load. Fronto frowned. 'Can four of you carry that?'

In answer, two of the men let go and stepped away. There was a groan of strain from the remaining four and the barrel dipped alarmingly, but they fought it steady and raised it again.

'Well done. Thank you, you four. Get to the boat and then the ship as fast as you can. You two, head along the beach in each direction. Tell every crew you find that Legate Fronto orders every unit back to their ship immediately, then get onto one yourselves.'

The men saluted and began to run, and Fronto stumbled off across the difficult terrain for the stream and the crews now filling their barrels or waiting patiently for their turn. 'Finish up,' he yelled at them. 'Take what you have and get back to the boats. Enemy riders spotted.'

It was stretching the truth a little, but it had the desired effect nonetheless, men stopping what they were doing immediately despite their desire for fresh water. 'Orderly and sensibly,' Fronto reminded them. 'Back to the boats and the ships, and take the barrels with you. Remember you're soldiers.'

The men moved swiftly back down the beach, and Fronto left them to it, scrambling instead up the slope, grabbing the protruding branches of trees to help pull himself up, and cursing the effects of advancing age. Those days when they'd followed the Helvetii into

Gaul, he'd have run up here in full armour, bellowing as he went. Now he was hauling himself up with difficulty, favouring his right knee in case the left gave way, and puffing and panting like an old man.

He reached the top and spent a long moment coughing and spitting into the sand, heaving in deep breaths. When he'd sufficiently recovered, he scanned the area, identifying the best viewpoint, a small cairn of stones standing on a low rise. Hurrying over, he clambered up them and stood on the top with difficulty, shading his eyes and looking this way and that.

There was no immediate sign of the riders, and it was his ears that identified trouble before his eyes. He turned and peered off to the northeast, squinting narrowly. The distinctive sounds of battle reached him from that direction and a moment later he could just make out the figures of the sailors fleeing from another similar wadi in that direction, scattering like the seeds from a dropped fruit, running for the boats, their barrels discarded.

Fronto closed his eyes. Damn it, but this was not good. When he opened them again, he saw exactly what he'd expected. Horsemen racing after the sailors, whooping guttural war cries. There were not vast numbers of the riders, but enough to put the sailors to flight, certainly, and they cut down the slowest runners before veering off and whooping with vicious delight some more.

As the desperate sailors hurtled towards the water, more and more riders swooped after them, cutting down the runners. The pursuit only faltered when sudden thuds and cracks announced that the men remaining on the ships had begun to man, load and release the bolt throwers mounted on the prows. The men were sailors, not artillerists, and the shots went wildly astray without much hope of causing any real damage, but their range made it clear that they *could* hit the riders, even if only by accident, at any time. The threat was enough and the horsemen suddenly broke off the pursuit, racing back to the men they had already cut down, hauling up those wounded sailors who still lived and throwing them over the backs of horses, and hacking the heads from those who did not.

Fronto closed his eyes again, took a deep breath, then scanned the beaches. Most of the men were almost to safety and many were still carrying their barrels. It was not an unmitigated disaster, at least, but they had been thwarted in gathering any more than perhaps a tenth of their water stock, and had lost a few dozen men in the process. Reasoning that there was little else he could now do, Fronto turned and stumbled with difficulty back down the slope, then began to pound across the sand, ignoring the ache in his knee, making for a small knot of boats that remained beached. As he ran, he saw one of the crews motioning each other to wait, and waving him on urgently.

He glanced to his right. The riders were far too far away to endanger him, but still he ran at full pelt, only slowing as his feet began to sink into damp sand. With no grace whatsoever he threw himself over the side of the boat and waved them into motion. They needed no urging and moments later they were rowing like mad for the ships.

Fronto lifted his face above the prow and watched the riders along the sand claiming their grisly prizes and their valuable captives, and thought for a moment he saw a flash of light from a reflection up on the bluff. It could be a signal. Most likely it was the chance reflection from a particularly shiny armour plate. Still, he couldn't stop himself watching. It never repeated.

The journey back was swift and Fronto was the first to clamber aboard this new vessel, not the one he'd arrived on, but the ship that belonged to these particular sailors. It was a Greek-style vessel, and he read the eastern script on the bow with interest as he climbed past it.

Chimaera.

Interesting. Looking back and forth, he noted the crew with a shrewd eye. They were of a lighter, swarthier look than the locals, but darker and more olive-toned than Italian Romans. Better still, though, each man seemed to be armed, each bearing a short Greek blade at their belt, something that few of the crews could boast. Smiling at the men, he turned and hurried along the deck to the trierarch at the rear, who stood close to his mate at the steering oars.

'Get us moving, Captain, and bring us close to Caesar's flagship.'

The trierarch, wearing an unconvinced expression but with respect for the chain of command, saluted, and began giving out orders. Moments later they were turning, making for the command vessel. Fronto sighed with relief, rubbed his knee and gestured to the trierarch.

'Sorry about this. You're out of Crete at a guess?'

'Rhodos, Legate. Welcome aboard the best ship in the fleet.'

'I hope that's true. I hate sailing.'

The trierarch grinned widely. 'Then I'll do my best not to go in circles too often, sir.'

Fronto laughed and then turned and watched Caesar's ship as they approached. His attention was suddenly caught by a fresh commotion and he peered off to the right, northeast along the coast. Another of the ships was navigating the fleet swiftly, making for Caesar's flagship the same as their own.

An odd, unpleasant premonition forming, he traced the line of that other ship's course and tried to pick out something in the distance behind it. For a moment he wondered whether he was just seeing what he'd expected to because of his overactive imagination, but the shapes gradually coalesced. Ships. Another fleet. That second ship heading for Caesar carried the warning, just as that flashed reflection from the cavalry had carried a message to these new enemies.

The warning being carried to Caesar was probably unnecessary. Others had now seen the approaching shapes and the alarm was echoing from vessel to vessel. Fronto hurried to the fore rail and waited as they closed on the flagship. As they neared, he waved and a small knot of senior officers closed on the rail to face him.

'What's the plan?' Fronto bellowed.

'We cannot fight them,' Caesar called back. 'Even if we have more ships, they are crewed by few sailors and no marines. An engagement would be suicide. In addition, the afternoon is late and soon the sun will go down. I have no intention of facing superior enemy ships in the dark.'

Fronto nodded. 'So what's the plan?' he repeated, slightly more urgently.

'Nepher here, my local guide, tells me that if the men row at full speed without pause, given the strong following wind, there is a promontory two to three hours away surrounded by dangerous sandbanks and submerged ridges. If we can make that and anchor at the coast overnight, the enemy will almost certainly avoid engaging us because of the dangers. We have enough knowledgeable locals aboard to help us get in close. That way we can wait out the night. The next morning we take the initiative and plough on to meet with the Thirty Seventh. Once we combine the fleets and have a full legion with us we can think about taking them on.'

Fronto shouted his understanding and agreement, silently biting down on his dismay at a potential three hours' sail at full speed and then a night aboard ship among dangerous sandbanks. But if that was the rest of the Aegyptian fleet following them, and it was fully crewed, the alternative didn't bear thinking about.

Orders were given and relayed from ship to ship, and moments later they were all turning and letting out the sails with a crack to billow in the wind, oars running out and beginning to dip in time with a frantic, energetic tune from the piper on each vessel.

The fleet started to move, racing west to perceived safety.

The one bonus of having been sick for a number of hours on the voyage here was that there was little left to come up for the rest of the journey, so Fronto found himself standing at the rail, retching a dry emptiness over the sea every now and then but with adequate time to worry about the enemy and the sandbanks rather than just his own digestion. After perhaps an hour he found himself finally taking a deep breath and looking up and about, since he had somewhat disappeared into himself on the journey. He was surprised at the amount of empty water he could see. Turning, he saw that most of the fleet was ahead. The Chimaera was falling slowly back, as if to play rear-guard.

'Why are we falling behind?' Fronto asked as he approached the helm. 'This seems to be a fast ship.'

The trierarch gave him a weird grin that reminded him worryingly of Salvius Cursor. The sort of grin usually given by someone covered head to foot in blood and smiling when they should instead be apologising. His two silver teeth gleamed.

'I thought we'd play shepherd to these sheep, sir.'

'What? We've no marines. We're no better off than them.'

That grin notched up two more worrying marks.

'On the contrary, sir. This is the Chimaera. We've got two pieces of artillery, not one like the rest of the sheep. Every man here is armed and a trained killer. We've got twelve bows and a stock of arrows, 'cause some of my men are damn good archers and gull meat makes a pleasant change from fish on a coastal voyage. We have a longer ram than many, and it's a single, bronze-sheathed beam that cuts through hulls, rather than your messy, three-pronged Roman ones that barge them open. And we carry a corvus like the biggest Roman ships. Above that we're the fastest in the fleet. And my lads lost a couple of friends on the beach, too. They're itching to make amends.'

Fronto's eyes narrowed. 'Fast. Secret armaments. Killers on the oar benches. You're pirates!'

The man laughed. 'I could take serious offence at that, sir. I'm Caesar's man, after all. But even an honest ship has to make a living between big voyages, and sometimes that takes you into dangerous waters. It's best to be prepared and to have an edge, just in case.'

'Bloody Rhodians,' Fronto said, rolling his eyes. 'I've half a mind to order you to get back in the middle of the fleet.'

'But we'd be no good there.'

With a sigh, Fronto nodded. It was true. Instead, he concentrated on watching the enemy in their wake as they sailed on west, the sun sinking towards the horizon. He began to count them, but looking at the rising and falling horizon did little for his ongoing health, and he kept having to swallow down his stomach's few remaining contents and recount. After some time, he reckoned Caesar's fleet probably outnumbered the enemy by three to two, but with no army aboard, the battle would be the enemy's with little doubt.

Discouraged, he turned and watched the coast flow past. It looked almost identical all the way. Featureless dun coloured landscape, sometimes low, sometimes a little higher, rarely with any greenery, dotted with local small hamlets that survived on the fishing industry and trade from the coastal caravan routes east to Alexandria and west to Leptis Magna.

By the time someone called out the second hour of the journey, Fronto was not at all surprised to find that they were now the very last ship in the fleet, almost as close to the lead enemy vessel as they were to the vanguard of their own force.

The next signal must have been given with flags, for the first Fronto knew of it was when the trierarch waved him over. He came to rest at the rail beside the Rhodian captain, who smelled of spice, strong wine, and deviousness.

'Message from the flagship: we're at the anchorage. The lead ships are already navigating the sandbanks, and word is being passed back to each vessel about their assigned position. I'd probably best warn you now, Legate, that we're not going in among them.'

'We're not?'

'There will only be limited room in there, and should the worst happen they will all be trapped, unable to adequately manoeuvre between the sand banks. The strongest advantage the Chimaera has is its speed and manoeuvrability, and I cannot compromise that by trapping us between sandbanks. We will stay at the edge of the fleet but in open water. If the enemy have sense they will leave us alone for fear of the sandbanks and of the rest of the fleet.'

Fronto glared at him suspiciously. 'And if they have *no* sense?'

'Then it's going to be an interesting night, sir,' grinned the Rhodian, the golden rays of the dying sun gleaming off his teeth and the rings of the hand that had gone down to clutch the hilt of his sword meaningfully.

Fronto hurried back to the prow and watched as the fleet slowed. Gradually the entire group came to a halt as each vessel in turn was guided in among the sandbanks and moved into position for the night. Fronto knew little enough about the ways of the sea, but he could picture what was in the general's mind. The fleet was all coming to a halt and dropping anchor still pointing west and still fully crewed. Every ship had sufficient food, and now adequate water, to see them through the night. And in the morning, probably before dawn while the enemy still dozed, they would start to slip west once more, heading out of the far side and making for the harbourage of the Thirty Seventh. If all went to plan they would be racing west before the enemy could do much about it, and could rendezvous with sufficient men and ships to make the battle theirs.

If everything went according to plan.

In Fronto's experience, that more often failed to happen than actually succeeding.

Gradually, he watched the ships slipping in through the bright blue-green waters, between the brown banks that were only visible from certain angles as they lurked just beneath the sea's surface. By the time there were only seven vessels still outside, he could make out the details of the enemy fleet following them. One thing was sure: they were well crewed, from the myriad shapes visible.

His misgivings about the possibly-mad Rhodian captain grew with every moment. Finally, he watched the last few Caesarian vessels moving into position and chewed on his lip as the Chimaera made no effort to follow them in, nor even to come close, remaining on the very periphery of the fleet, where they dropped anchor.

His suspicions about the piratical origin of this ship and her crew increased as he watched the crew settling in. Rhodos had once been a bastion against pirates, but even recently, the plague had begun to rise once more. Pompey may have rid the sea, officially, but who knew how many pirate vessels still quietly plied the east, every bit as dangerous as the ones that had captured Caesar himself as a young man.

Fronto looked aft. The enemy fleet had slowed some distance away and observed the Chimaera from there.

The crew of the Rhodian vessel did not prepare for their night in the same way Fronto had seen other sailors doing. Each man took charge of his own position. The oars were drawn in, but neither raised nor put away, simply lying across the decks and benches, ready to run back out at a moment's notice. Half the crew left the benches, while the other half settled down to sleep on them, pulling blankets the same colour as the deck over them and sleeping between the oars. The rest moved into positions of good observation for either lookouts or archers with more wood-coloured blankets. Fronto noticed several carrying bows and quivers with them. Other men lay beside the anchor chain, covered up. The trierarch and his steersman stayed in position, leaning against the hull side and covering themselves. A passing sailor handed Fronto a dun coloured blanket, and Fronto stared at the deck of the Chimaera.

In less than a hundred heartbeats it had gone from being a hive of activity to giving out the appearance of a deserted hulk. Unless you knew the men were there, in the growing half-light they were exceedingly hard to spot.

He mused worryingly for a moment that remaining in a position that granted the most manoeuvrability looked a lot like inviting an attack. He found a place to lie and sank to the deck, drawing his blade on a whim and lying it by his side. He pulled the brown blanket over him and bunched part of it under his head for a pillow. His last coherent thought was to liken the Chimaera to a lilia – those nasty little pits with a sharpened stake in the bottom, covered with grass to hide them from sight. Innocent and quiet, but with a surprise awaiting the unwary foot, which would lead to a really bad day. A few moments later, weariness from a day of retching overtaking him, he was asleep.

CHAPTER NINE

Aegyptian coast west of Alexandria, 11th December 48 BC

'Hush, Legate. No fuss. Quiet. Come.'

Fronto floundered blearily in his blanket, blinking in surprise. The sailor was an extraordinarily lucky man, in that Fronto had his sword to hand, and had he not managed even in the fog of half-sleep to remember where he was, he might have instinctively grabbed it and hacked off the man's arm as he shook the slumbering figure.

'Wha...' he managed in a low whisper.

'Come,' repeated the sailor.

As Fronto shook himself and extricated his cold, achy form from the blanket, he watched the shape of the sailor ducked low at the rail, moving with catlike grace away towards two other figures. He realised then that there were still signs of evening sunlight staining the sky. The sun had set but its glow remained. He could not have been asleep for more than a quarter of an hour, but had been so damn weary that he'd immediately fallen into a deep slumber.

Blinking and shaking it off, he struggled up to a similar crouch, wondering how many more years of sleeping rough he had left in him, and scurried across the deck close to the rail with considerably less poise than the sailor.

The trierarch crouched at the rail with one of his men, and turned, beckoning as Fronto approached. Reaching the man's side, Fronto came to a halt as the captain pointed off into the evening gloom.

'See there, Legate?'

Fronto shook his head. He could see the distant shapes of the Aegyptian ships gathered some way away, but in the twilight gloom could make out little more.

'They come for us.'

'What? I can't see anything.'

But as he concentrated he realised that he could. Some of those shapes were moving, slowly and indistinctly, but they were definitely breaking away from the enemy fleet and becoming larger as they approached.

'How many?'

'I make it three warships and five smaller civilian barques.'

'Warships to surprise and overwhelm, and barques full of men to seize the ship,' Fronto mused.

'Quite.'

'How do we warn the others? How do we raise the alarm without causing a full-scale engagement? Most of our ships are trapped in the sandbanks.'

The trierarch looked at him as though he'd suggested stripping naked and going for a swim.

'Alarm, sir?'

Fronto's brow creased. 'Well, yes. The alarm for the fleet.'

'We don't *need* the fleet, sir.'

Fronto blinked. 'Three warships? Five transports?'

'Three *slow* warships. Five *small* transports.'

'Don't be an idiot, Captain. There is a time for bravery, but hubris helps no one. Warn the fleet.'

'With respect, Legate, you have no authority on my ship. I'll not endanger anyone else when we are more than capable of dealing with the problem.'

Fronto clenched his teeth. 'Caesar will be exceedingly angry with you, even if you survive, which is unlikely. Give the signal.'

'No.'

He glared at the trierarch. 'Then how do you intend to beat such heavy odds?'

'By using the best muscle I have, Legate: the one between my ears.'

Fronto fell silent, staring at the man. 'You had better be as good and as lucky as you think you are, Captain.'

'I'm better.'

With a deep breath, Fronto nodded and, keeping low, scurried off towards the ship's stern. In positioning themselves out to the rear of the anchored fleet by some distance, the Chimaera had been swung slowly so that she faced the enemy, her stern to the rest of the fleet. A clear sign that the trierarch was more concerned with the ships behind them than being ready to depart swiftly with the rest. But then if the ship was as swift as the man said...

Still, Fronto knew over-confidence when he heard it, and he knew damn well what Caesar would think of all this. He knew his duty. Reaching the rear rail as the men of the ship burst into silent and very slow life, he gestured to one of the sailors. As the man crawled over, Fronto whispered.

'What is the signal for an attack warning?'

'Three flashes of the lantern, sir, but we're under an enforced darkness command. No lights on the ship.'

Fronto fumed. This was ridiculous. He gestured angrily at the man. 'Find a lantern, get it lit, and send the signal to the fleet.'

'The trierarch will throw me overboard, sir.'

'I'll do a lot bloody worse than that if you don't send the signal. Do it.'

The man looked into Fronto's eyes and for a moment was clearly considering refusal. In the end, though, he nodded, yet there was still more than a trace of disobedience in that gaze. How had Fronto had the misfortune after the beach attack to end up on a ship full of disobedient and suicidally insane ex-pirates?

Leaving the man and hoping to Hades that he was actually going to do as ordered, Fronto hurried forwards. He had to admit that he was impressed. The men who'd been asleep on the oar benches were now sat hunched low, still covered with their blankets, but gripping the oars ready to run out. Half those men who had left the benches were now back and in a similar state. The rest had made ready with the minimum of noise, movement and fuss. Hardly a breath of activity had shown aboard the ship, but now a dozen archers were crouched at the port rail, evenly spaced, and two men were raising the anchor with slow, quiet grace, the capstan well-greased to keep it silent. Men sat low, gripping ropes ready to pull and release, and crews were already at the twin artillery pieces, one loaded with a heavy stone ball and the other with a long bolt. Close to the latter a man crouched with a rag-wrapped torch and a small knobbly handful of something.

Fire fungus, Fronto realised. Deep in the fibrous mass there would be a glowing ember, and a few puffs of breath would reignite it. He was suddenly damn glad that these Rhodians were part of the fleet and not prowling the sea, looking for helpless traders.

As he neared the commander, the trierarch beckoned to him.

'Would you deliver three messages for me, Legatus? I don't want to take my eyes off the enemy.'

Fronto nodded and hissed an affirmative.

'Tell the ballista "target three", the scorpion "man down two" and the steersman "tactic one".'

Fronto pursed his lips. 'Ballista three, scorpion two, steering one. Got it.'

He glanced out to sea. Those other ships were coming closer all the time. Scurrying low across to the war machines in the bow, he found the crew of the ballista. They had loaded and primed their weapon slowly and in silence, and it now sat at maximum safe torsion, awaiting target and release.

'Trierarch commands target three,' Fronto hissed to them. The men nodded their understanding and began to move the machine ever so slowly, tracking the distant shapes. He hurried across to the scorpion and found it in the same state, foot long bolt ready for release. The man with the fire fungus now had it open in halves and was blowing on one, keeping it low, well below the rail.

'Man down two,' he hissed, receiving a nod. Leaving them to it, he raced along the rail, keeping low, to the rear of the ship. There the steersman stood with the other sailor nearby, striking flint and steel to ignite the oil lantern in his hand. Either the man was not having a great deal of success or he was deliberately failing, which Fronto certainly wouldn't put past this lot.

'Tactic one,' he told the man at the steering oars, who nodded.

Job done, Fronto hurried back to the prow. The enemy were noticeably closer now. The three Aegyptian warships had fanned out to approach like three claws, the transports in their wake, ready to take advantage of an overwhelmed ship.

Fronto hadn't realised how still the sea and the ship's motion had been, until they began to drift and the old familiar queasiness arose in his middle, threatening to overcome him. He fought it down as best he could. He'd eaten nothing for ages. There was nothing to bring up but a little drinking water.

The anchor was now in the ship and they were unrestricted in movement. Fronto glanced back at the stern, but nothing was happening yet. The oars had not been run out and the steersman remained still. There would be no use for the sail this evening, for not a breath of wind stirred the sea. Another glance forward and the enemy were getting worryingly close. Did they truly believe the Chimaera was still asleep? Quite possibly. The enemy vessels were still three abreast, perhaps two ship-lengths apart.

For a moment, Fronto wondered how long the Rhodian captain intended to wait in silence before making his move, but then he noted the trierarch's eyes. They flicked continually back and forth now between the approaching ships and the artillery mounted in the prow. Whatever he had planned was based upon missile range. Fronto knew the weapons well enough, despite these being of a slightly different, Greek-style manufacture, to know the rough ranges. The ballista with its fifty-pound stone ball would be the first to find range, and even if they were good shots, the longest range they could hope for a good level of accuracy was two hundred paces.

It was hard to judge distance at sea, for Fronto at least, and attempting to do so was made all the more troublesome by the fact that looking out over the undulating water did little for his stomach. Still, he bit down on the waves of nausea.

Four hundred paces, he thought.

Slowly, he became aware of something. They *were* moving. Barely noticeably, but they were. Without the power of oars or sail, still they were manoeuvring. The steersman was using the current of the water and his twin long oars to very slowly turn the ship. Even as Fronto watched, the central of the three enemy ships passed their direct prow line and to the port ever so slightly.

He grinned.

The devious bastards, these Rhodians. Without even the appearance of movement, they had shifted just enough to put the ballista in perfect firing line so that the prow beak was not in the way.

Three hundred paces...

He took several deep breaths and clutched his sword tight, though if he had cause to use it then they were probably in trouble and fighting for their lives. In momentary annoyance, he looked back and noted there was still no sign of a signal being sent out by lantern.

'Now,' whispered the trierarch close by, more to himself than to anyone else. A mere half dozen heartbeats passed before his word became law. The call to action was announced with a massive ligneous cracking sound as the ballista crew released their catch, and the cords snapped tight, launching the heavy stone rock at speed.

The signal having been given by the shot, everything sprang to life in an instant. Faster than Fronto could turn to catch it all, the oars were run out and the rowers counting, ready to dip them, the steersman heaved his apparatus, the ballista crew found the second stone and began to load, the scorpion crew tracked their own target, every figure threw off his brown blanket, and the man with the fire fungus set light to his torch and began to move. First he lit a small brazier by the scorpion, then raced along the port side, touching the torch to other containers of coals, which sprang to life.

Caesar's fleet would need no signal now. That something was happening would be clear.

Fronto watched the trierarch's plan unfold and was impressed despite himself. The ballista crew were among the better artillerists

Fronto had seen at work over two decades of war. That first shot had been aimed lower than he'd expected, and not directly at the ship in front. Instead of striking deck, rail or mast, it had instead hit the starboard oar bank, smashing several of the oars and knocking others back as it bounced along them.

Fronto winced. He knew enough of naval dangers to know what that meant aboard the Aegyptian ship. Far from just losing a few oars, it meant that several great heavy beams had just been slammed against the chests or backs of the men pushing them. Rowers would have died in their seats, ribcages crushed by the oars. Between the few men that would have suffered, the broken oars, and the utter chaos in rhythm it created, that central ship was now in trouble already, more than two hundred paces from engaging. With one bank of oars still dipping in time, they slewed dangerously, yawing off to the starboard.

The ship keeping pace with it at that side lurched immediately, their commander seeing the danger and being forced to turn away from the fight to avoid collision with the stricken warship. Fronto couldn't help but let out an exasperated laugh. With one shot of artillery the captain had, even if only temporarily, put two of the three ships out of the fight.

Now, the plan moved into its next stages. The steersman turned them gently, guiding them to the gap between the pair of troubled ships and the remaining active one. As he did so, the second artillery crew took advantage of the closer range and the angle, and released their bolt, touching flame to it beforehand. The fiery missile arced out from the prow towards the most distinctive figure on the deck of the stricken ship.

The central vessel's own trierarch was obvious, dressed in gleaming bronze and bright green and shouting out orders with a desperate tone. The bolt took him in the back and carried him halfway across the deck before pinning him to a rail, where his clothes ignited and he floundered, pinned, burning and screaming. Suddenly deprived of orders and command, the ship exploded in chaos, veering wildly away.

Fronto wondered why the archers remained still, when presented with such tempting targets, but the trierarch clearly had a plan. They were coming close now to the remaining ship, and a sudden blast from the steersman's whistle launched the next attack. The port oars continued apace, while the starboard ones shifted expertly into back-oaring, even as the steersman heaved his steering oar around. The Chimaera turned more sharply than any ship Fronto had been aboard, and his stomach heaved worryingly as they changed course in the blink of an eye. Six heartbeats and they were on an intercept course with the remaining ship, racing for their side. The oarsmen reversed their stroke expertly once more and all broke into a ramming speed with perfect timing.

The enemy vessel had nowhere near sufficient time to react. Their trierarch yelled urgently, and the ship turned, trying to veer away, but there was not enough time. Enemy sailors fled their oar benches and the rail in panic as the Chimaera bore down on them at a terrific speed.

They struck the enemy ship almost perfectly centrally, and just as they coasted into the kill, the oarsmen lifted their oars and leaned them back. Fronto grabbed the rail in the same manner as every other soul aboard, and held on for dear life as the two ships collided.

He'd never paid a great deal of attention to the shape of ship's rams – he'd never been a lover of the sea or committed to the fleet – but he'd seen enough used in his time to know what to expect, and was therefore surprised when what happened was totally different.

In his experience, the ram punched through the enemy boards and smashed and tore into the ship, then the attacking vessel would have to either desperately try and pull back, or stay lodged there and send men aboard to finish the enemy off. Not so, the Chimaera. As the ram struck, long and narrow and shaped like a blade, it sliced into the enemy hull like a sword. The ships lurched and slammed as expected, but on another whistle, as soon as the crew regained their footing, the oars were back in the water in a reverse stroke, pulling them away. The smooth shape of the ram made it a simple job to extricate, and in moments the Chimaera was reversing smoothly, leaving a neat hole in the enemy ship into which water was pouring in great torrents.

The ship was done for, and its crew knew it, for sailors were already leaping into the water. They were little more than five or six hundred paces from the shore here, and the water was not dreadfully deep, so any man with reasonable strength would likely make it to the beach, and every man knew it, trusting to their muscles rather than the doomed timbers of their ship.

Fronto gave a loud laugh. The mad bastard Rhodians were right. They knew precisely what they were doing. Indeed, those low transport vessels full of soldiers were now closing, and suddenly the archers were at work, dipping arrows into the burning coals of their braziers and loosing into the tightly packed boats full of men. The chaos that ensued among the enemy was impressive. Most of them began to turn immediately in a panic, racing back for the enemy fleet and away from this Rhodian nightmare.

The trierarch appeared from somewhere, grasping Fronto's shoulder. 'Feel like a fight, sir?'

Fronto nodded, brow creased. 'Where?'

'Let's take one of them.'

'*Take* one?'

'I'm feeling acquisitive, Legate. Up to it?'

Fronto gave another exasperated, slightly crazed laugh, and nodded. 'Why not.'

'There's one ship still untouched. We'll have that one.'

The Chimaera backed out of the fray and began to turn, and Fronto took in the carnage they had caused with wide eyes. The troop carriers were hurtling back to safety, some of them on fire. The holed ship was already disappearing beneath the surface, though the sea was shallow enough here that its position would in the end be marked by a mast still protruding from the water, even as it settled on the seabed. That left only two ships. One of those was only now starting to right themselves after the loss of one oar bank and their commander. The other was way out and having to manoeuver to bring itself back into the fight.

'Artillery,' bellowed the trierarch. 'Artillery and archers, put that fucking thing out of its misery.'

As the Chimaera turned with astonishing speed and grace, its missiles began to arc out at the ship that had not yet recovered from its damage. The starboard bank of oars took another rock, repeating the carnage of the first blow, while flaming missiles from both scorpion and a dozen bows struck again and again, hitting men and dry timbers alike. Unable to adequately row, and busy putting out endless fires, they were largely removed from the fight, and when one particularly well placed missile plucked the enemy steersman from the stern and hurled him into the water, it was clearly over for them.

'One left,' grinned the trierarch.

Fronto peered at the remaining enemy ship that was now racing towards them. In the distance he could see that several more enemy warships had detached from the fleet and were moving towards them, but at the same time half a dozen of Caesar's vessels were moving out of the sandbanks to come to their aid.

'This could end up in a full sea battle,' Fronto noted, 'and we'll lose that, you realise?'

The trierarch nodded. 'That's why we need to finish this fast and put them off the idea of another battle. Be prepared for a quick fight and hang on tight. This will be a little bumpy.'

Fronto tore his eyes from the approaching ships to each side, the light now almost gone, and squinted at the looming shadow of the remaining vessel hurtling towards them. He realised with a start that the Chimaera was turning gently, back towards the Roman fleet, which would present the enemy with a lovely side attack. He chewed his lip. What was the crazy Rhodian planning now, making himself such an easy target?

Watching carefully, he did as he'd been bid, grasping the rail with his free hand and holding tight, legs set apart for optimum stability. A fresh wave of nausea struck him, and he had trouble fighting it back this time. The enemy were coming for them at ramming speed, continually adjusting their course to keep on track for a perfect strike amidships. Fronto watched with interest as the Chimaera's crew readied. A few men were busy gathering up odd spilled coals that had fallen from the braziers during various manoeuvers, and slinging buckets of sea water over singeing timbers. Others extinguished the braziers with great columns of steam that rose into the dark sky. Archers nocked and remained poised, the only men not holding on. Artillerists had their twin weapons loaded and waiting, clutching the timbers tight.

'Steady,' called the trierarch.

Men waited.

The enemy closed, racing at them, sending up twin white horses of foam from the prow, oars working rhythmically to an unheard tune.

'Steady.'

Fronto clenched his teeth.

'Now,' the captain bellowed.

The oars began to dip, one side forward, one side back, as the steersman heaved his burden aside. The Chimaera began to move, sluggishly at first, but picking up pace with impressive speed. In heartbeats they were turning to face the enemy, who were now worryingly close. As soon as they faced the warship, prow to prow, the oars settled into a uniform rhythm and the Chimaera and its target hurtled towards mutual destruction.

The enemy prow swayed this way and that momentarily, its commander uncertain of what this crazed Rhodian ship was up to, and unsure how to react. The two vessels closed towards mutual collision, and suddenly the steersman gave two short and one long blast on his whistle.

In response, the starboard oars lifted from the water for a count of four as the port ones worked, turning the entire vessel to the right a touch. At that count of four, they fell back into the water and pulled again, straightening the line while the port oars were hauled swiftly inside.

The enemy captain realised what was happening too late. Desperate shouts echoed across the deck as their own rowers were ordered to pull in the oars.

They did not have time.

Having jogged slightly right, The Chimaera met the enemy vessel not head on, but smoothly side by side. The prow, sharp and designed to cut easily through the water, instead cut its way through the enemy oar banks, smashing them like kindling. Screams and the sounds of shattering wood rose all along the enemy rail as the oars pulverised their rowers, killing most in an instant. The two ships were robbed of most of their momentum immediately, and it was easy work for the Chimaera's crew to throw out grapples and pull the two ships together, before the corvus boarding ramp was swung out and to the side to drop to the enemy deck, its twin iron fangs biting into the boards and anchoring it there.

Even as the two ships came to a lurching halt, the archers and artillerists released and then grabbed for the nearest timbers. Twelve arrows, one bolt and a heavy rock smashed into the enemy crew, pulverising them. A few of the Chimaera's men fell with the collision, but most managed to hold tight.

By the time the ships were motionless, the Rhodians were moving. With the exception of the trierarch and the steersman, every crewmember had now torn a blade free and was racing for the corvus. Shaking his head in disbelief, Fronto joined them, gladius gripped tight as he sprinted up onto the ramp and across to the Aegyptian vessel.

He had to admire the enemy, that they still had fight left in them. In this state many a crew and captain would have surrendered, but the Aegyptians rallied their men to defend. Their crew was more numerous than the Rhodians, but not dangerously so. Clearly the bulk of their fighting men had been committed to the low transports, expecting the three warships to easily disable the Chimaera and leave her open for boarding.

Instead, they were in trouble. Fronto winced as he passed across the ramp between the two ships, partially at the sight of the lapping waves below, which continued to make his stomach gurgle and clench, but more so at the slaughter aboard the enemy ship. Bodies lay strewn, ruined and bloody across the benches, broken and torn pieces of oar among them from the terrible blow the Chimaera had struck.

He dropped to the enemy deck and avoided with distaste treading in what was left of a man who'd been struck by the ballista's stone ball. The Chimaera's crew were calling to each other or shouting cries of battle in the Greek tongue, but in such a thick regional accent that Fronto had trouble comprehending it.

The notion that these men had been, and potentially still were, pirates had never sat so comfortably with Fronto. They exhibited a strange glee in their viciousness, a chilling competence at combat, and clearly not one iota of remorse or shame over wanton butchery. They killed with impunity, and more than once, as Fronto pushed his way among them looking for a target, he saw scenes of savagery so far beyond the norm that it reminded him of Salvius Cursor. They were not just killing. They were making a statement.

In moments Fronto found himself facing a swarthy-skinned fellow with a stained grey tunic, wielding a kopis-style curved blade. The man bared his teeth and swept out with the sword, bringing it across in a back-slash at Fronto's middle. The legate threw his gladius in the way, deflecting the blow, but expertly twisted his wrist and managed to turn his parry into a slash that carved a narrow line across the man's upper arm.

The Aegyptian cried out and glared at Fronto, dabbing the wound with his free hand and noting the blood on his fingers as he pulled it away. Snarling, he lunged.

'Stupid,' announced Fronto as he simply leaned aside from the blow and brought his gladius up hard, slamming the point into the pit of the extended arm. It was not the perfect strike, which would carry it deep into unprotected torso and the vital organs there, because of its upward trajectory, but what it did do was irreparably ruin the man's shoulder before tearing out through muscle and taking part of his neck with it, smashing the collar bone in the process.

The man fell away, screaming, sword falling from helpless fingers. In a perfect world, Fronto would pause and drop to kill the man and put him out of his agony, for it would take him a long time to die from that. This was an *imperfect* world, though, and Fronto had other worries. He stepped over the body and advanced, looking for another enemy sailor, his attention suddenly drawn by a roar.

A man was running at him, spear raised. Fronto glanced around himself, taking in his position. His chances of parrying a spear from a charging man were small, and while he could probably sidestep, if he failed it would be the last thing he ever did.

Luck was with him. Space had opened up behind, and Fronto backed away carefully, footsteps precise. The man bellowed and leapt in for the kill, eyes on his opponent. His feet struck the fallen Aegyptian with the ruined shoulder, who lay, shuddering and moaning and hitherto unnoticed behind Fronto, and his eyes widened. He fell forwards with a squawk, the spear going awry and thudding into timber. Fronto immediately discounted him as a future threat and picked out another swordsman beyond. In reaching this new target he made sure to stamp down hard with a hobnailed boot onto the spear man's back with a satisfying crunch, keeping him out of the fight.

The new swordsman watched him carefully, blade held ready to strike or parry as required. Fronto was busy trying to decide how to play it when he noticed a Rhodian coming at the man from behind, teeth bared in a gleeful rictus. Fronto smiled sweetly at the swordsman, who frowned, wondering what the Roman was up to, right until the Rhodian's sword took him in the neck, ripped free in a welter of blood and flesh and a bloodcurdling scream.

The Rhodian gave Fronto a grin and nodded his thanks, turning and running off to deal with another.

The fight was all but over.

Fronto shook his head in disbelief. The Chimaera had taken on three warships and sundry transports. In a matter of perhaps half an hour, she had sunk one, disabled one and captured a third, causing the others to flee. Brutus would be envious of such a victory. Better still, where he knew damn well that Caesar would have come down like a ton of bricks on the Rhodians if they'd failed, he appreciated such insane bravery when it worked. Politicians were fickle like that, after all. There was a small chance of the Rhodians being disciplined, but there was a much greater chance of them being lauded and rewarded.

As Fronto wiped the gore from his sword with a rag torn from a body, and strolled back towards the boarding ramp, he smiled to see the Aegyptian banner being lowered from the ropes. The one that went up might have had some Greek slogan on it, but it was red, and bore Caesar's bull emblem. No one could doubt the ownership of the vessel now.

His gaze strayed out to sea. The enemy warships that had been coming for a second wave of attack had turned and were heading back to their fleet. Moreover, that fleet was on the move, diminishing gradually as they fled the shoreline. The crazy Rhodians had been so victorious and so terrifying that they enemy were retreating.

They had won. Night was almost falling, which put any further fighting beyond reason, too, so they would be safe now. Fronto grinned. This may very well turn out to be the first sea voyage he had ever actually enjoyed.

CHAPTER TEN

Approaching Pharos Island, Alexandria, 13th December 48 BC

Fronto watched as the small, light liburnian skipped across the whitecaps towards them. It was one of theirs, a fact confirmed by the existence of a red vexillum flying from the mast with an indistinct gold emblem that could only be Caesar's bull. Despite its allied status, Fronto felt a shiver run through him. Ships racing like that carried important news, and in the circumstances, any news was unlikely to be favourable. He turned and glanced back across the ships behind them.

The Roman fleet had doubled in number now since they had rendezvoused with the Thirty Seventh Legion, and better still, each ship now had a complement of veteran soldiers on board. Caesar had begun to divide the fleet up, with the ships of Rhodian origin now playing vanguard, after the almost suicidal valour one of their number had recently displayed. The Pontic ships, being built hardy and large, were positioned further out to sea, running along on the fleet's flank, while the various vessels that had long been part of the Roman military and not recently called up during the civil war, running as the centre and rear.

Fronto had elected to remain on the Rhodian ship after the rendezvous, which had surprised some, though apparently not those who knew him well. Caesar had warned him to be steady and careful, and not to act with his characteristic rashness. Galronus

131

had told Fronto he was coming too, as the legate clearly could not be trusted to stay out of trouble. And Salvius Cursor had also joined them. He'd given no reason, but the way his fingers twitched and played with the pommel of his sword made his purpose clear regardless.

A strong fleet, and now one with real teeth.

Why, then, was Fronto so jumpy at the sight of the liburnian?

'Ho,' shouted the Rhodian captain from the rail as the small light ship came alongside, slowing like the Chimaera, though not stopping. 'What tidings?'

The captain of the liburnian leaned across the rail, bellowing at pace to give his news before they were past, the smaller vessel clearly bound for Caesar's flagship.

'Enemy have Pharos. Fleet awaiting you,' was all he managed to impart before the liburnian was past and gone, racing for Caesar.

Fronto nodded and turned to the trierarch. 'You know the plan?'

'Take the right flank, kill the sons of sand-munching bitches.'

Fronto grinned. 'Succinctly put.'

It was little more than a matter of heartbeats before the fleet started to reshape itself, the news leaping from ship to ship before even reaching Caesar, and every vessel knowing the plan well, anticipating orders.

Caesar was determined not to be surprised again, not to be caught with his tunic up and forced to run or hide. With now adequate numbers to confidently commit to an attack, there was no longer a need to tarry, and the knowledge that Arsinoë's fleet was still at sea somewhere between them and the home port of Alexandria meant they needed to be prepared.

The plan was simple. The nine Rhodian galleys, all of whom it seemed carried a similar reputation to that of the Chimaera, would take the right flank, fighting close to the coast as befitted island folk, used to action around headlands and coves. One of their captains, a man called Euphranor, had been raised to admiral of the Rhodian contingent. That the Chimaera's captain approved of the choice suggested that Euphranor may well be another dangerous lunatic, in Fronto's opinion. The eight ships of Pontus, on the other hand, would maintain their seaward position on the left flank under their own admiral, while Caesar's fleet of seventeen Romans would drop back as a reserve force, forming the rear of a U shape. A Roman beast with Greek fangs.

Fronto stood at the rail, grey-green as usual while at sea, but long past the point of having anything left to throw up, and consequently as comfortable as he was capable of being on a ship. The fleet swiftly reformed itself according to Caesar's battle plan, orders from the flagship coming across quickly, supporting the manoeuvres already being undertaken.

The coast swept past on their left, an endless line of parched brown and yellow with intermittent signs of habitation. The sea continued a stunning bright blue-green. Here and there the fleet moved a little further out to sea or huddled together to hug the coastline, depending upon instructions from the native sailors aboard, for the coast was a warren of submerged sandbanks and narrow channels. At least the easterly wind had abated somewhat. The fleet had been making better headway against it than expected, anyway, but for the past hour or more the breeze had dropped to little more than a wisp, and the Roman fleet ploughed on at speed.

Anticipation was getting to Fronto as he finally saw the bulk of Alexandria looming ahead. Galronus appeared beside him and leaned on the rail.

'No sign of them?'

Fronto shook his head. 'Not yet. From what I gather they seem to have been lurking in the mercantile harbour on this side of the Heptastadion while their army try to take the Pharos Island. At least that's the rumour among the crew, gleaned from shouts from other ships. Whether they've taken the whole island or not we'll find out soon enough, but their fleet won't risk being caught and trapped in port. They'll be out to sea somewhere outside the Great Harbour, preventing us from returning. But they're going to get a bloody shock if they think we're the same fleet they met to the west.'

Galronus nodded. 'Bigger and better armed.'

'And confident.'

The two men fell silent at the rail and watched the shape of Pharos Island coming ever closer, the sprawl of urban Alexandria out to the right and the reaching arms of the commercial harbour before that. After a time, Salvius Cursor also joined them at the rail, his manner fidgety.

The fleet had begun to round the island when they first caught sight of the enemy, on both land and sea. Across Pharos lay small settlements, suburbs of the main city, and the men of the enemy force were visible on towers and rooftops, watching Caesar's fleet approach. The enemy fleet lay waiting at the far end of the island, guarding the entrance to the Great Harbour.

Fronto peered myopically into the bright distance.

'I reckon we outnumber them now.'

Salvius Cursor nodded. 'I agree, though not by a great margin. We have thirty four warships. I reckon they have a few short of thirty, but plenty of small craft to make up the numbers.'

Galronus pointed at them. 'They've mirrored our formation.'

Fronto squinted. It was true. The bulk of their fleet, all quadriremes by the look of it, were drawn up in two groups to left and right, with perhaps half a dozen larger quinqueremes in a rear reserve line between them.

'Looks like they plan to butt heads.'

A sailor standing nearby and coiling a rope paused in his work and pointed to the expanse of water between them. 'Formation caused by sea,' he said in a thick Greek accent. 'See the channels and the sandbank?'

Fronto turned his attention from the fleet to the sea that lay before them. Now that the man had drawn his attention to it, he could clearly see the problem. On the north side of the island, the coastal waters had once more formed into channels and banks. Here a wide shallow area sat before them, its depth inadequate for most ships, with a deeper channel to each side, which *would* afford adequate beam for the fleet. It would mean sending ships in small groups through the channels rather than sweeping forwards in a wide front, which would effectively negate any advantage Caesar could claim from numbers or manpower. The wily bastards.

'Can we not just go round them?' Galronus mused.

Salvius Cursor shook his head and pointed off to the right, towards the great Pharos lighthouse and the small fort that lay beside it. 'No time. This is a race now. See?'

And they could. The forces of the Aegyptian army were at the walls of the Pharos fort, swarming at it in an attempt to take it from the small Roman garrison. All three of them watched that fight, tense and horribly aware of what was at stake. They now had to beat the enemy navy with alacrity, for they needed to pass into the Great Harbour and send men to the fort's aid as soon as possible. If they delayed too long and the fort fell to the enemy, many ships could be sunk trying to gain entrance to the harbour once more. Arsinoë's new general knew what he was doing, clearly.

At a call from the flagship that echoed across every deck in relay, the fleet maintained its formation but slowed to a halt at the nearer edge of the shallows, facing the enemy. There they sat for some time, two fangs of heavy warships facing off along the deeper channels with the reserves facing across the submerged sandbank.

'They've got to move,' Salvius Cursor spat. 'Or we have.'

Fronto cursed. 'They have no intention of moving. The longer they delay the more time their army has to overwhelm the fort and deny us the harbour. In doing nothing they win by default.'

'Then why don't our ships move?' Galronus grumbled.

'Because no one, even these mad bastards, want to commit to sailing in more or less single file straight at the enemy. And Caesar doesn't know what to do about it. If Brutus was here and in charge, I suspect he'd have a plan already, but there's no clear solution other than throwing ourselves at the enemy and hoping and praying.'

Their tense concern was interrupted by a strangely positive roar from the Chimaera's crew, and the three Romans' heads snapped around. The crew were all facing out to sea and, looking past them, Fronto could see the Rhodian command ship, the Ajax, had moved slightly forward. A figure stood high in the prow with his arms thrown wide. He was shouting and at such distance, Fronto had to concentrate to make it out.

'...not be afraid of being the first into battle! Let the Pontics and the Romans quake at danger. We are men of Rhodos, sons of the sea. It shames us that soft Aegyptian sailors sit proud and watch us panic. No more. Not for me.'

Fronto grinned. Admiral Euphranor was clearly spoiling for a fight. Well, nothing was as sure as he'd get one.

'For Rhodian honour let us feed these Aegyptians their own gizzards while the rest of the fleet comes up behind. Four vessels to lead. Who's with me?'

There were distant roars from other vessels, and Fronto was unsurprised at the bloodthirsty bellowing that resounded across the Chimaera. Even as Euphranor gave the command and his ship began to surge forwards, so too did the Chimaera, ploughing into the deep channel on the shoreward flank, coming along beside the Rhodian command ship, two more of the fast and dangerous vessels falling in close to their rear.

Fronto turned his attention back to the enemy fleet and the stretch of sea in between as the voices of four Rhodian ships slid cacophonically from miscellaneous excited cries into a lively song, in a thick eastern Greek dialect that largely escaped Fronto's ability to translate. It seemed to be about blood, honour, blood, ships, steel and blood, blood and more blood. It sounded worryingly happy and carefree for a song with such a subject, but all four crews chorused their way through it as the vessels slid at breakneck pace towards the waiting enemy.

The distance to the lead Aegyptian vessels Fronto estimated at fifteen hundred paces now, as the Rhodian ships pelted forwards at an astonishing pace. At a signal from the command ship, the artillery in the bows were loaded and primed, ready for action. A second call had the archers take up positions. Fronto turned. Like all vessels in the fleet, the Chimaera was now host to a century of legionaries from the Thirty Seventh. He almost burst out laughing at the faces he saw among his countrymen, who clearly had drawn the short stick to be placed on board this vessel full of lunatics. The centurion did a commendable job of looking confident and unflappable, telling his men to be steady and prepared, though the way his fingers continually twitched showed a nervousness he had tried hard to hide.

A thousand paces. The corvus boarding ramps were unfastened to be ready, a move that spoke to Fronto of homicidal optimism, given the number of ships awaiting them. Eleven warships, he could count, all of whom might well be able to engage the Chimaera and its companion, the Ajax, before any support arrived.

He turned. The rest of the fleet was moving now. Caesar must have given his signal and the rest of the Rhodians were racing in the wake of the four lead vessels. The Pontic ships had begun to move on the other flank, and Caesar's Roman reserve were splitting and committing to one channel or the other. They would be of little use to the advance force, mind. Unless the Rhodians somehow managed to rout the group of eleven vessels that guarded the far end of that channel, there would be insufficient room to open up and manoeuvre, and it would all be down to the success of these lead Rhodians. Fronto just prayed they were as prepared as they had been last time.

Eight hundred paces. Three enemy vessels were concentrating on each of them now, the Chimaera and the command ship to their left. The other five had fanned out and were in position to support any of their fellows and prevent a breakout through the fleet. Commendable, of course, but Fronto knew what the Aegyptians were facing. If *he'd* been the enemy he'd have committed every ship he had to stopping those two lead vessels before the two directly behind them could come in.

Six hundred paces. Fronto gave up trying to pay attention to what Admiral Euphranor and his command ship did. Now it all came down to the Chimaera. Three vessels converging on them, two more close by, off to the right on the shore side. What had the insane captain planned this time?

Salvius Cursor drew his blade but Fronto shook his head. 'If you need that we're finished. Until we've broken out and evened the numbers, it's all down to the ships.'

A series of signals issued from the rear of the vessel and Fronto smiled. He had absolutely no idea what the man was doing, but it was peculiar and unexpected, and the enemy would be equally dumbfounded and wrong-footed by it.

Three warships were racing directly at the Chimaera, some thirty paces apart to allow adequate room for the oars without meeting and interfering. Fronto staggered, along with his friends, as the ship suddenly slewed to the left, heading almost on a collision course with the command ship. He clutched sickeningly at the rail as the others threw worried looks around. Fronto just grinned. The Rhodian captain was up to something, for sure.

When it looked certain there would be a collision with the Ajax, who had not flinched, suddenly and without shouted orders the Chimaera lurched back to the right, cutting through the water neatly in a beautifully executed high-speed turn. Fronto almost laughed out loud then, as he realised what they had done.

The enemy had seen them turn and had consequently moved to counter in perfect formation. All three enemy warships had turned to their right, still making straight for the Chimaera. Now, though, with only four hundred paces to clear, the Rhodian ship had changed direction sharply.

The enemy reacted with varying degrees of readiness, caught completely by surprise. The flanking ships turned slower than the central one. The outside flank, towards the shore, suddenly realising she was now in danger of her own collision, turned as sharply as she could manage. Even Fronto could see how poor that decision had been. They were going too fast for that. In order not to be rammed by one of the other ships sailing forwards on the periphery, they now had no choice but to try and turn back again, moving up to maximum speed. They avoided taking another Aegyptian ram in the side by mere paces, but the panicked manoeuvre had doomed them. Though the oars moved to desperate backwatering, they were out of space. The ship crunched up onto the shore of Pharos Island at a horrible angle as it tried to turn once more. Men fell and the ship toppled to its side, half-beached.

Laughing like a lunatic and aware that his friends were staring at him, Fronto turned back to the other ships. The remaining two who had singled them out were coming at them again. What would happen next Fronto could anticipate, though, for he'd seen it done once already by this crew. Sure enough, with little more than a hundred paces to spare, the Chimaera performed the now familiar, to Fronto at least, course correction a little to starboard.

The enemy ships were close together, distant enough only to stop their oars meeting. Suddenly the Chimaera was aiming itself into that gap, its own oars withdrawn and lifted.

To their credit the two Aegyptian captains tried their best, and reacted as swiftly as they could once they realised what was happening. The speed of oar strokes changed so that both ships began to pull apart, veering away to either side as sharply as possible, after which the oars began to pull in.

They were too late. The Chimaera ploughed in between them, smashing several Aegyptian oars that had been too late in withdrawing, as cries of pain and shock rang out from both vessels. As the Rhodian swept along between the two panicking Aegyptians, who reeled from the damage, the archers rose to the rails, nocking and releasing arrows in a furious cloud, their targets close and easy. By the time the Chimaera pulled away behind the two ships into the clear, the damage to the enemy had been brutal: oars broken, rowers crippled and dozens of men stuck with arrows.

More ships were now moving from the reserve to join the fray, and those other heavy warships that had been on the periphery were pulling forwards to engage. At a signal the twin artillery pieces in the prow launched at one of the other vessels, the bolt flying wide, but the rock striking somewhere mid-upper deck.

They were momentarily free of enemy vessels, and at a series of bellowed orders the sail was let out fully, the oars run out once more and the ship began to turn and sweep forwards, ready to engage another enemy. Fronto caught the boggle-eyed looks on Galronus and Salvius and laughed as he turned to take in the rest of the fight. 'They're so suicidally reckless I'm starting to think they may be related to you,' he grinned at the tribune.

Leaving them to gape in shock, Fronto looked back over their own fleet.

They were in a better position than they had any right to hope for. Admiral Euphranor's command ship had pulled off a similar coup with their own three enemies, and two of those were now reeling at the edge of the fight, getting in the way of the other ships trying to commit. Given the moment of freedom, Euphranor's ship had directly engaged another and was trying to board her.

Meanwhile the other two Rhodian ships who had come up astern were now free of the narrow channel and were moving out to commit to battle, taking on the other warships of the Aegyptian flank. Fronto couldn't make out what was happening out to sea, but it seemed that the Pontic ships were also either engaged or closing to do so.

Caesar's fleet flooded forwards from the rear, too, coming to threaten the Aegyptian ships that were numerically, and in terms of individual strength, now the weaker. It looked as though the Rhodian's fierce assault had pushed the enemy back enough to gain the freedom to fight, and now Caesar's fleet could fully commit and turn the battle their way.

He turned back to their own flank. The Aegyptians had begun to rally. Barring the one vessel locked in combat with the Ajax, the remaining nine enemy ships were pulling in to surround the four Rhodians. It might have looked bleak, but for the staggered, lurching manner in which several of those vessels moved, having taken damage to oars, rowers, crews and even the hulls themselves. Outnumbered the Rhodians might be; outclassed they were not.

His attention now fell upon a small flotilla of smaller vessels coming forth in support behind the troubled Aegyptian warships. Something about them seemed strange, and staring beneath his raised hand into the bright sunlight, he suddenly realised what it was. They were lit by several small fires. Concentrating, he tried to pick out the details, nudging Galronus, who he knew had the better eyesight. 'Look at the skiffs.'

Galronus did so and straightened suddenly. 'Fire pots and flame arrows.'

Fronto nodded. He'd thought so, but it was nice to have it confirmed by someone sharp-eyed. 'Go tell the trierarch.'

Galronus did so, even as new orders were being given. The Aegyptian ship wrestling with Euphranor had somehow managed to disengage and was limping away as fast as it could. In response, now threatened on all sides, the four Rhodian ships had begun to pull closer together and to circle like some Cantabrian wheel of cavalry. Fronto wondered what possible bonus this could give them, but realised soon enough as the oar benches were swiftly shuffled so that the weariest rowers were given the port oars which had only small strokes to keep the ship moving, the stronger men on the outside of the circle able to row harder. Moreover, the archers now all moved to the starboard rail and concentrated there, no longer having to divide their attention to both flanks. The artillery pieces both reloaded and turned outwards.

Fronto chuckled. Circling as they were, they might look like ready targets, but nothing could be further from the truth, and as the Aegyptian ships coming at them slowed, it seemed they now realised it too. There would be no chance to ram the Rhodian ships as they continually circled. This was now down to artillery and tactics, and clearly once more the men of Caesar's fleet had the edge.

New orders rang out across both fleets, and the enemy warships slowed, keeping pace with the circling Rhodians but out of missile range. As they did so, the fire boats began to close. Men swung pots of fire on cords with muscular arms, letting go as they spun, sending the pots hurtling towards the circling Rhodians, while others lit arrows and loosed at them.

Fronto frowned. The one problem with the Aegyptians' tactic was that it relied upon shock and panic, and the Rhodians showed neither failing, for they were prepared. After all, if the fire ships were in range to loose at the Rhodians, then the same was true in reverse.

As here and there fire pots or burning arrows thudded into the Rhodian ships, men hurried over with buckets of sea water and doused the flames. The response was appalling. The best archers and the finest artillerists on board the Rhodian ships waited for the word and the moment it was given, they went to work with horrific results.

Arrows, bolts and rocks burst from the circling ships like a ripple of death from a stone dropped in the water. Almost every shot had been carefully aimed until the signal, and then simultaneously every missile struck out at the fire boats round them, each of which had come to a stop to give them the most stable platform from which to work.

The same scene played out time and again on the fire boats. A man with a fire pot swinging about him ready to fling, or an archer with a flaming arrow nocked, was suddenly stuck with an arrow shaft or entirely run through with an artillery bolt, or his head smashed like an overripe melon with a hurled boulder. The result in most cases was the same. The fiery missile they had been preparing to send forth instead dropped, flew or tumbled from their dying forms into the boats. Boats that were filled with highly combustible materials.

In a circle of appalling destruction around the four Rhodians, the Aegyptian fire boats ate of their own bitter fruit as the majority of them burst into flaming death in an instant, beyond any hope of quelling with a bucket. Some, indeed, burst into such blazing sudden infernos that they more or less exploded where they sat, sending screaming men into the water, their clothes, hair and skin all afire.

It was carnage on an unexpected scale, and as men hurled themselves from doomed boats into the water, beginning the long swim to the shore of Pharos, those boats as yet untouched swiftly dropped oars back into the water and began to turn and race away from the fight.

Fronto felt it then: the tipping point of the engagement. He'd experienced it plenty of times on land. There often came a moment in a battle where two sides had struggled, tugging this way and that with huge levels of destruction, when even while both armies were still strong and committed, the scales would tip and the future of a battle would be decided. It might be when a unit breaks unexpectedly, as it had at Pharsalus. Or it might be when one side suddenly experiences a panic moment and their morale fails.

It was happening now. There was no visible sign as the ten Aegyptian warships moved in to engage the four Rhodians. In theory, the Aegyptians still had the advantage until the rest of the ships emerged from the narrow channel, which would happen any time now, but there was an atmosphere in the air. He could feel it. The Aegyptians knew they had lost, even though they continued to fight. Similarly the Rhodians, despite having used up all their tricks and now having to rely only on valour and strength, knew suddenly that they'd won.

Salvius cursor grunted angrily.

'They're going to withdraw.'

'Yes,' agreed Fronto. 'I can feel it too.'

'I never even bloodied my blade,' the tribune sighed wistfully.

Fronto turned and peered at the island off their starboard bow, then pointed. 'I'm confident you're not out of opportunities yet, Salvius. That fort is in trouble and the moment we drive off the enemy ships, we have to take that island. The whole damn thing, and the Heptastadion too, else the fort will suffer this again and again.'

Salvius nodded, his gaze playing over the beleaguered island.

Suddenly a whistle's shrill burst rang out, and all four Rhodian ships began to turn, emerging from their tight circle. Euphranor had spotted the vessel he had been trying to board earlier, and his ship was racing towards it once more, corvus boarding ramp wavering, men with ropes and grapples rushing to the rail.

Another Rhodian had picked a small sleek bireme and was mirroring the admiral's preparations, readying to take it down. The Chimaera and the fourth Rhodian seemed to have different ideas. The captain at the stern bellowed his commands and the Chimaera turned, tracking an enemy vessel and aiming for it, both artillery pieces loading and loosing in a continual barrage. The Aegyptian ship began to turn now as somewhere a signal was blasted for a retreat, but they were too slow by a mile.

They were almost perfectly side-on as the Chimaera moved up to ramming speed, their tireder oarsmen now better rested. Fronto watched the men on board the enemy ship crying out in fear as they saw the Rhodian with the unpleasantly long and pointed ram racing towards them.

A quick glance over his shoulder and then off to the left confirmed for Fronto what he had assumed was happening. The bulk of Caesar's fleet were now closing, having reached the end of the channel and the open water. At the same time the majority of the Aegyptian fleet was now racing east, away from the Romans and back towards the waters of the delta they knew so well.

The Roman fleet had carried the day, and, barring the threat the remains of the fleet coming up behind represented, and a smaller action from the Pontic ships on the far flank, four Rhodian vessels had achieved it alone.

The Chimaera struck their target amidships, every man on the Rhodian deck clinging tight to the ship as they lurched with the collision. As before, the perfectly-formed ram cut a neat hole in the enemy ship, and rather than battering it before them it simply came to a stop as the oarsmen began to backwater and extricate the prow from the enemy vessel.

As they pulled back, cheering and jeering, the Aegyptian vessel began to sink, water pouring in through the hole.

Fronto looked about as they moved away, joining up with the newly arrived ships of the fleet.

From what he could see three warships of the Aegyptian fleet had been sunk and one run aground on the island's shore, and two more were almost under the control of Rhodian boarders now. The charred remaining flotsam of fire boats showed how many of those had been destroyed, and the rest of the Aegyptian fleet, many of whom were at least partially damaged themselves, were already moving into the distance, racing east.

They had won.

His gaze slid to the island. The figures on the rooftops looked a lot more subdued now, but the fight for the fort was going strong.

That would have to be the next objective.

They had been beleaguered defenders long enough. Now they had water. Now they had an extra legion. Now was the time to fight back.

Pharos Island.

CHAPTER ELEVEN

Fronto sighed. Why was it clearly his lot, as the most seasick-prone member of Caesar's entire force, to spend the entire campaign aboard ships? He glanced irritably this way and that at the other vessels of the small fleet.

Following the battle out to sea, the Caesarian ships had entered the Great Harbour and put in at the jetties below the palace, though five ships had dropped their legionaries at the Pharos fort en route to bolster the numbers there. Fronto had initially been sceptical about Caesar's next plan, though the sense of it was coming clear.

The original notion of landing their full force at the fort and fighting out across the island from there had been abandoned, for Queen Cleopatra had pointed out patiently that the enemy could more easily defend one line across the island than they could an attack from all sides. Consequently, the fort's garrison had continued to hold against the enemy at their own defences and when the attack began they were to push west from their walls. But they were little more than a distraction, as was the fleet. Fronto was the true hammer here.

Pharos was about to be hit by three forces at once. One was already there and under enemy scrutiny, fighting across the walls of the fort. They would draw the Aegyptians' attention, certainly. But just to be sure, Caesar was sending part of his fleet back out to sea under Brutus' command to harry the north coast of the island with artillery and draw further attention that way.

Then, while the island's native army was busy trying to hold back the force from the fort and deal with the naval bombardment, the true insurgents would strike. Fronto looked around at the vessels in his force. The attack was being transported in smaller skiffs and merchant ships, not the warships that would draw too much attention. Ten cohorts of legionaries, three units of lightly armed infantry from the palace, and Caesar's favourite weapon: cavalry. Only three hundred of them, but they were veteran Gallic cavalry. Men who had fought across Gaul and at Alesia. Men who had crossed Greece and held the field at Pharsalus. Men on whom Caesar felt he could rely.

With Cassius remaining in charge at the palace alongside the queen, Caesar had taken personal command of the fort garrison, making himself highly visible in order to draw the attention of the enemy. With Brutus on the ships, that left the command of the landing force to Fronto, with Galronus in charge of the cavalry. The men buzzed with eagerness. He could feel it across the fleet. Caesar had promised a man's weight in gold to the first soldier who set foot upon the Heptastadion, having secured the island.

He tried not to pay attention to the roll of the boat as it approached the open mouth of the Palace Harbour. The entire force moved along the harbour walls, hidden from any watching eyes on the island. This was all about the timing, for there was no doubt that given adequate warning, the Aegyptians could put enough men on Pharos to swamp the Romans, though they would not risk pulling that many from the city force without good reason.

Fronto looked up at the sun. The attack *must* have started now, yet the fleet moved slowly still, settling into position in the Palace Harbour. He glanced back, tense, at the theatre rising above the water beside the palace, a natural high viewpoint, and was relieved to see the signal. Three flashes of a reflective lens, repeated to be certain.

Relief flooded him. The plan was moving forward, then. Stage one had been for the fleet to leave the harbour, which it had done over an hour ago, putting out to sea and then turning and coming against the north of the island, hopefully drawing the bulk of their artillery in response. Then, perhaps half an hour ago, Caesar would

146

have given the order for the fort's garrison, bolstered with men from the Thirty Seventh, to cross the walls and push west.

It was a good tactic, and one that the Aegyptians should have assumed a complete plan. A simultaneous push west by land and bombardment of the north coast, dividing the enemy strength. That a third move was yet to be played should hopefully not have occurred to them.

At the receipt of the signal from the theatre, the trierarch of this ship began to move, taking Fronto and his cohorts from the Sixth as the vanguard of this attack forward, and carrying them out through the arms of the Palace Harbour and into the open water of the Great Harbour.

As they emerged between the great stone piers, the mass of small ships and skiffs gathered tight together, they came into view of the island immediately, for the Palace Harbour sat within the southeast corner of the Great Harbour, while the Pharos Island formed the northern shore.

One mile of calm water lay between the piles between which they emerged and the island's shore that was their destination. It had been estimated that they could be beaching and disembarking in less than a quarter of an hour. That gave the enemy a quarter of an hour at most to see them coming, decide whether they posed more of a threat than the garrison or the fleet, and reorganise their force to face the landing ships, flooding men from other positions, between the buildings on the island, through narrow, vertiginous streets and to the harbour shore. In Fronto's opinion, he would have had trouble achieving that even with a Roman force of very competent officers, so the chances of the less professional and unprepared Aegyptians managing it were extremely small.

Still, he silently urged the flotilla to ever greater speed as he kept his gaze locked on Pharos Island. Sails were out and filled with what wind there was, to add a small boost to the speed, but it was the oars that dipped and circled, dipped and circled at the highest pace they could manage that pulled the ships towards their destination.

There was no maintained formation. This was about speed. Some of the vessels were naturally faster than others and instead of keeping their place in the fleet, they raced ahead. Landing men as fast as possible was the whole point.

Fronto was pleased with himself, though, that he had managed to select one of the fastest. His ship was still among the front runners, slicing through the water like a knife. He could see Galronus' ship some distance off to the left, almost keeping pace, and it gave him a wicked little thrill to note that Salvius Cursor's ship was slipping behind. He could imagine the tribune calling his trierarch very unkind names, desperate as he was to be involved in the fight.

Turning once more, he concentrated now on the island ahead.

They had been spotted. He could see movement on the rooftops facing the harbour. The question now was what would they do about it? That, and how fast would they do it?

He settled in, fingers gripping the rail, eyes on the island. The ship ploughed on and he fought down the urge to be violently sick. It had become such a common feeling that it came as naturally now as breathing.

Something was wrong with the shore.

He noticed it even as the trierarch shouted him, pointing at the island.

'I see it,' he called back.

The ship had been making for a wide thoroughfare on Pharos, a stone-flagged street running up through the heart of the island from a 'U' shaped dock on the water side. The problem was that from a distance across the harbour the dock looked fine, a deeply shadowed landing between high buildings. But now, as they approached, it became clear that the dock was not empty. That shadow harboured trouble.

A warship.

Fronto felt a moment of rising panic. How in the name of all the gods had the Aegyptians got a ship in there? His consternation was being echoed now across the landing flotilla as men shouted and pointed. Fronto, heart beginning to thump fast, shot his gaze back and forth along the shoreline, which was becoming more clear and distinct with every oar stroke.

Shit.

Every major dock along the coast seemed to be filled with an Aegyptian ship.

Had their attack been anticipated somehow?

Someone nearby was pointing in a different direction, off to the west, and Fronto's gaze followed it, heart sinking with realisation. There was a bridge built into the Heptastadion – the huge causeway that connected the city with the island and formed the western edge of the Great Harbour – which the Roman forces had long since discounted as any danger. It was narrow and low. A single ship at a time could pass through it between the Aegyptian-controlled commercial harbour to the west and the Roman-controlled Great Harbour to the east. With the Roman fleet waiting, they had simply discounted the probability that the enemy might send ships through there. It would be suicide, of course. What they had *not* considered was that the devious bastard now commanding the enemy force might slip one ship at a time through either under cover of darkness, or perhaps even in bold daylight while the Roman fleet had been in the west seeking water.

However they had done it, they had clearly used the bridge to bring a few ships in and position them along the southern shore of Pharos Island, blocking the main landing spots that were precisely the Romans' current target. Even now an Aegyptian warship was halfway through the arched opening, ready to engage the Roman flotilla.

'Bastards.'

The trierarch's expression suggested he shared the opinion.

'What's your order sir?' the man demanded, an edge of desperation in his voice.

Fronto felt a moment of uncertainty. The plan had been a simple one, and while he was perfectly at home commanding a legion in the field, ships were not his forte by a long shot. One thing was certain: if it came to naval combat, those big Aegyptian warships might have their work cut out against Caesar's navy, but that navy was on the other side of the island, and all Fronto had were small-to-medium-sized transport vessels, not one of which stood a chance against the bigger Ptolemaic triremes. They couldn't stop there. And there were few other places a ship could properly land to disembark a force of infantry.

He chewed his lip, eyes raking the coastline. They would be there in perhaps a hundred heartbeats now, and the entire plan had gone to shit before their very eyes.

His gaze fell on an area of the island further along the coast westwards, towards the Heptastadion. There grass and orchards came down to the waterside. It was not a huge length of coast, but enough to land perhaps two ships at a time, and in open ground. That solved the first problem that had leapt to mind.

'Signal the cavalry ships. Send them west to land on that grassy slope.'

As the man did so, his musician blasting from his horn and pointing, Fronto nodded to himself. That at least sorted the cavalry, and they would be in their element in such open ground. There they could race around and cause huge amounts of trouble without being hemmed in by buildings and streets. Galronus would make the enemy sweat there. But that didn't solve the problem for anyone else. It would take precious time to land the cavalry there, and if the infantry ships all queued up they would soon become prime targets for the enemy warships. Moreover, the time they took landing would give the enemy more opportunity to react and prepare, negating everything they were trying to do.

'Captain,' he said in a tone more decisive than he felt, 'I think it's time the men got their feet wet.'

'Sir?'

'There are no places to comfortably land a ship, but I remember when we landed in Britannia once. We stopped as we hit the beach underwater, all the ships grinding to a halt, and the men had to jump down into the waves and run for the beach. My own Tenth Legion. We're just going to have to do that again.'

'Sir, this is not a sandy beach we can run the ships aground on. It's shingle and rocks that break or deny ships, and difficult, rocky shoreline. You can't do that here.'

Fronto grinned at him. 'I hate being told I can't do things. Makes me want to do them all the more.'

'You'll wreck ships, sir.'

'Then you'll just have to be careful. See directly ahead, just a few paces east of that dock we were headed for?'

'No, sir?'

'Precisely. It's just a few rocks at the bottom of a grey wall.'

The trierarch peered ahead. '*That* sir? I think it would be generous even calling that coast.'

'Yes. Land there. A set of steps lies just off to the right. We can get the men to them. Send whatever signals you need to for the fleet. Just tell them to land wherever they can find room.'

The trierarch looked immensely troubled, but he did so regardless, watching the rocky coast ahead nervously. Leaving the other ships to land as best they could, Fronto peered at their own landing point. He had six centuries in this wide merchant vessel, all good men and well armed. If they could get close enough to that rock for men to leap ashore, they should be able to make that set of steps that led up into the town. From there, they could begin to take control of streets and blocks. It was tricky, but possible. His eyes drifted up to the rooftops. The enemy were still manning many of those places, giving them good vantage points. They would be ready to defend their positions, for sure, and they would have an advantage over the men on the ground below.

He turned to the men standing in the ship behind him.

'You're about to earn your pay, men. The enemy have denied us a good landing place, so we're going to try something stupid. We're going to get as close as we can to those rocks ahead and then jump ashore. I want you all to leap like horses. Anyone who misses will be in the water in armour, and we have no idea how deep it is. You understand?'

The men nodded nervously, a chorus of subdued affirmatives.

'It gets better from there. We have to funnel up a narrow staircase between two buildings with Aegyptians on top. You can bet money they'll drop things on you, so the moment you land, it's shields up and make a roof. Don't lower that roof until you're out of danger of falling objects, or whatever's on the ground in front is worse. Aemilianus' century, as soon as you find access left and right, I want half your men going each way. You lead one, your optio the other. Get into the buildings and up top faster than a rat in an aqueduct and neutralise the threats on the rooftops. The rest move and fan out. Once we have a good perimeter, we hold until other units meet up with us and then we move forwards. Everyone got that?'

Another subdued affirmative.

'And just to maybe take the edge off your nerves, I'll double the night's wine ration for any man who bloodies his blade on an enemy today.'

This raised more interest.

He noted the faces before him, and he couldn't really blame them their nerves. Taking the houses and streets was hard enough, especially while natives were trying to cave in your skull from above, but the thing that had every man twitching was the landing itself. Fronto turned to look ahead once more. It was going to be trouble. There would be losses, and that would damage morale before any true action.

He sighed, knowing exactly what he had to do. Like all the best Roman commanders, Caesar included, he knew the value of an officer sharing his men's peril. Caesar had stood in the shield wall against the Belgae, in among his men, and even now he personally led the advance from the fort, where he would be brandishing his sword and would undoubtedly find a way to plunge it into an Aegyptian in front of his men.

He eyed the rock that was now horribly close. It was probably a monumentally stupid idea. Even the oldest legionary in this ship was a decade younger than he. Lucilia would crucify him if she had even an inkling of what he intended. Thank the gods her and the others were safe off in Hispania.

He was too old for this kind of foolishness, and he knew it.

But times demanded foolishness regardless.

The ship closed. All along the coast transports were making for similar places: dangerous and impractical landing spots, which had the only advantage of being somewhere the Aegyptians had not considered worth defending. He couldn't see the cavalry vessels off to the west now, and had to hope they were doing well.

He peered down, then felt the bile rise as he watched the undulating waves. The harbour here was of dark water and even he, a sea-hater, knew that meant it was still deep. If the seabed rose in a slope here it should already be visible beneath the surface. It wasn't, which meant that there would be no slope. Just deep water and rocks. He swallowed nervously, trying not to show it to the men. His fingers went to the figurine of Fortuna hanging on the thong beneath his scarf, and he sent her a brief prayer that he make it to land and that his ragged body, and in particular his knee, see him through it all.

The ship closed, and he heard the trierarch praying fervently. At the last moment, the steersman heaved his oars over with the aid of another burly sailor as the oarsmen withdrew their poles, sending the ship into a sideways drift towards the rocks.

'Now is the time to pray there are no submerged rocks,' the trierarch yelled at him, wild-eyed.

'Hold on tight,' Fronto shouted across the ship, the men grabbing whatever they could, including each other.

The vessel hit the rocky shore side-on and none-too-gently. Men all across the deck fell and floundered, shouting in shock or pain as they were thrown about. There was a crash and the horrible straining ligneous sound of tortured wood. Fronto heard a crack, and saw the trierarch begin to panic.

'Everyone ashore,' Fronto shouted, biting down on his lip so that his next prayer to Fortuna came out muffled as he clambered up to the rail, shoulders hurting from holding tight during the collision.

He went for it straight away. No time to panic. Do it and hope.

He launched from the rail and hit the sloping rocks that were perhaps a foot higher than the ship. He made it, just, feet skittering wildly. It was then he remembered just how bloody awful hobnailed boots were on wet stone, as his left foot slipped, his leg flying out from under him. He swayed for a dangerous moment, about to topple back into either the boat or the water, and then instinctively threw his weight forward as Masgava had once taught him.

In a heartbeat he was face down on the rock. Behind him he heard the shouts of gods' names and various curses as the rest of the men began to jump across. Scrambling upright, Fronto managed to pull himself across the rock to the base of the grey wall, where he turned to watch his men.

They were leaping across the gap with what appeared to be enthusiasm until he realised it was actually increasing desperation. A hidden rock had indeed holed the ship, and already it was noticeably lower in the water. The men were not desperate to be on land, but they *were* desperate to be off the ship. Fronto didn't care. The end result would be the same.

He hardened his heart at the sight of men here and there slipping with a shriek and disappearing into the water between the wet rock and the sinking ship. They were done for and there was nothing he could do about it. Some of the lucky ones fell back into the ship and were afforded a second chance.

In fifty heartbeats most of his men were on the rock, shields held over their heads, moving close together to lock the boards in and make a more solid roof. Already Fronto could hear rocks and tiles and bricks thudding onto the boards from above. He looked down with dismay. The ship was already close to the waterline and the rock was now way too high to jump across. A few of the stronger, more lithe, men threw away their shields and leapt, grabbing the rock with desperate fingers, pulling themselves up onto land.

Sailors were now hurling themselves into the sea. Unencumbered by armour, they could safely swim the waters of the harbour, and would hopefully be able to make their way to somewhere safe to wait out the fight. Following their example, the legionaries still in the ship, who now had no hope of making the rock, instead began to strip off their armour and, down to just tunics and boots, joined the sailors in swimming to safety.

In all, surprisingly few had perished in the landing, though at least a score of men had been forced to disarm and swim elsewhere. A quick estimated headcount suggested that he still had five centuries of men, which was more than he had any right to expect after such madness.

A cry of pain reminded him that they were still in danger, as a heavy tile punched its way between the raised shields and crippled a man.

'On,' Fronto bellowed. 'Up the stair. Form line and move forwards. Aemilianus, look to the doorways.'

Taking a place somewhere in the middle and thanking the men to either side for the protection of their raised shields, he joined the centuries as they moved across the treacherous, slippery rock, men constantly sliding around and falling out of line, until they finally reached the rough staircase. This rocky shelf was probably used by local fishermen, the stair their access from the streets.

He was more grateful than he could have believed when his boot fell upon the solid and flat step. His men were chanting an old marching song to keep up their spirits as a constant barrage of rubble struck the shields above. Here and there men cried out as lucky shots managed to penetrate the shield roof and wound the men beneath, but they were holding off the bulk of it. He heard the shouts of the centurion and his optio as their men located doors into the flanking buildings and entered, charging through rooms and clattering up stairways.

They moved forwards at an inexorable but slow pace, a solid mass of men with a roof of linden boards from wall to wall, and covering more than a hundred paces of alleyway. It was only as someone ahead shouted a warning of enemy soldiers that Fronto realised that the thuds from the rain of masonry had thinned out and were even now still tailing off. Aemilianus and his men must have secured the roofs to either side.

'Shields down,' he shouted, hoping he wasn't being dangerously premature with the order. Odd pieces of stone still fell, but they were few and far between, and even now he could see legionaries atop the roofs, shouting encouragement to their fellows in the street below. What Fronto would have given at that moment for a couple of dozen Cretan archers to send up to the roofs. Still, he had done what he could with the resources at his disposal. Right now he had to create a perimeter until other men joined them. The entire force suddenly came to a stop, presumably at some unheard command from the front.

'Let me through,' he shouted, pushing his way between the men, 'coming forwards.'

In moments he was elbowing and shoving his way to the front in the press, men letting him past as best they could in the tight confines of the narrow street. Finally, with some difficulty, he saw the front line three men ahead and latched on to a centurion. Pushing his way forwards, he dredged his memory, finally beginning to comprehend why his grandfather had insisted on moving around with a *nomenclator* at his shoulder, to remind him who everyone was as he went about his daily business.

'Centurion Stallius?' he hazarded.

To his relief the man turned. Soldiers always liked you to remember their names. It made you more popular and your commands more palatable. He congratulated himself on this feat of memory since the Thirty Seventh had only been in Aegyptus a matter of days.

'Sir?'

'What's the situation?'

As he neared the front, he could make out enough ahead to realise that they were at a crossroads. Stallius pointed off down the three visible streets. 'I think we're about to be humped like a pretty sheep in a field of rams, sir.'

Fronto peered off ahead and found himself agreeing with the coarse appraisal. Down the road to the right he could see a barricade of timbers and junk with figures in white visible above and behind it. To the left there was no one for some distance, but some way off he could see, and hear, a unit of native spearmen advancing, a wall of bronze, white linen and colourful shields, spears held forth like a mobile hedge of deadly spikes. Directly ahead, a smaller Aegyptian unit of heavily-armed swordsmen were advancing, much closer but with careful slowness.

'Shit.'

'Quite, sir.'

Unforgiving sea behind, spears to the left, swords forward and a defence to the right. Not much to choose from. 'Hopefully other landing units will join us shortly.'

'I wouldn't bet on it sir. That street we came up curves west. We've come inland and further away from other landing places. They'll be on the other side of that barricade.'

'Bollocks.'

'Oratorically put, sir.'

Fronto flashed the man a quick irritated look. 'Well, the barricade shouldn't advance, so let's hold here until help arrives. Commit half the men to the left and half forward. Any men who still have pila with them should go left to help counter the spears. Let's see how long we can hold.'

'At least we'll have some help, sir,' the centurion said, pointing up.

Fronto followed his gesture to see legionaries appearing at the edge of the roof tops with masonry in hand, ready to do to the Aegyptians exactly what had been done to them. Fronto stood still as the centurion and his peers began to organise the defence of the two streets to the audible background of the advancing spear and sword units, chanting and stomping.

Giving them room to work, he stepped back and grabbed two men.

'You pair keep a close eye on that barricade. If they show any sign of breaking position and coming this way, shout a warning.'

The two legionaries saluted and took up position at the street corners, watching and waiting, hands on sword hilts. They had done all they could. Now they just had to hold until other landing units managed to hook up with them. Or until other landing units got here and found four hundred Roman corpses. He tried not to think about that.

His attention snapped back and forth between the spear unit and the swordsmen.

This was going to be a bitch of a fight.

CHAPTER TWELVE

Had the Aegyptians been more organised, Fronto pondered tensely, they might well have overrun the defence of the crossroads in mere moments. With little more than a hundred legionaries covering each road, and four or five times as many natives coming at them, had they concerted their attack and hit Fronto's force at the same time, they might well have pushed them back sufficiently to gain a fatal advantage.

As it was, the swordsmen came on slowly and carefully, while the spearmen ran at speed. Fronto sized them up on their approach in the little time he had. The swordsmen were heavy infantry, equipped in an archaic-looking Greek manner, but at a level comparable with the legionaries and with clear Roman influence in the shield design. Their general look suggested they were a native Aegyptian unit, probably of Alexandrians. As such, they were being very careful, not throwing away their lives, knowing their terrain and their enemy. The spearmen, on the other hand, had an entirely different colouring and a style that Fronto, even after only a short time in Aegyptus, could clearly see was not native. Probably Persian, he thought. Mercenaries. Their enthusiasm would be born of the belief that plunder and reward would be theirs for success, unlike the natives who would be ordinary citizens who fought for their king and their duty to the country.

As such, Fronto knew how to take advantage. With the difference between the two units he could take his time and attend to each problem with care. He turned to the man leading the defence of the northern road.

'They're being too cautious for their own good, Centurion. Give them the sword and shield fanfare. Put the wind up them.'

The officer grinned and turned, shouting to his men. In moments they began to rhythmically bash their swords against their shield edges, hammering out a beat. The chant of 'Ro – ma Vic – trix' that accompanied it had made many an enemy falter over the years, and it had the desired effect now. The swordsmen slowed further, some looking at their companions nervously.

Leaving them to it, Fronto moved back to the western street. The spearmen would be on them in perhaps ten heartbeats.

'Shields angled up and back,' he shouted. 'Deflect the blows then give them Hades on a stick.'

A roar echoed across the street as the men settled for the impact, legs braced, one back and planted firm, the other pressed against the inside of the shield. The second and third rows stood ready, pila raised.

With howls of fury, the mercenary spearmen launched themselves at the human barricade. As the front rows collided, the rear Persians stumbled to a halt and cast their spears up and over, hoping to take the rear ranks of the Roman defence, though few found a mark, most overshooting by a distance.

The men of the Roman front line took the hit well. The sheer momentum caused a ripple that threatened to knock the legionaries back, but they held. Persian spears struck the Roman shields and a few penetrated, lodging in the wood and making activity difficult for both attacker and defender. Some punched through the linden boards and slammed into the men behind, but such successes were few. Most of the enemy spears simply struck the shields that had been carefully angled, tearing through the painted fabric surface and skittering upwards to fly up over the top, past the hunched defenders. A few lucky strikes caught men in the second line, but most simply flailed off up into the air.

As the line rippled and bowed without breaking, injured men simply went down, replaced by the man behind in a heartbeat, with far too little room and time to pull the wounded to the rear. The second and third line began to slam their pila forward. They were primarily a throwing weapon and far from ideal as a spear, the tip too readily bending, but the men using them were good, and the effect was impressive regardless.

Iron points slammed into torsos, arms, necks and faces, and where they bent or broke on impact, the legionaries simply leaned a little further forwards and used the broken points to slam into the enemy again and again.

The Persians howled defiance and anger, but as they threw themselves with renewed vigour against the Roman line it was clear to Fronto that their rate of attrition was enormous. They were slowly eroding the Roman defence, but they were losing too many men doing it, white-clad corpses piling up before a Roman line that continually reformed as men fell.

Satisfied, Fronto ducked back to his right just in time to see the native swordsmen give a roar and burst into a charge. Once more he thanked Fortuna for their lack of coherent organisation. Had they timed this to join with the spear attack, the combined pressure might well have pushed the Romans back. Instead, the centurion in charge there simply called out his command and set his men to work.

The front ranks of enemy infantry ran at what appeared to be a Roman shieldwall, but in the moments before the lines met, everything changed at a centurion's whistle. Every other man along the line dropped back into a space left for them behind their companions. The enemy struck the now-intermittent line and the attack faltered instantly. Aegyptians hit the remaining men hard, but the legionaries were well-braced, a man directly behind them now, pushing them forward in support. As those natives hit the Romans, the legionaries all rolled their shields to the left, turning sharply, using the enemy's own momentum to send them yelling straight past and into the heart of the Roman lines where they were simply dispatched by dozens of brandished blades.

The momentum having been stolen from the enemy charge, the front line reformed once more and presented a solid wall to the enemy. The Aegyptians now began to fight hard, swords coming down and lancing out as best they could in the press, trying to overcome the Roman shield wall as the legionaries went to work, jabbing out with their gladii in the narrow cracks they created between shields.

Men began to die in droves, a few legionaries falling here and there, with a scream to be replaced by the next man in line, but the bulk of the dying went to the Aegyptians. Again, attrition would win the day. Satisfied that both sides would hold and they would survive the fight, Fronto stepped back out of the press and watched from sufficient distance to keep himself aware of all events.

Finding a set of steps to a house's upper door, he climbed the first few to get a better angle of vision. It was as he was congratulating himself on their success that he saw disaster looming.

A fresh force of men had appeared along that western street, and would be able to engage far too soon for comfort. More native infantry, they were swordsman like those along the northern road. Spotting the Roman line and the fighting, an enemy officer began bellowing orders and the reinforcements started to jog down the street.

Fronto chewed his lip, tense. He had to do something. If they hit his western blockade in the immediate aftermath of the spearmen, there was a good chance they would overrun the legionaries. He would have to pull men from the north to the west to help, but doing so would endanger the north.

He needed Aemilianus' men from the roofs. Here and there he could see them at the upper parapets, hurling down tiles and whatever they could find, harrying the enemy, but they would be required down here for much better effect. He couldn't see the centurion's crest up there anywhere, so he waved at them in general and bellowed for them to come back down.

'Sir!'

He turned at the shout and spotted one of the two men he'd left on watch waving at him and pointing east along the street. With plunging spirits he glanced that way, and could now see distant figures beginning to climb over and dismantle the makeshift rampart that had blocked the street there.

Then he frowned and squinted, shading his eyes.

His creased brow unfolded as his face opened into a grin.

They were Roman.

Better still, they were not men of the Sixth, men who had landed further along, but wore the uniforms of the Twenty Seventh. They were the men from the Pharos fort. Even as he breathed with relief, he spotted a figure in a white tunic, bronze cuirass and red cloak, sword circling as he urged the men on, grey hair cut short and aquiline features clear.

Caesar had arrived.

He turned back to the crossroads.

'The consul is here, lads. The Twenty Seventh are coming!'

The news had the desired effect and in moments the legionaries were roaring with fresh incentive, hacking and jabbing at the enemy. Fronto watched with satisfaction as the enemy began to quail under the increased pressure, and he even had to bellow orders for the centurions to restrain their men as the blockades began to push forwards.

Heaving in breaths of warm, salty air, Fronto removed his helmet and wiped a small lake of sweat from his brow, shaking his head with an effect like a dog shaking after a dip. Jamming the helmet beneath his arm, he turned and watched the general leading his men down the street. Even as they passed some side road, another landing force of the Twenty Seventh joined them, cheering, and the growing force moved towards the crossroads.

Their approach had clearly now been noted by the enemy. The already engaged units fought on, committed as they were, but that fresh group of swordsmen had now halted further up the street and were organising into a shield wall.

The consul of Rome strode into the crossroads like a conqueror, nodding his greeting to Fronto.

'Legate. You have contained things well here. Is this the current front line?'

Fronto made 'sort of' motions with his hand. 'In a way, General. The cavalry are operating somewhere ahead in the open ground. I think we were the westernmost landing force, so the rest will be behind you.'

Caesar nodded again. 'Many have already joined us. We have now cleared the island from the south and east. The northern coast is still held by the natives, though I sent a secondary force that way, clearing the streets as they went, and the enemy should be pinned down by the artillery barrage of the fleet. I have heard the sounds of fighting as we came west, so they seem to be enjoying reasonable success.'

'We're winning, then.'

Caesar smiled. 'Thus far the gods favour us, Fronto. Our great challenge will be at the far end, when we reach the Heptastadion. There lies a fortress we must overcome to control the island, and cavalry will, of course, be of no benefit there.'

'We can burn that bridge when we come to it, Caesar.'

'Quite. Let us move on.' The general turned to the growing force behind him. 'Gallus, take your men and fall in with Fronto here. Take that road and clear the island westwards. I shall take the rest north and clear from there, linking up with my secondary force.'

He nodded at Fronto. 'We shall meet at the Heptastadion.'

Fronto saluted and looked about him as his force suddenly increased by huge numbers, with the additional soldiers from the Twenty Seventh Caesar had sent his way. Moreover, Aemilianus and his men were now descending from the rooftops.

'Sir,' Aemilianus said as he hurried over from a doorway.

'Centurion.'

'The rooftops are largely clear from here. There are small groups we spotted here and there but the bulk had been committed near the coast to prevent our advance, and the other landing craft seem to have done the same as us, clearing them out. Anyone left nearby in the upper levels are already fleeing west to stay safely behind enemy lines. The last thing they want is to be cut off by us and unable to return to their own.'

Fronto smiled. 'Sounds like they're in retreat, then?'

'That's how it looks sir. What are your orders?'

Fronto turned. Caesar had taken his two centuries from the northern street and was already committing extra men, pushing the near-obliterated enemy swordsmen back along the thoroughfare.

Even as Fronto watched, the Aegyptians began to break, many of their number turning and running, fleeing along the dusty flagstones to the safety of their own men.

Looking back along the street behind him at the forces now dividing and peeling off to follow either Caesar or Fronto, he tried to estimate numbers. If he was right, he would have the better part of a thousand men now. What had looked like a dangerous and foolhardy foray into enemy held territory when they had first reached the crossroads now looked like a reasonable invasion force.

A familiar voice drew his attention, and he turned with a contrary mix of satisfaction and disappointment to see Salvius Cursor pushing his way through the soldiers towards him, Centurion Carfulenus close on his heel. It was no surprise to note that the tribune was already spattered with gore, what appeared to be a tattered shred of human being hanging from the bronze hooks of his chain shirt.

'Fronto.'

'Salvius. You met resistance then.'

'Briefly,' snorted the tribune. 'Orders?'

'Keep doing what you're doing. That way,' he added, pointing west.

The spearmen were more or less lost now, a few men still struggling on, a score of them already backing away with that careful, measured gait of the failed mercenary, uncertain of the reception they would receive from their own side upon retreat, but aware that to stay meant death. They backed up the street slowly, spears still levelled in case the Romans suddenly broke and decided to follow them.

'We can take them before they pass their lines,' Salvius said, peering ahead.

Fronto shook his head. 'Let them carry their failure and panic back among the enemy. We need to win the island, but I'd be happy if we didn't have to fight every last man to do it.'

Salvius saluted, though Fronto could see disapproval hovering in the man's eyes.

'We are not Morta of the Fates, Tribune. We do not have to personally bring death to the world. Let them run. It'll save us work.'

With another salute, Salvius hurried over to the legionaries as they drew themselves together into units, the last spearmen already down. Fronto wandered over, glancing ahead at the line of organised infantry awaiting them to the west. That would be a hard fight, but he had the suspicion that it represented the main force remaining against them here. Beyond that, not far away, Galronus and his cavalry should be at work… hopefully. A quick glance at his men told him that pila would be few and far between. This would have to be straight infantry work, then.

'Those centuries with more than one in five wounded drop back. You are now the reserve. I want the freshest men in front. We're going to do this the old fashioned way. Single time, then march and a half at eighty paces. Double pace at fifty, and charge at twenty five. Push forwards with every possible step, holding the line. I want their shield wall broken. Centurions, put your bruisers in the front line and keep your eye on me for each signal.'

There was a chorus of affirmatives, and as that died away they could hear the distinctive sounds of Caesar's force engaging somewhere a street or two to the north.

'Last thing: we need to make sure we clear the area. To the north, our friends are at work, but every southern street or alley we pass I want a small unit dispatched to make sure it's clear, then hurrying to catch up. Centurions' discretion for the dispatch of those units. Good. All set, so let's go.'

As those units who had fought down the spear men dropped back, joining up with the more battered units that had reached them from the east, the freshest centuries settled into the street, shields up and swords out and ready, the largest and most powerful men shuffled into the front line.

'Ready…' Fronto called. 'March.'

A score of whistles carried his orders to the men as every centurion began to move. The entire force stomped along the western street with the crunch of hobnailed boots landing perfectly in time. Fronto fell in beside a centurion some twelve rows from the front, and could just see Salvius Cursor about half way forward at the other side of the street, staying back just far enough to be respectable for an officer, but close enough to the action that he was almost guaranteed a chance to become involved. Fronto might have been tempted to upbraid him for that, but the simple truth was that a few years ago, he had been doing much the same.

The front line was eleven men wide, covering the width of the street, a solid wall of muscle and iron, crunching at the enemy. Fronto craned his neck to look over the men in front, an action not as difficult as it might sound, with every soldier hunching behind his shield as they stomped forwards.

They reached an estimate of eighty paces faster than he'd expected, and he cleared his throat. 'Pace and a half,' he roared, a chorus of twin blasts on whistles echoing his order. The men broke into that odd half-jog in perfect unison at the rhythmic calls of their centurions and optios, a pace that ate distance rapidly, yet with little exertion.

Fifty paces came quickly, then, the details of the enemy shield wall coalescing in the heat haze. They were solid and well-equipped, confident-looking. Their skin tone was especially dark, yet their equipment spoke of that strangely Greek citizen-soldier that was the mainstay of the Aegyptian force, and Fronto surmised that they were probably from somewhere far up the Nilus, deep into the land of Aegyptus. If that was true, then they were probably still unfamiliar with Rome, their focus traditionally on the desert peoples in the south.

'Double pace,' he bellowed, now that they were close enough the exertion would not rob his force of too much fighting strength. Three whistle blasts from every officer picked up the pace to a fast march, and Fronto was satisfied, peering ahead, that the enemy were starting to feel nervous. The line of native infantry rippled with the first faint tremor of worry. Eyes still on them, he counted to ten and then shouted once again.

'Charge.'

He had to hand it to the enemy, or at least to their officers and the level of control they maintained. That ripple of nerves became more pronounced at the sudden burst of activity, and there was a tremor along the line that Fronto recognised. They had almost broken and run, but calls and threats from their commanders seemed to have countered the worst of the nerves. Instead, the wavering stopped, and the enemy dropped a little, hunching behind their shields and bracing.

The Romans had almost broken the enemy without a blow, but at least they were nervous. It wouldn't take much, now.

As the legionaries broke into a run, shields held out ready to barge, swords held low at the waist, subsequent lines holding them up out of the way to prevent injuring a comrade, Fronto found himself swept along with the tide.

The men of the Sixth and the Twenty Seventh hit the Aegyptian infantry with a roar, like a winter wave crashing over a breakwater. Across the width of the street, legionary shields smashed into the defenders, shield bosses positioned perfectly to fracture and damage.

Two lucky enemy blows landed during that initial collision, and Fronto saw a man drop, another crying out but remaining in the fight. The enemy had no chance to capitalise on their success, though. The Roman line simply ran *through* the enemy, breaking bones, trampling the unfortunate fallen beneath agonising iron hobnails and rough leather soles, stamping down hard both for purchase and additional damage.

The second line of Aegyptians tried to push forwards, meeting the charge, but many were already falling back under the pressure of their own broken line. Fronto lost sight of the action then, as the clash became a matter of tense butchery and screams. He briefly caught sight of Salvius Cursor, at least head and shoulders above the crowd, and wondered momentarily upon what the tribune was standing to raise him so, though he suspected it to be a pile of corpses.

For just a heartbeat or two, he found himself surprisingly close to the front, and a desperate, wild-eyed Aegyptian threw a panicked thrust at him. Almost negligently, Fronto knocked the blade aside with his own and brought it back across in a slash at neck height. He was rewarded with a gurgling noise as a blood slick poured from the man's neck down onto his chain shirt, and he toppled, dying. Then suddenly Fronto was back among the lines again, and in the chaotic press he couldn't determine whether he had been subtly shuffled back out of danger by his men or simply bypassed by them as they tried to push forwards. Whatever the case, the result was the same. He was once more several lines back from the action.

A horn blared somewhere ahead, and a strange shiver of panic seemed to echo across the fight. It was only as the enemy began to disengage that Fronto finally recognised that honking noise.

Gallic horns.

Galronus and his cavalry were close ahead, and the sudden realisation that part of Caesar's force was behind them had finally broken the spirit of the Aegyptians. Indeed, as the honking of the Gallic horns repeated, becoming gradually louder as they closed, the fight broke up in a flurry, what was left of the enemy turning to flee. Legionaries did their best to take down Aegyptians as they ran, with varying degrees of success.

'Hold your positions,' Fronto bellowed as men began to lurch forwards in pursuit. Around the street, centurions blew their whistles and shouted orders, optios using their staves to jab and smack men who were too keen on the pursuit to listen. In moments the enemy were running away down the street, and the legionaries were re-forming into their units.

Fronto almost smiled at the aural tableau that followed. The din of desperate men running away, overlain with the hooming of Gallic horns, became the sound of ever-more-panicked men running back this way, overrun with those same horns *and* the noise of hooves pounding on stone.

'Blow your whistles,' Fronto yelled as the Aegyptians rounded a corner, once more heading back towards the soldiers. As the centurions did so, the Gallic cavalry appeared. Galronus was close to the front, swooping low over his horse's neck and swinging out with a sword to take the head from a screaming native. The cavalry were on them, then, riding down those poor bastards who had fled one enemy only to run straight into another. Their hasty attempts to surrender were too late as the majority went down under churning hooves or to scything cavalry blades, others fleeing into the arms of waiting legionaries who offered no quarter.

Fronto had been just in time having the whistles blown. It was almost certainly only the sound of Roman officers' whistles that had warned the cavalry of what lay around the corner, else they might not have had sufficient warning to stop in time and could have also ridden down lines of legionaries by mistake.

As the last few surviving enemy infantry raced up staircases or into narrow alleys or doorways to get away from this twin nightmare, Galronus slowed and trotted over to Fronto.

'You took your time getting here,' he grinned.

Fronto glared at him, and the Remi noble laughed. 'Seasons turn unnoticed here, don't they? I wonder who's consul now.'

'Shut up. We ran into difficulties.'

Galronus fell silent, but there was still an amused smile on his face.

'Caesar's force is clearing to the north. Have you seen them?'

Galronus shook his head. 'Not yet, but there's little resistance west from here now. The fleet has been battering the north coast with rocks and bolts enough that the enemy all fled south and ran straight into us in an area of fields and orchards. It was a mistake they won't get to repeat.'

'So not much for us to do now?'

Galronus gestured back along the street and to the bend they had rounded. 'There are maybe three blocks and side streets that way until you get to where we landed. There, it's nice and open and green from north coast to south. A sort of belt of fields between the houses and heppy-thingummy.'

'Heptastadion,' Fronto said absently. 'And what's that like?'

'Some enterprising fellow in the past decided that the bridge heppy-thing needed defending. It's more or less a little fort. Quite well-manned, since it had its own garrison, but it now has everyone who's fallen back across the island too.'

'A tough proposition?'

'For a horse, certainly.'

Fronto glared daggers at him, and Galronus continued with a sigh. 'Without siege equipment, or at least ladders, you're going to find it a hard fight.'

'Alright,' Fronto murmured. 'Let's go have a look.'

As he issued commands to the centurions and Salvius Cursor, whom he placed in command, Galronus had a second horse brought up. By the time the legionaries were beginning to march west once more, making for the last area of resistance on the island and the end of the Heptastadion, Fronto was mounted and with Galronus. At the Remi's command, the horsemen formed up and began to trot west, ahead of the infantry and picking up the pace as they went.

Sure enough, as Galronus had intimated, there was only a short stretch of the urban sprawl remaining before they emerged into open land. This fertile ground in a kingdom largely of desert had been made use of like all other cultivatable areas, given over to tightly packed farming with a few small orchards.

As they moved, they occasionally saw signs of remaining Aegyptian soldiers down the side alleys in one direction or the other, but as they rode, Fronto was aware of the infantry following on behind, dispatching small units along every street and alley to clear out lurking defenders. By the time they reached the Heptastadion what resistance remained would be negligible.

Feeling somewhat relieved, despite what lay ahead, Fronto and the cavalry rode out across the grassland and between the crops, trying not to destroy them. After all, not only were the farmers potentially not at fault in any way, but also the legion might be relying on those crops sometime soon.

He became aware of the increasing Roman control of the island as they moved through sizzling sunshine and lush fields. Further off to the north they could now see other units of infantry emerging from streets. Here and there, small groups of panicked natives ran for the southwest and their only hope of safety, and as they reached a rise in the open land, Fronto could see the shapes of Roman ships out to sea, just a few hundred paces from shore, where they continually released missiles at the land.

It seemed their plan had worked well. Now, if they could take the Heptastadion, their control of Pharos Island would be complete – no small coup considering the relative strengths of Arsinoë and Caesar's forces.

Fronto's first sight of the Heptastadion from this angle filled him with uncertainty.

The huge, straight breakwater marched from Pharos to the mainland, covering a distance of almost a mile, the arched bridge in it that the locals had used to sneak their ships through perhaps a third of the way along. He could make out little of the far end of the great work, for the heat haze made everything wavering and indistinct, but the near end had been fortified sometime in the past. What had once been a small residential area had been reworked with a view to defence. Houses in a horseshoe shape around the end of the great mole had been joined with ramparts, and their exterior windows blocked to form a fortress wall. Some of the houses had been raised to become towers of perhaps thirty feet in height. Only one gate had been left in the blank wall, and all other structures outside the ring of buildings had been torn down to make an open area around the fort.

It was surprisingly defensive for a structure cobbled together from old houses. Certainly it would cost the legion dearly to take the place, and take it they must if they wanted control of the island. If the enemy had sufficient archers on those walls and towers then many, many legionaries would die before they broke in.

Fronto's gaze scanned the upper regions, trying to determine the level of defence, and it was then that he realised there were not the strong archers he'd expected. More than that, there seemed to be far fewer figures up there at all, fewer than Galronus' comments had suggested they would find. The reason became clearer as he watched, more and more figures disappearing by the moment.

The defences were emptying.

Now, as they came closer, he could hear noises from atop the walls, and though it was too far away to make out words, the general tone was unmistakable:

Panic.

He turned, eyes narrowed against the sun. Roman legionaries were pouring from the streets of Pharos and out into the open land in speedy, triumphant units, following in the wake of the cavalry. Rome's power was on display as they finalised their hold on the island, and the last defenders, who had probably been given the command to hold this fort at all costs, had succumbed to fear and abandoned their posts.

The fort was rapidly clearing of men. Glancing off to the south he could see those fleeing Aegyptians running along the Heptastadion for the city of Alexandria beyond, and the perceived safety of their young princess' army. There were, in fact, so many people running now that some were pushed off the mole in the press and fell into the water. Others dived in on purpose, the better to get away from the approaching legion.

Fronto, a relieved smile crossing his face, gestured to a rider nearby. 'Take the word to the legions. The fort is ours for the taking. Get the door open and chase the bastards back along the pier to their mothers.'

Grinning, he watched the last defenders of Pharos leaving, granting them control of the island.

CHAPTER THIRTEEN

'The harbour will be ours entire within the day.'

Fronto nodded absently at Salvius Cursor's blasé prediction. He was probably right, of course. Something was nagging at Fronto, though, something unidentified that hovered on the edge of his awareness. The Caesarian army had rolled across Pharos like a runaway cart, demolishing all resistance in the way, but despite their seemingly easy victory he couldn't help but recall watching the enemy running back along the Heptastadion, and the piles of dead that had been gathered afterwards as the island was consolidated.

For such a hard fought victory, the number of enemy dead was still rather minor. Unusually so. Fronto had seen enough battles in his life to know what kind of toll to expect from this sort of action, and this was not it. Many of the enemy had fled back to their own lines without falling. It was almost as though some enemy officer had given them orders not to throw their lives away but to withdraw and defend in the face of destruction. A very sensible approach, in Fronto's opinion.

Yes, they had gained control of Pharos, and they were on the brink of controlling the Heptastadion, which would grant them complete control of the Great Harbour, but the enemy were yet strong. They still outnumbered the Romans and were now playing a sensible game. That worried Fronto. When Achillas had been the Aegyptians' commander, they had thrown away men and made poor tactical decisions. This new general was not doing that. He had pulled back his men and rallied in the city, and as yet they had seen no real sign of the heavy fist of the enemy – the Gabiniani. What would he do next?

'The fort is going to fall,' Salvius said with an air of satisfaction.

Another nod from the legate. Yes, it would. But the fort was not what bothered Fronto.

Sweeping across Pharos, they had overrun the abandoned fortification at their end of the great mole with ease. They had managed to take a few prisoners and kill a few of the last fleeing soldiers. The captives had been tight lipped, even under torture, and the Romans had gained little from them they had not already known. The common soldiery could not be expected to know the minds of their senior generals, and so the need for information from them had not been pressed.

In control of the island-end fort, Caesar had garrisoned it and set his men to clearing the island of resistance. There, they had encountered the first unpleasant surprise. What they had assumed to be a small civilian suburb of Alexandria had turned out to be something quite different. No families were to be found therein. Instead, traps had been set in some of the buildings, while others had been sealed tight and housed fanatical archers or slingers who would wait for legionaries to pass by and then drop them with shots unseen from windows.

The mess the problem caused had led Caesar to drastic action. Over the rest of that day and the next, while the fort was consolidated and garrisoned and supplies and equipment procured and shipped, the legion was set to work demolishing the houses of Pharos. Now, as the morning sun beat down on the third day since their island landing, little remained of the small town but a field of rubble punctuated by burial pits. From the Heptastadion fortress, they could now see clear all the way to the fort by the great lighthouse over a field of broken stones.

Pharos had gone.

Then, today, the next stage of consolidation had begun. Stones from the demolished houses were being carried along the great work to that arched bridge in the mole, and there dumped into the shallow harbour's waters, more rubble being brought there by ship. Hour by hour tons of stone were being submerged, gradually blocking the bridge against any future traffic, leaving the harbour mouth the only access, controlled by Caesar's forts.

Everything seemed to be working smoothly.

But there were nagging doubts for Fronto.

The enemy force had simply watched all this happening from the city, waiting patiently. And while the Romans controlled the arms of the harbour and the island that enclosed it, the Great Harbour's docks and jetties remained under enemy control, Caesar's ships being berthed in the smaller Palace Harbour. The Aegyptians had a few ships that simply sat waiting, like their army. What they had planned worried him.

And now the enemy were pulling back again, a little further, like the tide. The problem with the tide going out, though, was that it inevitably came back in.

Caesar had brought artillery and the few archers he commanded along the Heptastadion and begun to rake the ramparts of the fortification at the city end with missiles. A few men had died and then the enemy had been sure to keep their heads down. Now there was an uncomfortable silence as the archers and artillerists waited, saving their ammunition, preparing for the next time a head popped up.

'They're not there,' Fronto said finally.

'What?' Salvius Cursor frowned at him.

'They're not ducked down behind the walls. They've gone. They've pulled out while we weren't looking.'

'Why?'

'Fronto chewed his lip. Well, this place is not all that defensible. After all, it's designed to stop attackers getting *onto* the Heptastadion, not off it. All its main features point at the city. As you predicted, the place would fall easily, but they know that too, and their current commander is not in the habit of wasting men.'

'I think you're reading too much into this,' Salvius grunted. 'You credit them with more intelligence than they have. They panicked and fled from the island. It wasn't some grand military withdrawal.'

'I thought that at the time. And yes, perhaps those last men pulling back from the other fort did panic, like the men trapped in the street between us and the cavalry, but I think that was just a mistake in an otherwise solid plan. We are a smaller force than they. They're wearing us down with attrition. We lost men taking the island, but we lost more to the nasty little surprises they left for us in the town. For the sacrifice of one archer left in a house they could take out half a dozen of our men before we got to them. They're making us work hard, wearing us down and tiring us out.'

'But we've nearly done it. In half an hour we'll control the harbour.'

'For how long?' Fronto mumbled.

'What?'

'They're building up to something. I just can't quite grasp what, but they've more or less given us the harbour with little cost to them. They'll come back at us, and soon, but they're waiting for something and I can't work out what.'

'You *are* a storm crow, Fronto.'

'Mark me: trouble is coming our way.'

'Shall I give the order to the men?' Salvius said, changing the topic.

Fronto peered at the empty battlements of the fortress and sighed. 'Might as well. We don't know what they've got planned, and we're probably walking right into whatever they intend, but what other choice do we have?'

Salvius Cursor rolled his eyes and turned to the signifer and the cornicen behind him, telling them to give the signal. As the horn blared out, Fronto watched the last stage of the harbour battle unfolding. The twin artillery pieces sitting at the sides of the great stone walkway remained pointed at the battlements, but the unit of archers split and moved from their solid lines to either side, gathering with the artillery and leaving a clear passage through the middle. The steady tramp of boots arose as the three cohorts lined up along the Heptastadion began to move. The front century had left their shields behind, instead carrying a huge timber beam from the Pharos ruins.

He watched the legionaries reach the gates of the fortress without incident and begin to swing the beam, smashing it against the gate repeatedly, every blow of the timber heartbeat bringing the sound of cracking and splintering, as the gate gradually broke and gave. It took less than a quarter of an hour to smash the gates open sufficiently to grant the men access.

At Carfulenus' command the next three centuries ran through the gate, swords out and shields up, ready for any lurking enemies. Almost a dozen went down in agony just inside the gate before the attack was halted with urgent commands. Fronto nodded to himself glumly as he and the tribune hurried towards the gate where a centurion was waving to them.

'See?' he said to Salvius as they peered into the heart of the deserted fort to see the hundreds of small caltrops spread across the ground, barely noticeable in the shadow of the gate. Men sat or leaned against the wall, clutching crippled feet with barbed iron points buried deep in them.

'It's just a few caltrops. The men will recover.'

'But they're out of the fight. More men out and looking at a month of healing before full effectiveness, and all at no cost to the enemy. They're planning something. They continue to pull back and make us pay for every foot we advance. There will be other surprises in the fort.'

Salvius gave him a despairing look, but nodded. 'I shall take charge of occupying the fort. We'll go carefully.'

Fronto waved him on, turning instead to look across the water at the city, an enemy lurking there, out of sight.

'What are you up to, Princess? What are you planning?' he fumed as he turned back to watch the three cohorts moving into the fortress and taking control. Occasionally he heard cries of alarm or pain as the men discovered traps or nasty surprises left by the enemy. Back along the Heptastadion he could see other men on board two triremes completing the infill of the bridge which was yet still well below the waterline. Then, back across the harbour on the island, he could see the bulk of the Roman force embarking.

Their army was so spread out now. That was another worry. They had been in control of the palace and its redoubt with only a

179

small force and had been careful and conservative with their activity. Yes, they now had a much larger force, but the push to control the island, the mole and the harbour had resulted in that force being so divided that, if anything, their territory was less well defended than before. Men at the palace redoubt. Men at the twin forts at the harbour mouth. Men at the fortifications at both ends of the Heptastadion, and the lion's share now boarding ships.

This, Fronto couldn't help but think, was a mistake.

Other officers had thrown their support behind the idea of pushing to control the city's waterfront and thereby deny the enemy any naval capability in the Great Harbour. The idea was to man the Heptastadion fortification with three cohorts, the maximum force that could realistically be housed there, and to bring the rest of the force across on ships, along the side of the great mole. Then, when all was prepared, to land the men at the same time as the cohorts sallied forth from the fort, and seize control of the shoreline.

What Fronto had pointed out in a tired tone at that briefing was that the shoreline was the very place from which they had pulled out when the enemy first arrived, as it was far too difficult to hold. Yes, he'd argued in the face of opposition, the army was now far more numerous, but they were also more widespread. It was a mistake. But it was a mistake they were determined to make.

To the background melody of soldiers occupying the fort, with the occasional scream of an encountered trap, of the general hum of city life, and of the two Roman triremes busy dropping stones into the water to fill the arch bridge, Fronto waited and fretted.

He was almost expecting it when it happened.

A series of honks and blarts across the city cut through the aural tapestry like a sword. Clearly everyone else had heard it, too, for all activity in the fort ceased instantly, and the Roman force at the city end of the mole fell silent, listening to the discordant chorus.

Then they came.

An area some four hundred paces across stood clear and empty between the Heptastadion fort and the nearest blocks of the city, open flat land that had been left clear deliberately to give the fort a good field of missile range.

Into that open space poured the Aegyptian army.

They did not look panicked. They did not look like they were reacting, or on the defensive. They looked like a well-organised field army going to war, and forming the front centre of the force: two thousand Gabiniani, like some parody of a Roman legion, their equipment akin to that of Fronto's men, but adorned with Aegyptian accoutrements, their shield design a weird native one, animal pelts over their shoulders. Once again, Fronto cursed the fact that the young princess had escaped the palace and removed the headstrong and foolish Achillas from command. Their new general knew what he was doing.

Thousands of men began to assemble in careful lines, armed and ready, confident of victory.

Given time to prepare, the Romans could have mounted artillery on the fort's ramparts, gathered every missile they could, and put them up there. But they'd had no time. The enemy stood in a perfect killing zone for missiles, and Rome had nothing to throw at them. The legion had teeth but its mouth was shut.

Legionaries began to line the walls of the fort, looking down at the assembling force, and even in the silence Fronto could sense the air of nervousness. Rome had placed three cohorts into the playground of the enemy.

Fronto turned, looking over his shoulder. Their only hope of holding this end of the Heptastadion and perhaps, in fact, not being wiped out entirely, was the rest of the army. He felt a few moments of tentative relief as he spotted the ships bearing their soldiers ploughing through the harbour's waters at a fast pace, aware of trouble and trying to deliver relief in time. As such, the fleet was shunning formation, each hurtling as fast as it could on its individual path.

That could be their undoing.

His relief evaporated at the sight of what lay beyond them. Where just moments ago there had been two Roman triremes dumping rocks into the water back beyond the last approaching ship, halfway between the fleet and the island they had just left, there were instead two blazing infernos.

Fronto's eyes widened in shock. The triremes had been fired with speed and efficiency, and now he could see how. Other, smaller ships from the Aegyptian fleet were hurtling through the bridge that was not yet blocked. The cunning bastards. The Romans had dropped enough rocks there over the past hours that no deep-keeled warship stood a chance of getting through the gap, but the small, shallow boats were coming through, straight over the blockage that had not yet become deep enough to stop them. Just like those boats they had tried to send against the Rhodians in battle, these small vessels were crammed with combustible material. Even now several had passed the flaming triremes and were racing across the harbour in the wake of the fleet.

Finally, some of the ships of the Roman relief fleet noticed the disaster occurring behind them, but there was nothing they could do about it. If the fleet halted to deal with the threat closing on them from behind, then they could not deliver the reserves to the shore, and the Aegyptians would annihilate the cohorts there with ease. Instead they had to hope they could get to shore, drop their men and still have time to turn against this secondary threat before the Aegyptians could fire the entire fleet.

Damn that cursed cow Arsinoë and the clever shithead she had put in charge of the army.

Signals were given across the fleet as a few of the vessels slowed. Somewhere on one of those ships Brutus was in command, and he would now be forming a plan. No man stood a better chance of solving this than him, unless that be Tiberius Nero, the hero of the pirate wars, who, thank the gods, served alongside Brutus.

A roar drew Fronto's attention back to the enemy. Thousands of men now stood in the space before the city, and at a new signal units sidestepped to make space. Archers with very dark skin and brilliant white tunics, hair straight and black, shuffled forwards with shields of mottled animal hides. These they dropped and crouched behind, drawing up in a line three men deep all across the space.

Fronto prayed Salvius and Carfulenus had the sense to keep the men in the fort in cover as another command began the barrage.

Arrows struck the top of the parapet and many sailed over, arcing high in order to drop from the sky like a rain of death inside the fort.

A cacophony of cries suggested that not all the men in there were out of danger. Likely the officers had not considered the likelihood of the enemy dropping arrows over the wall like that. The disaster had already begun. Only something bold was going to change things now.

Hoping Brutus and Nero knew what they were doing, and praying that someone had carried news of this to Caesar, who was somewhere further back with the army, he committed himself to action. Racing forwards, he passed from the Heptastadion into that beleaguered fortress. The sight that greeted him was bleak. Men clutching injured feet hid in the safety of the gate passage, while out in the open courtyard area, between the north and south gates, half the century of men who had been given the task of clearing away the caltrops now lay dead in the blistering sun, arrow shafts jutting up like accusing fingers. The only active soldiers he could see, which was astonishing given that three cohorts were now based here, were small groups of legionaries hiding in the lee of walls or crouching behind battlements, the rest safely inside.

In mere moments he spotted Salvius Cursor lurking in the shadow of the exterior gate opposite, fuming at his impotence and desiring nothing more than to get his teeth into the enemy. Fronto moved to rush quickly across the courtyard, but even as he did so the next flurry of arrows dropped from the sky, putting out of their misery several of the wounded men floundering on the ground and yelling. Fronto pulled himself up short and waited for the barrage to die down, then ran for it across the sandy flagstones. Salvius seemed genuinely glad to see him, which was alarming in itself.

'Tribune, keep the men under cover, but have them ready to sally on command. As soon as I give the word I want them pouring out of that gate.'

Salvius gave him a horrible feral grin. 'Time to bloody our blades.'

'Hades, yes. I have no intention of sitting here and waiting. If we don't do something to break them, we're going to be annihilated. I need to time it with the landings, though. What's left of three cohorts charging against that lot would look like an angry child charging a century of veterans waving a stick.'

Salvius saluted and turned to the standard bearer beside him, who looked as though he might sweat to death under the weight of his burden and the horribly impractical wolf skin he wore over his helmet. 'Pass the word to every officer to form their men under cover. Have every century move as close to the front gate as they can, while staying under shelter from arrows, and be ready to sally from the gate at the legate's signal.'

He then turned to the men lurking nearby at the gate.

'Get that bar removed and the gates ready to open at a heartbeat's notice.'

'Sir? What if they attack?'

'Then you draw the pointed thing at your side and you stick the sharp end in them, soldier. Get the damn gate ready to open and stop questioning my orders.'

Flushing, the soldier saluted and ran over to the gate, readying his men. Leaving Salvius and the legionaries to it, Fronto looked this way and that and spotted a man emerging from a rooftop onto the wall, shield held over his head and crouched low. Reasoning that the nearest stairs must lie there, he took a deep breath and ran once more across the courtyard to the door of that building. For just a moment he panicked that he was going to fall as his knee gave way, but he gritted his teeth and lurched back into a run, disappearing in through the doorway as the next barrage of arrows began to fall where he had just been. Grabbing the Fortuna amulet at his neck, he thanked the goddess of luck for her continued care and peered around.

An entire century of men and more stood silent and worried in the dim interior, hiding from the rain of iron-headed destruction. They lowered their eyes respectfully in the presence of a senior officer as Fronto spotted the staircase in the corner and began to push through the crowd. As they tried their best to pull back and make room, he gestured to the corner.

'Up to the walls?'

'Yes, sir.'

Nodding his thanks, Fronto forged on through the tense crowd of men to the stairs and began to climb. It came as no surprise when he emerged onto a second level equally full of men. The only real open area here lay in another corner where sunlight announced stairs emerging onto the ramparts. Hurrying across, he noted with a sour look the arrows lying there where they had dropped. No wonder the men were not gathering in that corner.

'Anyone here wounded?'

Two or three men, looking nervous, raised their hands. Fronto looked at them and selected the worst of the three, a man who still had an arrow jutting from his forearm, snapped off below the flights. 'Lucky you, soldier. You get to stay here when we sally, 'cause I want your shield.'

With a grateful look, the legionary handed over the scarred shield with his uninjured arm. Fronto took it, raised it with difficulty in the press and approached the steps. Taking a breath and hunching below it, he scurried up the steps, emerging into the sizzling sunshine.

Almost instantly, he heard someone yell 'Down!' and saw the soldiers up here crouch lower and push themselves against the wall. Fronto hunched under the shield and ran. Time was too short now. Hearing the clatter of arrows on stone all around him, he reached the area of wall closest to where the Heptastadion and the shore met and clambered into the tower there, hurtling up another set of steps and emerging onto the top.

The soldier there looked as tense as everyone else, but stood tall with his shield at his side.

'Not finding cover?' Fronto breathed at him, sucking in air after all the climbing and running.

'Too high here, sir, and too far away. No arrow's come close.'

'Good.' Lowering the shield, Fronto hurried to the edge and looked down.

He was immediately relieved. The fleet had almost reached the shore now, and Brutus had been at work. The larger ships with the greater numbers of soldiers on board had been given priority and had moved to the front in a line six vessels wide, ready to disgorge their cargo simultaneously. Lesser vessels followed in two more

185

lines, the smaller fire ships still chasing them but unable to quite catch up with the fast Roman warships. Fronto smiled to see the Ajax and the Chimaera among the front line.

He looked down from the tower and spotted a signifer and a cornicen standing together in the shade of the next tower.

'You there.'

The men looked up, squinting into the sun, straightening and saluting as they spotted the senior officer.

'How loud can you tootle your horn?'

The cornicen looked faintly offended at the phrase, but yelled back. 'If I try hard, they'll hear me in Tartarus, sir.'

'Good. The moment I give you the signal, I want you to sound the Sixth's, the Twenty Seventh's and the Thirty Seventh's orders to advance at double time. All of them. You can do that?'

'I can, sir.'

Fronto turned back to the sea to catch the first ship striking the dock. As it rocked to a halt, men were leaping to the jetty even before the ramp was run out. Ropes were thrown and looped around the cleats but nothing was tied, the men holding the ships to shore with simple muscle power as the soldiers disembarked as fast as they could. He couldn't tell whether they were the Twenty Seventh or the Thirty Seventh, but it mattered not. All the calls would be given.

Moments later the second and third ship were mirroring the action, cohorts of men hurrying from the quay to fall into formation along the shore. Even as he watched, that first ship unloaded its last man and the sailors pulled in the ropes swiftly, never having fastened them. In heartbeats the ship was pulling away from the quay and arcing wide to allow the next ship in. As it put back out to sea, Fronto watched the sailors dousing the sail and ropes and what they could of deck and hull with water, while artillerists loaded the weapon in the prow. They then began to pick up speed, slipping back past their own fleet and making for the fire ships that closed on them. Brutus was on form, clearly. Even as the first wave of men were landed, their ships changed role from transport to warship and raced back at the secondary threat.

Good. He could trust Brutus and leave the naval activity to his friend. The big threat now was the army gathered up before the fort.

He could hear them chanting in their weird language. It sounded warlike and angry. They were trying to make the Romans nervous, and from the sight of the men in the fort, it was working. But the Aegyptians had made one error. They had assumed they were untouchable. Just because they had the fort pinned down, the fleet under threat, and superior numbers, they felt they were on the cusp of victory.

Fronto was about to change that.

Holding his breath, he watched the last of the lead ships, the Ajax, land its men and begin to pull away, the second line of vessels approaching. The moment the last hobnailed boot of the first wave struck stone, Fronto turned again and gestured to the cornicen.

'Now. Advance at the double.'

The man saluted hurriedly and lifted the great curved horn to his mouth, taking a deep breath and blowing into it, unleashing three loud sequences of notes in quick succession, at least one of which the men down by the ships would recognise. Fronto turned back, looking down at the shore, and grinned as the men, startled by a call to advance being given from the fort and not their own officers, began to move in formation at a double march.

Even as they started to advance, Fronto heard other orders relayed across the fort and the legionaries there also began to move, pouring from doorways, heedless now of potential death from above as they made for the main gate, beyond which lay open ground and the enemy force.

This was it.

The legion was moving to engage the enemy. The Aegyptians might outnumber them, but if they thought Rome was going to bend the knee in fear, then they were sadly mistaken. He just hoped the men had it in them to make the enemy regret offering battle.

Something nagged at him, like someone pulling his sleeve, and on instinct he turned and looked down at the newly arrived cohorts on the shore, now marching into battle. Behind the front line, a man on a white horse with a scarlet cloak was looking up at him with a furrowed brow. Caesar had arrived and been immediately swept into an unexpected battle.

Ah well. That was an argument they could have later. Right now there was an Aegyptian army to attack.

CHAPTER FOURTEEN

Fronto stood atop the highest of the fortress towers, giving him an excellent view of the northern, southern and eastern sides of the place. The Heptastadion mole behind them was dotted with men from the three cohorts and other support units on various tasks, but remained solidly in Roman hands.

The east, where the Great Harbour's quayside and many jetties lay, was now filled with Roman ships, while others sat out in the water, engaged in a conflict with a myriad of smaller Aegyptian vessels. Brutus might have planned his reaction better than anyone could have expected, but he was still having trouble. The Roman warships were to the Aegyptian skiffs as a bull to a fly, but like flies, the small vessels continually shifted, darting this way and that and harrying the bigger warships with fire arrows. Consequently the Roman ships, lacking military manpower, were expending much of their sailors' time extinguishing fires. Brutus would carry the day, certainly, but it would be a long job and a difficult one, with attrition, and would keep the ships out of action elsewhere.

The south, though, was where the main battle lay. The vast forces of the Aegyptian general were engaged with the Roman army that had disembarked, along with the lead elements from the cohorts in the fort. To make matters complicated for the observers above, the Gabiniani fought now, and it was somewhat difficult at times to quite tell what was happening given their similarity to the legionaries with whom they struggled.

One thing was sure, though: the enemy's early confidence had swiftly begun to waver. Where they felt they had the Romans pinned and terrified, they were now fighting hard, the legions having advanced in a swift, professional manner and launched into battle without fear.

It was hard to tell from here what would happen. The Roman force was fighting with a more coherent and forceful approach, and was making headway under Salvius Cursor, trying to drive a wedge into the enemy centre in an attempt to cut their force in half, and perhaps gain access to their command at the rear. But the enemy were still steady and remained more numerous by far. Fronto would not be willing to wager even a denarius on the result just now. Either side could break at any time, with just the slightest sign of trouble.

Salvius was just visible in the press as a gleaming silver and crimson figure at the forefront of the central push. He was a mad bastard, though some of that seemed to have ebbed since arriving in this benighted country and the death of Pompey, but once his blood was up and his sword bared, there were few men better prepared to wade screaming into the enemy and give heart to their men.

On the flank, conversely, Caesar was being far more strategic. Accompanied by members of his praetorian guard, he darted in and out of the action, swiftly, bloodying his blade in places where he could appear heroic with the minimum of true danger, yet his very presence and his flowing scarlet cloak brought courage to all those around him.

Fronto thought back on the Caesar who had personally stood with the men against the Belgae, part of the line in a desperate fight, and he realised that this man was not really the same Caesar. The one who had stood with his legionaries had been a reputation-hungry general, struggling for political position and more at home with the soldiers than with most noblemen. But over the last few years, since the end of Gallic resistance and the rise of the consul's feud with the senate, he had changed. He had become a more political animal. Cassius had seen it. Others too. Fronto hadn't really, until now.

He sighed. In truth they were *all* changing. He himself was getting too old for this profession. Ten years ago that would have been him down there at the head of the wedge. Instead now younger men led the fight, while Fronto had joined the old men at the back.

All things changed.

Some changes were less welcome than others, though, as he was rudely reminded by a sudden desperate series of whistles off to the northeast. His gaze pulled back from the ebb and flow of battle before the fort and to the ships of the Roman fleet docked along the harbour. Sailors from the vessels were mobilising, grabbing weapons and moving to the front of the ships.

Aegyptian units had begun to put in an appearance from various streets along the waterfront, off to the flank of the main fight. Fronto felt his spirits sink. This enemy commander was a constant series of unexpected tricks, the devious bastard.

With the Roman forces committed to the fight, the enemy, who had huge numbers, had brought a few more of them sneaking through the streets to come from the flank. There, only the sailors of the fleet could react.

They would not be enough.

Fronto watched, heart in mouth, as units of sailors dropped from the ships and took what positions they could find on the dock. A few had bows, many slings. More had darts or simply a handful of stones. Conversely, the enemy now emerging from the harbour streets were a mix of light spear men, skirmishers, and medium infantry in chain shirts and with solid shields.

As they formed in the open and began to move forwards, flanking and endangering the entire fight, the sailors started to act. Fronto had to hand it to them: they had courage, if not much in the way of common sense. Perhaps if Brutus had been among the commanders here he might have found a better solution, but he was out across the harbour, dealing with the enemy boats, and this would be the work of Tiberius Nero, the pirate hunter.

Slings whirred, arrows thrummed, and stones and darts arced silently up in the air.

The legate atop the tower watched tensely. Against all odds, the sailors were having an effect. They might not be professional soldiers like the legionaries away to the south in the open ground, but many had honed their missile skills aboard their ships over the years, bringing down birds or spearing fish, if nothing else. They might not be well armed and armoured, but their accuracy was impressive.

The enemy were trying to keep their formations and advance, but they were hampered by the detritus and general junk across the dock, forcing them to continually slow and navigate around obstacles, and all the time missiles were thudding into them or plummeting from lobbed shots down into the heart of the mass. Indeed, even as Fronto watched, whole units of infantry slowed their advance to a crawl, trying to maintain cohesion under a constant hail of stones, darts and the occasional arrow. Men with shields began to raise them and advance in imitation of the testudo.

Fronto's gaze snapped back and forth now, teeth biting into lower lip. Just as the Roman army was spread dangerously thin across Alexandria, so the forces currently at their command were equally thin here. Perhaps a cohort of the Sixth remained on the Heptastadion, but they were all involved in the shipping forward of equipment, supporting the infill of the bridge which had recently become a priority, or launching missiles against the Aegyptian boats that continued to threaten and to approach the bridge. No one could realistically be drawn from there. The main fight was ongoing, the ebb and flow of battle quite noticeable. Only Roman efficiency and unit cohesion was making sufficient difference to stand up to the superior numbers of the enemy. There were men there who could easily peel off and hurry along the port side to aid the ships' crews, but to remove any unit, even the smallest, from the main Roman force would endanger the entire engagement. A tiny change could see the enemy triumphant there.

No men could be spared to aid the sailors, and Fronto could see the trouble there already.

The enemy were struggling to navigate the dock side, between the obstructions and the constant hail of missiles, but that was not going to be the case for long. More men were appearing behind them now, and the presence of a better reserve was boosting the morale of those beleaguered enemy units. Moreover, they were finally coming close to clearing the obstacles into an open space, which would give them a clear run at both the sailors and the flank of the main Roman force.

But all of that was not what was about to ruin things. That pleasure went to the sailors themselves. They were doing well; better than they or Fronto had any reason to expect. But they were becoming overconfident. They were jeering at the faltering enemy units, failing entirely to notice the fact that that faltering was coming to an end, and that they were beginning to move properly. Men had even paused in their barrage to turn and hoist their tunics, baring their backsides at the Aegyptians as though they had already won. They felt victorious. Unbeatable.

Over-confidence can kill an army every bit as easily as fear.

Fronto watched with a sense of foreboding as the first Aegyptian troops cleared into open ground. A light infantry unit armed with swords and shields but just tunics, they suddenly dropped into a square, shields clacking together in a wall, eyes low and glowering over the top, as fierce-looking as any advancing legion.

The sailors nearby continued to pelt them with darts and rocks and smooth sling stones, laughing and invoking gods. Fronto shivered. Had Brutus been down there, or even Fronto himself, he would now have those men withdrawing to the ships in good order, but swiftly, and the ones still aboard the vessels untying ropes and manning oars ready to move.

They still stood a chance as long as someone made the decision to withdraw to the ships and put out to sea, but the window of opportunity was closing rapidly, and no one down there seemed to see it. Over-confidence. The men were feeling victorious and heady valour was overwhelming their sense of danger. Desperate now, watching the point of no return edging closer, Fronto turned to that cornicen on the wall.

'Do you know naval calls?'

The man frowned. 'No, sir.'

'Not even a retreat?'

'No, sir. I know the general command order to retreat that applies to all units in the field, but that probably doesn't include sailors.'

Fronto grunted. 'And that would pull our men out of the fight anyway.'

Nothing he could do. No one down there was preparing, and no one up here could tell them to. If the sailors pulled back, the main Roman force would turn to meet the flanking attack and might just hold the enemy, especially if accompanied by missiles from ships out on the water and untouchable.

But that wasn't happening.

The officers of the ships had little experience in combat, other than vessel to vessel, and they had no clue what was coming. Fronto did, and he watched in gloom as the fight along the dock changed nature in a heartbeat. Had they been prepared, the sailors would even now be pouring onto the ships, which would already be moving away. But they remained in port, and the sailors continued to loose missiles and jeer, all too late.

The first ship load of sailors realised their mistake as that front unit of light infantry broke into a charge, roaring as they ran. The sailors exploded in panic, their triumphant exultation turning to terror in an instant. They raced for their ships, but only a few would make it safely.

Now, all along the port, enemy units were clearing their obstacles and running at the sailors who had been bothering them through their advance, and with nothing in the way, the Romans stood no chance. Spearmen and swordsmen piled into the Roman sailors and began to massacre, even as a general rout began, every Roman sailor running for perceived safety individually, ignoring the rest. Chaos broke out as men swarmed back to their ships, with Aegyptians howling at their backs, men dying in droves.

Fronto rubbed his temple. He could see no way to salvage this. It was a disaster, just as he'd anticipated. They'd been doing better than anyone could have hoped, but the tipping point had now passed, and the enemy were ascendant.

He fought against the urge to have the cornicen sound the general retreat. If they fell back now, they could still rally and withdraw professionally. But his mind furnished him with the memory of being shouted down in the briefing by men who were confident that controlling the dockside was imperative, and that doing so was feasible. If he sounded the retreat now, there would be repercussions. Still, he almost did so.

'Wet your lips,' he called down to the musician. 'Any moment now, we're going to call the general retreat. Watch for my signal.'

He chewed his lip again. Every heartbeat they fought on meant the faint chance that they might break through the main enemy force and turn the tide. But every heartbeat also put them one step further from an orderly withdrawal and towards a rout.

Salvius Cursor fought on with his men amid the enemy, unaware of the danger. Caesar, out on the flank, now had to be aware of the plight of his ships, yet he continued to press. Some of his men had reformed facing the dock side, so *they* knew what was happening, but the consul had still not sounded the call.

Caesar would not retreat.

Damn the man, but pride was less important than saving the army.

Fronto turned to the cornicen, ready to give the order to retreat in spite of his commander, when everything went wrong.

Someone on the Roman left flank, close to Caesar's position, had seen the destruction on the dock side and had panicked. As all along the quayside men fled to their ships or perished while attempting to do so, and the more precipitous of captains tried to pull their ships out to safety, even with inadequate sailors, so the Roman flank crumbled. The chaos that reigned across the shoreline spread to the main force and took hold there.

Fronto pointed at the cornicen. 'Sound the retreat.'

'Sir?'

'Do it. The army's about to rout. Let's see if we can save some order.'

But it was too late. As the musician blared out the call to retreat, the entire left flank of the Roman force was already pulling back in a disordered and chaotic manner, running for their lives. Fronto spotted Caesar in the middle of it, somehow separated from his bodyguards and waving his sword in the air in an attempt to rally the men who were fleeing past him, ignoring him. Fronto was suddenly reminded in an unpleasant way of that debacle at Dyrrachium, when the standard bearers had fled the field past their furious general.

Was this to be another Dyrrachium? Perhaps that was what had Caesar so determined. Perhaps he intended to make this another Pharsalus, not another Dyrrachium. If so, he was going to be sorely disappointed.

The army was disengaging now. Fronto was relieved to note that his timely call, while it had been too late to avert disaster entirely, had at least saved the Roman centre and right, who were pulling back in order, presenting a united front to the chanting Gabiniani, and preventing a slaughter. They were retreating towards the gate of the fort, whence they could surge through to safety. Not all were so ordered, though. The left flank that had routed in panic were now racing for the ships along the port. There was no hope of them pushing their way through the forces rushing to the fort, and with the more numerous and currently victorious Aegyptian army following them, the few units that had started this along the dock were of little import.

Desperate legionaries were surging up the boarding ramps already, while others had been caught and bogged down by those enemy units. The dockside was utter chaos, and Fronto could see barely-manned ships already pulling out into the water, while others were trying to leave, but failing as fleeing Romans and howling Aegyptians all tried to board them. Fronto could see that they were going to lose ships here. Even if they weren't captured, they would be sunk.

Worst of all, there was nothing Fronto could do about it. He had started them pulling back, even if it had been too late. All he could manage now was watching the effects and hoping that something could be saved from all of this.

The dock was a disaster. Those flanking enemy units that had swamped the shoreline had formed into small blocks of men that sat like islands amid the torrent of fleeing Romans. Due to the panicked nature of the retreat, none of the routing men were concerned with removing that danger, and so those Aegyptians went on untouched, islands of violence in a stream of fear. As Romans fled past them, heedless of the danger, enemy swordsmen and spear men lanced out and slashed, cutting down swathes of desperate, running men.

Romans were pouring onto ships, but so were Aegyptians, and some legionaries were even engaged in fighting with their own sailors as the men of the fleet fought to protect their ships and prevent them being flooded by far too many soldiers. Fronto shut his eyes and sent up a prayer to Fortuna, for clearly only she could save them now.

Things were at least going better in the open space before the fort. The careful withdrawal to the gate had been ordered enough that the enemy only advanced in their wake slowly and cautiously, aware that running after the Romans might just swing things back once more. Men were pouring through the gate by the century and hurtling across the fort, heedless of the corpses and caltrops, running out onto the Heptastadion, and making for the island of Pharos and Roman safety, almost a mile distant.

The bulk of the army should make it back, but the debacle at the dock could yet prove serious enough to end Caesar's ambitions in Alexandria.

This sudden recollection of the consul struck Fronto, and he scanned the surging armies for a sign of the white tunic, bronze cuirass and scarlet cloak of the general. Caesar had been on the left flank, which had collapsed and fled in panic. He had no way to enter the fort with the main withdrawal, and would be caught in the general flight for the ships.

* * *

Aulus Ingenuus struggled this way and that in the press. Once or twice he caught sight of his men, each identified by the red plume on their helmet, but the chances of pulling any kind of unit together in this chaos were negligible. The worst thing, though, was losing sight of the consul.

As the Roman force had suddenly turned and broke, fleeing to the ships, the praetorians, just eight of them here right now, had pulled in to protect the general, but Caesar had pushed them back, cursing. Finding adequate room without the protective press of his guards, the consul had managed to stand tall and cry out the orders to stand fast. For effect, his sword whirled in the air, continually catching the blazing sunlight and flashing blindingly.

The dazzling steel and his iron voice went unnoticed, though, in the rout, and as the press thickened, the guards around him had gradually, one by one, been pushed back and forced away by the flow of humanity.

Ingenuus tried to rise above the crowd, continually knocked back by fleeing, desperate soldiers with no care for propriety or the order of rank. His ruined hand with just three fingers, the remnant of an engagement a decade ago in Gaul, came up to shelter his eyes as he searched among the tide of human heads, his good left hand wrapped around his cavalry blade.

Then he saw it. Caesar's head, bare and grey-haired, among the shining helmets of the legions. The general was being gradually forced back, but continued to exhort his men to stand their ground. No cornicen or signifer stood nearby, though, to echo his commands, not that it would have made the slightest difference. The battle was lost, and no amount of charisma or Romanitas from their commander was going to stop that.

Briefly, Ingenuus noted two red plumes converging on the general, and thanked the gods that his men were still carrying out their duty. Taking a steadying breath, he turned in the direction of his commander and began to heave his way through the sea of men, trying to cut across the retreating flow. Here and there he foundered as men struck him with elbows, shoulders and knees in the press. Someone trod heavily on his boot and he felt the hobnails bite down painfully, but ignored it as he forced his way on. After some time pushing through the press, he rose once more, trying to get his bearings. It took precious moments to spot the general, during which he was once more pummelled and occasionally forced down below the press of men. The grey-haired consul was still there, with the two red plumes denoting his bodyguards. He was closer to the shore again now, the tide carrying him inexorably that way even as he fought to halt the rout.

It was then that Ingenuus spotted the enemy. A banner of some weird design bobbed and weaved above the sea of heads some forty paces from the general. A banner meant soldiers. Enough soldiers to protect it. The general was in extreme danger.

Ingenuus snarled and pushed on, angling towards the general once more. He was not going to let Caesar fall now. Not here. Not in such a stupid situation. Raised from lowly cavalry command on the fields of Gaul, Ingenuus had been made commander of Caesar's praetorians and had been faithful to that position for a decade, following the consul across the world and doing what had to be done to keep him from harm.

Here, now, in Alexandria, the general was in as much danger as he had ever been, whether it be from the enemy unit closing on him, or even from his own panicked and routing men. Ingenuus would not have it. He was the general's bodyguard, and he would protect Caesar no matter what.

Another pause, and he rose with difficulty above the crowd. He was tantalisingly close now, but so were the enemy. That banner was not much more than a dozen paces from Caesar, and only one red plume was in evidence, the second bodyguard having somehow disappeared, either cut down by the enemy, or simply trampled by panicked Romans. Even as he watched, he saw the consul disappear beneath the crowd for precious heartbeats before re-emerging, hair awry, cloak skewwhiff.

Last push.

Ingenuus struggled on. Suddenly, the colour of the bodies through which he was pushing changed, and he realised with an odd shock that he was among Aegyptians, both forces so tight in the press that there was no space between them.

His sword cut and stabbed as best he could manage in the tight confines of the mob, and he found that using his other elbow, forehead, knee, and even once teeth, was as viable as a true weapon. It was with regret that he head-butted a fleeing legionary by accident, suddenly bursting free of the Aegyptians.

He spotted Caesar, then. The general was furious, his face almost puce with anger as his own men pushed him this way and that in their flight. The remaining guardsman struggled to protect him, but there was little he could do other than act as a human shield and fight off the worst of the press. Those Aegyptians were there now, too, right on the general.

Ingenuus threw himself forwards, diving at the enemy. In a moment, his man was there with him, and he caught sight of Caesar, just behind him, as Ingenuus and his guardsman went to work, hacking and carving at the advancing Aegyptians. In a worrying moment, the general was pushing forwards, still purple-faced and breathing like a bull, but Ingenuus turned even amid the fighting and shook his head.

'Go, Consul. Go now.'

With that, he concentrated on the enemy. A man landed a lucky blow on his right shoulder and for the first time in ten years Ingenuus was grateful that he'd been forced to retrain with his other hand, as he felt that arm go numb beneath the blow.

They were being pushed now, and space was opening up between the fleeing Romans and the few units of Aegyptians who had pressed forwards, spotting the enemy commander and desirous more than anything of being the man to kill Caesar.

For a moment, Ingenuus considered selling his life here to buy his commander time, but the sudden loss of his fellow guard, under a horrible scything blow from a weird-shaped sword made that seem less reasonable. Alone he would last only moments.

He backed away, as fast as he dared, feet questing for space amid the detritus and the fallen bodies. It was slow work, but he felt a grim satisfaction that he was delaying the enemy advance. For some reason the Aegyptians were wary of him, and their push had slowed, keeping pace with his retreat, their eyes and swords tracking his every movement, waiting for an opening.

He could smell the brine now and hear the commotion at the ships, the lapping of the sea.

He stopped and gripped his sword tight in two hands.

'Come on then, you bastards. Who's first?'

There was a tense pause and then they came at him suddenly. One man lunged, overextending, and Ingenuus caught him in the side, a debilitating blow that would lead to a slow and lingering death. Another swiped down, but the officer had ducked to the side, out of the way. He caught a third swing with his blade and knocked it aside before cutting up and into a man's groin. As blood sluiced down from the man's crotch and he howled, staggering away, a blow caught Ingenuus, and he lurched back, reeling from the sudden pain in his chest. He glanced down and could see blood among the rings of his metal shirt. It might not be critical, but he had the distinct feeling it was. Indeed, as he fought on, he could feel his breathing becoming tight and shallow. As he swung his sword, so he fought for breath. Something was wrong.

Snarling his defiance, he cut a man across the midriff and spun, slamming his blade into someone's arm so deep it bit bone. Wrenching it back out, he prepared for another attack, but something struck him in the side of the head, and his helmet moved so that his vision was momentarily blurred and obscured, a gong ringing through his head, pain like a thousand hangovers wracking his brain.

He fell. Reaching up with his numb arm, he tried to use his three fingers to undo his helmet strap, but failed. He realised with dismay that his sword was no longer in his left, and reached up with that one. His helmet came free and a fresh thick flow of blood came with it. He felt light-headed.

Desperately, he tried to stand. He managed to get upright on shaky knees for a moment. Aegyptians were between him and the Romans now, chasing the last fleeing men to the ships. It took his fuggy mind precious moments to spot the general. Caesar was on one of the ships now, high in the prow. His wonderful scarlet cloak had come free and he now held it bundled in his hand as he gestured with his sword.

Ingenuus shook his head at the sight, an action that made him feel distinctly nauseous. The general was far from out of danger. Ingenuus had been on enough ships now to realise that the one Caesar rode was doomed. There were so many men aboard that there was no room for more to crowd up the ramp, and men were even hanging from the ropes and the rails, dangling over the harbour. The ship rode so low in the water that the largest waves were reaching the rail. She was going to go.

Ingenuus winced, ignoring the pain running through him.

'No sir. Don't die like that. Not after all this.'

He watched in horror as more desperate soldiers, being hacked at from behind, grabbed onto the starboard rail or swarmed onto the ramp. He saw Caesar recognise the danger then and begin to move, pushing through his own soldiers. The consul was high in the prow, close to the shore, but the shore was now in enemy hands, and the ship was slowly rolling to starboard, towards the jetty. It was going to capsize. Ingenuus watched in dismay as the ship finally gave under the weight of the men trying to board it. As it lurched to starboard and tipped, the general reached the port rail and, without pause or care, threw himself into the water. All along the ship, men were hanging on for their lives, few having the sense to drop into the harbour.

Ingenuus lost sight of the consul as he plummeted from ship to water, cloak in one hand, sword in the other. At that same moment the ship crashed down onto the jetty, the mast shearing, ropes entangling, the roaring of tortured wood overshadowing everything as the ship's hull gave way.

The vessel sank, amid the screams of doomed men.

Ingenuus watched for just a moment more, sighing and wiping torrents of blood from his face.

He dropped to his knees. Everything felt so cold, his body heavy like lead.

'Look to your son, Venus Genetrix,' he breathed, wishing fortune on the general with his last breath.

He was, mercifully, dead before a passing Aegyptian, angry and cheated of victory, took three goes to hack off his head and carry it back   as   a   prize.

CHAPTER FIFTEEN

Fronto's head snapped back and forth between the army flooding back through the fort and the disaster at the port.

He'd seen Caesar's ship sink, crashing through the jetty and taking hundreds of souls with it, but he'd also seen the general dive into the water at the last moment. He knew that, as senior officer at the forefront of battle, his duty was to oversee the withdrawal here, but he could not help but watch the harbour debacle, for the consul's survival was critical.

Without Caesar, why were they here. What would they do?

His gaze scoured the dock side for a quarter of a mile. Aegyptian units were now in complete control of the port, and the few Romans he could see were either rolling around on the ground clutching deadly injuries, or were being herded away as prisoners by whooping natives. The ships had pulled away into the harbour now, or *most* of them had, anyway. Of the twelve ships berthed at the quayside, two were lost to the deep, one already only visible as masts jutting from the surface, the other caught up in the ruined jetty and lying on its side. A third remained docked, though now under enemy control and swarming with Aegyptians.

Nine were pulling back out across the water, packed with fleeing Romans. It was an ignominious sight, for certain. Not one that Fronto felt Caesar would put in his missives to send back to his adoring public in Rome. At least, not unless he could yet turn the tide and make it glorious, as he had done between Dyrrachium and Pharsalus, or Gergovia and Alesia.

Finally, his heart thumping, Fronto caught sight of the general. The shape of Caesar was visible among dozens of other Romans swimming through the waters. Many soldiers who had plummeted into the harbour had drowned before they could remove their chain shirts, and others were already struggling with the weight of their other gear, occasionally dipping beneath the surface. Most would not make it to safety.

Even as Fronto watched, tense, Caesar, struggling to swim in his bronze cuirass, suddenly disappeared beneath the gentle waves of the harbour. He held his breath, staring at the water, and felt a surge of despair as that glorious crimson cloak suddenly bobbed up to the open air. He almost exploded with relief when a moment later Caesar broke the surface once more, having managed to struggle out of his cuirass in the deep. Treading water while regaining his breath, the white-clad consul gathered his red cloak under his arm and began to swim, arm windmilling and feet kicking, carrying him further and further from danger.

Still, it was a mile to the safe shore, and the ships in between were busy. It was a long way. A young, fit legionary would have difficulty with such a task, let alone a man of fifty some years. His gaze slipped ahead and he realised with a little relief that Brutus had finally got the better of the smaller Aegyptian vessels. One of his warships sat ablaze in the water, its crew having abandoned it, but apart from minor damage, the rest of the fleet there seemed to be intact. The ships that had fled the shore during the disaster were too weighed down with men to consider returning, but a fast, light liburnian from Brutus' fleet was already heading south once more, making for the troubled general.

Confident that Caesar would be safe, Fronto returned his attention to the task at hand. Cohorts were now through the fort and pounding along the Heptastadion in formation, at a run, making for Pharos once more. At a rough count, there would be perhaps a thousand men still either in the fort or pushing to get inside.

Trouble was far from behind them, though, as the Aegyptian army had clearly sensed their fleeing enemy were getting away and someone among them had kicked them into fresh speed. Instead of cautiously following the retreating cohort, the Aegyptians had begun to engage them. A brief sight of the uniform of a tribune told him that Salvius Cursor was fighting the rear-guard action with his men, keeping the enemy at bay, but he was having trouble. The legion was fighting well, but they were so hopelessly outnumbered now that they could not hold the enemy for long.

Fronto watched the legionaries pouring in through the gate, tense as ever.

'Sir.'

He looked down at the voice and caught sight of Centurion Carfulenus in the courtyard gesturing to him.

'What?'

'You should retreat to the Heptastadion with the others, sir.'

'Crap. I'm staying right here and commanding the fort. We have to hold the Aegyptians, man.'

The centurion gave him a disapproving look, but Fronto ignored him and peered at the troubled rear-guard. Salvius was in the shit, now, his men being forced back into the crowd of retreating soldiers funnelling into the gateway. His gaze slipped to the north once more, just to confirm that the ship and his general were converging. They were. That at least was no longer a worry.

He watched now until he lost sight of the rear-guard fight, the angle from this rear tower making it impossible to see what was happening right in front of the gate and south wall. He stood, tense, watching his army hurtling back through the fort and onto the great mole, running for the island.

Then a new sound began to manifest, among the din of desperate men. A panicked sound. That worried Fronto. Thus far, the men fighting back to the fort had avoided panic, reacting with solid professionalism, but that thread of sound was something new and ominous.

He peered down into the courtyard, full of seething masses of men trying to get back to the Heptastadion, looking for the source of the panic, and then he spotted it. At the southern gate, men were pointing and shouting into the shadowed archway. Half a dozen soldiers suddenly fell back, clutching arrows that thudded into them.

Fronto felt his heart lurch. The enemy had managed to reach the gate before it was closed. Salvius Cursor had fought as hard as any man could, Fronto was sure, but the numbers were just too much.

Heart thumping, Fronto hurried across the tower top and pounded down the stairs, then along the perimeter wall until he reached the north gate, above the exit to the Heptastadion. There, the angle allowed him to see into the main gate opposite, and what he saw was not an encouraging sight.

Legionaries were still flooding through the fort and out through the other gate beneath Fronto, and Salvius and his men had created a block of iron and bronze in that tunnel, attempting to deny the enemy, but they were in trouble. The Aegyptians had archers placed behind them and periodically raked the Roman lines with arrows, heedless of the fact that a few struck their own men. They could spare the manpower, Salvius could not, and access to the fort was at stake.

He watched, breath held, as legionaries tried desperately to force the great gates closed, but even as they pushed, men fell back with arrows thudding into them, while the enemy pressed in ever greater strength. Then, suddenly, the Aegyptian crowd parted and a cart appeared from the press, hurtling forwards. As the desperate legionaries forced the great gate closed, that cart slammed between the timbers, holding them apart. In desperation, the legionaries tried to push the cart back out, but the weight of men heaving it inside was too much. The gates were lost, and Fronto knew it at that moment.

If the gates were lost, then so was the fort. If the fort fell, then their control of the Heptastadion was in danger. The enemy had withdrawn carefully all the way from the island, drawing the Roman forces forward, extending them, like a clever swordsman tricking his opponent into fatally overextending himself. Then they had struck with confidence, ravaging Caesar's army and pushing them back.

Damn them.

Carfulenus had seen it coming, hadn't he? That was why he was urging Fronto down. Sensible.

Shit.

A new focus of panicked screaming drew his attention and, already anticipating the worst, he turned to look back along the Heptastadion. The enemy's ships that had been out in the undefendable commercial harbour to the west, on the other side of the Heptastadion, had closed on the great mole, staying a safe thirty paces from the stonework, from which they had begun to launch a barrage of missiles into the soldiers fleeing along it at Carfulenus' direction..

Fronto snarled. This entire damn battle the command had insisted upon had been *invited* by the enemy, allowing them to let Rome put their head into the lion's mouth. The lion had then snapped its jaws shut. Rome was fleeing back to the island, losing everything they had gained since they set foot on the Heptastadion, but while the status quo could settle once more, Aegyptian losses had been paltry, while the Romans had fallen in swathes.

They had to get out. Now. Fast,

His gaze flicked across the harbour once more, and he was grateful to see that the navy was moving. Caesar was being hauled out of the water aboard a fast courier ship. Brutus' fleet had split. Half had gone towards the bridge in the Heptastadion to prevent any further Aegyptian ships breaking through, the others racing for the southern end of the great mole and the troops now fleeing under enemy missiles. Help was coming. It would be too late to save the fort, but it might help preserve men in the face of this almighty fuck-up.

His attention turned back to the courtyard. Salvius had determined that the gate was lost, and was even now pulling back from it, his men forming a shield wall, with an angled roof from the second row and a straight cover of shields from the lines behind, a testudo without sides that pulled back across the fort, presenting a painted wooden wall to the enemy.

In a way it was the Aegyptians that had made it possible for the tribune to retreat. Their use of a cart to jam the gates open prevented them from sending enough men in at speed to hamper the Roman withdrawal. They would get out, and then have to run the gauntlet of enemy artillery along the Heptastadion to reach safety.

Fronto became aware that he was being shouted and looked down. The cornicen and signifer were now down on the ground level, amid the press, gesturing at him. He realised with a sudden wave of alarm and foolish chagrin that he was the last Roman on the walls, and already the enemy had pushed the retreating Roman line back past the staircase he had used to get up here. Why hadn't he listened to Carfulenus?

He fretted. He was trapped. Probably. There would be other ways down, for these forts had been cobbled together from housing, but what if the only stairwells were already also behind the enemy. And if he spent time looking for one, he might end up trapped here with them.

With a sinking feeling, he began to hurry back around the wall to the eastern side, with its commanding view of the corner where the Heptastadion almost met the port, separated only by the fort wall. He sighed and began to unbuckle his cuirass. His helmet he could do without. He would need his sword, and he damn well wasn't getting rid of it anyway, but the rest was all replaceable. Lastly, he crouched, untying his boots. It would be easier with bare feet, after all.

Finally ready, he approached the parapet and looked down. His stomach lurched unpleasantly.

It was a lot further down than he'd thought. The water looked dark green here, which suggested depth, but Fronto was well aware of the nature of harbours and sea walls. It might look nice and deep, and yet have big, pointed rocks just a few feet below the surface.

He was a good enough swimmer. He'd swum all his life, for sea-sickness didn't touch you when you were immersed in it, oddly. Still, despite everything, Fronto hesitated. It is simple human nature to fight against the suicidally idiotic, after all. Hoping there might still be another way out, he glanced over his shoulder at the courtyard. One look answered that question. The Roman lines were closing on the north gate now, and the enemy were gaining control of the fort. Aegyptians were flooding in through the main gate. Archers were setting up in the courtyard, men hurrying up staircases to walls and towers, and he could even see a native bolt thrower of Greek design being manhandled through the arch by half a dozen burly men. Time to go.

Still he delayed, heart thundering every time he looked down at the deep green sea below, which could be harbouring anything beneath its intractable surface. It was only as the first arrow clattered against the stonework a few feet to his left, and his hasty turn revealed half a dozen archers nocking arrows to bows and looking up at him, that the stupidity of throwing himself from a high wall was overcome by the stupidity of *not* doing so.

Taking a deep breath, left hand grasping the twin figurines of Fortuna and Nemesis around his neck, he clambered up onto the battlements. A second arrow struck the merlon just beneath his left foot.

He jumped.

It was not supposed to be an ignominious and graceless plummet into the brine. It was supposed to be a beautiful dive executed in the manner of which a Roman officer could be proud, knifing into the water and emerging to swim to safety. Instead, Fronto fell feet first like a lead weight and hit the water like a boulder, sending up a great crown of foamy droplets.

He struck the surface so hard that it robbed him of breath and all sense for a moment, and he seriously worried he might black out. Indeed, after some time he suddenly realised that he was simply sinking into the deeps, and finally began to take control, panic thrilling through him at the thought of drowning. His feet kicked, mercifully not finding any of the great pointy rocks of which he'd been afraid.

He broke the surface a moment later and heaved in deep breaths, coughing and spluttering. Taking a last look up at the fort they had controlled so briefly, he put his head down and began to swim towards those ships coming to collect survivors.

* * *

The Paneum, central Alexandria, January 7th 47 BC

Arsinoë leaned on the table, fuming, her face pale.

'Send him in.'

The eunuch bowed and hurried out backwards, grateful for a reason to leave the angry princess. Moments later, Ganymedes entered, striding confidently, tall and muscular, dressed in the garb of a general. Some days she regretted having raised him so. When he was simply her man, he'd had no ideas above his station. These days he seemed to believe he was in control, just because he commanded the army. She glowered at him, lip rising into an unpleasant sneer.

'Highness?' he said.

Her glare hardened to diamond. '*Majesty* is the correct term of address for a queen.'

Ganymedes nodded. 'I concur, Highness. And when we have your brother and sisters' heads on spikes I will be the first to announce such. Until then palace propriety should stand.'

She seethed. Should she have him killed? He was becoming an affront to her. And she had been willing to overlook his attitude initially, because he had been doing so well. His new strategies and plans had been wonderfully effective. He had taken the useless war of Achillas and turned it into something that had the Romans reacting and fighting for even a toe-hold of power. She had been pleased with him.

And it had culminated in the battle of the Heptastadion in which Caesar had been dealt a severe blow. They had lured the stupid Romans into spreading themselves thin and putting their neck under the Aegyptian sword. Ganymedes had brought that sword down, but had stopped just short of severing the neck.

The Romans had retreated across the Heptastadion under a shower of missiles from the ships, and their fleeing force had returned to the island of Pharos to lick their wounds, even taking their ships back to there and to the Palace Harbour. They had manned the fort at the northern end of the Heptastadion and begun to dig in, adding to the defences there and filling the wall tops with missiles and artillery.

Why Ganymedes had let this happen had struck Arsinoë as something of an important question. At the time and, indeed, over the days that followed, she had demanded to see the general for an explanation. In a move of the most astounding disobedience, Ganymedes had declined to see his queen, claiming more important matters demanding his attention.

So she had watched, irritable, as the Romans once more drew their lines. Admittedly, the royal force had taken control of the Heptastadion once more, and were even now using great lines and hooks to clear the boulders that were blocking the arched bridge to larger ships. But the fact remained that while they were almost back where they had been, they could have done so much more.

Finally, when she was seriously considering having Ganymedes assassinated, for there seemed no other way to get to him, he had sent word that he was coming and sought a royal audience.

She cursed herself silently. She had let herself get so wound up that she was leaning over a table snorting angry breaths when he arrived. She'd meant to be sitting on her throne and looking unattainable and imperious, like a true daughter of the Nilus. Instead, she was worried that she more resembled a petulant teenager. Straightening, she forced herself to calm down, clasping her hands behind her back and stepping away from the table.

She could not allow herself to be overcome with rage. It would make her do rash things. This interview had to be undertaken with her as the strong position. As such, she gave a nod and the doors were shut behind the general. Ganymedes turned, an eyebrow rising at the sight of the two hulking bodyguards that had closed the door. Two more stood behind the throne, as well as the usual lackeys and slaves. She was surrounded by the loyal, the faithful and the dangerous. Ganymedes was alone.

It irked her that he showed no sign of nerves at that.

'General, I demand an explanation for our failure to complete this war.'

Ganymedes gave her a look that threatened to make her fly into a rage once more, somewhere between the condescension of the tutor to the foolish student, and the commander to the soldier.

'Perhaps you could elucidate, Highness?'

'We had them on the run, Ganymedes. We had them fleeing. We could have pressed and retaken Pharos Island and the fort. Once we had the fort, we would have had a strangle hold on their shipping. They would be back to having just the palace and the Diabathra, as they had in the beginning. Then we could have squeezed them until they burst. Why did we not press home our victory? I remember in our planning sessions before all of this, that our goal lay in pressing them right back to Cleopatra's bedroom and destroying them there.'

Ganymedes shrugged. 'That was always *your* plan, Highness. I never concurred with it. To do so would be to overreach in the same way we tricked Rome into doing, and to let them have their revenge. I stopped short of such lunacy.'

She shook and forced herself not to leap at him and tear his face off with her nails. Once she was sure she could speak without open venom, she continued.

'We let them retain the island. Why could we not press for that at least?'

'Because we would have lost an unacceptable number of men, Highness. That is the sort of move Achillas kept attempting, which depleted the army. The Romans had already fortified the northern fort. Their fleet had freed itself and could operate and, though their legion ran back across the Heptastadion, they were not running in panic. They withdrew like an army, in the control of their officers. Once they secured the far end, had we pressed them, we would have been funnelled along the mole into their maw. We would have lost thousands with little chance of gaining their walls. To do so was futile. Instead we consolidated what we had retaken and watched them limp away. Now we have the bridge clear again and can harry their ships if we decide to. We weakened them considerably and pushed them back.'

'And now? What do you intend now? We are once more at that impasse. My accursed siblings remain alive in the palace, and Rome remains in our city.'

'Now we do nothing, Highness.'

'*Nothing?*'

'For the coming days, at least. I am reluctant to commit until I know better how things will look by the end of this month.'

'What?' This sounded important.

'Highness, we have the superior army, but we do not have the power to take the palace from them by force without risking everything. I am not a man given to such risks. I have called up every soldier, every piece of artillery, every weapon we can secure. They are on the way to Alexandria. If they reach us and the odds remain as they are, then I will commit to a final push.'

'And if not?'

Ganymedes approached and began to jab the map on the table with his finger. 'We have intelligence of Roman reinforcements. I cannot as yet confirm numbers or timescales, but we have been informed of infantry and archers coming from Crete and the west. From Syria and the north come at least two more legions. From the east, from the twin-faced traitorous client kings of the desert lands come archers, infantry and cavalry. Rome is hurrying to their general's aid.'

'Then we must push now.'

'Do not be foolish, Highness.'

She bristled again. One more phrase like that and she might just have him quartered and peeled.

'Explain,' she hissed in acid tones.

'This has become a race, and a balancing act, all at once. We cannot put an end to the Romans until our men arrive, but Rome cannot defeat us until theirs do. Whoever gets here first will have the upper hand and will secure victory. There is nothing we can do now but wait and see whose dice come down favourably: ours or Caesar's. In the meantime, we must be careful. We cannot afford to commit too heavily and risk everything, but we also cannot leave the Romans in peace. We must keep them on edge, for if our army arrives first we will be able to use that. But if we are careful and circumspect, then if their army arrives first we may yet be in a position to negotiate.'

Arsinoë's lip twitched again.

'There will be no negotiation. If we must lose every man, we will continue to fight Rome.'

'That will not be a popular idea with *every man*, Highness,' he replied calmly. 'We are in a strong position and I will not readily step out of that position without good reason. If you wish to put your divine power to good use, Highness, I would entreat the gods to move our reinforcements faster than theirs.' He looked back down at the map. 'I may yet consider diverting our reinforcements to stop theirs mid-delta. It all depends upon timing and numbers.'

The princess fumed. Replaying their earlier conversations in her head she was certain that Ganymedes had been fully supportive of the plan to wipe the Romans out in this one great push. Now it seemed that he had been simply indulging her, while harbouring an entirely different opinion. Men who purported to serve, yet went against their mistress's wishes were little more than traitors. She wondered once more whether to simply do away with him here and now.

No. Irritating and disobedient he may be, but he was still a shrewd military man, and she was not blind enough to her own skills to believe she could step into his boots. Until she found a suitable replacement, Ganymedes would live.

'Go,' she barked. 'But do not presume to exclude me or keep me waiting in future. I shall require constant updates of our situation, and if I call for you and I am told you are too busy, the next time you see me will be while your eyes are being plucked out. Do you understand me? I am your *queen*.'

'I understand, *Highness*,' he replied with a stress on the title of a princess, and blistering impudence. Leaving Arsinoë shuddering with anger, he bowed, turned and left. She entirely failed to notice that her oh-so-loyal bodyguards at the door gave her not a single glance, but threw open the exit at a simple nod from the general.

* * *

Royal palace, Alexandria, January 7th 47 BC

The room had polarised into two camps at the first growled disapproval.

'We still need control of the Heptastadion if we are to be secure,' the queen said in those honeyed tones that seemed to win men over despite themselves.

'The Heptastadion *cannot* be controlled without securing the forts at either end,' Cassius snapped, and not for the first time. 'And look how well that worked out for us the last time.'

Fronto nodded at the officer. Cassius had been the only man who had leapt to his defence during their debrief after the disaster, and through the same arguments that had been raging for a week now.

'Which is why I am still exasperated at the utter failure of certain men to consolidate their control,' Cleopatra murmured, with just a flicker of a glance at Fronto. 'Your men had the entire harbour in their grasp and fled at the sight of my sister's army.'

Fronto had meant to stand back and not put himself in the way of verbal arrows this time, but he simply could not help himself and stepped forwards, wagging an angry finger at the queen.

'For hours I argued against the entire bloody campaign. I told you the dockside could not be taken and held with the men we had. I had already tried exactly that once before, remember? And just to make my gods-cursed life complete, you put me in command of the push that I knew damn well we couldn't win.'

'You ran away,' the queen said, narrow eyed. Fronto was exceedingly irritated to see Caesar nod. The general should damn well know better than that, but the wiles of the seductress queen of Aegyptus seemed to be making the old man blind to the truth.

'I sounded the retreat, and only once the flank had broken and the battle was lost anyway. If I had not done so, we would now have at least a thousand fewer men. I recognise your authority here, queen of Aegyptus, but you are not *my* queen. Do not presume to lecture me on strategy. You have fought as many battles as I have ruled countries, to wit: none, while I walked the fields of Mars covered in the blood of Rome's enemies when you were still playing with child's toys.'

He stopped, breathing heavily, aware that he'd gone much further than he'd intended with that, but they had lost good men, the image of Caesar's bodyguard returning without their commander a particularly bitter low point. The queen's eyes were filled with fire.

'I cannot see how much can be gained by hauling out the same arguments and dusting them off at every meeting,' Brutus said, stepping into the middle of the room between the ireful queen and her consul consort, and the pairing of Fronto and Cassius.

'Quite,' Caesar said finally, with a careful look at the queen, who paused, silent for a moment, and then gave a sharp nod.

'Why the Aegyptians haven't pressed home their advantage yet is the main mystery,' Cassius grunted. 'We've no word of support, and they outnumber us by some two to one at least. They could at least make a try for the island. Instead we have constant sallies by one side or another, pushing back and forth with no real purpose or strength. On the bright side, our men seem to have recovered their morale in the face of the enemy's indolence.'

'Do not mistake silence for indolence,' Cleopatra snapped at Cassius. 'Because you cannot see and hear them does not mean they are doing nothing.'

'And yet they merely send out light sallies,' countered Cassius with a sneer.

'Time will tell all,' Caesar said. 'For now, let us continue to meet their half-hearted pushes with similar of our own. It gives the men a chance to recover their spirit with the occasional small victory, while a major campaign could break them.'

The conversation moved on, but for Fronto it never seemed to go anywhere new, and no matter who spoke, or what they were speaking of, the focus for him remained the fact that the queen's glare returned to rest on him again and again, and when it did not, it fell acidly upon Cassius. Following what the other officer had said to him earlier in the winter, Fronto could not help but notice that every time the queen's eyes fell upon the consul, Caesar ended up nodding at her words, whether they made tactical sense or not.

He had never before seen Caesar under the sway of anyone. Indeed, quite the opposite was the norm, and this was a worrying development.

The faster they got Aegyptus under control and were out of here, the better.

CHAPTER SIXTEEN

Royal palace, Alexandria, January 17th 47 BC

The arguments had raged once more, as they had repeatedly over the past half month. It was, to Fronto's mind, a fitting simile for what was happening in the city: two great powers in conflict. One a royal court, be it Arsinoë and her general Ganymedes or Cleopatra and her Roman consul lover, the other a military command, be it Caesar facing Arsinoë or Cassius facing Cleopatra.

In the rich rooms of the palace, the ebb and flow of angry politics forced everyone to side with one power or the other, even if there was no official rift, and arguments, opinions and recriminations fell from the air like arrow storms, defendants putting up verbal shield walls, while the artillery of over-confident design launched fresh assaults.

And in the city the war had settled into a strangely stagnant toing and froing. Rome was content to retain mastery of the harbour, the palace acropolis and the island of Pharos, while the Aegyptians were happy to operate from the commercial harbour, to control the Heptastadion and the bulk of the city. Fighting continued, for this was war after all, but there were no grand plans or hard pushes for control. Skirmishes and occasional attacks of opportunity occurred, reminding everyone that they could not become too complacent.

Fronto was a veteran of every kind of war, and he knew this type, knew what was coming, and that knowledge made him pensive and irritable as he lurked in the background of the strategic meetings, staunchly behind Cassius but keeping quiet and avoiding incurring fresh waves of accusations over the failure of the Heptastadion battle.

He knew what would happen, if not precisely how or why. Rome was waiting for more reinforcements – the other legion from Syria or the army Mithridates had promised – and until they got them there would be little chance of putting an end to this. Rome had approaching ten thousand men now in Alexandria, and even that figure was dwarfed by the Aegyptian number. To launch a major offensive until further reinforcement would be to invite a repeat of the last disaster, and everyone knew it. So Rome sat and simmered. The enemy had to be waiting for something similar. They had the numbers, but without something special they could not hope to overcome the palace redoubt. So they too sat and simmered. Both sides waited, occasionally jostling and pushing. But they waited.

At some point the wait would be over.

If Caesar's reinforcements arrived, they might be able to finally end this nightmare. If it was the enemy's hope that manifested, then Rome's ambitions in Aegyptus were over and Caesar would have no choice but to tuck his tail between his legs and run, which would likely be the end of him politically. Everything was at stake. And unless something happened, it seemed they might as well flip a coin to decide the future.

Not an enviable state to be in.

It was because of his disinterest in the latest arguments that Fronto happened to become aware of the visitor before the others. As Cassius harangued the queen and stopped just short of accusing Caesar of being her latest eunuch, Fronto had turned his back on the room and leaned on a wide flat windowsill, beneath a painting of a wide-winged blue bird and a collection of lotus flowers.

His gaze took in the complex of the palace and the city beyond, separated by the massive defences of Cassius sizzling beneath the hot sun that continued to sear the land even in the heart of winter. And that was where he saw the emissary.

He was clearly an ambassador, for the white-clad nobleman was accompanied by several slaves and a small bodyguard of veteran Ptolemaic cavalry, all under the careful accompaniment of two score men of the Thirty Seventh and a detachment of Caesar's praetorians. They were moving along the wide street from the gate in the improvised walls to the palace itself, the figure of Salvius Cursor, currently assigned in place of Ingenuus as the praetorian officer, leading the way.

'Stop bickering for a moment,' Fronto snapped at the heated debate in the room behind him. 'We've got company.'

There must have been something in his tone of voice, since such insolence commonly earned him a dressing down from Caesar and spiteful comments from the queen, but on this occasion the room fell silent and all eyes turned to him.

'It seems the enemy have sent a diplomat. He's being escorted this way and will be here any time.'

Caesar shared a glance with the queen. 'I would respectfully ask that you retire from the room while I meet with this new arrival.'

Cleopatra bridled. 'This is my palace, Consul, my city and my country. Do not presume to...'

Caesar held up a placating hand. 'No disrespect, but this emissary is doubtless from your sister. If it is an address to yourself, then I will personally retire from the matter and send them to your throne room. But Rome is the power with whom she has locked horns in the city, and it should be Rome her ambassador meets. Your presence will be inflammatory and could make negotiation difficult.'

Cleopatra narrowed her eyes. 'Beware negotiating the future of my nation without me, Caesar.'

'Please?' It was polite, and said kindly, but there was a firmness to Caesar's tone that they all knew. Still unhappy, but accepting it regardless, the queen gestured to her entourage and turned, striding from the room.

'Need we negotiate with them anyway, Caesar?' Hirtius ventured from his place a little behind the general's shoulder. 'We are in no urgent danger.'

'I have no idea what an ambassador might be here to say,' the general replied, 'but in a situation like this, Aulus, it can only be a matter of import. As such I need to hear what they have to say, and I need to mull it over as a consul of Rome, and not an overseer of the Aegyptian throne.'

He peered around the room. 'It has not escaped my notice how divided this command has become. I am less than encouraged by it, but the healing of such rifts is a matter for another time. Now, I need solidarity in appearance at least. Gather and act like a unified council of war, for when our visitor leaves once more, I need him to report our strength and unity of purpose, not our division and rancour.'

With a collection of nods the room shuffled and repositioned, the entire Roman command forming into a half circle behind the general, like some senate hearing. There they waited tense for a few moments more before the tell-tale noise of many booted feet echoed along the corridor outside the chamber.

A rap at the door received a nod from Caesar, and the two praetorian guardsmen at the entrance pulled on the handles, opening the room up. For a moment, Fronto felt the pull of grief at the sight, and had to fight it down in the current circumstances. The loss of Ingenuus on the battlefield had been keenly felt by all those who had fought alongside him since those days in Gaul when they had faced the Helvetii. The officer's body had not been recovered, which did little to improve the mood, and they had been forced to hold a strange ceremony, praying for peace in his afterlife. To see Salvius Cursor in his place was oddly fitting, but not overly comforting.

Fronto shook it off. Time later for grief. Ingenuus was not the first good Roman to die in this damn war. Salvius Cursor marched into the room and bowed to the general as his men fanned out, and the native nobleman entered with a haughty step and no sign of deference.

'Consul, this is Sarapas, who introduced himself at the gate as the 'Voice of Aegyptus'.'

Caesar cocked his head to one side. 'Did he indeed? Well met, voice of Aegyptus. I am Gaius Julius Caesar, consul and dictator of Rome. Say your piece.'

The Aegyptian's kohl-rimmed eyes narrowed, and his fingers drummed on the golden cane upon which he leaned.

'Roman, I come from Ganymedes, general of the armies of the Black Land.'

'Not from the princess Arsinoë, then?'

'Do not play games, Roman. You must know by now that this land is strong and will not simply roll over and allow Rome to order the throne around. The general Ganymedes is moving his senet pieces into position and when the board is ready, Rome's days here are numbered. We have the strength, the advantage, the popular support, and the gods on our side.'

'Yet you are here in supplication,' Caesar noted archly.

'Not in supplication,' the noble spat angrily. 'There is a hatred endemic among the children of Ptolemy, and the queens and princesses of the line are the cause of all strife and trouble in our land.'

Fronto blinked. Though his memories of the foolish and flamboyant young king who languished in rich solitude in the palace were hardly kind, he had been of little danger to Rome. Ongoing exposure to Cleopatra, though, had led Fronto to decide that she was a thousand layers of trouble all wrapped up in a pretty package, and her sister Arsinoë no better. The ambassador might be an arrogant arse, but the truth of that statement hit home in Fronto. From the look on Caesar's face, it had struck him too.

'General Ganymedes recognises that there must be a child of Ptolemy on the throne of the Black Land, but he also has an eye on the future. It is his opinion that while a daughter of the line claims the double crown there cannot be peace, and Rome will continue to war with us. With a king on the throne, especially one who owes his place to the consul, the ties between our nations could be reforged. Ptolemy the Thirteenth, Theos Philopator, was crowned as a true king, and remains so, popular with his people. It is

General Ganymedes' hope that you will see your way to releasing the king from your care back into the arms of his people. In return for the release of the king and the removal of his sister from the royal line, General Ganymedes will agree terms, stand down the army, and similarly remove the princess Arsinoë from the line. One king alone, with friendship to Rome. This is our offer, and I urge you to accept it, Roman.'

Caesar's face remained unreadable as he watched the man. Finally, he turned to the praetorian commander. 'Salvius, please escort the mouth of Aegyptus here to the grand triclinium and offer refreshments to he and his men.' To Sarapas: 'Please wait in the triclinium while I discuss the matter. I shall have an answer for you shortly.'

With a nod of the head, the Aegyptian turned on his heel and left, gold stick tapping the floor as the soldiers accompanied him. The door closed with a click, but Caesar said nothing until the sound of footsteps faded, then turned to the officers.

'What do you make of such an offer?'

Cassius was the first to chime in. 'If you do not snap the man's hand off accepting this offer, then everything we have been trying to achieve in Aegyptus has been a joke and a lie, Consul.'

There was a tense silence. Fronto might agree with him, but there were more politic ways to put things.

'*If* they can be trusted to hold to their side of the bargain,' Hirtius put in. 'The perfidious nature of the rulers of this land is becoming a theme for our time here.'

There were several nods.

'The fact remains,' Cassius pointed out, 'that we fight here to maintain a foothold purely to satisfy a woman to whom we owe nothing.' Caesar gave him a cold look, but Cassius shrugged it off. 'Caesar, I was your enemy, yet I joined you willingly, for I serve Rome and not the ego of any of its sons. As such, I will not honey-coat my words or tell you simply that which you wish to hear. I speak for the good of Rome and, though you may not currently realise it, also for the good of yourself.'

Fronto could see the coldness in the air between the two men and, taking a deep breath, stepped forwards. 'While you all know there is no love lost between the queen and myself, I wish her no harm. Caesar, there is an issue here that has not been mentioned. In addition to the release of the king, Ganymedes has also essentially demanded the death of his sisters.'

'And that is a small price to pay for Rome,' Cassius argued.

'Perhaps. I dislike the queen and her influence, and she and I will never see eye to eye, but I cannot condone her death. Remember, we began all this from the strong legal standpoint of upholding their father's wishes in his will, and attempting to secure the siblings together on the throne as had been intended. To instead favour one over the other has been niggling me all the time the queen sits on the council while her brother languishes in locked rooms, but to execute one of them and support the other is going a step too far. Rome does not have the right to kill foreign kings. To do so is to send a message to the world about the republic that we do not want to send. Besides which, from a practical viewpoint, there will still be sectors of society that support her. This, Caesar, is not a straightforward decision.'

'If it ends the war and ties them to Rome, do away with her,' Cassius insisted.

Brutus now stepped into the fore once again.

'Caesar, you termed this a "negotiation". The point of a negotiation is to put forward possibilities and hammer out an agreement. Can we not take back to this Sarapas man a counter-proposal?'

Caesar frowned. 'You propose a compromise?'

Brutus shrugged. 'Offer to meet half way and see what transpires?'

Fronto nodded now, stepping forwards again. 'Offer to give them their king back, but refuse to remove the queen. They were made joint rulers. With his time in our care, Ptolemy might now be persuaded to see the value in shared power. And the queen will have to be pressed into accepting it. Then the only issue is their sister.'

Hirtius stepped next to Fronto. 'Princess Arsinoë is clearly an impediment to peace, and while Rome could not openly condone her removal, what the Aegyptians do to secure their own throne is none of our business.'

Fronto gave him a disapproving look and opened his mouth to argue, even as Cassius, lip wrinkling with distaste, prepared to deny the whole thing, but neither managed to speak, for Caesar was there first.

'It is a plan with merit. We cannot consult with the queen, clearly, and the task of persuading her as to the wisdom of this path I shall take on in due course. For now, I think the way forward has been made clear. Come.'

Without further ado, Caesar marched from the room. At the doorway he paused and spoke to one of the praetorians, who scurried off at speed. With the Roman command in close pursuit, Caesar strode through the palace, making for the grand triclinium. As they travelled, Cassius hurried forwards to Caesar's side. 'I urge you, Consul, not to put the needs of the queen above those of Rome.'

Caesar nodded. 'I will do what I must, Cassius. Your loyalty to the republic has been noted and does you credit.'

The officer dropped back once more to walk beside Fronto. 'He will not relinquish her, you know? If he has to bring the entire republic down in order to fluff up the cushion on her throne, he will. I will follow him as long as to do so will not endanger Rome, but I am growing increasingly uncomfortable with his reliance upon that woman.'

Fronto could only nod. It was a difficult situation, and at the heart of it he agreed with Cassius. Now, though, Rome needed unity, not division.

Shortly thereafter they arrived at the triclinium, where Sarapas sat eating fruit, his slaves fawning around him, guards standing at the rear under the watchful gaze of legionaries. The Aegyptian rose with the aid of his gold cane and bowed his head.

'You have reached a decision?'

'I have.'

There was a pause, then, during which Sarapas began to look confused and uncertain, until the sound of footsteps echoed from another door, and the figure of Ptolemy the Thirteenth, King of

Aegyptus, emerged from another doorway, followed by his slaves and escorted by praetorians.

'Sarapas, voice of Aegyptus and ambassador of Ganymedes, into your hands I deliver your king. Let there be an understanding of peace between us. The young princess in your camp is your own affair, though for our part, Rome requires that she be denied any true power in your state. In return for peace and a cessation of hostilities, I relinquish the king back to his people. I will not, however, harm the queen, who was granted an equal share of rule by their father. Rome came here in the wake of Pompey's flight and sought upon our arrival simply to support the wishes of the former pharaoh. Nothing has changed. We support the joint rule of Ptolemy and Cleopatra. Let that be the decision to stand and see the country at peace.'

The young king stepped out uncertainly into the room. 'Your words are calm and reasonable, Consul, but you reckon without my sister. I am the very soul of compromise,' he added with a surprisingly straight face, 'but Cleopatra will never deign to share the throne with me. I charge you with this, force her into acceptance and I will welcome Rome as friends of the house of Ptolemy. But I fear you fight an impossible fight there.'

Caesar nodded slowly. 'Ptolemy, King of Aegyptus, take the government of the country into your hands. Look to the welfare of your kingdom in the wake of this dreadful war. Settle them into fidelity with Rome. Go with the friendship of the republic.'

Sarapas looked unsure as to whether he should leave, his conditions not entirely met and, clearly struggling with his internal debate, he finally bowed. He had secured the release of the king, after all.

Fronto frowned as he caught an odd look pass across the Aegyptian's face, and watched as the man shot a glance momentarily at his king. He saw a nervous flicker strike Ptolemy, and the young ruler stepped just a little closer to Caesar.

'Come, my King,' the ambassador said, and began to walk from the room, his slaves and guards gathering around him. The king, navigating the furnishings of the triclinium, contrived to pass close to Caesar, which had the general's praetorians shuffling forward protectively, and as he came close he hissed, loudly enough to be heard only by the officers nearby.

'Do not send me back, Caesar.'

The consul frowned, and Ptolemy threw a worried look after the ambassador, who hadn't yet turned or noticed the king's delay.

'It is no longer Achillas there who I wished to rejoin, but my sister's creature Ganymedes. I will become but a puppet to them, and nothing will change, for my sister will continue to wish my death. Don't release me.'

But Caesar stood silent, and Sarapas reached the door and turned, waiting. With a last, silent plea at the consul, Ptolemy the Thirteenth turned and joined his countrymen. Fronto waited until the Aegyptians had left under the escort of men of the Thirty Seventh, and then joined the Roman command on the wide balustraded balcony, where they watched. The Aegyptian embassy emerged a short while later. At some unheard command, the king's full entourage had joined him in the vestibule, and someone had fitted him with his accoutrements of state. The man who had been a frightened teenager in the triclinium left the building a king of Aegyptus, if a worried one.

Fronto drummed his fingers on the balustrade.

'Have we just made a mistake? I didn't like his parting message.'

Caesar sighed. 'I was under the impression that it was largely your idea, Fronto. But it was our best hope at securing peace now. Better to seize an opportunity proffered than to wait for the coin to flip and see what the Fates have woven for us. My trouble now will be soothing the queen, whose fury will be truly mighty.'

* * *

Arsinoë the Fourth, queen of Aegyptus, narrowed her eyes.

'What have you done?'

General Ganymedes, who had become less and less ingratiating and respectful over the preceding days, barely cast her a sidelong glance. She seethed at such insolence. One more example of this disobedience and she would have the man dealt with. There would be another who could take his place, she was sure.

'Ganymedes, you serve at my pleasure, and the well of that particular resource is fast running dry. What is this commotion. What have you done?'

The general, finally paying her attention, turned, arms folded resolutely.

'Your army falters, Highness. In the early days, Achillas pressed upon them that the reason they labour is to remove your sister from power, on the basis that she is a conniving and dangerous woman. The Black Land might have a history of such queens, but they never end well, after all. The hatred he encouraged against the queen has had the unfortunate side effect of making the army look at you in much the same way. Officers and men alike wonder why we fight a conniving queen, on *behalf* of a conniving queen, when a legitimate king languishes in captivity.'

Arsinoë felt the rage rising within her. How dare he?

'General...'

'No, Princess of Aegyptus, the time for your imperious commands has passed, now. You are no longer a figure to rally behind, but rather an impediment to victory.'

The princess, eyes wide with ire, gestured to her left, motioning one of her guards beside the door.

'Kill this dog.'

Nothing happened. Indeed, Ganymedes breathed deeply, arms still folded, and a small smile crept across his face. 'Oh poor naïve young princess. Do you really think loyalty is so easily maintained? Not a man in this army would stand against me for you.'

A ripple of fear ran through her then. Her gaze spun to take in her guards, not one of whom had moved in obedience to her command. Her heart chilled.

'No.'

'But *yes*, Highness. Caesar, clearly a man as naïve as you, has sent us back our king. Even now he passes through the camp to this place to regain his throne. And when he arrives, I will mount him on the prow of my ship as a figurehead for the people and then remove the Romans for good. Our forces are almost here now, a few days' journey upriver at most. And you? I had even contemplated sending you back to the Romans.'

Arsinoë shivered and stepped towards the doors, which seemed to open, offering her freedom. It was hardly fitting for a queen to run for her life, but the alternative was unthinkable. She spun, only to realise that no safety was to be found through those doors.

Her brother, Ptolemy the Thirteenth, strode towards the room, surrounded by eager-looking officers. Soldiers lined the walls outside.

Her brother had aged in his captivity, and his eyes had a haunted look.

'Majesty, I am overjoyed to welcome you back to the arms of your people.' Ganymedes bowed from the waist. Arsinoë, close to panic now, backed off against a wall.

'Ganymedes.' The king looked... tense. Uncertain. With good reason, of course. He caught sight of his sister pressed against a wall, half in shadow.

'Kill her,' he said to the guards.

Arsinoë tried to melt back into the stonework. There was an odd silence and complete lack of movement. In a clearly-orchestrated move, the doors of the room were then closed behind them, neatly shutting out most of the eager soldiery and leaving in the room only Achillas' men, Arsinoë's former guards, and a couple of officers.

The king spun, looking at the men around him, none of whom had leapt to obey his command.

Ganymedes simply maintained his smile, arms folded.

'I fear you are labouring under a misapprehension, Majesty. You are not in command here. You might *rule,* but *I* command, for now at least. In time I am confident you will grow into a fine king, but you are still young and given to foolish notions. Achillas made the mistake of obeying you, and together you almost lost control of our land to Rome. I will not make that mistake. I will prosecute this war and end Rome's interference, and to do so with an eager army, I need their king looking regal and strong. *That* is your role.

Look powerful for me, and in return I shall win control of your kingdom. I shall then maintain governance of it until you are of an age to do so confidently. When that time comes, I pray you will understand why I do what I do, and forgive me my methods. But there is too much at stake now to allow faltering leadership.'

Ptolemy sagged. 'I am to be a symbol.'

'And an important one. But your sister here will not die. I am half inclined to send her back to the Romans, I admit, but one thing we learn from games of senet is not to needlessly sacrifice any piece that may become useful later.'

Arsinoë shivered. She was to live. For how long, she did not know, and as a captive of Ganymedes and her brother, no less. But at least she would live.

* * *

Royal palace, Alexandria, Kalends of February 47 BC

Fronto paced through the palace to the latest meeting with the Roman command, and turned to glance over his shoulder at the sound of approaching boot steps, spotting Cassius emerging from a side door. The officer fell into step with him.

'You've heard the news?'

'What news?' Fronto snorted bitterly. 'The news that the Aegyptian hydra has another head? That Ptolemy reneges on his deal and leads the army with Ganymedes against us? The news that Cleopatra has denounced you and I as traitors to her cause? The news that the Aegyptians gather troops once again? Or perhaps the news that the queen has missed her monthly bleed?'

Cassius shot him a look. 'For the love of Venus, Fronto, stop spreading that rumour. That kind of talk needs to be trodden down.'

'Oh come on, Cassius. Her maids leaked the word and it's all over the palace. The only reason anyone pretends they know nothing is political expediency. And soon enough it's going to become too obvious to hide. What are we all supposed to do when the queen is waddling around, lugging a belly the size of a grain sack? Do we keep pretending nothing is amiss? Do we claim she became pregnant by miracle? That it was a slave or her brother-husband? The world will soon know she carries a child, and when that happens the world will know it's Caesar's. Hold your nose and take a deep breath, Cassius, 'cause we're going for a dive in the shit pit.'

Cassius fell silent. Fronto was right, of course, but until the queen announced something, or Caesar made an admission, no one wanted to be the man to broach the subject.

'Anyway,' the man said, waspishly, 'I meant the news from the Cypriot merchants.'

Fronto shook his head. 'No. Good or bad?'

'Good, at last.'

'Thank Saturn's shiny golden knob for that. We could *do* with a bit of good news. What is it?'

'Reports of a huge body of allied troops marching south along the coast of Judea, closing on Aegyptian lands. Reports of strength vary, but they're all high. Looks like legions and client armies from Syria and Cilicia, perhaps Mithridates' army comes at last, and Aegyptus' neighbours rally to our cause. Seems the Aegyptians are none too popular with their eastern neighbours.'

Fronto snorted. 'The Pharaohs spent thousands of years conquering them all and enslaving them. That sort of thing makes people bitter.'

He tried not to think what that said about Rome, and shook off the thought.

'It'll take them time to get here, though. Ganymedes controls the delta and any reserves he has will get there easily from upriver. Reinforcements will have to fight their way through to us. We might be smouldering corpses by the time relief comes. Some days I wonder if being a smouldering corpse might not *be* a relief,' he added bitterly.'

'Gods, but you're a breath of light air, Fronto. Galronus is right about you.'

The two men strode side by side towards the meeting.

'I don't understand you, Fronto.'

'I'll take that as a compliment.'

'Facetiousness aside, you're from a distinguished family. A minor offshoot of it, I'll grant you, but your ancestors have been consuls, tribunes, praetors and governors. Fought the Carthaginian fleets and produced lawyers. Gods, but one of your ancestors was made dictator to save the republic a century and a half before Caesar was given the title. You are in every way his superior in the republic, yet you roll over like a pup and let Caesar warm his feet on you. Days like these, when we are in over our heads and proud men steer the republic's interest, why don't you stand on centuries of your family reputation and speak up?'

He stopped, aware that Fronto had fallen still and was now twenty paces back along the corridor.

'Where did all that come from?' Fronto said quietly.

Cassius sighed. 'Someone has to defend the republic, and it clearly isn't going to be the man made dictator for that purpose. He's little more than bed slave to a foreign queen now.'

Fronto made motions for his friend to keep quiet, but Cassius shook his head. 'I stand for the republic, Fronto, but increasingly I seem to stand alone. Caesar and his woman have everyone under their spell, with people like Hirtius too impressed to argue, and men like Brutus more intent on keeping the peace than solving the problem. In our meetings, the only man I find standing consistently behind me is you, and yet you won't open your mouth to argue when I'm shouted down. In fact, when we were finally offered a way out and all it required was the death of one foreign queen with delusions of divinity, suddenly you were arguing against it. And look what your leniency got us. Fresh war. Why won't you stand with me?'

Fronto deflated. 'I'm old, Cassius. Old and tired. I've fought for Rome for decades. And I stood up for what was right in my time. I faced Caesar when I thought he went too far, and went looking for a better way. You know what I found? A dozen *worse* ways. Rome has become a tangled web of intrigue and corruption, and it's gone way beyond the days of Marius and Sulla. I don't think there's any help to be had. Rome has become the playground of powerful individuals, not an honourable senate. And when you find yourself in a war where the only option is which bastard to side with, don't choose the bastard who means well. *None* of them mean well. Choose the bastard who'll *win*. And choose the bastard who'll do the least damage doing it. Did you know my father?'

Cassius shook his head. 'Your grandfather, by reputation.'

'My grandfather was noble and just, but none too bright. He meant well. He lost. My father was out with Sertorius in Hispania. He only avoided having to throw himself on his sword by being too incompetent and unimportant for anyone to care about. In the wars in Hispania, he went from a doting and clever father and an honourable son of the republic to being a pointless drunk. Do you know what his last words to me were?'

'Of course not.'

'Well I remember them vividly. I've spent my whole life trying not to see any sense in them. To think the republic was still strong. That Romans cared. But the older I get, the more I see the wisdom in my poor fallen sot of a father.'

'Fronto?'

'The last thing he told me was "Don't stand out. Don't make a name for yourself. Don't be a success. Being a hero just earns you enemies. If you want to sire children and live to be a happy old man, move to the country. Hide in a villa. Be a nobody".'

'Hardly great advice for a patrician family.'

'On the contrary, it's *sage* advice, Cassius. Rome seethes with civil conflict, and we're here trapped in a foreign land fighting a war that's not ours. Had I been a useless drunk, I'd be on my estate now, bouncing my two boys – who I've not seen for years, by the way – on my knee. I'd be of too little value here. Too late I saw that, and I was already tied to the wheel of history, but I saved my family. I sent them off to the countryside. They will live in obscurity. Safety. If this all somehow ends well, I'll join them and live to be an old drunken sot handing out salutary advice. But if not, at least they're safe.'

'So you still do want this to end well?'

'I do,' Fronto sighed. 'But I'm past the days when I'm going to stand proud and shine and tell people what they should do for the good of the republic. I just want to end this all and go home.'

'Then stand behind me and at least nod when I speak. Caesar has to have someone around who will argue against excess and foolishness.'

The two men walked on in an awkward silence. Somehow the delay of their short debate seemed to have been longer than either man thought, and the meeting was already beginning as they pushed their way into the room.

'Ah, good,' Caesar said quietly. 'Now we are all here. You are both aware of the news of Asian reinforcements?'

The two men nodded, falling still as a praetorian shut the door behind them.

'Good. The latest, then, is that Ganymedes and his puppet king have reequipped their navy and strengthened it with every vessel they could find. Their fleet departed the commercial harbour yesterday and we assumed they would be once more on their patrols of the coast, but intelligence has it that they are intent on cutting off our supply lines. Since they cannot take the harbour from us, they now turn to piratical activity, harrying our supplies. Those that come across the sea are in danger, but also those that come from inland along the Canopic branch of the river. As such, I feel it is time to send forth the fleet once more. With reinforcements on the way, keeping our supplies adequate is a matter of prime importance.'

Brutus cleared his throat but Caesar shook his head. 'Tiberius Nero, step forwards.'

A thickset man with almost white hair stepped out of the rank of lesser officers at the rear. Fronto frowned. He knew of Nero. A man who served as a quaestor. Once one of Pompey's pirate hunters.

'Brutus,' Caesar said quietly and kindly, 'you consistently serve well in grand scale naval actions, but this is Nero's ground. Nero here helped Pompey clear the Cilicians from the sea. He knows about hunting pirates. Nero, I am granting you command of the fleet. Sea and river both, I want clear. Take the ships and obliterate Ptolemy's navy.'

Fronto watched Brutus' face fall into a mixture of disappointment and disapproval. Nero might be good at what he did, but he had been Pompey's man in his time. Brutus did not like him.

But then Salvius Cursor had once been Pompey's man, and had Fronto himself not briefly borne that label too?

'Alright,' Cassius said. 'Let's destroy the Aegyptian navy and clear the way for the reserves. Time to gather and end this thing.'

CHAPTER SEVENTEEN

Canopus, on the coast of the Nile Delta, February 6th 47 BC

Julius Meleager, trierarch of the Chimaera, eyed the situation with an appraising glance. The grand temples of the city of Canopus sat to their right on a headland, impressive and ancient, older even than Julius' own people in Rhodos. To the left of that, at the near end of a long, wide bay, the branch of the Nilus River known as the Canopic surged off inland to the south, wide enough for several ships to manoeuvre.

Somewhere just a few miles upriver, or so rumour said, a large grain shipment from sources loyal to Cleopatra sat waiting to be able to sail out into the sea safely, and make for Alexandria to supply the trapped army. They themselves, though, were confined, for just inside the entrance to the river sat a fleet of Aegyptian ships, blockading it effectively. Fewer ships than the fleet behind the Chimaera, but well positioned in a river not wide enough to press a serious Roman advantage.

Numerous horn calls blasted out from the ships at the rear of the Caesarian fleet and Julius turned for a moment, peering over his shoulder. The ships of the Roman navy had drawn up in a formation off the coast, facing the enemy, and were moving towards the river mouth only at the slowest possible rate. The Rhodian contingent sat at the western edge, and the Chimaera formed the very flank, as was Julius' favoured position. He could see the Ajax just a little behind him and to the left, flying the flag of their admiral Euphranor.

The new Roman commander, Tiberius Nero, had given orders that all ships were under his direct command and that no individual officer was to display their colours, but Euphranor was hardly about to listen to such a command. Nero might be a good admiral and a Roman hero, but he was not yet known to Euphranor, and the Rhodians were, after all, their own men.

Even as the fleet slowed, preparing to sit immobile, facing the land, the Ajax put on an extra turn of speed and came alongside. Julius grinned as the Rhodian admiral strode across his deck and leaned on the railing of the flagship, gesturing to the Chimaera's trierarch.

'Meleager!'

Julius reached his own rail opposite the admiral and waved. 'What will Tiberius Nero do?'

The admiral threw an insolent gesture back towards the Roman fleet. 'Nero does not want to commit within the narrows of the river, of course.'

Julius turned and looked into the mouth of the Canopic channel. He nodded. 'While I hate to agree with the man, he has a point.'

'Yes, but it's under his helmet,' snorted Euphranor. The man's too cautious, for sure. We outnumber them two vessels to one. We need to engage, and while the day remains light.'

Julius winced. 'True, Admiral, but his caution might be warranted. Once we're in the river, neither side will be able to field more than three ships at a time. We lose our advantage of numbers. Nero knows that. No admiral worth his salt would throw his fleet into that situation with such an uncertain chance of success.'

'Nero got his experience fighting Cilicians. They're a different breed to these Aegyptians. He thinks he can draw the Aegyptians out into open waters by simply sitting there and looking Roman. He thinks they will run out of patience and attack him.'

Julius shrugged. 'Such a thing seems unlikely, I'll admit, but these Aegyptians have made the odd reckless blunder before, so perhaps he is right. Launching at them in tight confines is not a favourable option, regardless.'

238

Euphranor harrumphed. 'So *we* sit and wait in the hope that they will get bored and come out, which is unlikely. *They* sit and wait because they know they are in the best position and our supplies cannot reach us through them. No one moves. And then soon night will come and we will be forced to put to shore and abandon this. They can resupply from the riverbanks and sleep aboard. We must seek a safe harbour. This is like two stone lions watching one another. They're impressive and pretty and both quite dangerous, but the chances of either of them leaping and ending it are rather small.'

Julius Meleager chuckled. 'Without someone impulsive, the status quo is unlikely to change.'

'So we need them to be impulsive. What do you think will goad them into that?' Euphranor called, a slow grin spreading across his face.

Julius smiled knowingly. 'I know what you're suggesting, Admiral, and it's reckless. Dangerous.'

'Right up your channel then, eh Julius?' the man grinned. 'But impulsiveness breeds its like. Recklessness can be infectious.'

The Chimaera's captain sighed. It *was* feasible. Everything they had seen of the enemy, both at the engagement by the sandbank anchorage and the battle off Pharos Island, had suggested that the Aegyptians were at best moderately disciplined, and that they tended to be reactive by nature. That could be used against them. It was a balancing act. Their commander's level of control against their native impulsiveness. If that balance could be tipped...

Certainly *something* had to be done. The Roman fleet could not sit off the coast facing the river indefinitely, and committing to fighting in the channel would be foolish. And all the time they were wasting here, the grain ships upriver remained in danger from other enemy attacks.

But it was still a dangerous gambit.

He nodded at the admiral. 'Just the two of us?'

'There's no space for more than three ships at best, and with only two there's more room to manoeuvre. We need to goad them. We need to keep poking them with a stick until they get angry enough to lash out, and the moment they look like giving chase, we need to turn fast and run for the fleet. With luck we'll drag them *all* with us.'

'Alright. Let's do it.'

Euphranor laughed, saluted, and raced back to his place at the rear. In moments a jaunty tune warbled out across the deck of the Ajax and the oars began to dip in time, pulling the ship forwards. With a gesture to the *keleustes*, Julius Meleager strode back to his own position, shouting instructions to the helmsman. The keleustes began to march back and forth along the deck between the banks of oar benches, shouting encouragement as his piper started to pick up the melody from the Ajax, keeping perfect time. In moments, Chimaera too was knifing through the water, racing for the entrance to the river in the wake of the Ajax.

A small thrill of nerves ran through him at the cacophony of sounds that followed, though that shiver was swiftly overcome by the exhilaration of impending battle. Back across the fleet, horns honking the command to come to a stop and to maintain formation blared out with increasing volume and urgency as the Roman fleet tried to rein in the two errant Rhodians.

'Let's hope they're ready when the time comes, sir,' the helmsman said, eyeing the Roman fleet rapidly dwindling behind as they raced for the river.

'Nero's not daft. He's just being a Roman, playing it safe. You know what they're like. That's why they need men like us. Men like the admiral over there.' Laughing, Julius turned and peered off ahead between the rigging and beneath the limp sail. The two Rhodians moved at pace and he could see the Aegyptian fleet sitting silent and still in the waterway. What would they do?

The Ajax had a slight advance on the Chimaera, having burst into motion a little sooner, and she was almost a full ship length ahead. For just a moment Julius considered upping the pace to fall in beside her, but decided against it. Better to maintain pace and not risk confusion with two rhythms going on side by side.

As he had noted, the enemy fleet was drawn up in rows of three ships, all they could realistically fit in the river and still be able to turn. They had been sensible in that the three vessels that made up their first line were clearly their three most powerful warships – a very Roman notion. The republic always fielded their heaviest infantry at the front as a shock force, legionaries advancing in a shield wall, clad in iron, steel and bronze. It often worked, of course, and could do as much at sea too. Their commander probably thought that the Romans would baulk at launching an assault on three massive, powerful ships, and that if they did, they would likely end up as floating wreckage at the hands of those three monsters.

Again, it was a reasonable assumption. The Ajax and the Chimaera were both warships, but nothing close to the massive size of those three. But what they lacked in size, they made up for in deftness. They were fast and manoeuvrable, more so even than the swift Roman liburnians, something the huge Aegyptian ships could not claim to be. And in tight situations that changed the odds entirely. They would be short on space. When you're trapped in a barrel, it's better to be a hornet than a hawk.

'Ready, men,' he bellowed. 'Artillery and archers: "man down" to left and right. Helm, target four then sharp turn to starboard. Oarsmen to ship on approach.'

He glanced left to see the Ajax racing on, still the better part of a ship length ahead as his artillerists began to load and prime their weapons. Then, suddenly, the flagship's musician changed pace, bursting into a high-speed melody. With a roar, their crew obeyed the new command, and Julius watched with just a flicker of nerves as the Ajax began to surge ahead, the oars rising and dipping faster, picking up the pace to a ramming speed.

He prayed to half a dozen gods, most notably Poseidon and Ares, that Euphranor knew what he was doing. It was the admiral's favourite tactic to start any conflict with a sinking. It struck fear into the enemy to see such a thing, and gave the rest of the allied ships heart. And with the sharp narrow rams the Rhodians bore, it did not necessarily remove them from action as they tried to extricate themselves, as was so often the case with Roman rams. It was dangerous, though. An unlucky strike and they would be lodged and at the mercy of the Aegyptian fleet until they could withdraw.

Julius was in no mood for such risk. He would pull off his own favourite tactic. His only real peril was whether he would have the room to follow up with the strategy they needed to get away afterwards. It would certainly be tight.

Ajax was concentrating on the leftmost enemy vessel alone. Julius would take on the other two. If they could enrage them sufficiently, they might draw them out. Sinking one was a gamble, as it could prevent pursuit from those behind. Julius did not want to sink these two. Just to anger them and make them follow.

That was the moment it all hinged on, of course. If things worked out right and the gods were feeling benevolent, the loss of one Aegyptian ship and the sight of the other two pursuing the Rhodians could just drag the rest of their fleet out into conflict in the bay.

The two Rhodians closed, and now the front three Aegyptian ships were moving. They might not be intending to sail out to sea, but the enemy commanders knew they had to be at least moving to fight these two Rhodians off. One benefit of the Ajax disappearing further and further ahead was that Julius could watch his admiral's initial attack before he himself was committed.

Sure enough, he saw Euphranor's flagship turn a little to the left, just as Julius would have done. As they closed on the single ship ahead, they began to veer to their port side, just a touch. There was a moment of tension, and finally the enemy reacted. The leftmost Aegyptian ship turned, tracking the Ajax, making sure to keep facing it. There was a strange faltering then, as if their captain couldn't decide what to do; couldn't read the plan of the Rhodian. After all, if both ships continued to turn thus, they would end up parallel and both crunching bow first into the bank with insufficient room to complete the turn.

But Euphranor knew what he was doing. Even as the enemy committed to the turn, Ajax was already straightening once more and closing at killing speed. The enemy realised what was happening just too late. They had presented a ready target to the Ajax now, at a three-quarter angle.

In desperation, the enemy captain tried to turn back, at the same time bellowing to his artillery to loose. The Rhodian admiral's attack was underway, though. As the distance closed inevitably, the artillery on the prow of both Ajax and its target loosed. The enemy bolt slammed into the woodwork of the Ajax, sending a cloud of deadly splinters up, but failing to slow them. With beautiful precision, a heavy stone shot hurtled through the air from the Rhodian ship. Due to the movements of the two vessels it missed its *prime* target, the ship's mast, glancing from the heavy timber pole before raking on across the deck, killing two men and ploughing into the steering rudder and the man controlling it. The helmsman reeled, injured and shocked but intact, yet for precious moments he was torn from the rudder grip. The enemy ship slewed further into their turn, making the angle of approach for the ram all the more perfect.

That was when the Ajax hit them.

The enemy ship was moving at a steady, easy pace, but the Ajax struck at ramming speed. The Rhodians' perfectly knife-like ram cut through the boards of the Aegyptian vessel and the Ajax continued on with powerful momentum, oars withdrawn now, the wedge of its prow continuing to force the hole in the enemy hull wider and wider.

Taking his eyes off his admiral's attack, Julius concentrated on his own action now. The enemy vessels were running side by side towards the Chimaera. They were too close to one another for comfort, really, due to the narrowness of the river. With a smile, he watched his own prow shift again with the latest in a series of minor course corrections from the helmsman. The Chimaera was aiming directly between those ships, and the enemy didn't seem to be able to decide what to do about it. They couldn't turn towards one another for, with the lack of room, they would simply collide. They couldn't both turn left, or they would beach on the shoreline, and to both turn right would put them in the midst of the Ajax's own nightmare attack. Clearly they couldn't diverge, either, for they would then do *both*. All they could do was come on, parallel and in formation. Aware of what could happen if the Chimaera slipped between them, they continually jogged left or right, trying to force the Rhodian into a new path, but the Chimaera's helmsman continued to correct and make for the gap.

The enemy finally slowed, seeing what was coming and fully aware that they couldn't stop it. The Rhodian ship was going to go between them. Knowing what that would do to their oar banks, just as Julius' rowers shipped their own oars for protection, so did the men of the two enemy warships.

The three vessels met, the narrower, lighter Rhodian sliding between the two larger ships with grace. But it wasn't the oars Julius had been after. He didn't *want* to cripple these ships, after all. One sunken enemy was trouble enough. He needed these two enraged and active enough to follow him, and in doing so to drag the rest of the enemy fleet with them. The Chimaera slid between the ships, and the captain almost laughed at the stunned and confused expressions of the enemy sailors as they passed.

Then the true nature of his attack became clear. As the ships passed, so close they could have shared wine together, the Rhodian artillery loosed, and the archers rose from the rails where they had let go of their oars, to retrieve their bows.

The heavy stone shot arced right, the iron-tipped bolt left, both accompanied by half a dozen arrows. The captains of each vessel were easily identifiable, and so were the oar masters – the keleustoi, or whatever the Aegyptians called them – and they made perfectly visible targets at this range. The captain of the left hand ship was plucked from the deck and carried, screaming, over the rail and into the river by a scorpion bolt the length of a man's forearm in the centre of his chest. At the same time, their keleustes, who had been stomping up and down between the oar banks yelling at his men, became the repository for three arrows, squawking and tumbling among the benches.

A similar scene played out to the right. The captain there disappeared in a spray of gore as he took a stone ball the size of his head full in the torso. What was left of him slid unpleasantly across the deck to wobble to a halt by the rail, shaking rhythmically even in death. Most arrows missed their keleustus as he waved his rod at the oarsmen, but one shaft thudded into his bicep, making him scream.

That was it. In a heartbeat they were past, having shot between the two ships and emerged beyond, between them and the second line of three ships in the Aegyptian fleet.

'Bring us about, full speed to starboard, watching for the bank. Return to the fleet.'

Grinning from ear to ear, Julius watched his men lower their bows and grab the oars as they were run out. In moments they slewed so sharply to the right that even though Julius was gripping the rail he still almost fell. At a stomach-churning pace the Chimaera arced right, around the rear of the enemy.

Julius watched the riverbank nervously as they came closer and closer, and half expected the oars to touch the mud at any moment, but somehow they managed to stay clear. Fifty heartbeats and they were facing north again, racing past the two ships they had just attacked and making for the open sea. They just had to hope the enemy were sufficiently enraged to follow, that their impulsiveness overrode the strength of their commander.

He was gratified at least to see what effect they had already achieved as they passed the two Aegyptian ships. They had been very careful to kill neither the helmsmen nor the pipers that set the pace. They had not damaged the oars or sails, nor harmed the rowers. They had done nothing to impede the ships' ability to fight. But they *had* taken out the two men on each ship with the authority and sense to prevent the ships following. Even now the Aegyptian crews, furious at the damage and the loss of their captains, were launching into a pursuit. Some minor officer or brazen crewman had given an order to advance, and the oars began to dip in time to a frenzied tune.

The enemy's blood was up.

They had done it. Now if only the rest of the fleet took the bait and followed.

With a sigh of relief and a grin of contentment, knowing that the Chimaera was fast enough to outpace the enemy, Julius allowed himself a moment to locate the Ajax.

His heart climbed into his throat at what he saw.

The Ajax had utterly destroyed her target. The hole she had torn in the side of the enemy ship had been so large that already little could be seen of it other than masts and torn sails jutting from the river's surface, men swimming for shore, and pieces of ruined timber bobbing around on the water. The Ajax had clearly extricated herself cleanly and swiftly from the sinking wreck.

But Euphranor had not ordered the withdrawal after the attack. Quite the opposite, in fact. Spirits sinking, Julius watched his friend's ship sailing straight at a large vessel in the second line now, a ship flying numerous colourful banners – likely the enemy's flagship. Julius shook his head. *No.* The admiral had sunk a warship himself, and had watched Julius harry the other two, but had then taken in at a glance the lack of movement from the rest of their fleet.

Two vessels were following the Chimaera, intent on making her pay. The rest of the Aegyptian fleet had not fallen for the goad. But Euphranor had been determined.

'Steady,' Julius bellowed at his crew. 'Don't outpace them too much. If we race away they'll give up. Just stay a little ahead. Tantalising, like a twenty sestertii whore. Draw them on.'

But even as he issued his orders, his eyes were back on the Ajax. He watched as Euphranor's ship collided with the enemy flagship, holing her. The Rhodian admiral had to know that he was doomed; that it was a suicide attack. Even as the Ajax punched a fatal hole in the hull of the enemy ship, grapples and ropes arced out, hooking into the Rhodian vessel and pulling her close.

The enemy flagship was going down, but she would take the Ajax with her.

Julius squinted. The increasing distance as they raced back for the fleet made it hard to see, but he could make out fighting on board now. Men from both ships were leaping back and forth. A few dived into the water to swim for shore, but more were fighting frantically.

He saw a figure then. It could have been Euphranor. Probably was, in fact. The figure burst through a crowd of tussling sailors and clambered up to a high point, then let forth a loud ululation and lifted a head to display to all present. It was in a helmet with three long green plumes. It had to be a senior man. At least a trierarch, if not an admiral.

The figure held its prize aloft, warbling loudly to attract attention, and remained in position for a dozen heartbeats until the first arrow plunged into him. It was followed by a second and a third before the figure and his important trophy toppled from the timber and into the water.

Heart down in his boots, Julius watched the disaster unfolding. Even as the fighting raged aboard the decks of both vessels, they began to sink. Tied together, they took longer than they would apart, for the Ajax remained undamaged, but finally the weight of the sinking Aegyptian carried its enemy under the surface.

The effect among the enemy fleet was both instantaneous and unanimous. Where they had watched their three foremost warships sunk and damaged, they had retained formation and remained in position. Whether it was the sheer audacity of the Rhodian vessel charging them and sinking their flagship, or whether perhaps it was the insult of hacking off the head of their commander, Julius would never know. But the enemy fleet was moving. Whistles and horns were blowing back there and the entire Aegyptian fleet was on the move.

In his sacrifice, Euphranor had goaded them sufficiently at last.

With a slow exhale of regret, Julius turned back towards the sea. He could see the Roman fleet out there. They too were moving now, reorganising to meet the enemy. He had little doubt that in open sea the Roman ships with their superior numbers and stronger discipline would carry the day. Julius made a small vow to Athena that, when they returned to the city, he would make sure those in command knew that while Tiberius Nero had commanded the fleet and won the battle, it was Euphranor of Rhodos who had made it possible.

CHAPTER EIGHTEEN

Royal palace, Alexandria, March 23rd 47 BC

Fronto rubbed his eyes, scraping away the sleep in the corners, yawned and scratched himself in a most un-patrician manner. Squinting, he focused on the shape of Galronus in the doorway, the Remi horseman almost vibrating with energy. Damn, but how was he so alert at this time of the morning? No, Fronto decided firmly. Night. Not morning. Morning was some way off yet, and even the larks were still chirping into their pillows.

'Wha?'

'Something's happening with the Aegyptian forces. Looks like they're pulling back.'

'Wha?'

Fronto pulled the sheets back, grateful for the faint waft of air that reached his sweaty form beneath, and swung his legs out over the edge of the bed, sighing with pleasure as they slapped down onto cool marble.

'About an hour ago someone first reported it, but it looks like they've actually been thinning out for hours.'

Fronto frowned. 'Thinning out?'

'There's still men on their defences and their ships remain in the commercial harbour. They still have artillery manned and so on, but the numbers of men visible have been decreasing throughout

249

the night, if reports are to be believed. They're pulling back, Cassius reckons, but where to is the question, and why.'

'Cassius is up and about too? What's the matter with you all? Are you allergic to sleep?'

'Fronto!'

'Alright, I'm coming.'

As he struggled into a clean tunic, belting it and slipping his feet into his boots, he pondered the situation. A thought nagged at him. As he raked a bone comb through his salt-and-pepper hair, he narrowed his eyes.

'They're trying to sneak away and get a head start.'

Galronus nodded. 'Seems reasonable. But where to, and why?'

Fronto slipped his sword baldric over his shoulder, a finishing touch that finally made him feel dressed. 'It's what we did numerous times,' he said, 'including to Pompey at Dyrrachium. And there's only one reason to need a head start. We're in a race. We just don't know it yet. Come on.'

Hurrying out of the chamber and heading through corridors towards the room Caesar used for his headquarters, Fronto worked his mind through everything he knew was going on, teasing the pieces of information together like a child's puzzle to see if they fitted. They did. Alarmingly well, too. By the time he reached the command room and the praetorians threw back the doors for him, he was confident of both what was happening and what they needed to do in response to it.

Caesar was standing with the queen, Cleopatra, looking out over the balcony, towards the city where Ganymedes and King Ptolemy still held control. The armies had been in a deadlock now for two months since the battle at the Heptastadion had ended in a stalemate, but if Fronto was right – and damn it, but he knew he was right – then not only had that deadlock finally ended, but Alexandria had in fact just become entirely unimportant.

Cassius was poring over a map with Brutus and Hirtius. Orfidius Bulla and Uttedius Pollio, the two senior officers, were locked in debate in the corner with the commander of the palace guard, and other officers stood at the periphery, quiet and pensive.

'It's a race, and we're losing with every moment we waste,' he announced as he entered, halting all other conversation and drawing every gaze.

'Fronto, good morning.' Caesar said calmly. 'I am inclined to disagree, however. Many possible explanations have been bandied about, but the most likely answer is not one we should rush into. We know that our relief comes by coastal route, while the enemy are expecting their reserves from the south, inland. Our legions move faster than their army and are prepared for trouble all the way. It is the general belief, based upon the queen's knowledge of geography and our understanding of the forces involved, that Ganymedes is sending a sizeable escort to bring in his reserves, lest they meet our own reinforcements in the delta with disastrous results.'

'No, Caesar, that's not what's happening.'

'It is the most plausible explanation, and fits with their command style thus far,' Cassius offered from across the room.

'Bollocks. Ptolemy is not in command, because he would be weak and cower behind his walls. Arsinoë can no longer be an influence, and Achillas is dead. Ganymedes is still running this war for the enemy, and he is a man given to considered action. Moreover, he is willing to sacrifice to gain strength, as we saw at the Heptastadion. He's not the sort of commander to panic over the safety of his reserves and weaken his position here because of it. At best he will have sent scouts who know the delta to pass word to his approaching reserves. But that isn't what's happening. We need to move. This is a race.'

'Where to?' Hirtius queried.

Fronto marched over to the table and turned the map so it was the right way up for him.

'Here. Pelusium.'

'What? That's ridiculous. It's all the way across the delta and of little importance now. What are your reasons?'

Fronto walked across to the window and peered at the enemy defences. What he saw – a thin, skeleton force at best – supported his theory. He waved at the enemy lines.

'They've taken nine men in every ten by the looks of it. They've only left enough troops behind to hold their walls for a few hours. Enough to look like they're still there. Those men out there are like my men at Dyrrachium, manning empty walls until the last minute so the army can get a dozen miles from Pompey before he realises it. They don't care what happens here now. Alexandria is no longer of importance to them. They just want to delay our realising it.'

'But why?' Cassius pressed.

'Pelusium. It's all there. Think about it. When we first got here the queen had an army but they were bogged down at Pelusium by Ptolemy's forces.' He gestured to Cleopatra, who nodded.

'We were held there,' she confirmed. 'Achillas had occupied an old fort at the main crossing. A powerful one, and we couldn't realistically pass it.'

'And because we've been concentrating on Alexandria,' Fronto ploughed on, 'we've ignored Pelusium. We've labelled it unimportant and assumed it no longer mattered. But we were wrong. Ganymedes and ourselves have both been playing a waiting game, knowing that whoever's reserves reached the city first could win.'

'This is all common knowledge that proves nothing,' Hirtius grumbled.

'Listen to me. I think that Ganymedes is brighter than any of us have given him credit for. He's not panicking about his reserves bumping into the relief. In fact, I think that's his very plan. He could probably have had his forces here first, but he's decided that if he does, and he assaults us, he'll deplete his force just in time for our reserve to thrash him. No, he's decided to remove our support from the field.'

'What?'

'I would wager that a week or more ago his reserves were rerouted to Pelusium. In fact, I'd wager that for the last month, ever since the navy battered him at Canopus, he's concentrated on winning the land war. He's gathered all possible forces at Pelusium to stop our reserves the same way Achillas did to the queen.'

Cleopatra straightened, eyes wide. 'He will not have the men to destroy them, just hold them, as Achillas did to me, but…'

'But if the army can hold our reinforcements there long enough for Ganymedes main force to arrive from Alexandria, then he can obliterate our reinforcements at Pelusium with overwhelming numbers. Then there will be no more help coming for us and he can simply stroll back to Alexandria and wipe us out. By then our numbers will be the same, but his will have doubled once more. This city is unimportant now. The critical fight is going to be at Pelusium. We can sit here and watch them gradually thin out, or we can try and reach the reserves and turn the tide. A race. See?'

Cassius nodded. 'Gods, but if you're right and we don't get there in time, our reserves will be massacred. This place is now of no strategic value.'

Caesar looked back and forth between his officers, settling finally on Fronto. 'You're sure? Confident? Everything might rest upon this decision.'

Fronto nodded. 'It's what I would do, Caesar. On your more impulsive days it's what you would do, too. We're in a race but we haven't even put our shoes on and found the starting blocks, while the competition is already halfway to the first turn.'

The general rubbed his temple. 'Our legions can force march faster than their men, but they know this terrain much better. I think our speed advantage is negligible at best in the circumstances. Moreover, if we race there we arrive with exhausted men, a situation far from ideal.'

Brutus looked up from the table, a finger moving slowly from Pelusium to the coastline on the map. 'Ships.'

'What?'

'Send them by ship. The winds are no longer unfavourable. We can sweep east along the coast with ease.'

Cassius shook his head. 'Tiberius Nero still has more than half the fleet prowling the open sea and the river channels looking for the rest of Ganymedes' ships. We don't have enough vessels to carry the army, and it will take days to bring them all in.'

Brutus let a sly grin slide across his face. 'There are ships here for the taking. When we first got here, Fronto took the ships in the Great Harbour. Yes, he later burned them, but he initially took them, and without much difficulty. Now there's a sizeable fleet in the commercial harbour – the one that pinned our men on the Heptastadion – and the enemy forces in the city couldn't hold back an angry dog, let alone a Roman legion. We impound the vessels they left behind – bit of a mistake, that – add them to our own fleet and then ship the army to Pelusium.'

'Will they get there in time?' Pollio put in with an air of uncertainty.

Brutus made a waving motion with his hand.

'All things being equal, if we can secure the fleet today and get the army boarded, I think the ships could be at Nicopolis by nightfall. As long as they don't run into trouble, they'll be offshore at Pachamounis the night after, then Tamiathis, and finally Pelusium. With good captains you could squeeze an extra day out of that, but you have to allow for not all the ships being as fast as our warships.'

'And at best guess,' Cassius replied, 'that's one day less than a land army would take on the speed march. But they left half a day early. It's going to be tight.'

'Then we'd best get going,' Fronto said.

* * *

Fronto peered from the alleyway, the half-light of dawn illuminating the fort. His gaze was drawn inevitably to the corner of the wall from which he'd plummeted gracelessly into the harbour's waters, and he had to drag it back. There was no sign of life on the walls, but torches guttered, so someone was in there.

Carfulenus appeared next to him.

'Looks deserted.'

'It isn't, though. Someone is keeping the torches lit. It's a gamble. Either Ganymedes pulled out every man he could spare and abandoned the fort, which is what I lean towards, with just maybe half a dozen men keeping the gates shut and the torches lit. Or... he filled it with horrible surprises for us. I doubt he's had time, but he has a habit of such underhanded nastiness. It's a risk.'

'It's one we need to take, sir,' the centurion urged him.

'Agreed. Pass the word. No horns or shouting. Move out fast. Whistles only when we're on the dock. You know what to do. Two centuries to each ship.'

Carfulenus nodded and ducked back into the alley.

Moments later, men of the Sixth Legion poured from the streets around the recently contested Heptastadion fort and swarmed along the seafront beneath the walls of the fortress. It was eerie to Fronto. He'd had legions moving quietly before, but it never seemed quite right. Rome charged to war with loud and proud statements, not sneaking hither and thither. Around him, like a sea of ants, shadowy centuries of men poured through streets nominally controlled by the enemy, and into the commercial harbour.

They had not seen a single Aegyptian, though they had kept well clear of the enemy's defensive line, just in case.

Taking a deep breath as a signifer, struggling under the weight of his heavy standard, charged past, Fronto began to run along with his men. Out from the alley, amid the streams of legionaries, he pelted for the harbour. He had passed the gate of the Heptastadion fort before the enemy alarm went up. Someone halfway alert within the fort had noticed the army flooding past the walls, and was now shouting and waving a torch atop the rampart. He would be too late to make a difference. Already men from the legion were hurtling along the dock and making for boarding ramps.

The Aegyptian ships, largely wide-bottomed civilian merchants, were open to them. Each ship would have a small private guard aboard to prevent thieves and other local trouble from boarding uninvited, but half a dozen native toughs would be no match for the men of the legion.

As a horn call finally announced that something important was happening in the port, Fronto was already along the harbour side and choosing which ship he felt like being sick over the side of for the next few days. Something wide and flat and heavy and less given to bouncing around, he decided.

The ships were largely unmanned. Being civilian ships on the whole, their crews were ashore, with only a few guards aboard. As such there was little chance of any of them escaping the closing Roman grip.

Selecting a ship, Fronto followed a century of men up the boarding ramp. Two natives lay dead at the top, two more bodies floating in the water below, a fifth clutching his head and cowering by the rail as a legionary threatened him.

Behind the second century to board came the half dozen really important figures. Each unit had been assigned a man who could pilot the vessels, another who could keep a tune and four men who knew what to do with the many ropes and cleats. Without them, the Roman force would stand little chance of putting to sea.

The helmsman took his place as the piper stood by the mast. Two centuries of men threw themselves into the oar benches, while the remaining sailors loosed the ropes and pulled in the ramp. The last legionary to board pushed the injured native into the water, and in moments the pipes were issuing a rhythmic tune and the legionaries were undergoing on-the-job training as rowers.

There were an alarming few moments as the soldiers seemed unable to fall into a rhythm and the oars continually thumped and clacked into one another, threatening to break, but finally they found something like a rhythm and began to move.

Fronto took a deep breath as he looked this way and that across the harbour. There was as yet no sign of enemy interference, and most of the ships were pulling out into the water. They'd succeeded, and the ease with which they'd done so and the lack of interruption confirmed the situation. There were too few Aegyptians left in the city to contemplate fighting back.

Well, the Romans had acquired their secret weapon now.

The chase was on.

* * *

Off the coast of the delta, March 25th 47 BC

'What's that?' Galronus murmured, pointing from the rail.

Fronto lifted his green face. 'Probably vomit,' he grunted.

'It is beyond me how you can be so sick on calm water over such a short distance.'

'I could be sick floating in a bucket if I could fit. What is it?'

'Horseman,' Galronus said, pointing again.

Fronto followed his gaze and tried to spot the man. The morning light was still dim and vague on this, their second day out of Alexandria, and he had to squint and focus to make out any detail on the land, trying hard not to notice the water in between.

He could see nothing, but now the Rhodians around him were spotting something too.

Bloody Rhodians!

Once the fleet had been loaded, Fronto had planned to sail on the flat bottomed slow merchant he'd helped take, but Caesar had assigned his officers and had placed Fronto on a vessel of which he already had experience, with orders to try and keep the Rhodian contingent from doing anything unexpected and precipitous. Thus, rather than his stable, slow merchant, Fronto had found himself aboard the Chimaera once more, which knifed through the water like a race horse. Worse than that, a ship whose steersman seemed to enjoy throwing the ship into sharp turns to left and right every now and then, apparently for no better reason than to laugh as the Roman officer nominally in command ran across to the rail to deluge the waters with yet more stomach lining.

He ignored the Rhodians, concentrating.

Galronus had better eyes than him. Fronto could still see no rider.

'Are you sure?'

The Remi nodded. 'A small group. Can't tell whose, though.'

'Can you tell how many?'

There was a pause as Galronus made a headcount several times and confirmed his math.

'Six.'

257

'Not the enemy, then, I reckon. They'd either be large cavalry units or individual riders. Six is about right for a Roman scout patrol in enemy territory. Few enough to be subtle but enough to be a tough proposition for bandits or lone enemies.'

'Shall we signal the flagship?'

Fronto looked back along the rail. He couldn't even see Caesar's flagship. The Chimaera's captain liked to keep on the edge of the fleet and even the rest of the Rhodians were some distance back, the lunatic trierarch Julius Meleager happy to be way out in front.

'Let's confirm things first.' He turned and waved to Julius. 'How close to shore can you get?'

'Close enough for you to piss on land, Legate,' grinned the Rhodian.

'Do it. Get close to those riders,' he pointed in the direction he hoped they were, and finally spotted the shapes, wondering if it was possible for your eyes to age like the rest of you. Presumably. He could swear his eyesight wasn't as good as it used to be.

Still, he watched as they closed on the shoreline, where half a dozen horsemen sat on a bluff overlooking the water. If they *were* enemy riders then they could hardly miss the Roman fleet, but they had made no move to ride away with the tidings. As the ship came ever closer, Fronto could see that they were neither Roman nor Aegyptian. They wore white, hard-linen cuirasses, bronze greaves and helms with pteruges of green hanging from their shoulders, each man armed with a long, Greek-style blade. All had curly black beards, and the slightly olive umber look of the men of Anatolia.

Aeolians.

The reinforcements! What were they doing *here*, so far west of Pelusium? Had they managed to slip scouts past the enemy into the western delta?

'Slow,' he shouted to the trierarch. 'Stop, in fact.'

The Chimaera slid to a halt, the oars backwatering at pace, closer to the shore than Fronto would have dared to attempt, aware as he was of how much damage beaching the ship could do. As they bobbed, the Roman fleet approaching behind, one of the riders walked his horse forwards. Fronto glanced over his shoulder to see that the fleet was slowing, aware that something was happening, then turned again to the man on the shore.

'Identify yourselves,' Fronto bellowed to the riders.

'Theotimus of Astyra,' the rider shouted, 'Ilarch of the Astyra asthippoi of Pergamon.'

Fronto let out a relieved breath. Prince Mithridates had to be close, then.

'Identify *yourself*, Roman,' the man bellowed in turn.

'Marcus Falerius Fronto,' he replied, 'Legate of the Sixth Legion and lieutenant of the consul of Rome Gaius Julius Caesar, who follows in the flagship. What news? Is the prince thwarted at Pelusium?'

A momentary shiver of panic rippled through him. The idea suddenly struck him. What if he'd been wrong? What if the others had been right after all and the enemy had all met up inland somewhere? Even now they could be marching into Alexandria and fortifying the place against them.

'Pelusium?' snorted the rider. 'Your information is old, Lieutenant of Caesar. We assaulted the fortress of Pelusium days ago. Pelusium fell to the forces of Mithridates with great success, though after many casualties on both sides.'

'Pelusium fell?' Fronto felt his heart beat faster.

'Yes, Roman, and our army grows larger once more. The Jews of the Delta had proclaimed for Rome and the Queen of the Nilus and threw in their lot, fighting the enemy and encamping nearby. They have supplied and guided the army onwards. We are currently camped by the river some fifteen miles upstream, and the enemy are closing.'

The enemy. Then it still *was* a race…

'Where are they?'

'Not far away on the western edge of the river. My lord and his officers have decided to dig in rather than meet them head on, for scouts put their numbers at significantly larger than ours, bolstered by the forces that fled from Pelusium. Units such as mine have been dispatched to locate your army, Roman, in the hope that we can redress the balance in numbers.'

'Well you've found us,' Fronto said. 'Is the river navigable?'

Only for a short distance on this branch, due to sandbanks.'

'What numbers are we talking about on both sides?'

'Their force is estimated at in excess of twenty thousand. Ours is a little over eleven thousand.'

Fronto chewed his lip. Add the fleet contingent to that and the numbers would be close enough to par to make no odds. They had a *chance*. One chance, but they needed to get to Mithridates and his army before Ganymedes managed to deal with them.

'Ride for your camp. Tell the prince that we're coming. We'll sail upriver as far as the ships can and then disembark and force march the rest of the way. We shall be with you by sundown.'

The rider nodded his understanding and then turned and rode back across the bluff, gathered his men and disappeared inland. Fronto eyed the inlet of the river, one of the myriad branches of the Nilus, as it snaked off inland through the green fields and forests.

This was it. An end to the war at last. No more skulking in palaces or besieging buildings and harbours. They could meet Ganymedes in open ground and face him on *their* terms. And with the numbers close to even, they would win. With good morale, open ground and no disadvantage, the army of Rome was in its element. They could beat them now.

* * *

The Nilus river, March 25th 47 BC

The sun began to set as the lead elements of Caesar's force caught their first sight of the army of Mithridates, and a welcome sight it was. Like a strange eastern parody of a legionary camp, the fortified area was filled with tents in ordered rows, and pickets saluted the Romans as they passed along a raised causeway between well-tilled fields.

Fronto was recovering his colour at last and feeling considerably better on four legs than one keel, riding with the rest of Caesar's staff at the army's fore. He approved of the camp they approached, and the sight of it gave him heart. Mithridates and his officers clearly knew what they were doing.

At a command from the consul, the tribunes hurried about, giving out orders and sending the various units to places where there was still room for men to pitch camp, while the officers and their military escort made directly for the command tent at the centre, surrounded by officers' pavilions and displaying strange flags with which Fronto was unfamiliar.

As they approached, men in Aeolian armour that looked oddly similar to that of a Roman officer stepped out of the tent and threw out salutes of greeting, gesturing for the newly arrived Romans to enter. Respect shown in their movements, but without the usual deference. It seemed odd to Fronto, watching these officers treating Caesar like a foreign diplomat rather than fawning all over him, but one had to adjust one's perceptions sometimes. Caesar *was* a foreign diplomat here, and while Mithridates might have come to his aid at a summons, Caesar was but a Roman politician, while Mithridates was a prince.

The Roman officers dismounted and followed the Aeolians inside, into a spacious and lavish tent, filled with luxuries, yet the man on the throne at the far side resembled more a military commander than an extravagant prince.

'Caesar, well met,' Mithridates said with a warm smile, rising from his throne and striding across the tent before grasping the general's hand and pumping it up and down in a powerful grip. 'I was concerned we might not cross paths before one of us had to do battle with the pharaoh.'

Caesar laughed. 'We are indeed fortunate, Highness. We were bound for Pelusium, presuming you were held there.'

'Oh we were,' the prince smiled. 'For a number of days, in fact. In truth we might well still be there, but a number of local cities suddenly declared themselves our friends and denied the pharaoh's army support and supplies. It seems that Rome and Pergamon both are warmly regarded by the Jewish communities when compared with the pharaoh. With their lines of supply and communication hampered, the royal forces at Pelusium held out only briefly and then fled west to join with their pharaoh.'

Caesar nodded. 'So now the entire force of Ptolemy awaits us?'

'Quite. I fear it will still be a hard fight, Consul. My scouts tell me that his army is fortified some ten miles from here on the west bank of the Nilus. The river there is very much uncrossable and his eastern rampart therefore largely unassailable, barring a narrow strip of riverbank. To the south lies an area of swamp and mire, which defies any advance, and the northern approach is defended by a steep escarpment. Only the western angle is feasible, and that has been well fortified. I can only assume that the pharaoh has become aware that he has failed to prevent our combining forces and therefore is securing against our attack.'

'A wise move,' Caesar said seriously. 'Had he agreed to meet us in the open field, we would be a bull to his sheep. His army would have broken within an hour. Fortified, he forces us to play his game. Still, we can do so with confidence of victory, I believe. How, then do we approach, Highness? You have the advantage of having scouted the region.'

Mithridates shrugged.

'There is a native crossing point roughly halfway between us and the enemy position. If we wish to cross the Nilus, we must either travel back north to where you will most certainly have disembarked from your ships, or south almost twenty miles to a wide crossing, unless we tackle this one in between. Of course, the enemy will also know this, so the likelihood of our army getting that far unmolested is small, I would say.'

Caesar straightened. 'Yet we must do it. We finally have all our forces together, and with the entire enemy military gathered close by. Here is our chance to bring to a conclusion the Aegyptian issue, and we must not waste that opportunity. Are your army well-fed and well-rested, Highness?'

'As well as one could hope in this place. The Jewish communities have been most helpful.'

'Good. Then we move at first light. Time to end this.'

CHAPTER NINETEEN

The Nilus river, March 26th 47 BC

The Nilus river, March 26th 47 BC

It felt good. In *several* ways, in fact, it felt good. It felt good to be in the open countryside and able to plan and see for a distance, rather than being cooped up in a fortress made of buildings in the heart of one of the world's largest cities. And it felt good to be at the front of a massive force, comprised of legionaries, auxiliaries and the great and powerful professional army of Mithridates, rather than worrying about the chances of survival, cooped up with a small force staring out at a massively superior enemy.

It felt good.

Good enough even that the oppressive sticky heat of the delta, and the rivers of sweat running down him and sticking the tunic to his skin, was a small niggle. Best of all, the sea was a distant memory and his stomach had finally settled down. He had eaten properly this morning for the first time in days, and he felt all the stronger for it.

The army travelled in column, but it was a wide and strong column, not some long winding line of drawn out men awaiting easy ambush, for the lands of the delta were flat and easy and given over to agriculture. Many a farmer would curse all the nailed boot prints ruining his crops, but it was certainly easy going for the army.

Fronto had contemplated walking. In the old days he'd shunned horses on campaign, in those earlier years in Gaul. He'd walked with his men and let his horse travel at the rear. His knee still troubled him, though, and age brought with it an increasing desire for ease.

He reached down and ruffled Bucephalus' mane. It occurred to him that his faithful steed, once the horse of Longinus back in that first year of the war, was getting a little long in the tooth himself. He'd never really questioned how long horses lived, but he had a feeling it was perhaps two score years at most. Bucephalus must be an old man himself. Guilt struck him then about the pressure he must be putting on the old boy.

He glanced to his left, contemplating raising the subject with Galronus, but the sight of the Remi made him force down his maudlin age-based worries. Galronus was a decade younger than he, still lithe and in his prime. And the grin on his face had been there since they broke camp this morning. In fact, it had been there since the previous evening, even through sleep.

Following their initial meeting with the prince of Pergamon, there had been a long logistical discussion, during which a highlight had been the discovery that a unit of Germanic cavalry had made their way down from Syria alongside the army of Mithridates, bolstered by Galatians from Asia. Galronus had gone to see them almost straight away and had been in their company ever since, Caesar assigning him to their overall command, adding them to his existing Gallic cavalry. Given that they served under three different leaders, a single unifying commander had seemed prudent. Galronus was in his element now, back where he belonged: on a horse and leading other riders, somewhere where he could be effective, in flat, open country. It was what the Remi were born to do.

Fronto gazed back at the force behind him. He had elected to ride at the front with the horsemen – some eight hundred riders, all of Celtic blood despite their disparate origins, acting as both scouts and vanguard for the army. Behind them came the Sixth Cohorts of the Sixth, Twenty Seventh and Thirty Seventh legions, followed by the staff and the general, along with the prince of Pergamon.

Around and behind the rest of the officers rode the commanders' guards. The companion cavalry of Mithridates in their Tyrian purple and white, covered with gleaming bronze, were impressive, and their officer was almost as richly bedecked as the prince himself. In response, and in order not to be outdone, Salvius Cursor had had his praetorian cavalry spruce themselves up, drawing what fresh kit they needed from the baggage. Fronto smiled at the sight. Salvius was a different animal to Ingenuus, but he was just as focused in his own odd way.

Then, after the officers, came the bulk of the infantry, both Roman and Aeolian, with the baggage train following on, slaves amid the beasts, hauling gear, driving wagons and leading herds, and then a rear-guard of cavalry supplied by Mithridates. A solid army, altogether.

Fronto turned his attention once more to the land before them. They had moved several miles from the prince's camp in the morning sun, along the eastern bank of this particular branch of the Nilus, making for the known crossing point, and the terrain had continued easy and clear.

Something was happening now, though. Fronto frowned, peering into the distance, trying to make out details, though Galronus and the cavalry had clearly already seen it. The shapes coalesced into those of riders pelting back towards the army. The scouts.

Fronto felt a shiver of anticipation run through him. That had to mean the enemy had been sighted.

The scouts hurtled towards them, and as they approached, two thirds of their number rode on past, making for the general, the prince and their officers. The rest fell in alongside their fellows, horses and men alike lathered with sweat.

'Enemy sighted, sir,' one of them confirmed in a guttural German accent.

Galronus nodded. 'Details?'

'About half a mile ahead there's a tributary – the one we were expecting from the map. A narrow enough river flowing into the main channel, but with steep banks on both sides and no sign of the bridge we'd heard of. The Aegyptians have positioned an army on the far side. Looks like a large cavalry force and a small veteran unit of infantry armed with spears and shields.'

'Trouble?'

'It's going to be a total shit getting across the river,' the man replied without a trace of deference in his tone. 'The enemy don't worry me, but getting to them will be nasty.'

Fronto leaned across. 'Their choice of ground seems good, but not their choice of men.'

'How so, sir?'

'Spearmen can stop anyone getting up the far bank, yes, but what use will their horse be?'

The rider looked at him as though something odd had suddenly sprouted from his head. 'Sir?'

'Cavalry can hardly hold a riverbank, surely.'

The man threw a sidelong look at Galronus, who grinned and nodded. He then looked back at Fronto with creased brows. 'With respect, sir, I'm of the Boii. No greased-up, make-up wearing, bird-buggering Aegyptian with a spear is going to get in my way. Cut us loose and we'll *show* you what use the cavalry can be.'

'But you won't be able to get down and then up the steep banks.'

Again the man shared an insolent look with Galronus, who nodded once more. 'Take the horse and do your worst, Gauto.'

The Boii warrior grinned a wolfish grin and whooped. In moments the riders were peeling off and racing away to the east, without the need for horns or whistles or other signals. It sometimes surprised Fronto how a decade of serving under a Roman general and alongside the legions, even if only as mercenaries, had done little to change the tribal nature and habits of the cavalry, and he had to repeatedly remind himself that Galronus was the exception to the rule, rather than an example of it.

As he watched some five hundred horsemen racing off to the east, the rest remaining with the column, Fronto turned to his friend. 'Go on, then.'

'What?'

'You're twitching to go with them. I can see it. And you're their commander, anyway.'

Galronus looked for a moment as though he might argue, but then gave a bark of a laugh, saluted Fronto and turned his horse, racing off to catch up with his Germanic and Gallic men. Fronto turned in the saddle. The majority of those left with him in the column were Galatians from lands bordering those of Prince Mithridates, and he wondered whether the division between those who'd gone and those who stayed was because of that vague cultural divide.

As the column moved, Fronto and the horsemen slowed down to allow the gap with the commanders to close, the bulk of the horse having now departed. Fronto peered off to the east. The cavalry would presumably look for a way across the river somewhere upstream, then flank the enemy. If they managed to find a crossing, they might spring a nasty surprise. With half a mile to go and no loud signals given, it was unlikely the Aegyptians would know the horsemen had gone. Certainly with the well-irrigated farmland of the delta, the cavalry did not raise the huge dust cloud that they did on more parched ground to betray their movements.

As the Sixth Cohorts slowly caught up with them the thunder of hooves arose, and Fronto spotted the officers and commanders cantering along the sides of the column, surrounded by their personal guards, making for the head of the army in response to the tidings of the scouts. Caesar drew up alongside, eyes narrow.

'Our Remi friend and the cavalry?'

'Went east to find a crossing, General,' Fronto replied.

'My native advisors tell me that it is many miles to any reasonable cavalry crossing,' Caesar murmured.

'Thank the gods these aren't reasonable cavalry, then,' smiled Fronto. 'They'll find a way. I've yet to see the Germans miss a fight.'

Brutus barked out a laugh at that.

'We still need a way to get across for the rest of the army,' Cassius said. 'There used to be a bridge, apparently, and that was what we were making for, but the enemy have presumably brought that down. Given the number of men they've fielded on the far bank, even if the cavalry get across, they'll be massively outnumbered without infantry support.'

Fronto nodded. 'But if there *was* a bridge across then that means it's crossable. I have an idea.'

The army surged on, the commanders now at the fore, with men of their guards riding ahead to clear away any potential dangers. It seemed only moments later when the enemy came into sight. Off to the left lay a stand of tall old sycamore fig trees and acacia, and to the right the sluggish wide flow of this branch of the Nilus. Centrally they could see what Ganymedes had sent against them.

The veteran Aegyptian spearmen formed a solid wall on the far bank, four rows deep, cavalry sitting in ordered ranks behind them, the odd plume of an officer visible amid the lines and blocks. As a force it was considerably smaller than Caesar's army. To Ganymedes, it probably represented all he thought necessary to keep an enemy from crossing. Of course, they had little familiarity with Rome, and the ingenuity the legions' officers and engineers had shown, along with the experience they had gained during their time in Gaul, would give them an edge in situations like this.

'How wide would you say that is?' Cassius asked, gesturing ahead.

'Perhaps forty feet,' Hirtius mused.

'Closer to fifty,' Fronto corrected.

'And the banks are supposedly steep,' Cassius said again.

'Quite.'

'The far side is higher, I think. Could be trouble here.'

'Perhaps I could have my archers clear them?' Mithridates mused.

Caesar shook his head. 'It would be a waste, Highness. They would have to loose from a distance of perhaps sixty feet, and the enemy have large, solid shields. The vast quantity of ammunition you would use to make any real difference could leave us deficient when we encounter the rest of the enemy. The Aegyptians know this land. If they have not fielded archers against us, then they know this to be true.'

'Then what do we do?' Cassius muttered.

'We bridge the river,' Fronto said brightly.

All eyes turned to him.

He grinned. 'I'm not talking about sinking piles into the water and shaving planks under the eyes of the enemy. Even Pomponius and Mamurra couldn't build us a bridge quickly enough here. But a makeshift crossing would do. We only need to get sufficient men over quickly to get stuck into them.'

'What are you suggesting, Fronto?' Caesar asked, frowning.

The legate pointed off to the east as they slowed their horses to a gentle walk. 'Sycamores. Several dozen of them. Ignore the acacia, but those sycamores are old. Some of them have got to be fifty feet tall at least. Bring them down and take off the branches, then drop them across the water, and there you have it. A bridge.'

'It'll be difficult to keep balance,' Brutus said doubtfully. 'Rounded surfaces and at an upward slope too.'

Mithridates shook his head. 'Then, gentlemen, why not build a mound this side. The trees could be made level with the far bank.'

Caesar smiled and turned to Fronto. 'Well?'

'Give me half an hour.'

Driving his heels into Bucephalus' flanks, he wheeled and rode back along the line of men to the Sixth Cohorts. It was standard practice in marching order to place close to the front of the column, between the vanguard and the main force, a unit of engineers and pioneers, for at the end of a day's march it would be their duty to begin creating a marching camp, while the rest of the army pulled in and joined them. As such, the Sixth Cohort was filled with the best technical minds of the legion, as well as the biggest, strongest arms and backs.

None of these cohorts were carrying their poles hung with pack and equipment, for those were transported in the baggage train, allowing the pioneers to concentrate on their primary tasks, and three men in every four had a pick, shovel and mattock over their shoulders instead, the rest with surveying *groma* and other equipment.

Their senior centurions marched at the head of the Cohort, alongside a junior tribune from the Thirty Seventh, who looked a little older and considerably more natural in uniform than most of his ilk. Dropping into a walk alongside them and pointing off towards the stand of tall trees, Fronto explained his plan. The tribune, clearly a cut above the usual glory-hungry politicians' sons found in the role, sucked his teeth. 'It's feasible, sir, but it wouldn't take a lot of imagination or work among the enemy to mess it all up for us.'

Fronto frowned. 'Go on.'

'Well, sir, they only need to heave the logs about a bit and they'd tip our men off. If they can chuck water over the trunks, they'll make them slippery too. There's endless ways it could be made bloody awful for the men.'

The centurion beside him shook his head. 'A little extra work and we can stop them moving about anyway, sir. Nothing we can do if they sluice them down with water, but we can make them stable. Then it's down to the footing of the lads.'

The tribune nodded slowly, then looked up at Fronto. 'My advice, sir, is to send the Second Cohort of the Thirty Seventh over first once we've built it. Their officers are proud. Call them the "Mountain Goats" sir. Should have seen them at the Heptastadion. Up and over narrow ramparts in the blink of an eye. They're your men.'

Fronto grinned. Let's do it. Get to work. You lot deal with the trees and I'll get the ground level for you.

* * *

Less than a quarter of an hour had passed since they had come within sight of the enemy at the river, and Fronto had spoken to the engineers, and just half an hour in total since Galronus had ridden off with his cavalry.

The officers sat astride their mounts off to one side with their guards as the army continued to position itself, the baggage still arriving from the north, escorted by Mithridates' horsemen. Four cohorts were at work or preparing, the rest saving their energy for what was clearly to come.

The Second Cohort of the Thirty Seventh stood in solid lines, stripped of all unnecessary kit and ready to attack at the signal. The Sixth Cohort were hard at work as was evidenced by the sounds of sawing and chopping, planing and hammering from the copse of sycamores upstream, and by the occasional almighty crash as one of the larger trees suddenly disappeared from the canopy top. All the while, as the enemy watched them with a clear mix of trepidation and interest, two more cohorts worked with shovels, removing earth, rubble and turf from a field off to one side and ferrying it forward to the riverbank where they were rapidly constructing a mound, with a sloping ramp that would crest at a height equal to the far bank.

The Second Cohort, lined up with the ramp and twitching to move, waited.

Fronto had dismounted and stood nearby, far from the other senior officers, where he periodically stretched or dropped into a crouch, loosening his muscles. Ostensibly, to any other officer in view, he would be recovering from the ride, but the truth was that he too was preparing. And it was Fronto, who was renowned for roving about, so no one would question why he wasn't with the Sixth now.

The longer he had watched the preparations and seen the men waiting, the more he had become convinced that it was time to take a more active part in matters. Since the day they had tried to hold the harbour when Achillas had arrived in Alexandria, Fronto had stood at the rear. Occasionally he had been forced to defend himself, but rarely had he put himself in that place that had ever been his position of choice: in the midst of battle with his men.

He had grudgingly admitted to himself that he was not that same vital younger officer who had faced Ariovistus or the Nervii. Too many parts of him ached, and he ran out of breath quicker. His eyesight wasn't what it once was, either.

Perhaps that was what this was: a challenge to himself. A desperate need to prove that he wasn't past it all. But the more he had watched, the more he had recalled those early days in Gaul, sneaking along a riverbank with his men at Bibrax, storming bridges and attacking forts, and he couldn't help but see them as halcyon days.

He was going over the bridge with the Second Cohort. He hadn't told anyone yet, and the officer corps were far away, leaving him to his planning. But he'd removed anything he didn't need to fight with and had left them with Bucephalus, who had been walked back to the baggage.

He was determined.

He listened to the general murmur of the army as it waited, overlain with the sound of hard labour as men dug and shovelled earth, and adzed and shaped timber. He felt a sense of relief as he realised that the chopping and sawing had died down and almost out. All the trees they'd identified had been brought down and were now being tidied and prepared.

He cocked his head to one side. The decrease in the volume of their labours allowed a new sound to filter through the din.

A horn.

His gaze rose to the army across the water, trying to identify what had changed and what signal had been given, before realisation struck him. That had not been one of the strange hooming noises of the Aegyptian signallers, but a much more familiar sound.

His gaze slipped from the Aegyptians, who were looking equally alert and concerned, eyes sliding this way and that, and off to the east. Sure enough he spotted them quickly, now that he knew what to expect.

That had been the honk of a Gallic cavalry horn.

The blurred shape of a mass of distant horsemen was moving at an astonishing pace along the far bank, making for the ordered lines of the enemy. An explosion of panic suddenly burst out amid the Aegyptians. Fronto almost laughed as he watched officers bellowing out orders, half of which contradicted each other.

The line of spear men at the top of the far bank broke up to move, following an order to come about and face the threat of the cavalry approaching from the east, then became tangled and confused as other officers and signallers told them to remain where they were, as the cavalry behind them milled about in response to half a dozen different orders of their own.

This was the time. They had to move, or Galronus and his men would be trapped on the far side with a much larger opposition. He turned to the nearest centurion, who was overseeing the ramp, bellowing orders to his men.

'That'll have to do, Centurion. Pull your men back.'

The officer looked faintly offended. 'It's not finished sir. Not level.'

Fronto waved aside his protestations. 'We're out of time. Call them back into position.'

Leaving the centurion to it, he turned to find the nearest rider, who sat beside a cornicen, awaiting orders. 'Go and find the Sixth. Tell them…'

His voice trailed off as his gaze rose above the man and caught sight of the activity beyond.

'Never mind.'

The legion's engineers had appeared, trudging slowly but steadily from the tree line, hauling their new construction between them. Fronto stared. No matter how long he served alongside them, he never failed to be impressed by what legionary engineers could do with a vague brief, few resources and less than half an hour to work with.

What they carried resembled more than anything a giant version of a ship's boarding ramp. As they came closer they became aware of the cavalry approaching on the far bank and thus of the sudden urgency of their task, breaking into a rhythmic jog, accompanied by a breathless chant.

Fronto watched as they neared him, ogling the massive ramp. Formed of six wide trunks, they had been pegged together, holes drilled in them and wooden connectors, which they must have had ready beforehand, driven in to hold them together. Even as they ran with the construction, others of their unit ran alongside, throwing ropes back and forth, lashing the trunks together on the move.

'Get it in place,' Fronto yelled as they hurtled towards him.

They were going to be late to the banquet, he knew, but every moment counted now for the cavalry. Fingers twitching at the urgency of it all, he watched Galronus and his riders close on the enemy flank. Someone across the river seemed finally to have pulled together order among the Aegyptians, and the reserve infantry had been moved east to form a thin hedge of spear points facing the fresh danger, their own cavalry pulled back into a square now behind an L shape of infantry.

Galronus had seen the defensive formation, Fronto realised, for the riders split up, the bulk of them racing around to the south, still trying to flank the much larger enemy. The rest continued to race for that wall of spears, and Fronto winced, knowing full well that no horse willingly charged such a thing, and that what was about to happen could be a massacre.

As he watched, Fronto rubbed his eyes, wondering if they were getting worse, if they were playing tricks on him. For precious moments he was sure the entire German cavalry racing into battle on the far bank were gleaming like Noric steel, and as he realised why, he let out a disbelieving laugh.

They were soaked.

All of them, men and horses alike, were completely soaked. They had not been able to find a crossing, and so they had found another way. They had *swum* across. Fronto shook his head with a grin and promised to find the Boii officer Galronus had called Gauto later, and buy him a large drink.

If he survived.

He laughed again at the ingenuity and sheer crazed bravery of the German cavalry as he watched their response to the enemy's hedge of spears. They knew their horses wouldn't charge that line, and that if they did many of their prized mounts would die. And so, as they closed, the moment the horses became nervous, the men simply threw themselves from the saddle and drew their blades, hurtling on foot at the astonished Aegyptians while bellowing guttural war cries.

'How the hell did we ever beat them?' Fronto sighed, before having to grudgingly admit to himself that they might have beaten the German tribes more than once, but all they had done was knock the crazed bastards back for a time. The day they could be brought into the empire like the Gauls, gods help the rest of the world.

The Germans crashed into the shield wall, diving between the spears and stabbing, slashing and hacking at the natives. In moments they had driven several gaps in the wall, and Fronto had the fleeting notion that they were simply going to win the fight on their own. Then he shook off the fantasy as he took in all that was happening. The Germans had certainly made their mark and shaken the enemy, but the Aegyptian force was far from done. Indeed, unless they received support soon, every rider across there was going to be butchered. The shield wall along the river bank had not thinned out, though another reserve line from behind them had been moved. Those men were being brought to bear against the Germans, and the initial success of the dismounted tribesmen had been overcome. They were being pushed back, and now German bodies were falling, adding to the carpet of corpses. Moreover, the rest of the riders who had veered south to flank the enemy had met fierce resistance from the Aegyptian cavalry.

The butchery had begun.

He turned to watch the engineers, sweating and chanting, bearing the huge bridge forward, carrying it to the recently-created mound. As they began to stump up towards the crest, he turned to the Second Cohort, who stood tense, waiting.

'Hit them fast and strong. Our only hope to help the cavalry is to hit them hard enough to break them and gain us a foothold on the far bank. Don't stop once you cross. No careful formations and lines. Centurions, keep an eye on your units, each contubernium look to your mates. Form into whatever small units you need to to survive, but push your way in and kill the bastards.'

This received a roar of approval from the men.

The officers nearby peered at him for a moment, and then wrote him off as simply egging on his men. They thus didn't see him draw his sword and fall in beside a tall centurion with dark, hairy ape-like arms. The man looked at him with a frown.

'Shhh,' said Fronto, and grinned.

He watched, tense. The engineers reached the top of the mound, shuffling forwards with irritating slowness until their officer called a halt. The enemy watched, nervous, as men stepped back, away from the river, hauling on ropes. As they pulled, the men carrying the tree-trunk bridge moved slowly forwards and, as they did, the entire apparatus rose until it was near vertical, the men underneath struggling so hard to move forwards that they often cried out in pain.

It all happened at once, then. At a triple blast from the centurion's whistle, the men simply dropped the bridge, which hit the fresh mound so hard that the timbers sank deep into the earth. Then the men began to let out the ropes. Slowly, at first, then more and more, until another whistled signal came and they let go.

The tree trunk bridge hit the far bank hard, and the line of spearmen there scattered in panic, not wanting to find themselves crushed beneath its weight.

Fronto never heard the signal to advance, so all-encompassing was the noise around them, and suddenly found himself surging forwards with the men. He wondered briefly whether any of his fellow officers would spot him among the infantry. Then, amid the front runners, he was suddenly clambering up the mound at the fastest pace he could manage. He tried not to be disappointed and irritated by the fact that others overtook him, reminding himself that he was a generation older than every last one of them.

As he put his first foot on the logs of the bridge to cross, he wondered if this had been a terrible mistake. His legs wobbled as he tried to keep his footing, and he felt a sharp pain in his knee as he slid a little on the smooth, curved surface. Quickly, though, he regained his stability and began to hurry across, ignoring the throbbing of his knee.

With a roared oath to Nemesis and Fortuna both, he hurtled across, falling slightly further back as legionaries with catlike grace skittered past him. Still, as he reached the far bank he pushed his way past two small knots of men struggling with Aegyptian spear men, and forced his way into their midst.

An enemy soldier came into view, finishing off a fallen legionary with his spear, and the man only just managed to turn in time before Fronto was on him. The spear came round in the press and Fronto spun, sweeping down with his blade and hacking the shaft in two half way along. As the spear man recoiled, Fronto stepped forwards with a roar, raising the blade again. He slammed it into the man's neck, feeling it carve through muscle and sinew, twisted and pulled, the man falling away, screaming. Another white-tunic'd and chain-shirted Aegyptian appeared from somewhere, having abandoned his spear in the melee and drawn a blade. The man spotted Fronto and the panic on his face vanished in an instant, to be replaced by hunger, as he saw a Roman officer and realised what a prize Fronto was.

He leapt, sword thrusting, and Fronto almost died in that moment. As he tried to sidestep, his knee trembled and jarred, and he fell against another man. The sword that had been meant for his armpit instead slammed into the leather pteruges hanging from Fronto's cuirass and carved a deep gash along his left arm.

He cried out in pain but as the man, triumph in his eyes, drew back for another attack, Fronto brought his own sword down in a crossed slash. He couldn't kill the man through the chain shirt he wore, but it was enough. There was sufficient strength in the blow to snap ribs beneath the shirt and the Aegyptian fell back with a bellow of agony. Fronto righted himself, pushing away from the man he had fallen against. Putting a little weight on his left knee he stepped forwards, preparing to finish his opponent, but a casual stab from a nearby legionary did the job for him.

Fronto paused, heaving in a breath, hissing at the pain in his left arm and testing his tender knee, then straightened and looked for another opponent.

There wasn't one.

Staring, he realised that almost every figure he could see now was either a German or Gallic cavalryman or a soldier of the Thirty Seventh. Only a few Aegyptians remained, and only then because they were locked in deadly struggles. The rest had gone.

Staggering forwards into an open space, he tried to take stock.

The enemy were running. Cavalry and spearmen alike, they were hurtling south.

A legionary nearby shouted something derisive and made a rude gesture at the retreating Aegyptians, calling them cowards.

'If that's what we're facing,' someone laughed, 'then break out the victory crowns now.'

Fronto shook his head, though he did realise that he too was smiling.

'We might have beaten them back, but this was just a test. Just a hurdle to jump. And those men aren't gone from the conflict. Even now they're withdrawing across the river to join with the rest of their army. The big fight is still to come.'

'We'll still pound the bastards to snot, sir.'

Fronto laughed and rubbed his knee.

'I hope so, man. I hope so.'

CHAPTER TWENTY

Fronto reached round and touched his arm, wincing. The movements of the horse seemed to shake the wound open every few heartbeats, or at least that was how it felt. The medicus had assured him that it would begin to knit and heal in no time and that the cut was so clean and straight that there would be hardly a mark in the end, but to Fronto it still felt like an open chasm in his flesh.

Bucephalus walked steadily, once more alongside Galronus' horse at the head of the column. The general had suggested, rather blatantly, that Fronto might want to stay back with the officers. No one had reprimanded him for being part of the attack across the log bridge, but he could feel the disapproval radiating from the other officers, and when the others had been out of earshot briefly, Cassius had called him a 'bloody fool'. That at least had made him grin as he declined the offer of safety and rode to the van.

He wasn't grinning now, and the reason was only partially the pain in his bicep.

The rest was the Aegyptian army that lay ahead.

Reports of the defensive strength of their position had not been exaggerated. The fort they occupied would be a tough proposition for any army. Clearly this had once been a garrisoned fortress, though long since out of use, its thick mudbrick walls now cracked and ancient yet still strong. It would take a determined legionary to climb them, especially under a hail of missiles. The entire place was on a slight rise by the river, a huge, square monstrosity. To the south apparently lay a wide marsh that denied access for the Roman army. To the north, facing the approaching legions, Fronto could see a steep escarpment rising from the flat earth of the delta before even the walls began. To the west lay a gentle slope that constituted the most reasonable approach, yet was the strongest fortified. And to the east lay the river, with just a narrow strip of land separating fortress from water.

Clearly, the northern approach would be an insane proposal, and the southern marshes impossible for sufficient numbers. That left both east and west, each of which had been discussed by the officers on their approach. The west would be the most straightforward, but the best defended. To the east stood a dock on the river and a gate in the wall for access from the waterside. That had been an attractive option.

Until now.

He sucked his teeth and looked the scout in the eye. The man's gaze did not falter.

'How many?'

'I counted eight, sir.'

Eight warships. Damn it.

'And there's no hope of taking them down?'

'Not without ships of our own, sir. They're anchored mid-stream. They're bristling with men. I would guess that the fortress itself is not quite large enough for the royal army, and the excess have been pressed into secondary locations.'

Irritatingly dangerous ones, it would seem. For a moment, Fronto pondered how the enemy had managed to get ships here, when the Roman fleet couldn't reach this far upriver without grounding on mud banks. Still, he had been told that the entire delta region was a criss-crossing and winding network of interconnected branches of the river, along with a few man made canals. Probably the ships had come via another branch. He sighed. Where they came from was irrelevant. The fact was that they sat untouchable out in the water, and their presence made the riverside approach far less favourable. Attacking along that narrow strip of land under a barrage from the walls above would be hard enough, but to do so while being pounded with missiles from eight ships out in the water too would be horrendous.

'And this other fort? How defensive is that?'

The scout huffed. Fronto was asking for confirmation of things he'd already said in his initial report.

'It's an easier proposition than this one, sir. About the size of a vexillation camp for a single cohort. Mud brick walls, but with no natural defences. Houses maybe five hundred, with stabling.'

Fronto nodded. A second fortress, perhaps a quarter of a mile from the main one, off to the west, seemingly housing the cavalry, those men who had fled the last fight to return to the main force. The Caesarian army could attack from the west, but they would need to deal with the outlying cavalry fort first, which would give the enemy time to prepare and could at least slightly weaken the Roman force.

Sagging, he nodded to the scout and turned to Galronus. 'I'm going to consult Caesar.'

Gesturing back north, Fronto turned his horse and rode back along the line of cavalry with the small scout unit, racing the rumour, spreading by word of mouth along the line, that the Aegyptian navy had come to the enemy's aid. They reached the staff officers swiftly, and Caesar, Mithridates and the others pulled out to the side of the column to meet the riders.

'What news?' Caesar demanded. Fronto sat back and once again let the scout repeat his tidings, emphasising this time every bit of detail Fronto had drawn out of him. When he had finished, Caesar tapped his lip with a finger and turned to the prince of Pergamon.

'A tough nut, Highness. No approach feels adequate.'

Mithridates nodded. 'If the enemy are both prepared and spirited we will be forced to fight hard. I might humbly suggest that the only realistic advantage we can hope for is to inspire fear. We occupied a poor position by the previous river but the suddenness, unexpectedness and ferocity of our attack drove terror into enemy hearts and saw their resolve crumble. If that success could be repeated, then perhaps we might improve our chances.'

Caesar continued to tap his lip. 'Quite. Ferocity and unexpectedness: a powerful combination. Let us keep them off guard and unprepared. It is afternoon now, and any assault we launch runs the risk of continuing into the hours of darkness. Let the men rest and relax. We shall make camp within sight of their walls, where they might brood over our numbers, strength and confidence. Let them spend the evening and the night worrying over what we might do.'

'And what *shall* we do?' Mithridates enquired.

'At dawn, the centurions and your officers will have the entire army ready to move at a moment's notice. We shall launch our attack immediately, and without pause to dissemble the camp or pack the tents. This fight will end on the morrow and we shall not worry about leaving an abandoned camp thereafter.'

'But *where* do we attack?' Fronto mused. 'The riverside? Or do we take on the cavalry fort first and then the western slope? Or perhaps a division of forces?'

'*All* of this we shall achieve,' the consul said with an odd smile.

'Caesar?'

At dawn the army will answer the call, each man having broken his fast quietly in his tent, unseen by the enemy. At the horn's cadence, the army will advance at a fast march against the cavalry fort and overrun it.'

Cassius frowned. 'Caesar, there cannot be more than half a thousand cavalry in the fort. Twice that if they pack tightly. It will not take an army of twenty thousand men to overwhelm it.'

'Absolutely,' smiled the general. 'But the victory of such a huge force against such a minor one will be both swift and total. Let the enemy watch their external fort fall in mere heartbeats to an army that only moments earlier appeared to be abed. Imagine if you will the consternation and nerves this will spread among their number.'

Brutus smiled too now. 'It will certainly be a shock.'

'And we shall give them no time to rally. The very moment the cavalry fort falls, the army will divide. My lord prince, I propose a division of labour. Your force contains a number of cavalry and archers, as well as trained infantry. I suggest that your army marches upon the easier western slope, along with my cavalry, the Thirty Seventh and the depleted cohorts of the Twenty Seventh, where numbers will be crucial, and where both horse and bow might be of effect.'

Mithridates nodded. 'And the Sixth, Consul?'

Fronto waited, tense, listening carefully.

'The Sixth will assault the east, along the river side. It is a dangerous approach, but the strip of land is narrow and more suited to heavy infantry. Your assault,' he added, turning to Fronto, 'is considerably more difficult and destined almost certainly to fail. However, in pressing there you will force the enemy to divide their number. You should be able to draw sufficient defenders to the east to weaken the men facing us on the west, granting us adequate advantage to overcome them.'

'That's a bitter task, General,' Fronto said, reservedly.

'But an important one. It is a task I can only give to a veteran force with a history of such engagements. That describes both the Sixth and yourself, Fronto.'

Mithridates laughed. 'You are a wily fox, son of Venus. Gods be praised I am not your enemy. It shall be as you say. Our army will tackle the western slopes upon the fall of the fort.'

Fronto tried not to feel put upon. He'd been assigned the shitty end of the sponge stick, and they all knew it, but the idea was sound, as was the reasoning of assigning the Sixth.

'Good.' The consul turned to the rest of the staff. 'Fronto, Brutus can advise you on the most advantageous approach, given the enemy ships' capabilities. Cassius will command the reserve, which we will keep out of missile shot of the walls and ships. I shall remain with the command and guide the battle as best I can. For now, have the men make camp and be certain that they are in good spirits. Let the Aegyptians see them drink wine, eat hearty and sing songs of battle.'

* * *

The night was sultry, with the heat of the day still evident and the waters of the delta providing humidity. The camp seethed with life, more resembling a legion in garrison during winter months than an army on active campaign. The atmosphere was positive, almost festive, even. The only men not relaxing were the pickets watching the enemy fortress.

Fronto strolled between the tents until he found the First Cohort. He'd not got to know many of the officers from the Sixth personally, as he'd done with the Tenth in the old days. He'd not felt the same connection with this likely temporary command, after all. Yet now, facing the brutal task assigned them, he was regretting it. In such times, it was important to know the men upon whom success or failure might hinge.

 First he sought out the tribunes. The five junior ones were the usual chinless adolescents looking for a reputation to carry them into office in Rome. The *senior* tribune was a solid man, though. A career soldier looking to gain a position as a legate and therefore open to sound tactical thinking and a good link in the chain of command.

Having familiarised himself with the nominal commanders of the Sixth, he'd moved on to the senior centurion. Carfulenus he had fought alongside, of course, and had spoken to repeatedly since their arrival in Aegyptus, and yet he realised now that he still knew nothing about the man. Not even where he came from.

He found a soldier on guard at the centurion's tent, and with only the briefest of introductions was admitted. Upon entry, Fronto immediately formed a positive opinion of the man. The tent was missing many of the home comforts senior centurions tended to gather, resembling much more an ordinary soldier's accommodation, or Fronto's own, of course.

Carfulenus sat on the edge of his cot, buffing his sword's baldric and periodically taking a bite from the bread and sausage on the platter beside him. As Fronto entered, the centurion rose and saluted, placing his sword on the bed.

'Sir.'

Fronto nodded a greeting and motioned for the man to sit.

'You're familiar with the plan for tomorrow?'

Carfulenus nodded. 'Yes, sir.' He began to polish once more as he sat, and Fronto frowned.

'Don't you have a man to do that?'

'Somewhere,' the centurion smiled. 'One of the lads is always offering, but I'm from a family of modest means, sir. I'm not used to having people to perform such simple tasks. Besides, when you do it yourself, you know it's done right.'

Fronto grinned. He liked the man more with every encounter.

'I'm not worried about the cavalry fort,' the legate said, 'but the riverbank attack is going to be nasty, and I intend to keep as many men alive as possible. We've only got to draw their attention and keep them busy. Caesar and the prince will storm the camp then. Most of the Sixth will make an assault on the eastern river gate and wall and form a roof of shields. I want the First Cohort forming a wall against the ships, though. We have to hold off any barrage as much as possible.'

'That's not going to be easy, sir. Even disregarding arrows, there will be artillery.'

'Yes, I've been pondering that. This is why I want to keep the units on separate assignment. I want a new signal. Distribute spare whistles among your men. I want a whistle every ten or fifteen paces along the bank. The moment an artillery bolt or rock comes your way, I want a signal given, and the entire unit can open up a passage, stepping out of the way of the missile. It's far from foolproof, but it will save men. Can you do that?'

Carfulenus nodded. 'We'll need to take extra whistles from the Thirty Seventh, but it can be done.'

'Good.' Fronto leaned back. 'Keep your men alert and alive, Centurion. And keep an eye and an ear on me. The situation tomorrow is going to be very changeable and fluid, and I need every man ready to react at a moment's notice.'

Again Carfulenus nodded, and Fronto grinned. 'Now let me introduce you to a habit I learned from the tribes of Hispania. A fortifying of the spirits for coming war.' With a grin, he produced a small jar of wine.

Carfulenus smiled.

* * *

Fronto moved between the tents once more, watching the glow of dawn rapidly blossoming and driving back the indigo gloom. Scratching himself absently, he adjusted his helmet strap and rolled his shoulders. This was it.

Every tent flap displayed a collection of eager faces, fed and watered and battle-ready, waiting for the call.

He reached the camp gate just as the other staff officers drifted in. Caesar sat astride his white horse, red cloak bundled up ready to let loose. No point in alerting any watchful Aegyptian too soon. In moments they were ready.

'Every man knows his place?' the consul asked quietly.

Cassius nodded. 'All is set, Caesar.'

'Then let us begin. Jove and Mars watch over us.'

The gathered officers made votive motions to the sky and then finally Caesar turned to the nearest signaller, who held the general's red and gold "Taurus" vexillum. 'Give the signal.'

The flag waved once and Fronto watched the massive camp, impressed as always with the efficiency of the legions. The flag signal was picked up by others and then, as men began to pile from their tents ready for war, whistles started to blow. In heartbeats columns of legionaries were streaming between the tents and past the officers out into the open ground before the gate, units of the army of Pergamon keeping pace.

As soon as the First Cohort was assembled, a cornu hoomed and there was a clattering of swords on shield edges. The First Cohort of the Thirty Seventh began to jog. They had gone little more than a hundred paces when a light unit of speedy Aeolian spearmen caught up and fell in on their flank. Behind them two more cohorts from the Twenty Seventh formed and ran, with Mithridates' heavy infantry alongside and following on. Fronto turned to the other staff officers as the entire army moved out.

'See you either in Ptolemy's tent or in Elysium, gentlemen.'

Similar sentiments were shared by the others as Fronto jogged off to join the Sixth, who were almost formed up. A signifer held the reins of Bucephalus close to the knot of six tribunes, all of whom were mounted ready.

'Let's go.'

The ranks of the Sixth moved off in columns and Fronto mounted, the officers riding forward. As they moved, Fronto noted the activity that burst into life all across the landscape. While the Roman force moved at speed for the cavalry camp, accompanied by the vast army of the prince of Pergamon, a rumble like thunder from both sides announced the presence of the Roman and Aeolian horse. The Gallic and German cavalry raced along the left flank, with Galronus briefly visible at its head. The cavalry could do little in actually assaulting the fort, but their presence on the periphery to harry any stray enemies was a given.

The enemy were aware of the danger, now. Men flooded the walls of the royal fortress, preparing to fight off the massive army, peering into the growing light at this alarming and unexpectedly swift assault. It was only as it became clear that the Caesarian force was moving at a tangent, not aiming for the fortress, that their true goal became clear. Desperate horns honked from the fortress, sending warnings to the cavalry camp. In response, panicked signals arose from there. A gate opened as someone made the decision to flee to the safety of the main camp, but no horses emerged as a senior officer commanded the gate shut once more. Even had there been room for them in the main fortress, they would be unlikely to make it without meeting Galronus' howling Germans and the horsemen of Mithridates first.

Fronto nodded to the other officers and the seven of them began to move aside, riding to the periphery of the Roman force. The situation would require close attention when they moved on to the main fortress, but the centurions could handle this initial attack without great difficulty. As such, the Sixth's officers sat on the highest rise they could find with a small group of musicians, standard bearers and dispatch riders.

They observed from their vantage point. Just as some fool in the cavalry fort had made to open the gate and flee, before being overridden, another fool in the main fortress opened their west gate and a unit of light swordsmen began to emerge, rushing to the aid of the cavalry until desperate calls pulled them back inside and the gate was shut once more.

Ganymedes was not fool enough to risk his security to save the cavalry. They had to be sacrificed. Fronto approved of the sense of it, despite the loss of men, as he watched the Caesarian army flood up to the mudbrick walls of the smaller fort. No one was going to be able to prevent this. Within moments of reaching the walls, legionaries and provincial Asian units were pouring over the ramparts and into the fort. The Aegyptian cavalry put on a brave show, dismounted and using their longer swords and spears to try and hold back the tide, but even as Fronto watched, he could see the light of Aegyptian defiance winking out. As more and more Caesarian units poured into the fort, hacking and stabbing at their enemy, all without the howls of victory, just an eerie professional silence punctuated by orders or bellowed oaths, finally the enemy broke.

The gate that had been opened briefly was now swung back once more, and this time riders poured from it in desperation, pelting for the safety of the massive fortress on the riverside bluff. Perhaps thirty riders of the hundreds stationed therein made it out of the gate before the attacking infantry closed in and blocked it, penning their enemies while they butchered the trapped men.

Those thirty put heels to flanks and raced with every iota of speed they could manage for safety. It was clear from the start that few would make it. Galronus had been ready for them to break, and as they emerged and charged eastwards, the Caesarian cavalry fell on them without mercy. A dozen Aegyptians died within bowshot of their former fort, others being brought down one after another by the pursuing Gauls and Germans. Fronto counted six that escaped the cavalry alae, for Galronus was not foolish enough to follow them within arrow shot of the enemy fortress.

It was over in the blink of an eye. In less time than it took to dress for battle, the cavalry fort had fallen. The Caesarian forces, with precious few casualties, finished off the enemy, administering mercy kills to critically wounded allies, and swift executions to the remaining enemies, who'd hardly had the opportunity to surrender anyway.

A shrill blast signalled the end of the assault and immediately new signals were being given. Barely had the last kill been made before the army was on the move once more. Fronto took a deep breath.

'This is it.'

'Give the order, sir,' his senior tribune murmured, watching as the men of the Sixth flooded back out of the smaller fort's north and east gates, forming on the move to save both time and momentum, guided by the shouts and whistles of their centurions and the staves of their optios.

'This is where it gets dangerous,' he muttered. 'Let's move out.'

Following Fronto, the tribunes and the various signallers and riders trotted down the low slope and moved to intercept their troops before they closed on the enemy fortress. Fronto gave one last glance back at the second force, still assembling and rushing for the western slope of the fortress in the wake of the fleeing horsemen. Caesar, Cassius, Brutus, Salvius and the others would all be over there, all in the company of Mithridates of Pergamon, as they led the majority of the army at that accessible but well defended slope.

'Double time,' Fronto said. 'We need to get to the eastern ramparts quickly enough to pull men away from the western slope.' In response, the senior tribune issued orders to the signallers, and cornua blared out the sequence.

The Sixth suddenly burst into speed, a swift jog from the steady march, centurions' whistles urging them on. Fronto looked ahead, his heart beginning to pound. He could see the strip of shore now. There was perhaps room for ten men to move and act abreast between the water and the ramparts of the fortress. A terrible area to be trapped in. He could also see the Aegyptian ships now, anchored fifty paces out into the river, unreachable. Briefly, he contemplated sending men into the water to take the ships, but decided that it would be futile and a terrible waste of men. He had to stick to the plan and pray they could pull this off with as few casualties as possible.

'To your units,' he said to the others. 'But keep an eye on me.'

As the force pounded along the northern side of the fort towards the river, the officers among the units went to work, acting on Fronto's instructions, imparted in detail the evening before and hammered out with the officers.

The First Cohort filtered inwards, a four-man column becoming only three men wide. Similarly the eight-man column of legionaries from the other cohorts dropped to being six wide. At another signal, as they closed on the fortress, the units formed a loose testudo, tight enough to be protective but still loose enough to allow for a double time jog. Their timing was perfect, and the shields slammed into place above, just as arrows, darts, bullets and rocks began to hurtle out from the fortress walls. Here and there a man fell, but the bulk of the unit held steady as they passed from the northern rampart with the difficult escarpment, and into the narrow riverside access.

As they rounded that corner, the legion began to shift once more at yet another signal. While the bulk continued with a roof of shields, hurtling along under the walls, the First Cohort rearranged themselves. The leftmost line, along the shore, dropped their shields back to the side and hunched behind them as they jogged. The middle line and inner line kept theirs raised.

Moments later the ships began to loose their barrage. Arrows and darts thudded into shields. The first artillery shot was a disaster, the units still moving and unprepared to deal with it. A stone the size of a man's head ploughed into the shield wall, obliterating the front two legionaries and maiming the pair behind them, even crippling the two in the third line. A new signal picked the speed up once more and now the men were running, shields only loosely covering them. Getting into place was the critical thing now.

Fronto watched, nervous, from his vantage point a few hundred paces away. He almost cheered with relief when the men reached the position of the river gate and stopped. At least stationary they could better protect themselves from the incoming storm of missiles.

The men of the Sixth began to pound at the gate and walls, and Fronto watched a battering ram being manhandled into the throng, passed forwards under the roof of shields towards the gate where it could be employed. He chewed his lip. The chances of the gate falling were minimal. The enemy leaders were astute and would almost certainly have bolstered and blockaded the gate inside against just such an eventuality. But the fact was that they weren't here with the expectation of breaking in. They were to provide sufficient threat to drag enemy troops away from the *real* battle.

Finally fully in position, all the men fell silent, no more standard signals blaring out for fear of interrupting the all-important warnings. Then it began. Three blasts in sharp succession from somewhere near the northern end of the stretch, and the men around that whistle threw themselves left and right out of the way. The bolt that had thudded free of the shipboard ballista passed between the men and slammed into the mudbrick wall.

It was going to work.

Of course, that would only save *some* of them. Even as the first missile failed, another set of blasts rang out, and then another, as again and again the naval artillery loosed at the packed men on the bank. With the third shot, soldiers failed to get out of the way in time, and screaming ensued as men were pulverised. At the same time all manner of missiles, both forged and scavenged, were dropped from the walls and archers loosed in continual volleys from the ships. In the first fifty heartbeats few shields remained untouched, most displaying up to ten protruding arrow shafts. Some were pinned to men's arms or torsos, and rocks occasionally dropped between shields, crippling the soldiers beneath.

The gates were now being pounded with the tree-trunk ram in a steady rhythm, and soldiers were busy trying to mine a way into the ancient mud bricks, loosening them and pulling them away in the hope of forcing a hole in the wall. They would not live long enough to do so. Even as Fronto watched, the attrition rate was appalling. He couldn't *imagine* how bad it would have been, had he and his officers not taken what steps they could to minimize the damage.

This had damned well better be worth it.

His gaze slid up to the ramparts. Certainly the walls were thicker with men than they had been when he'd first looked, which suggested they had drawn defenders this way. The sun was now putting in a full appearance, and the mauve glow that had accompanied the fighting so far gradually slid into azure, becoming brighter and brighter.

Fronto turned his gaze upon the far side of the massive fortress, trying to identify what was happening over there, and as he did so something struck him. He paused, brow furrowed. With the increase in light his sight was becoming clearer and clearer. Was it possible?

His command position was on a slight rise for the added field of vision, but it was also a little too close to the ramparts to see much of the interior of the fort despite its slanted angle. He *thought*...

In a heartbeat, to the surprise of the signallers and couriers around him, he turned and raced his horse north, away from the fortress. Finding a spot several hundred paces further away with a low rise, he trotted up it, turned and shaded his eyes.

A smile rose to his lips.

There *was* a chance. The *enemy* had given them a chance. But who should take it? Not Fronto. He was too old for that sort of thing. And clearly not the tribunes. Carfulenus. He seemed solid, and was clearly used to leading them. It had to be him.

Grinning now, he gestured to his companions as he cantered back towards the fight. At the beckoning finger, a courier pulled in beside him.

'Sir?'

'Ride into that nightmare and find Centurion Carfulenus. Tell him that the *south* fortress wall is clear. Tell him to take a few centuries into the marsh quickly and seize that south gate.'

The man frowned, and Fronto pointed at the fortress. 'They've pulled so many men forward to hold against Mithridates and to batter us that they've left hardly anyone on the south wall. A few centuries could get through the swamp and take that wall, and once *they're* in, the rest will fall. Go, man.'

As the courier raced off, Fronto took a deep breath. There was a chance. Carfulenus would have to get to that gate and assault it before the enemy realised he was doing it, but if he could take that wall, they could secure it for others. The enemy would have to pull more men south to stop him, and that would give both the legions and the Aeolians the chance of breaking in.

He looked at the rapidly dwindling force on the riverbank, being mercilessly pounded with missiles. The battle could be won or lost in the next few moments.

CHAPTER TWENTY ONE

'**M**ake your family proud.'

Those had been the last words Decimus Carfulenus had heard from his father's lips when he had left Aquileia and signed on to join the legions. By a curse of timing he'd hit just the wrong moment for recruitment. A few years later the region would be seething with recruiters manning the legions Caesar would take into Gaul, and a few years earlier, recruiters were filling the ranks of Pompey's legions for the war against the king of Pontus. But when Carfulenus had been of the right age, the only men who were being sought were burly frontline pioneers to ship around the republic for depleted units.

Decimus Carfulenus had known he was no such type. Oh, he had no fear of combat, and was content to do his part, else why join the army, but he knew his strength to be a little lacking, while his mind was as sharp as a gladius point. He knew with unpleasant irony that he was perfectly suited to commanding a force of men, but the low rank of his birth made that extraordinarily unlikely.

They were not a rich family. They had no lineage like officers from the rank of tribune upwards, who could trace their family line back to the noble patricians who had ousted the kings of Rome centuries ago. Little more than a hundred years since, the Carfuleni had been tribal. Members of the Veneti. Now they were members of the plebeian order. Romans given Latin rights.`

And so he had done the only thing he could. The only way he could use his natural talent for the military. He had signed on as a clerk, given his ability with letters and numbers. Within days he had found himself on a ship, whisked away across the sea to Hispania and the arms of the Ninth Legion, serving under Caesar. He'd had a grand total of four months of honing his craft there, before an accident of geography and timing had left him as the senior soldier among a unit of thirty, in a tiny outpost during the revolt of the Lusitani.

When the howling tribesmen came for them, the men had gone entirely to pieces, and it had only been Carfulenus' calm demeanour and sensible brain that had managed to pull them together and beat a fighting retreat from there, back to the main body of the Ninth. Better still, they managed to pull out with all the supplies from the outpost intact and with the loss of only two men and three walking wounded.

When they had found the legion, the Ninth were already engaged against more of the natives, and it took the best part of a month to complete the suppression. In the aftermath, with the high number of casualties among the centurionate, as usual, Carfulenus had found himself nominated for a posting on the strength of his actions the previous month.

He had served as an optio for the next few years, learning the role well and quickly, achieving a level of popularity with others from both above and below. The first year of the war in Gaul had seen a stray blade remove much of his centurion's neck, and Carfulenus had been promoted in the field, selecting his successor as optio.

He had served throughout the campaign well, though never quite attaining dizzy enough heights to reach the notice of the legate or the general. It had only been on the invaliding out of the Primus Pilus of the Sixth, last year, that Carfulenus had suddenly found himself offered a move to a new legion, in the most prestigious command a man could have below the rank of tribune.

He had been nominally just about old enough by then to legitimately hold a centurion's vine stick.

A funny old career path.

He *had* made his family proud, though. Who knew, he might even be given a horse and land and raised to the equestrian order when he finally returned to Italia.

If he finally returned to Italia.

Because right now he was seriously questioning why he'd sought a military career at all, and not just gone into pottery like his father.

An arrow almost parted his hair, and two guilty-looking legionaries closed the gap in their shields over his head. Three shrill whistles blew and the source had been too close for comfort. In a heartbeat, men were scrambling away. The two legionaries forgot all about covering him with a shield and leapt for safety. Carfulenus instinctively threw himself forwards, slamming into the backs of other desperate men as a head-sized stone ball thrummed past, taking the leg clean off a man who'd not moved fast enough, before slamming into the base of the mud brick wall.

Carfulenus looked past the poor crippled sod who lay staring at his pulverised stump in horror, and noted sourly that the accidental strikes by the shipboard ballistae were actually having more effect on the walls than the soldiers trying to pull them apart.

He hoped their sacrifice here was giving the main army under Caesar and Mithridates the edge they needed. He hoped it would happen soon, too. The men of the Sixth were being annihilated here, between the constant barrage of missiles from the river and the endless rain of death from above. Estimates were impossible in the press, but the fact that with every breath he heard a new shriek of agony or saw a man disappear, crumpling under the weight of a dropped rock, suggested that the Roman force was not going to last long here. The only real question was whether they would panic, break and flee, or stay and die to a man.

'How goes the gate?' he bellowed, catching sight momentarily of the optio of the Fourth Cohort, Second Century. It was worth knowing every man of rank, he'd realised early, and his exceptional memory kept them all locked nicely away.

'Like hitting a pissing brick wall with a carrot, sir,' the man replied wearily.

'This is damned ridiculous.'

He stepped back and looked up, trying to gauge the number of men on the wall. His luck was holding, for he saw the heavy, lead-weighted dart coming at him in time to leap to the side, where a legionary helped steady him for just a moment before falling back to the dirt with an arrow pinned through his throat from side to side.

'Centurion?'

It took him a moment to realise someone was shouting him.

'Centurion Carfulenus!'

Turning a full circle, and leaping out of the way of a foot-long dart at the warning tweet of a whistle, he caught sight of a man in a red tunic with a leather satchel, making his way through the press. The man was unarmoured, and it was a miracle he'd made it thus far. As if to confirm that idea, an arrow clacked off Carfulenus' bronze cuirass, striking at a tight angle and deflected away into the press.

'Get down man. You'll get yourself killed. What are you doing here?'

The man took a deep, nervous breath, and Carfulenus couldn't really blame him as he tried to get the centurion between himself and the river. 'Fresh orders from Legate Fronto, sir.'

A tiny seed of guilt flowed through him at the name. Fronto had told him to keep an eye and an ear on him for any change, and he'd completely forgotten about the legate until now. But then no one in this carnage could be expected to keep popping up to see if his commander was waving at him.

'What is it?'

'The legate says that the south wall is clear. It... argh!'

A sling stone smacked into the courier's shoulder, smashing the bone and throwing him back. Carfulenus reached down and grabbed him, ignoring the yelp as he grasped the broken arm. 'Finish your message.'

The man winced. 'The legate says to take men into the marsh. Take the south wall.'

Carfulenus let the courier fall back and risked looking up again. There were men packed along the wall top. The idea of sloshing through a swamp with dozens of legionaries and attacking a different wall was far from appealing, but it didn't take much to realise that almost *anything* had to be better than this.

He looked this way and that and spotted another centurion's crest in the press.

'Geminus!'

The man glanced round.

'Gather your men and follow me.'

At a nod from the man, Carfulenus began to shove and pull his way through the press, heading south along the strip of land. During a brief pause at another whistle, while the men just in front threw themselves out of the way of an artillery shot, another centurion appeared.

'Modestus, follow me with your men.'

On he went, pushing and heaving, pausing for temporary disasters, climbing over the dead and ducking missiles, shouting every time he saw a centurion's crest. It was, in a way, a relief as he reached the southern edge of the struggle and the press thinned out. In another way, it was not. The press might have eased, but that simply left them more open to shots from the ships or the defenders on the wall top.

Carfulenus peered ahead, trying not to flinch at the various missiles still being cast their way. It looked even less inviting in person than it had in his head. It *appeared* to be pleasant, ankle deep grass with occasional tufts of harsher, taller reeds. But there were pools and streams winding across it. It *appeared* easy.

But he had been born and raised in Veneti lands at Aquileia, where swamps were common, and every boy and girl knew of the dangers. Where every boy and girl knew someone who had not come back from playing in the marshes. He turned and lurched back out of the way of a cast stone. He could see five centurions. At full complement that would mean almost four hundred men following him. Of course, they were at little more than half strength even before the battle. They would be lucky to number two hundred now.

'Sir, we're getting h… shit, that was close,' a centurion hissed as an arrow whirred past his shoulder.

'Into the marsh. Everyone. Now.'

And without pause, as two more legionaries went down to weapons cast from the wall, Carfulenus started to run, passing the slope of dry land beneath the wall and descending to where the channel of the Nilus had flooded and invaded the land to the south.

'Be bloody careful and stay with me,' he shouted as he disappeared suddenly up to the thighs in what had looked like solid turf.

Behind him, soldiers and officers alike lurched to a halt in horror as their commander half-vanished into the ground. Then Centurion Modestus simply changed his stance and his leg slid from under him into wet ground, forcing him to his knees as he tried to pull himself back up using his vine stick.

'Sir, that's crazy,' someone shouted. Carfulenus turned just in time to see two men sprout arrows and fall, gurgling, to the dusty ground.

'If you stay there, you're all dead,' he shouted pointedly, and began to half wade, half swim out away from the fortress to the south. He was aware as he went of the sounds of utter panic behind him.

'Control yourselves, you 'orrible bastards,' snapped another centurion, and Carfulenus turned.

'On the contrary. Be panicked. Shout and scream like tortured womenfolk if you wish. *Run* into the swamp. Let the enemy think you're on the run, then they'll forget about you.'

A sling stone plopped into the water nearby, and Carfulenus forged on urgently. Assuming the others were following, he pointed ahead. 'That thick vegetation is solid. Make for it.'

Another step and suddenly the ground disappeared beneath his feet. Struggling back, he managed to regain his footing and turned. Spotting an optio, he held out his hand. 'Give me your staff,'

The man did so, somewhat reluctantly, and Carfulenus began to move again, using the long staff to test the depth as he walked. It was slow going, but gradually they moved further and further from the fortress. He had been moving in peace for some time before he realised it. The missiles had stopped. They were out of reach of the ramparts and had been written off as fled by the defenders, who now concentrated on the rest of the Romans below them.

'To that line of thick reeds, then we move west and start to turn and come back,' he shouted back at the men labouring through the marsh behind him. 'Follow me precisely, try to hold on to the man in front. If anyone falls, grab them and help them back up. Centurions and optios, use your staffs and sticks to test the ground.' He laughed, perhaps a little too maniacally. 'We're going to get pretty wet, but those Aegyptians in the fortress aren't going to know what's hit them, when we get back.'

* * *

In all, it took almost half an hour by Carfulenus' reckoning before they neared the safety of dry land once more. They had fled deep into the marsh, away from the walls and to the cover of that line of vegetation. There, they had turned and moved inland from the river. It had been clear from such distance that the south wall had barely a man atop it, so sure were the Aegyptians about the inapproachability of that side. He could count three heads in total. There were probably more up there, but all attention would be focused east and west, where the brutal attacks were ongoing.

'Stay low and keep close to the reeds,' he said, loud enough that the next dozen or so men could hear, and pass word on along the snaking line of sodden legionaries. They had managed to pull closer together once they turned north again, for there were numerous reed beds and patches of vegetation which helped obscure them, and after the first quarter of an hour the men had swiftly acclimatised to the terrible marsh conditions. At least the water wasn't cold.

'Pass the word,' he said, as his foot found stronger ground with shallower water. He was almost out. 'Every man at that wall. I want all five centuries attacking, one point each. See the buttresses on the wall. Every third buttress gets one century of men. The mud brick should be easy enough to climb with the buttresses jutting, and there are few men to fight you back. As soon as you gain the wall, clear it for the rest.'

The message went back, relayed from man to man.

Carfulenus looked up. Still nothing. Either the men up there were half asleep, or, very likely, were so bored with looking out over empty marshland that they had given up and were instead intent on watching the battles happening at the other walls.

He almost laughed as he clambered up onto solid ground and, shivering, began to hurry up the slope to the base of the defences. There was a rise of perhaps four feet above the grass and dirt before reaching the base of the mudbrick wall. Unlike the fortress's other walls, this one had been braced with external buttresses, likely because of the erosive nature of the marsh below it. Climbing an old pitted mudbrick wall would be easier than Roman stonework anyway, but given the angle with the buttress it would be even more swift and simple.

Turning, he watched as his men clambered from the water and split into their centuries, shuffling along the wall into groups. The din of battle was enough to cover the muffled sounds of men sloshing up out of the water, and he was beginning to wonder if they might get inside before they were even noticed when the accident happened.

A legionary simply lost his footing and fell forwards into his comrade. The crash of metal with the collision might still have gone unnoticed had not both men cried out with shock and dismay.

Almost immediately a cry went up on the wall above them.

They had been discovered.

'Up!' he bellowed. 'Up the wall now. No quarter. Secure and hold.'

The legionaries were still struggling out of the water, but there were sufficient men here to constitute a reasonable assault already. Almost a hundred. Taking a deep breath, Carfulenus muttered a prayer to Minerva and then grinned. 'Hope you're proud, dad.'

Then he began to climb. As he felt for holds in the crumbled mud mortar, and his feet scrabbled, digging into pits, he laughed at the insanity of it all. He'd signed on as a clerk to avoid exactly this sort of madness, and look at him now.

There were distinctive sounds of panic, organisation and activity above now.

As he struggled upwards, Carfulenus looked this way and that. The men of all five centuries were swarming up the walls, faster and easier than him. He tried not to feel disappointed at that. He was brave enough, fast enough and strong enough, but these men were bulky front-liners and it had always been speed and wit that had marked out Carfulenus among his peers.

Somewhere off to his left, a man managed to reach the parapet. There were shouts and curses in both Latin and Aegyptian, and the sound of metal scraping on metal. Trying to concentrate on his own approach, he made sure to find the very best hand holds. He was high up now and a fall would likely break bones. He almost heaved a sigh of relief, as he glanced up and realised he was mere feet below the parapet. Then the worst happened. A figure appeared, looking over the edge, and then in a heartbeat a spear came out and over, jabbing down.

Carfulenus had no choice. He let go with his right hand and pulled his left foot from a crack, swinging out over emptiness, held by the tips of four fingers and by his toes, as the spear lanced down past him. He marvelled as a burly legionary who'd been climbing up below him snarled angrily and, keeping two feet and one hand wedged, released his right to wrap a grip around the neck of the spear and jerk hard.

The spear came out of the Aegyptian's hands, but not before pulling him out across the parapet and almost off the wall. The spear clattered away down to the ground, and Carfulenus was moving before he'd really considered the dangers of his decision. Not certain he could find those same handholds before he fell, he grasped the flailing arm of the Aegyptian hanging out over the edge and then let go with his left hand. Trusting to the gods, he began to climb the shouting warrior, using him as a human ladder, pulling himself up and over the top.

As the man cried out at the pain, Carfulenus dropped over the top and onto the rampart, then turned in a swift movement and pulled the man's leg upwards, pitching him out over the wall. He tried not to feel guilty, as that legionary who had probably just saved his life cursed the centurion for dropping a body on him.

Ripping his sword from its scabbard with a wet, sucking sound and half a gallon of marsh water and bits of weed, he glanced this way and that along the wall. There were less than a dozen men on the parapet. They had been taken by surprise. Even now they were realising the danger, though. Men were being pulled back from the fights to both east and west, making their way along the wall top to counter this fresh threat.

He sucked his teeth. They had the chance here and now, but if they lost impetus, they would end up bogged down and forced back. He couldn't just struggle to control this wall, or it would do little good. He had to keep pushing and break them. Taking another breath, he found two of the centurions who had clambered up now, fighting off the last of the wall's defenders.

'They're coming to retake the wall,' he bellowed. 'Look to the corners. Take your centuries and stop them getting any closer.'

The men saluted and began bellowing their own orders. In moments units of legionaries were running along the wall top and blockading the enemy relief, stopping them retaking the wall. That was only half the job, though. He looked out across the centre of the massive fortress.

The vast majority of the enemy were at the fortress's edge, either on the walls or below them, supporting their fellows. The bulk of the place consisted of hastily repaired wooden huts or tents and pavilions.

He smiled. Nothing put the shits up a fighting force than something unexpected going on behind them. As another centurion climbed over the edge onto the wall top, Carfulenus gestured to him, and then looked down over the lip. The other two centurions were on the way up.

'All other men not assigned, here's your orders. Get into the camp and cause chaos. Burn buildings and tents. Kill anyone you find, no matter who they are. Tip things over and throw them around. Get lost in the tent rows and cause havoc.'

With a grin, the newly arrived centurion saluted and began to lead his men to the nearest wall steps.

Carfulenus stretched and prepared himself. It was not over yet, but he had a feeling. This was right. This was going to work. Whirling his sword above his head, and with his gaze fixed on a glowing brazier nearby just begging to be tipped into the dry wooden doorway next to it, he laughed like a madman and ran into the fray.

* * *

Ptolemy Theos Philopator the Thirteenth, Mighty Warrior of Horus, He of the Two Ladies of Upper and Lower Aegyptus, Divine Beloved of Gold, Lord of Two Lands of Sedge and Bee, Father of the Black Land and son of Ra, chewed his nails nervously. His gaze snapped this way and that, taking in the carnage around him from his excellent commanding position at the northeast corner of the fortress.

How had it all gone so wrong? They'd had sufficient strength, they'd had the edge with terrain, a tough fortress and support from the warships in the river. Rome had nothing but their men. Yet they had come on like lions at gazelle. Fearless and implacable.

He should have known. He'd spent time among them in Alexandria, and if he thought about it now, he could have said in advance that there was no way the Romans were going to end this, other than either victorious or dead to a man.

He'd not wanted this. Oh, he wanted to *rule*, and he wanted that bitch Cleopatra out of the way, but he never wanted a war to do it. That wasn't the way of the Black Land. A phial of poison. A deadly serpent. A knife in the night. *That* was the way of the kings and queens of Aegyptus. Not damn great sieges and the like. Ganymedes was behind all this, and Arsinoë behind *him*.

And now it was all going wrong. Ptolemy knew little of war. He'd never drawn a sword in his life, and had overseen any important conflicts from the safety of a throne room a minimum of forty miles away. Yet he knew it was over. He could see it in the eyes of General Ganymedes, who stood nearby, bellowing at people and pointing this way and that. He could see it in the uncertain gaze of the officers. In the stance of the Gabiniani's commander. He could see it in the fear-sweat of the soldiers around them.

It had been bad enough facing Caesar's army when they had overrun the cavalry fort so easily and so swiftly. Then they had made the insane decision to attack along the riverbank too. Ganymedes had been certain that approach would be so costly the Romans would never try it. Then they did, and the general had had to pull away precious men from the main defences to help there. And just when they thought they had it under control, a small unit of Romans had emerged from the marshes to the south like strange swamp demons, and had swiftly gained control of the south rampart.

The Aegyptian command had responded well, but the Romans continued to respond better. Faster. Ganymedes had pulled yet more men from his defences to retake the south wall, but they were being held at the corners by small determined groups of legionaries, while the rest of the Roman dogs flooded into the fortress itself.

Now buildings were ablaze, and the precious reserves and slaves, and all those needed to support the massive army who had been cowering in the safety of the heart of the fort, were dying in droves by the blade, or worse still, trapped in burning buildings. Chaos ruled in the fortress, and Ptolemy could see no way they could realistically regain control now. Indeed, the realisation that the fortress was on the brink of collapse had redoubled the Roman efforts. Those men by the river bank had forced a hole through the mudbrick walls and were only being kept outside by throwing men at them in waves. And the Romans' Aeolian ally was forcing the western gate, on the brink of success.

They had lost, and they all knew it.

Ptolemy had made his decision even before he saw others doing the same. Soldiers, panic filling their very marrow, were dropping down from the walls, risking injury to escape this place that had begun as a sanctuary and now seemed destined to become a mausoleum. They were dropping over the very corner where the pharaoh watched, where they could attempt to flee to the north or, best of all, into the water where ships waited to spirit them away.

The pharaoh looked left and right. He was under no illusions that he was in control here. He was a prisoner of Ganymedes as much, if not more, than he'd been a prisoner of Caesar. The soldiers by his side were his jailors, not his 'protectors'. They were distracted. *Everyone* was distracted. The war was ending in chaos and oblivion. Who was going to care about him?

Without further pause, Ptolemy leapt forwards and jumped from the rampart, turning well and reaching out to grasp the parapet. With shouts of alarm his jailors came after him, but they could do little. He was hanging by his fingertips. The drop was perhaps forty feet in total, just over thirty from where he hung, but a good seven or eight feet of crumpled bodies lay down there to break the fall.

As hairy hands reached down to grab him, he let go.

Ptolemy, renegade king of Aegyptus, hit the cushion of the dead hard, but managed not to twist or break anything. He was forced to pause to recover, but was soon up and moving again. The knowledge that the fortress was lost must have been all consuming now, for men were throwing themselves from the walls with wild abandon, risking everything rather than be butchered or burned inside. He was one of hundreds, thousands even, fleeing the walls. The Romans were still clamouring to get in just fifty paces away, and some turned and shouted, pointing at the king.

He ignored them. They would never catch him. He sprinted from the dust down the bank and threw himself into the water. The nearest ship was already receiving survivors who had swum across. Ptolemy set his sights on it. As he swam, desperation giving way slowly to relief, he glanced back. He was immensely gratified to spot both Ganymedes and Arsinoë high on the walls, surrounded by Roman standards. Good. At least they could pay for this mess.

And when Rome had settled it all, Ptolemy would approach Caesar and explain that he had been an unwilling prisoner. That he had begged Caesar not to send him back. He could yet turn this to his advantage.

He would…

The crocodile came from nowhere.

One moment, Ptolemy Theos Philopator was a refugee king, with plans to regain his throne.

The next, he was food.

CHAPTER TWENTY TWO

Alexandria, Kalends of April 47 BC

Fronto felt for Carfulenus. The man had been instrumental in the victory at the Nilus, after all. Hades, but they might well not have won at all, had the centurion not achieved what had initially been deemed impossible by both sides. Certainly it seemed highly likely that the Sixth would now constitute just a handful of wounded men with a mangled eagle, had the centurion not caused destruction and panic within the heart of the enemy on an unprecedented scale.

And yet he was not here to revel in his victory, as the place for a centurion was with his legion, and so Carfulenus busily slogged through the delta a couple of days behind, while Fronto had joined the officers with the cavalry for their triumphant return to the city.

Fronto relished the memory of that victory.

The clash had swung in a single moment.

They had been fighting a battle that could go either way, with a huge scale of loss and bloodshed on both sides, the masses of Rome and Aeolia being held at the walls by the determined forces of Ganymedes. The Gabiniani in particular had been a thorn in Caesar's side, for their Roman origin gave them the same siegecraft that the general's own legions displayed, making the battle all the more difficult.

The army in its massive glory had been kept at the western ramparts, while the Sixth were busy being metaphorically pounded with a meat tenderiser between the east wall and the river. Then Fronto had seen the mistake in the enemy's organisation and had passed word to Carfulenus. It had taken perhaps a half hour of continued brutality, for all those men at the walls, for the centurion and his small unit of insurgents to make their way unnoticed through the marsh and assault the barely-defended south wall.

The moment they had crested the battlements, everything had changed, and it had changed quickly. Fronto and the others fighting their desperate fight outside hadn't seen or understood what was happening, of course. They had only seen the effect. Suddenly, columns of black roiling smoke had begun to curl up into the sky from the interior of the fortress. Then here and there the missile troops on the walls had begun to lift their barrage of the attackers, turning their bows, slings and darts on something unseen inside, instead.

It had not taken long then before panic set in. The enemy went to pieces very quickly, the Gabiniani the unit who held things together the longest. But with the enemy's attention so utterly divided, the main force at the western wall had easily managed to overcome the rampart and the gate.

The enemy had broken. With no hope of regaining control of their own fortress, the bulk of the men simply tried to flee the field. More than half the enemy force was composed of conscript units from distant parts of upper Aegyptus, who had no intention of being butchered or enslaved by a victorious Roman army for a lost cause, or of foreign allies or mercenaries, none of whom had any inclination to stick around.

Only the Gabiniani and a few small local units from the great city fought on, surrendering only at the very last in the heart of their own fortress. Those enemy soldiers who'd dropped over the walls and run for their lives invariably escaped. The Romans still had to fight on at that point and overcome the Gabiniani, and many of those fleeing were just farmers who would be needed for the grain supply in times of peace, after all.

What had happened to the king was a matter of some debate. Some said he was seen to drown in the river, others that he made it to a ship which then simply sank under the weight of refugees. This last was possible. That very fate had struck three of the eight ships after all. Every account of eyewitnesses, whatever they said, uniformly involved the death of Ptolemy the Thirteenth.

Without the evidence of a body, Fronto would never be certain that the young idiot hadn't escaped, but it didn't really matter. If he ever put in an appearance, he would gain no support. His sister would now be the uncontested ruler of Aegyptus. The army and the country entire would bow to her. Nobody would support the failed king.

And the really dangerous leaders of the enemy had been captured. Princess Arsinoë had been taken by men of the Twenty Seventh atop the walls, where she claimed to have been attempting to surrender to Rome anyway, wishing to help them bring down the general who had deposed her. Her wiles came to nothing. She had been chained like a common slave and added to the column bound for Alexandria.

Ganymedes had fought to the last, and when it had become clear he had lost, and he found himself at the mercy of the victorious Romans, he had spat hatred and curses at them, and then raked his dagger across his own throat before anyone could stop him.

All that had remained was the mopping up, securing of prisoners and burial of the dead. The officers had spent one further night there, overseeing it all, before departing and leaving it to the low-rankers.

Alone among the enemy, the Gabiniani had been treated differently. As Roman citizens, they could not be taken as slaves, and no officer, no matter that they had fought on the other side, had any desire to execute so many of their countrymen after years of civil war. Everyone had seen enough of Roman bodies, after all. When the leader of the Gabiniani had lowered his weapon and pledged to take an oath of allegiance to the victors, that solution had been accepted by all parties.

The war was over.

The following day Caesar and Mithridates, along with the senior officers of both armies, had begun the journey back to Alexandria by the fastest of land routes, accompanied by cavalry units. All along the return trip they found evidence of check points, outposts and depots that had until very recently been manned by Aegyptian soldiers, but had been abandoned by the time the Romans arrived. Tidings of the victory had apparently raced across the delta with far more speed than any cavalry unit.

Now, as they crossed the dusty Plain of Eleusus, and approached the Canopian Gate, it became abundantly clear that the tidings had long since hit the city. Allowing for the fact that the news probably moved a day faster than the cavalry, and that they had remained by the Nilus for one day after the fall of the Fortress, the city had likely had just less than two days between discovering that Caesar had overcome the Aegyptian army, and his triumphant return to the city.

The people had worked hard.

The last time Fronto had seen the Canopian Gate, in the middle of the previous month, it had been awful, and with the small skeleton force left behind, they had likely done little to improve it. The gate had been left broken and open, for Ganymedes' men had controlled the land both within and without, and it was easier to move supplies through it without rebuilding. The walls and towers had been battered and damaged, scarred and blackened. Beyond that, the wide thoroughfare of Canopus Street had been a nightmare of broken stone, piles of refuse, pits and holes and rubble, the worst of it covered over with temporary plank bridges.

The sight that greeted the travellers suggested that the people of Alexandria, both pro- and formerly anti-Roman, had worked together at incredible pace to rebuild. The walls and gate were as new, festooned with flowers and displaying hanging banners, bearing the eagle of the house of Ptolemy and the golden bull of the Julii. It had an oddly festive look.

The street beyond had been repaired. In truth it had been a very quick bodge job done by local labourers, and any legionary engineer would have a fit if his men had carried out such work, but for locals short on time and resources, it was still impressive. The buildings along the street had been hung with flowers and drapes.

As the column, with the officers at its head, approached the gate, they had seen the populace filling side streets in droves, held back by men that looked like a combination of the palace guard and the legionaries that had been left as a tiny skeleton force in the palace. They were cheering, in Latin, in Greek, in Aegyptian, even in Aramaic. Fronto smiled, taken as always by humanity's adaptability. Without a doubt there were men standing there, and hailing the great conquerors as saviours and liberators, who just two days ago had been part of the force left behind to pin the Romans in.

His emotions upon first sight of the next scene were more complex and a little darker. Some two hundred paces down the Canopus Street sat a golden throne surrounded by palm leaves and a crowd of courtiers and soldiers. Cleopatra, undisputed queen of Aegyptus, sat upon it, smiling at the new arrivals. Men in rich clothing, some of them certainly military commanders, stood to the sides.

The Roman officers closed on the throne, the cavalry behind them beginning to filter off and secure the city around them. Caesar brought his steed to a halt before the throne, his eyes almost level with the queen's, due to the carefully measured height of the seat's pedestal.

Cleopatra bowed her head slightly. Caesar did the same. Fronto failed to show any deference. His eyes had fallen upon the clear rounding of the queen's belly, now perhaps halfway through carrying the child. The sight brought an unwanted tic to his eyelid.

'Greetings, Caesar, consul of Rome and friend of the House of Ptolemy.'

Very good friend, Fronto thought acidly, still looking at the pregnant bulge before finally tearing his gaze from it.

'Cleopatra, queen of Aegyptus,' Caesar replied with a warm smile.

Fronto listened as the queen and the consul lauded one another. He vaguely heard her telling him how the city had come out with cheers in her support, when it was said that the pretenders were dead and Ganymedes defeated. He heard the officers there, clearly the surviving opposition in the city, telling Caesar how they had pledged to serve the queen and offered Rome their unconditional surrender. Various weird religious items that seemed to be important to the Aegyptians were given to Caesar in some odd symbolic ceremony. Fronto only vaguely heard the rest...

...because he could feel wave after wave of bitterness and disapproval battering them from his left. He didn't need to turn to see the source, for he knew damn well who it was.

Cassius.

Formality finally dealt with, they passed the various parts of the city that had been bastions of one side or another and arrived at the palace. At the first opportunity, Fronto found an excuse to slip away to his room, which was largely how he'd left it, if a little cleaner, though some interfering soul had organised his things and folded the clothing. Shoving them roughly aside into a creased heap, he sank onto the bed and opened the cabinet beside it. To his relief the wine was still there, and so was the cup. That same helpful soul, undoubtedly, had placed a large ewer of cold water on the tray above the cabinet. Though it was almost certainly good water, Fronto eyed it suspiciously and poured his wine neat. Not only had there been months of dangerous water in the palace, the ever present danger of poison probably had not yet passed.

He sat there in silence, sipping the wine.

'Here's to a settled Aegyptus,' he said to the empty air, holding up his cup in a toast.

'Settled under a whore,' said an unwelcome voice in reply.

Fronto looked up wearily to see Cassius in the doorway. 'Unpleasant choice of word,' he noted.

'What else do I call a woman who sells her body to a foreign power to secure her own advancement? Especially one who was technically married.'

'So is he,' Fronto replied, and immediately regretted it.

'Well it's over, Fronto, for good or ill. The question now is what will Caesar do? Will he lay down his imperium and try to heal the republic? Or will he take his Aegyptian queen and try to found a new monarchy for Rome?'

'Cassius, I've fought a battle and ridden scores of miles over the last few days. I'm tired. Can we not do this now?'

'If not now, then when?'

'Do you never stop pushing?'

'Not when the republic is at stake,' Cassius sighed. 'I fear the influence of this oriental witch. She is a queen with her hooks in Caesar. I fear it is only a matter of time until he sees himself as a king. He's looking far too comfortable in the role of a Ptolemaic monarch these days.'

'The war isn't over yet, Cassius.'

'For me it is.'

'What?'

The dark-haired, serious officer leaned against the door frame. 'If there are enemies of the republic to deal with, then I shall do so without complaint, but we are at a turning point now. Pompey is gone, and his support is fragmented. The republic can be put to rights now with speech and negotiation. No more citizens need to die.'

Fronto shook his head. 'Cato remains in Africa with plenty of support, both military and political. Afranius, the young Pompey, Petreius, Attius, and of course Scipio. As long as they remain in strength, they will never agree terms.'

'Don't be naïve, Fronto. All men have their price, and I fear theirs is surprisingly low. No one wants this war to drag on. I know these men. They can be brought to terms, as long as Caesar is willing to compromise.'

'Oddly, it's one thing he's very good at,' Fronto agreed. 'For a politician and a general, he can be quite generous and merciful. But there is yet an impediment. Now that Pompey's gone men like Scipio may be in charge, but there is one man there who will continue to rally the enemy and who will never submit. And while Titus Labienus stands against Caesar, others will join him.'

'Didn't Labienus used to be your friend?'

'He was,' Fronto said. 'He was always a good man. A great commander and a noble man. But he is also totally inflexible. He set himself against Caesar, and Caesar will never forgive that. Not from the man who was once his right hand. Those two cannot be reconciled. There will be fighting as long as Labienus stands. The war is not over, Cassius.'

'For me it is,' he repeated. 'As I said, I will fight Rome's enemies, but I will fight no more Romans. If Caesar insists on pursuing victory without the hope for a negotiated peace, I will not be a part of it.'

'But you won't stand against him?' Fronto urged.

'Not now. Not as long as he remains a son of the republic. Should that change, I cannot say what I might do.'

Fronto shivered at the tone in the man's voice, remembering the very same tone from two other conversations in his life, both concerning the consul: the dying breaths of his brother-in-law in Hispania, and the fallen officer Paetus, pledging revenge on Caesar. The consul was slowly but surely racking up a worrying collection of enemies. Gods willing Cassius could yet be kept from that list.

'Anyway, I came to tell you,' Cassius said in a lighter tone, 'that there is to be a banquet tonight to celebrate the restoration of the queen to the throne. You slipped away before it was announced. Attendance is "expected".'

'You tried to cry off, then?'

Cassius barked a humourless laugh. 'See you there.'

* * *

Alexandria, late May 47 BC

Fronto spotted Cassius on his way to the meeting and swiftly backtracked, finding another corridor. The last thing he wanted was another bitter lecture on the importance of the republic from the man. He liked Cassius, and certainly respected his ideals, but there came a time when it all became repetitive noise. And almost two months of idleness in the city had done little to improve that.

Some of the officers, men like Hirtius and Salvius, itched to move on to Africa and put an end to the war. Others, like Cassius, believed that Rome's job here was done, and that a peaceful solution could be found, that a return to Rome was now the way.

Caesar was determined to stay for now, though. Reasons were cited, and they were all good reasons. The country had suffered a year of war, and the disruption to the infrastructure had been dreadful. The presence of Roman legions full of engineers held the promise of getting the country back on its feet much faster than without. And in return for the military helping put Aegyptus right, the queen had pledged grain and gold for the republic. Besides, with the cessation of hostilities, the city was once more a hub for produce, and the legions were living well, better than they had done for half a year, so none of the common soldiery was complaining.

And throughout the days that had followed the victory at the Nilus, Caesar and his officers had aided the queen's government in removing anyone who posed a continuing threat or stood against her, securing their army and reorganising it under new officers of certain loyalty.

Plus, of course, it took time to recover supplies and call in all the ships of the fleet.

There were many very good reasons to stay.

And only one that no one mentioned.

The queen's condition became more and more pronounced as the days wore on, and it was the private view of all concerned that Caesar had no intention of leaving the country until his offspring was born. In a way, Fronto could understand. The man had never had a son, and celebrated only one child through three marriages. Moreover, Julia, too, had died a few years ago. Oh, the consul still had family, and Fronto had seen how close he had been at times with his precocious great nephew Octavian, but the notion that he might sire an offspring here, and soon, would be a central factor in everything he now did.

How that ate away at Cassius, Fronto could see every day.

Nothing had annoyed the man as much, though, as the triumph. Cassius had been set against it in conversation with all others, though he had at least learned now to keep his mouth shut in the presence of the queen and the consul. But he had almost exploded holding in his opinions as the triumph was planned. A triumph, he had spat in private, was held in *Rome*. It was voted by the *senate*. And it was *only* given when deserved. For Caesar to vote himself and his bitch a triumph in this godsforsaken latrine of a country – Cassius' words – was unacceptable.

Yet he had stayed and frowned and sneered throughout, as the consul and the queen, with their retinues and armies, had paraded through Aegyptus on vast, luxurious barges. They had sailed upriver as far as Memphis to the adulation of the people, where they gathered the youngest of the siblings, yet another Ptolemy. Their captives were paraded in chains along the bank, including the princess Arsinoë. When it was finally over, and the ships deposited them all back in Alexandria, the decision had been made about the younger princess' fate. Despite Cleopatra's demands that she be executed, the consul sent her with a solid military escort aboard a ship for Ephesus, where she was to spend the rest of her life in the sisterhood of the temple of Artemis.

None of it did anything to diminish Cassius' rantings, and Fronto had begun to avoid him as far as possible.

The meetings of the officers that had been held every market cycle had become little more than civilian planning meetings, deciding how best the Roman forces based here could improve matters for the locals and their queen. The meetings had, in fact, become so mundane and humdrum that many officers had stopped attending regularly, which was why it seemed so worrying and important that the entire officer corps had been summoned to today's gathering.

There had to be news of import.

Couriers came in every now and then from Rome or Syria, or other odd locations, including Pergamon since the prince had taken his army and departed. It was usually dismal news, too, but nothing enough to stir Caesar from his intention to stay in Alexandria.

Fronto entered the room and found somewhere to stand safely far away from Cassius, awaiting the last of the invitees. Once Salvius Cursor nodded to show he was the last and closed the door behind him, Caesar straightened behind his table. He picked up a scroll tube and tapped it meaningfully, then indicated another lying nearby.

'Gentlemen, we are presented with a troubling quandary.'

A wave of uncertainty washed through the room. It had been so long since anything important had happened, it seemed strange now. Caesar looked around the room, then picked up the leather tubes, one in each hand.

'Neither of these missives represents Aegyptus, where we reside and where in the perfect world we would continue to do so into the winter, allowing full settlement of this client state into the position we require, and securing the queen as our link with it. Neither, equally, represents Africa, where Cato now gathers our enemies, creating a redoubt against us, filled with men of military strength and intelligence. Both of those are places where our presence is required in the best situation. Neither of those is one of the options now upon the table.'

He waved the scroll case in his right hand.

'Rome. Tidings from Antonius are far from encouraging. It is one thing to have enemies gathering in Africa, at the edge of empire, but it seems that Rome begins to seethe once more. The decision to confirm my dictatorship going onwards to deal with the continuing threat, it appears, was not universally popular, and Antonius compounding it, by extending his own position as Master of the Horse, has enraged many.'

Fronto could imagine it well. It would be seen as an attempt to extend personal power, especially as he seemed to be dallying in Aegyptus and not dealing with that threat for which the dictatorship had been conferred.

'Moreover, Cornelius Dolabella, along with Pollio and Trebellus, have been making trouble, attempting to secure the cancellation of debts owed. Had I been present, perhaps I might have managed to play down the situation, but unfortunately Antonius is a man of action, and charisma is no replacement for political wit. His rather heavy-handed approach did more than just fail to put an end to their trouble; it exacerbated it, and has driven many a senator to their side. Senators who owe their career and wealth to me alone are becoming my naysayers.'

His voice had become bitter. This was not good news, and they all knew it. Left alone, Rome would fester and more and more voices would be raised against the consul. He needed to be there. Cassius had been right about that, at least. And Antonius might be able to persuade people of many things with his glib tongue, but he also had a temper, which worked against him in political circles as much as his charisma worked for him.

'Finally, there seems to be trouble among those legions we sent back to Italia after Dyrrachium and Pharsalus. A triumph is seemingly expected in Rome, and those legions who fought so hard in Achaea wish to be publically recognised. It seems that our little display here for the benefit of the queen has been seen as an affront by many an officer and soldier who fought at Pharsalus.'

Fronto winced, turning to look at Cassius. The man's face was a picture as he bit down on all the 'I told you so's he'd built up over the weeks of complaining about that lavish triumph on the barges. Cassius looked as though he might burst at any moment and shower them all with anger and bile. How he managed to remain silent, Fronto could never guess.

Caesar sighed. 'Rome, you see, demands my presence, and the continuing support of my own legions requires us.'

'And the other scroll, Caesar?' Hirtius muttered, pointing.

Caesar looked at his left hand and gently shook its contents.

'The only reason we are not already planning the journey to Rome. The news that might be considered more urgent.'

There was a tense silence, all breath held as they waited.

'Pharnaces the Second. The situation in the east continues in decline, though now at a sharp angle. Domitius Calvinus, along with several of Rome's allies and clients, has been defeated rather disastrously and fled back to Syria to lick his wounds. While Calvinus simmers in Tarsus, Pharnaces rolls over the entire east in a war of conquest. Styling himself the king of Pontus, he appears to be trying to pull together all the territories that Pontus once held.'

There was a collective intake of breath. Such a move, way beyond defeating Calvinus, was a direct challenge to Rome.

'Yes,' Caesar said. 'I can see by your faces that you understand the importance of this. Pharnaces has seized large areas of Cappadocia and Armenia, parts of Syria and other local states. He has bludgeoned the allies of Rome, overrun our loyal client kings, and even seized cities that belong to the republic. Left unchecked, which it seems he is since Calvinus' defeat, we may be watching the rise of a new empire in the east.'

Cassius finally spoke, and Fronto was impressed at how controlled he sounded.

'Then you must go east, Caesar.'

'It is a difficult decision,' the consul replied, with uncharacteristic uncertainty.

'No, Consul, it is not. Not for the man made dictator for the safety of the republic.'

'Oh?' Caesar seemed genuinely interested.

'Of course. Rome displays troubles and political difficulties, and the legions feel ignored and disenfranchised. But these are all affronts to you personally. They are matters that concern your place in the republic. The invasion of Cappadocia is a challenge *to* that republic by an enemy of Rome. That automatically takes precedence. That is of far greater import. If you cannot see that, Caesar, then you do not deserve the imperium of dictatorship that has been granted to you.'

There was a shocked silence, even from Fronto. Few people had ever been so brazen and near insulting to the general. Oh, Fronto had, but only in private. This was *public*. Cassius had upbraided his own commander in front of everyone.

Eyes, nervous and twitchy, slid from the general to Cassius and back, awaiting the response.

Caesar stood silent and still, his arms gradually lowering until the scroll cases touched the table.

'Cassius,' said Hirtius, disapproval in his tone, but Cassius waved him down. 'No, Hirtius. I am only saying what you all think. If our general has the good of the republic at heart then his decision is simple and this is no insult. If self-aggrandisement is more important than the republic, *then* it becomes an insult, and it is one I will stand by.'

He narrowed his eyes and pointed at Caesar. 'If you march on Pharnaces of Pontus, then you can count on my sword arm by your side and my utmost loyalty, Caesar, but if you turn away from the republic's enemy to deal with your own opponents, then I was wrong to bend the knee last year at the Hellespont, and I shall follow you no further.'

The tense silence returned, and Caesar stood regarding Cassius with an unreadable expression.

Finally, he nodded, dropping the scroll case from his right hand.

'You are, of course, entirely correct, Cassius, and I am forced to thank you for reminding me of my duty. Rome must wait. I will send a few men there to support Antonius in his efforts and, at times, restrain him if necessary. Then we shall march on Cappadocia and Pharnaces, the enemy of Rome.'

There was a sense of deflation and relief in the room. Cassius stood silent for a moment longer, gaze locked on Caesar, as if willing him to change his mind. Then finally he nodded.

'It will take perhaps a week to gather sufficient ships to move the army,' he said.

'That will not be necessary.'

'What?'

'This place is still unsettled and Rome will soon become reliant upon Aegyptian grain, with Cato in control of the African wheat supply. We cannot leave Aegyptus free to do as they please. The queen rules only with Roman support. The Gabiniani might renege upon their oath, after all. No, we shall leave the Twenty Seventh and the Thirty Seventh here to continue the work of securing Aegyptus.'

Fronto blinked. 'That's dangerous, Caesar,' he said. 'You mean to take only the Sixth?'

'And the cavalry, yes.'

'Calvinus had five times that number, and still lost to Pharnaces.'

Caesar peered across at Fronto, and an odd smile crossed his face. 'But Calvinus lacked something we do not.'

'And what is that?' demanded Cassius.

'Me,' replied the general, without a hint that he recognised the hubris he displayed.

CHAPTER TWENTY THREE

Tarsus, July 17th 47 BC

F ronto rubbed his sore rump and shifted slightly between the saddle horns as Bucephalus plodded stoically towards the walled city, which lay at the northern edge of the plain in the shadow of the mountains beyond – a smudge of blue-grey that rippled with the heat haze. He had to remove his helmet for a moment and wipe the sweat from his head, with his only slightly less sodden scarf. He'd thought that leaving Aegyptus would mean an end to the steaming heat they had suffered for more than half a year. What he had not counted upon was that winter in Alexandria was not a great deal hotter than Syria in high summer.

He reminded himself, and not for the first time, that he should stop complaining and think himself lucky. Bucephalus was probably suffering under his weight and in this heat every bit as much as Fronto himself, but at least they weren't at sea.

It had taken longer than expected to leave Alexandria. There were many official and very rational reasons for this, yet a person only had to be in Cassius' company for a short time before he began to suspect the general was simply struggling to leave his exotic queen behind. But leave her behind they had. The queen now had all of Aegyptus subjugated, and with no strong opposition. Her army was supported by the Twenty Seventh and Thirty Seventh legions, and a cadre of very sensible Roman officers, who had been tasked not only with securing Rome's favoured ruler, but also with remaining loyal directly to Caesar, and not sliding into local politics as the Gabiniani had done. To legitimise the royal house once more and prevent the insidious Aegyptian worry over the sole female ruler, Cleopatra had agreed to marry her youngest brother, the boy now known as Ptolemy the Fourteenth, and rule with him. It was a formality, for there could be no doubt who truly commanded in *that* relationship.

Fronto had initially been somewhat surprised at how easily Caesar had handed his lover over in marriage to another, but had quickly shaken off notions of propriety. After all, Caesar was already married himself, and there was no romance in this royal match, especially with Ptolemy not yet old enough to lose the bulla of childhood, or whatever the Aegyptian equivalent was.

So, finally, they had been ready to depart, with Aegyptus settled and safe.

Taking only the Sixth Legion, which, when allowing for the dead of the past few months, the number of wounded after the dreadful fight by the Nilus, and their being below strength in the first place, put their numbers now at less than two thousand, the consul and his staff had finally left Alexandria. Despite her wonders, Fronto was quietly glad about that, and even more so that there was very little chance that he would ever be called upon to return to the place.

To his relief they had decided not to travel by ship after all. Though it would be swifter and less bothersome to most, Caesar as always had practical reasons for choosing a land route. Rome had allies in the east, many of whom had joined with the army of Mithridates and helped the general win his war. When that same army had departed, those allies had gone with the prince, unaware that Caesar might have to call upon them for another campaign. Given the need for manpower, the consul had elected to travel along the coast with the legion and his cavalry, collecting units as he went. It were not a vast horde of men that they collected, but even small units of missile troops could make a big difference in the field.

Finally, after weeks of travelling, the army had moved into northern Syria and arrived at Tarsus, the great ancient city at the crossroads of the world. A thriving trade city on the silk route, and a metropolis brought under Rome's wing by Pompey just twenty years ago, Tarsus had swiftly been transformed into the heart of the Roman east, a suitable capital from which the Roman governor could maintain control. Thus it was that this walled city by the Cilician shore had been the place to which Calvinus had retreated, licking his wounds after his latest defeat.

Caesar had been tight-lipped on the subject of Calvinus. The man had, after all, lost huge numbers of troops and important land in a failed war against a foreign king, and it was only a combination of the ability he had shown commanding the centre at Pharsalus, and his clear, known and unswerving loyalty to Caesar, that kept him from disgrace.

Now, as Fronto rolled his shoulders and anticipated the rest they would enjoy tonight in a real bed, he could see the small detachment of well-dressed men riding out from the city's great square gates to meet them. As they neared, the scouts ahead of the column signalling that nothing untoward awaited them, the officers kicked their horses into speed and moved ahead of the army.

Gnaeus Domitius Calvinus sat astride a white mare, half a dozen officers at his back, as well as a few local dignitaries seated on litters and wrapped in togas. Two centuries of legionaries stood in lines to the sides – an honour guard for the commander.

As they converged, Fronto noted with interest a scar across Calvinus' cheek, which looked relatively fresh. It seemed that despite his loss at Nicopolis, Calvinus had not withdrawn without a fight. Caesar had also noted the wound, and Fronto could see the consul reappraising the man with this fresh insight.

'Consul,' Domitius Calvinus said, bowing his head. 'Welcome to Tarsus.'

Caesar nodded. 'Domitius, thank you for the welcome. We shall not be tarrying more than a single night here, however. Pharnaces of Pontus must be made to pay for his presumption, and his territorial gains returned to Roman control. We march on in the morning, and other than leaving an appropriate garrison in this city, I need you and your forces to join us. How many men can you muster, excluding walking wounded?'

Calvinus seemed somewhat surprised and taken aback. He straightened.

'Caesar, I have the bulk of the Thirty Sixth, numbering approximately three thousand. Beyond that there are surviving vexillations of other legions counting a total of not more than one and a half thousand. Given time, a further thousand allies could be drummed up locally, though not in time for a march on the morrow.'

Caesar drummed his fingers on his belt. 'With my current force, that brings our strength up to perhaps seven thousand. Given their veteran status, this is beginning to look like a strong force to field against the Bosporan invader.'

Calvinus frowned, shaking his head. 'With respect, Caesar, even after the losses Pharnaces suffered at our hands at Nicopolis, he will still be able to put a force of near twenty thousand in the field. Moreover, his men are also veterans and in high spirits. Marching on him with a force of seven thousand is tantamount to suicide.'

He winced at the end of this, well aware that he was still riding the ignominy of failure against that same enemy.

'We do what we must with what we have, Domitius,' Caesar said flatly. 'Though I do not intend to meet Pharnaces with *quite* such uneven numbers. We will bring our number over ten thousand with the aid of Galatia.'

Calvinus' frown deepened so much that his brow threw his eyes into shadow. 'Caesar, I strongly advise that you move to the west coast and bring in Mithridates, skirting Galatia entirely.'

The consul shook his head. 'Mithridates has served well already. He was instrumental in our victory in Aegyptus, and he now has his own house to put in order. I will not lay upon him demands that will weaken his strength in his own lands, nor risk his ongoing goodwill by asking too much too often. No, Mithridates is not within my sights. Galatia is our next stop. It is, after all, directly between us and Pharnaces according to the latest reports, unless you have any contradictory news for me?'

'No, Caesar. Pharnaces and his army wait in the highlands north of Cappadocia. He compounds his vile actions in his victory. It is said that he tortured his Roman prisoners to death and that execution has become the norm for any Roman found within his lands, whether they be soldier or civilian. For sure, Pharnaces must pay, but a march through Cappadocia and Galatia will likely weaken your force, rather than strengthen it, Consul. Deiotarus of Galatia is no ally of yours.'

Caesar nodded. 'Deiotarus is a gamble, but I feel he is the correct choice.'

'Consul, Deiotarus was so far inside Pompey's purse he was buried in coin. He took the field against us at Pharsalus as part of Pompey's force. He has ever been your enemy. Marching up to him and requesting his support is madness. He is most likely to fall upon you with his army, and then seek the adoration of your enemies in Africa.'

Caesar continued to nod. 'Of this I am aware. But only bitter fools now place themselves against me. Men like Cato. Pompey is no more, after all. Deiotarus may have sided with Pompey against me, but he has never wavered in his loyalty to Rome. He and I may have been enemies, but his reason for that is gone, and he will help Rome against her foe. Of that I am convinced.'

Calvinus sagged. 'Then if you are set on such a course, Caesar, at least march into Galatia in strength and prepared for a fight.'

The general smiled. 'All the strength we can muster in one night, Domitius. If you would be so kind as to show us to suitable lodgings, and send out the call for your legions to muster, we march on at dawn.'

* * *

Blucium, Galatia July 28th 47 BC

The hill town of Blucium sat atop a strong rise on the northern end of a narrow valley, amid high, bleak-looking peaks. Its walls were old and exotic, its buildings somehow oddly eastern looking. Fronto shifted in the saddle once more. He was twitchy.

They had been watchful and prepared, from the moment they had passed beyond the bounds of Roman Syria into Cappadocia, close to the lands now controlled by Pharnaces' men, skirting their territory and making for independent Galatia. Some officers shared Calvinus' worry about the danger of approaching the staunchly Pompeian king. That he retained his independence in a region where Pharnaces seemed intent on conquest suggested that Deiotarus already had some treaty in place with the Bosporan aggressor.

Fronto was acutely aware that however much they might be prepared, if Deiotarus had designs on war, he could very easily spring a trap here in this valley, and the Roman force would take some time to put into battle order, without even considering artillery and the like.

His memory furnished him with unhelpful memories of their journey across Achaea the previous year, between Dyrrachium and Pharsalus. How many towns had they come across, sitting behind high walls and closed gates and denying the general? Blucium looked just like them to Fronto, and there was no sign of the gate opening as the officers walked their horses slowly up the sloping road towards the city, the Galatian king's capital.

'Give the signal to deploy the legions, Consul,' Hirtius urged Caesar as they neared.

The general shook his head. 'Wait.'

As the army in the valley below slowed and came to a halt to a chorus of whistle blasts, the officers came close to the city's southern gate and stopped at the consul's signal. Salvius Cursor filled the silence, barking orders at his praetorians, who spread out in a protective cordon, men close enough to throw themselves in front of the general with a raised shield if required. After all, they were now within missile shot of the walls and towers, and though there was no sign of life up there, neither the tension nor the threat diminished.

They sat in silence for a time, the only sounds the distant din of the army forming ordered lines, the gentle hum and sizzle of bees and sun-seared land, and the kites soaring on thermals, trilling and screeching in warbling tones. Finally, once even the legions had come to a tense standing silence, the quiet was suddenly filled with a ligneous thud and the sound of creaking iron. The gate of Blucium swung slowly open, its movement stately.

Fronto felt himself tense, anticipating danger.

After a further pause, a shape appeared in the shade of the gateway. Slowly, it emerged into the light. A figure on horseback. Just one.

Fronto stared, narrow eyed, uncertain what this was. The other officers were equally cautious and confused. They watched, many hands going to sword hilts as the single rider began to descend towards them. He was an older man, dressed in a plain grey tunic with a beige cloak over his back, head bare. Fronto had to remind himself that the Galatians were related to the Gauls he had fought both with and against for a decade, as he realised the man wore long trousers in the Gallic style. His face was bearded and his hair long and curly with a single braid to the side, like some odd fusion of Greek and Gaulish styles. Indeed, as he came closer, they could see that the entire ensemble resembled the garb of a standard Gaulish rider, yet the patterns at hem and neck were of a very traditional Greek design. Very odd.

But not as odd as the simple fact of one low-born peasant riding out to meet a consul of Rome at the head of his army. The rider came to a halt not far from the outer praetorians, and bowed his head low.

'Deiotarus,' Caesar said quietly, sombrely, in greeting.

Fronto blinked. Surely not? This man was a commoner. Even his jewellery was plain and of low quality. The rider raised his head.

'Consul.'

'Perhaps you could explain for the benefit of my somewhat mystified officers,' the general said, gesturing to the rider.

'I offer myself to you as supplicant, Caesar,' the man said. 'Not as a king, but as a citizen of Galatia.'

Caesar nodded. 'Humility is a rare and valued quality in a leader, Deiotarus, but perhaps this is a step too far?'

The king shrugged. 'With news of your approach, and the knowledge of my past, I found myself in a position with several options, Caesar. Perhaps I launch a pre-emptive strike against you, knowing that you may well be here to put an end to my rule? But in doing so, I would break solemn vows I made to Zeus and Apollo both, to support the republic, and I am not a man given to breaking vows. Moreover, there is a dangerous aggressor in this region with whom I have enjoyed at best a tense stand-off in recent months, following a military defeat at his hands. Should I fight a costly battle against you, I would open my kingdom to the depredations of Pharnaces.'

Caesar simply nodded.

'Or, of course,' the Galatian went on, 'I could lead out my army and greet you as I would have truly preferred, as an equal. Representative of Rome and leader of a great force here to put an end to Pharnaces. My own court and generals would also have preferred that. My current garb is not popular with them. But to do so to you, a man to whom I have so recently been opposed, and whose banner I sought at Pharsalus with blade bared, would have been presumptuous at best. Childishly hopeful in truth.'

Another nod from Caesar. Deiotarus gave a shrug.

'And so I come to you as supplicant. I place my fate and that of my people at your mercy knowing that you are capable of both great clemency and powerful revenge. I do this that if vengeance is your heart's course, it be aimed at me, as the leader of these people, and not at they.'

'Would you like to explain your loyalties of late before I contemplate matters?' Caesar said easily.

'I have of necessity taken arms with your enemies, Caesar. Pompey and others. But I would remind you that we are far from your power centre here, Consul, and surrounded by fractious peoples and hungry enemies. This region was Pompey's heartland for many years. It is only natural for a man in my position to side with the most advantageous power for the future of my own people. Now, with Pompey gone, and *Caesar* the power in the east, I come to *you* for the strength of my kingdom. I have not been a supporter of Pompey, Caesar, but a supporter of Rome, whose rod of rule was here *wielded* by Pompey.'

Caesar nodded. 'Your vow to Apollo and Jove is enough for me. I ride for Pontus and the fastnesses of Pharnaces the invader. I will end his reign of terror in this land and impose once more the rule of law. In doing so, I would of course value the support of the Kingdom of Galatia, who have long been the allies of Rome. Deiotarus, King of Galatia, will you lead your army with us to destroy our mutual enemy?'

The king bowed his head, and oddly, to Fronto, few men had ever managed to look quite so regal, even with robes of state, as this simple, humble man did now.

'I have an army of four thousand heavy infantry, and less than a thousand horse, who can be mustered presently. More can be gathered, but it will take time. I did not wish to field too large a force here, lest I be seen by yourself as an aggressor.'

Caesar nodded. 'Your men will be invaluable. With my own force, we will still be short of the numbers Pharnaces can field, but I am confident of our men's strength and morale, and of our officers' quality. Were the enemy three to our one, I would still feel sure of victory.'

For the first time, King Deiotarus smiled. 'My men will tear out their throats in the name of Rome, Consul.'

'Return to your palace, King of Galatia, and attire yourself correctly for rule and for war.'

Deiotarus bowed his head once more and threw up a hand in signal to the city. Despite himself, Fronto flinched. He had seen enough betrayal in his life that the simple gesture immediately filled his imagination with fears that the signal would have artillery and archers along the wall top release missile after missile, down into the Roman contingent.

No such thing happened, of course. Figures did appear at the parapet, but they were gripping standards. The eagle of Galatia snapped and fluttered all along the walls, interspersed with the eagle of Rome, Pompeian standards carried over from the days they had been fielded against Caesar at Pharsalus. Now they were in *support* of him.

Deiotarus, regal in his humility, turned his horse and rode back towards the city, beckoning only once for the Romans to follow him. Salvius Cursor looked to Caesar for approval, who nodded and gestured for the staff officers to accompany him, urging his own horse on after the king.

Fronto tried not to imagine just how easy it would be for a treacherous king to have a deadly ambush set within the city gates, his eyes strafing the parapet in search of drawn bows and primed artillery, yet finding none. As they passed beneath the great heavy gate and into the city itself, he tensed, prepared for a sudden attack, or the gates to close behind them, trapping them within. None of it happened.

The soldiers Fronto could see inside the city stood by the sides of the street, at attention and with a professional stance. It seemed odd to him. These were a strange people, both Greek and Gaul wrapped up in one bundle, with hints of Syrian and Pontic and more thrown in. They had Gallic beards and Greek hair, Germanic braids and Syrian skin, a true mix of cultures. But the thing that really surprised him was the soldiers themselves. Had he not known who they were, he would have assumed them a Roman legion, even down to the madder-dyed red tunics and the pila they shouldered. Indeed, the only thing that readily marked them out was their shields, which were painted with the jagged stylised eagle of Galatia, and their unit names in Greek text.

The people of Blucium cheered as they passed, the only silent figures being the soldiers – these odd Galatian legionaries – who stood watching with professional stoicism. Fronto finally began to relax as they neared the royal palace at the heart of the city. More soldiers awaited them here, including officers who looked so like the consul's staff that they could easily be mistaken for them. Citizens cheered and laughed, and had their higher classes worn togas and forgone the long trousers that seemed the norm, Fronto might have assumed they were in a Roman city.

As they entered the gateway of the palace itself, the king dismounted, the Romans following suit. The king bade them follow one of the officers while he changed his clothes, and would meet them in the hall of state. As he disappeared, one of the officers stepped forwards and addressed them in perfect Latin.

'If you would care to follow me, sirs?'

As some lackey took their horses away, the officer led them in through an impressive door and into a wide vestibule lined with trophies and banners, lit by braziers and oil lamps, providing a rather oppressive heat in a room that would otherwise have been blessedly cool after the hot Syrian sun. Through another corridor they were escorted, and finally into a great hall of decorated marble with more banners, and a large throne on a raised dais.

A man who looked disturbingly like a druid to Fronto stood close to the throne, leaning on a tall staff, and finally the officer stopped and turned to them. 'I apologise for the nature of your wait, sirs. We were not sure whether we would be hosting you or not, and a banquet seemed an unlikely proposition. I can have couches brought for you, and food?'

Caesar shook his head. 'This is perfectly adequate, thank you. The king will be with us shortly?'

The officer nodded. 'His majesty will be prepared swiftly.'

Fronto stepped out of the line of officers. 'Might I pry into something?'

The officer's eyebrow rose. 'Go on?'

'You faced us among Pompey's forces at Pharsalus, yet I do not remember seeing your men on the field. I'm sure I would have remembered them. Yet they are clearly a legion. They might so easily be one of Caesar's own.'

The officer smiled. 'We were among Pompey Magnus' forces, Legate, yes. In fact half our unit were committed in the thick of the action alongside Rome's legions, though you would be unlikely to identify them in the press. The rest were held back in reserve and managed to depart the field without pursuit and destruction. This is why we can bring only four thousand men to your aid. Without wishing it to sound like a recrimination, your own men destroyed the other half.'

Fronto nodded sadly. 'Such is the peril of civil war.'

The man glanced down for a moment and then lifted his gaze to Fronto once more. 'As to their similarity with your own forces, this dates back some years, to Pompey's first contact with the kingdom. The king's fascination with the efficiency of Pompey's legions led to a complete reorganisation of the royal guard. Our numbers remained the same, some eight thousand, but we were modelled on the Roman legion. Pompey lent us instructors, armourers, engineers and more. Within a handful of years our guard went from being modelled on the forces of Alexander, the scourge of Persia, to being a reflection of Rome's legions.'

He looked oddly embarrassed for a moment. 'Of course, after initial successes in the Mithridatic wars alongside your legions, we have encountered something of a losing streak recently, first against yourselves at Pharsalus and then more recently against Pharnaces. Our men remain optimistic and strong, however, despite those losses.'

Fronto smiled. 'They seem very professional. You are to be commended. And the Pompeian centre at Pharsalus gave us a real struggle, so there is no cause for chagrin there.'

'Our forces will make a good showing in the coming days. The men are twitching for an opportunity to give Pharnaces of Pontus a sound beating and, Pharsalus notwithstanding, they are ever comfortable standing alongside the legions of Rome.'

Fronto turned and glanced out of the door at the men standing there, straight and professional and reeking of military might. For the first time since they had left Aegyptus with just one legion, he felt that they might just be able to beat Pharnaces, despite his advantage of numbers.

CHAPTER TWENTY FOUR

Taouion, July 30th 47 BC

The ancient city of Taouion was one of Deiotarus' more important fortresses and production centres. Like the capital, it sat on the crest of a hill, a weird echo of Gaul imprinted with Greek style, where it lorded over a wide valley and numerous peaks pocked with rich mines. No wonder these lands were continually contested and fought over, Fronto mused, looking at the resources they produced.

The army spread out in the valley below, filling it from slope to slope and stretching back into the heat haze with the baggage train still invisible. His gaze rose east to the pass and the hills beyond. Some three days march that way, if reports were to be believed, Pharnaces waited with an army twice the size of theirs. Caesar was brimming with confidence, and it was honest confidence too, not a show of bravado for the likes of Calvinus and Deiotarus. Fronto had known the man long enough to tell the difference. Fronto was *less* full of confidence, and disinclined towards shows of bravado. Pharnaces' men might be inferior, but the odds were still stacked in his favour, and this was his land. Fronto had learned time and again that an army imperils itself if it faces an enemy on their home ground. Any general knew that.

'We shall overnight here,' Caesar said, sitting astride his white mare on the peak at the valley side facing the city, officers

337

gathered around him. He turned to Deiotarus. 'It is acceptable that the army encamps in the valley? This will not impede your citizens?'

The king smiled. Geared for war, he now looked totally different to the poor supplicant who had met them on their arrival. Like some Macedonian conqueror of old, yet with nods to his Gaulish origin, he gestured towards the city.

'Taouion relies little upon fertile land, Caesar, for there is so little of it. Goats and hill beasts are their diet, and the rest comes in trade for the minerals mined all about. Indeed, if your officers allow it, the people of the city will be grateful for the opportunity to trade with the soldiers.'

Caesar nodded and turned to Cassius. 'See to it that orders are distributed. The locals are permitted to approach and to set up their stalls and trade with the men. The usual warnings against fights and drunkenness, mind.'

Cassius saluted and walked his horse off down the slope towards the massing army.

'You know Pharnaces?' Caesar said, peering off into the distance.

Deiotarus shrugged. 'We have crossed paths, not just on the field of battle.'

'What is he like. As a man, I mean. Not as a ruler.'

'Arrogant. Headstrong and arrogant. Indeed, if it were Pharnaces himself leading his army, I would say that we have little to worry about, Consul. He could easily be goaded, and might act with dangerous rashness. Unfortunately he is also no fool, and his army is commanded by competent men. Still, there is in the Bosporan character a certain impetus to immediacy that might work against them.'

'Is he wily? Will he attempt to gain through deviousness as well as through war?'

The king pursed his lips. 'I would not put it past the man, certainly. After all, Rome has had hegemony in the east for many years and no ambitious man dared push for personal gain for fear of incurring the enmity of the republic. Pharnaces is no different than any other in that. Yet the civil war pulled from the region the strong rulers and their veteran legions. The moment Pompey fell, his allies gathered far away in Africa, and you were besieged and trapped in Aegyptus, suddenly Pharnaces takes advantage of Roman weakness to begin his conquests. His timing speaks of a man of wheedling deviousness. In men, I find that such guile is usually at dangerous odds with arrogance, but a man who can tame both such sides of his nature and make them work in concord? Well, he could be a dangerous man.'

Caesar nodded absently.

'I feel that the rogue king of Pontus might just be about to attempt to lull and court us, even as his forces prepare. Your intelligence on his army?'

Deiotarus sat back in his saddle. His lands abutting those of Pharnaces, his scouts were Rome's primary source of information. 'Our intelligence places his army in the region of Zela, some seventy to eighty miles east, along the mineral trade route.'

'Apart from one small group,' Caesar murmured and lifted a finger, pointing along the valley.

The others followed his gesture. A small force was making its way down the eastern slope in the late afternoon sun, which filled the valley with golden light from behind the Roman force. Fronto squinted. Maybe two hundred riders, many in bronze, which shone even at this distance. 'Can't be a danger to us,' he noted. 'Even the most headstrong man wouldn't send such a small group against his enemy's legions. And they're not scouts. Not armoured like that.'

Caesar nodded. 'An embassy. Duplicity hangs in the air like a miasma.' He turned to the king. 'I see your enemy's dual nature at work, Majesty. I see his arrogance settled with his army in the peaks, daring us to challenge him, but I see his guile riding towards us this very eve, bedecked in bronze.'

'Do not allow them to approach, Caesar,' Salvius Cursor said quietly, gesturing to his officers to draw up the rest of the praetorians who were lagging further back down the slope.

'You think we need fear them?' Caesar smiled. 'I do not. I have no intention of showing fear or weakness. This is no true deputation, but an intelligence gathering mission and delay tactic by the Bosporan invader. Let his embassy return with news of a confident and powerful enemy. By all means, Salvius, have the praetorians form up and on hand, but I will meet personally with this embassy, and his honour guard will be permitted close.'

Salvius Cursor's face radiated disapproval, but he saluted and began to order his men into the best possible position to move at speed and take down an enemy, should he make a single false move.

'Send a rider to guide them in,' Caesar told him.

They sat and watched, wondering what to expect, as Salvius' rider reached the approaching party, and escorted it along the line of the army as they prepared to camp for the night. Fronto smiled. He knew centurions, and knew damn well that at the first sniff of a foreign deputation, every man they passed would be perfectly kitted out and defiant. The strongest men would be on show. What the emissaries of Pharnaces would encounter were the ideal legionaries – the best of the best – and it was these men whose description would be carried back to the enemy.

Gradually, the group became clearer as they approached. Amid an honour guard encased in helms and cuirasses of bronze, with laminated arm plates, skirts of white pteruges and horses clad in coats of bronze scales, came the emissaries of Pharnaces. Dressed in rich robes, their hair oiled and elaborately curled, even their horses displayed wealth in gold accoutrements. Fronto felt disdain rising at the sight. As they approached, they slowed. The honour guard dropped slightly back, though Salvius' hand still went to his sword hilt at the closeness of so many heavily armoured men.

There was a stoic silence and a stony-faced look to the soldiers, though Fronto had seen such men as the emissaries often enough to recognise a veneer of bravado over a sea of nerves, so thin and brittle that it might snap and peel away at any moment.

'Greetings, Roman,' the head man said in thick Greek, raising a hand.

Caesar sat still. 'I am Gaius Julius Caesar, consul of Rome and representative of the republic in all matters. Say your piece, men of Bosporus.'

The emissary narrowed his eyes at the flat response. He leaned back, placing one hand over the other on his reins.

'His great Majesty, Pharnaces the second, scion of the house of the Mithridati, King of the Bosporus, King of Pontus and Cappadocia…'

'*Invader* of Pontus and Cappadocia,' Caesar corrected him, butting in.

The man's lip twitched and he paused, glaring at the consul.

'His Majesty entreats you to lead your forces no further into his lands.'

He paused, clearly waiting for Caesar to correct him once more. That the consul did not seemed to irritate the ambassador even more. He straightened. 'In return for you standing down from a war footing and leading away your forces, his Majesty will agree to terms beneficial to Rome and vows to stand by them. He sends you this as a gift appropriate for a royal friend and victor of such wars as the consul can claim.'

His shaky hand held a purple linen wrap, which he unfolded to display a golden crown in the form of a laurel wreath.

'Your master's vow is as solid as morning mist, and almost as long-lasting,' Caesar said pointedly, ignoring the rich gift.

The ambassador's twitch returned as he lowered the crown. 'I am instructed to remind mighty Caesar that his Majesty had staunchly, for years, refused support to Pompey in his war against you. More than once, the general sent requests for troops and supplies as he fought your forces. From his Majesty, Pompey received not one man. Not one loaf of bread.'

'And in return he believes we will sit back in gratitude and watch him carve an empire out of our territory?' Caesar said, his tone becoming dark.

The twitch heightened. The man was close to losing his temper, Fronto noted. 'Might I remind *mighty* Caesar,' the man spat, 'that the would-be hegemon sitting on the horse beside him not only supplied Pompey with the tools to help destroy Caesar, but even took the field against him personally.'

Caesar glanced at Deiotarus, who simply nodded, then resumed.

'The king of Galatia and I have agreed amicable terms. Such is easier to do with a man who does not claim swathes of Roman land for his own. A man who might have fought a Roman general, but did so in the service of another such Roman general.' As the ambassador wound up for another tirade, Caesar held up an assuaging hand. 'Very well, man of Bosporus. I will say this to you, which you may carry back to your master.'

He walked his horse two paces forwards so that he was uncomfortably close to the ambassador, at which point the differences between the two men escaped nobody. The Bosporan with his rich tunic, oiled curls and copious golden jewellery, sat before the consul in his armour, with sword at side, hair severe and grey, eyes like a hawk. Put the two men in an arena, Fronto smiled, and Caesar would wipe the floor with the ambassador, despite the thirty year gap in their ages in favour of the Bosporan.

'I am a fair man, and known for it,' Caesar said. 'I am as renowned for my clemency as for my military victories. In fact, nothing gives me greater pleasure than granting mercy when it is humbly and reasonably sought. As such, I recognise the strength in the man beside me who may have been my enemy but sought amends and peace like a true leader. All this, I might add, while your own master displays not one iota of humility as he invades Roman lands.'

His hand shot out, a finger levelled at the ambassador, and he was now so close that the pointing finger almost put the man's eye out. The Bosporan leaned back in shock.

'Do *not*,' Caesar snapped, 'dare to take a moral high ground with me. Not when spouting such obfuscating bilge.'

He leaned back and watched the man struggle upright in his saddle.

'In point of fact,' the consul went on, 'I see your master seeking to use such acts of loyalty as an excuse to save him from war, while my own victories I do not seek for vainglory, and are granted by the gods for the betterment of the republic.'

He stepped his horse back once. 'As for the great and serious outrages perpetrated against Roman citizens in Pontus, since it is not in my power to set them to rights, I accordingly forgive Pharnaces.'

Fronto frowned. This he had not expected. In fact, disapproval emanated from the rest of the Roman officers too. Caesar glanced round and they kept silent at the look in his eye.

'I cannot, in fact,' he resumed, glaring at the ambassador, 'restore to murdered men the life they have lost, nor to the mutilated their manhood; and such indeed is the punishment, worse than death, that Roman citizens have undergone in your master's stolen realm.'

He left the accusation of torture hanging in the air like a foul smell, and the ambassador, unable to deny it, for it had become common knowledge, lowered his face for a moment.

'Here are my demands,' Caesar said loudly. 'Pharnaces must immediately withdraw from Pontus and Cappadocia. He must release all slaves he has taken in his campaign of conquest, and make appropriate restitution to all those who have lost or suffered as a consequence of his actions. Once this is done, *and not before then*, he may send tribute and gifts to us, as appropriate for friendly rulers in the arms of the republic.'

With this last, he pointed at the crown. The ambassador dropped it as though it had suddenly become hot, the rich bauble clattering into the dirt by his horse's hooves. Fronto tried not to see the victor's laurels ground into the dirt as an omen. He failed.

'This is your last word on the subject?' the ambassador hissed.

'It is.'

'Then I shall take your proposal to the king. Farewell, consul of Rome.'

Turning his horse and gathering his party about him, the ambassador began to ride away, his honour guard close by. The Romans watched them go, and Fronto cleared his throat.

'You don't expect him to actually leave, of course.'

Caesar shook his head. 'He is playing with us. Possibly buying time to prepare against us in some manner. Certainly, after committing to this conquest as he has, he is not going to relinquish all his gains and return to obscurity. No, but I would be willing to wager that he will string out the debate. Perhaps he hopes that we will weaken through lack of supplies. Perhaps he believes that

King Deiotarus here will abandon our cause. Whatever the case, he speaks through one face and leads his army with the other.'

He turned, scanning the crowd of officers, and singled out Galronus.

'Take five of your best riders. Follow the ambassador discreetly. Find their camp and watch what happens, then report back as swiftly as you can. It would be greatly advantageous to us if you were not seen by their own scouts.'

Galronus nodded and wheeled his horse to go find his best riders.

Caesar squinted off into the distance. 'I wonder what his plan is. Why is he trying to buy himself time?'

'We'll know soon enough,' Fronto muttered.

* * *

It was early morning two days later, the kalends of the month, that the next encounter came. The army marched at speed along the valleys of Cappadocia, bearing down on this Zela, where Pharnaces was said to have gathered his force. As the legions stomped along the valleys, raising dust with their thousands of tramping feet, the deputation once more appeared ahead in a saddle between hills.

Caesar brought his officers out to the side and climbed to a spur of land that overlooked the valley, Salvius Cursor gathering the praetorians around them. There, they waited patiently as the two hundred strong, gleaming deputation of King Pharnaces closed. It was no accident that Caesar had chosen this position, for the enemy were forced to climb a steep slope to meet them, the going difficult. When they finally came to a halt in front of the Roman officers, the horses were clearly exhausted, and it took long moments for even the unarmoured ambassador to recover. Finally, he held up his hand in greeting.

'Good day, Consul of Rome.'

'That remains to be seen,' Caesar said quietly. 'You have my reply from Pharnaces?'

The man nodded. 'His Majesty sends greetings to the representative of the mighty Roman republic. He acknowledges that perhaps a certain over-zealousness had overcome him, and that he had occupied more territory than he had originally intended. His Majesty agrees to Caesar's terms. Even now his army begins to disperse to home garrisons. However, he begs Caesar's indulgence.'

'Oh?'

'The consul is a career military man, and must be aware of the sluggish nature of such a great undertaking. The consul, he believes, cannot expect the entirety of half a year's campaign to be undone in a matter of hours. He begs that Caesar grant him a month to complete his withdrawal from Roman-claimed territory.'

Caesar narrowed his eyes.

Fronto glanced sideways at his commander. He had been watching the ambassador carefully, and there was something about his manner. Everything here was façade. There was nothing genuine at all, and the consul had to be aware of that.

Caesar was as inscrutable as ever, though. The consul straightened.

'The king is most reasonable,' he said. 'Though we shall, of course, require a sign of complicity and good faith. I will grant until the calends of next month for his Majesty to complete his withdrawal from all occupied lands and the release of prisoners. The appropriate restitution may draw out beyond this, of course. But as a gesture I shall expect the army of the king to have withdrawn from this region and dispersed within a matter of days. That should be more than possible for any army, no matter how poorly-disciplined.'

This last jibe seemed to stab the ambassador like a knife, and his lip twitched in irritation. However, he bowed his head. 'The king will accede to the consul's demands, of course, though I would remind Rome of her own promises to withdraw and to advance no further.'

Caesar smiled, and Fronto now knew something was going on, for he knew that smile well and knew that it masked other intent. The consul turned to find Cassius. 'Have the signals given to halt the column.'

Cassius looked extremely disgruntled at the command, but saluted and rode off to carry out his orders. The ambassador looked satisfied for the first time in two meetings. Straightening, he pulled out of his repertoire the most oily smile imaginable, which stretched its fake line so far from ear to ear that it looked as though his head might fall in half.

'It is a matter of great joy that accords such as these might be met between Rome and Pontus,' the ambassador said.

'Would you care to stay for a while?' Caesar asked in a pleasant voice. 'To celebrate such great accords, we should feast.'

The ambassador slipped into his most contrite expression. 'Would that were possible, Consul. However, the process of withdrawal is a complex one, and the king requires our presence. Perhaps when all is settled, we can celebrate further with a true meeting of equals.'

Caesar bowed his head. 'Far be it from me to stand in the way of the king carrying out his withdrawal. Rome extends its gratitude for such easily-agreed concord.'

The ambassador continued to smile that horrible smile as he turned and rode away, the other nobles falling in with him as his honour guard shifted into protective lines. Caesar and the officers sat silent as they watched the group descend the hill, and then begin the long journey east up the valley. Once they were some distance away, Caesar sat back in his saddle and raised his voice.

'You can put in an appearance now.'

Fronto frowned and turned in time to see Galronus and one of his riders emerge from behind a small stand of maple and scrub bushes. Their horses were exhausted, clearly, and both riders looked tired and worn. Galronus threw up a half-hearted salute and reined in next to the consul.

'What news?' Caesar said

'Estimates of their numbers are more or less accurate, Caesar,' the Remi nobleman said. 'Twenty thousand or thereabouts, including more than a thousand horse.'

'Are they, perchance, showing any faint signs of withdrawal?'

Galronus shook his head. 'Far from it. I'd say that they are entrenching with every expectation that they are here to stay.'

Caesar turned to the others. 'As we suspected. Duplicity abounds. The question is what they are attempting to buy time for.'

'I think that is clear, Caesar,' Galronus said. 'Their army occupies a peak close to the city. It would appear that this hill is the site of some ancient fortress. It could be extremely defensible, but the walls and ramparts have long since eroded and tumbled down. The enemy are currently in the process of fortifying the place, building strong walls and digging new ditches.'

'Ah,' Caesar said with a nod. 'This explains their attempts to delay the inevitable. They seek adequate time to construct their defences.'

'Why use a ruined fortress then?' Brutus muttered. 'Why not occupy one of the strong fortresses that needs no work? Jove knows but we've passed enough of them.'

'Logistics,' Caesar replied. 'None of the fortresses we've seen would be of sufficient size to contain an army of twenty thousand with horse and supplies. It may be that Pharnaces has simply made the best of an unacceptable selection. Better to house his army in one strong position and be forced to fortify it than to split his men into extant fortresses. Now we know for what he is buying time. To prepare defences against us.'

'And we've halted the army?' Brutus prompted.

'Temporarily,' Caesar smiled. 'Pharnaces now thinks he has delayed us, and that we will encamp or retreat and grant him adequate time to turn the region into a great redoubt against us. And some might. Some might even believe his vows. But note that the ambassador claimed an accord between Rome and Pontus, suggesting that the king continues to lay claim to the land, and moreover he suggested we might be equals. He believes we might leave. He is wrong, but it is important that he does not realise as much for as long as possible. We will allow two hours for the enemy riders to depart. As soon as our scouts signal that the embassy is gone, the army will begin to march once more. Better still, we will now march at speed. Leave the baggage train behind. Every man carries three days of supplies and the cavalry the spare equipment. The slaves following on can port what they can manage. We move at double time. Pharnaces believes us held here, and will be in disarray when the army arrives unexpectedly.'

Fronto grinned. The poor Bosporan bastard had no idea what was coming.

CHAPTER TWENTY FIVE

Zela, August 2nd 47 BC

'**N**o movement in evidence?' Caesar said.

Galronus shook his head. 'Their preparations continue with desperate speed now that they know we are coming, but they show no sign of retreat.'

'And why would they?' Cassius sighed. 'Outnumbering us two to one and in a position of strength.'

Fronto nodded. The army had marched at speed on Zela, scouts ranging ahead. They had found the ancient city, fortified on its hill, rising in the centre of a wide plain amid the mountains, but that was not where Pharnaces would be found. Galronus and his riders had given the king's position as a hill fortress some three miles north of the city, approachable only along a narrow, winding valley.

The Roman army had arrived late the previous evening and had encamped close to the city. Word could no longer be kept from the enemy of their approach, for clearly Pharnaces would have eyes and ears around the city, watching the Romans arrive unexpectedly and at speed. At least Caesar's army had managed to close to three miles unanticipated, which would send the edge of panic through the enemy. The large remaining question, of course, was how to deal with the final approach.

Zela, August 2nd 47 BC

That question had raised great debate in the headquarters during the evening. Galronus had not been part of it, for he and his best riders spent the hours of darkness riding around the locale, keeping a watch on the king's fortifications, and attempting to identify any other approach.

That had been Brutus' favoured tactic: a surprise assault via some unexpected and unidentified secondary approach, such as the Persians had achieved at Thermopylae, flanking Leonidas and his three hundred Spartans. Unfortunately, try as they might, Galronus and his men had been unable to find anything more useful than treacherous shepherd's paths that would allow only for very slow and painful going, which could easily be spotted and blocked by the enemy. Inadequate by far for a legion.

That approach had failed.

Cassius had been in favour of simply digging in at Zela and occupying the plain, fortifying the approach to the valley along which the king's army lay. It was a long-term tactical approach, and a very traditional one. The enemy would be trapped in poor mountainous territory, their access to good supplies and forage cut off. It was, in truth, probably the most sensible notion. But it would also likely carry them into a siege through the inhospitable months. Caesar had cited such problems as the unknown territory, mountain winters and the distance from Roman supply routes as reasons for setting this plan aside. The undertone that everyone understood was that Caesar could not personally afford to dally over winter, no matter the cost. Rome was slipping further from his control every day he campaigned in the east, his mistress languished in Alexandria, closing on giving birth to a potential heir of the Julii, and last but far from least, Cato, Scipio, Labienus and the others continued to gain strength against him in Africa.

No, Fronto knew the general could not stay long enough to effect a siege. He needed to end this.

There was only one way, then. They had to march up that narrow valley and risk everything, deploying in the ground between peaks where the king had fortified. And no officer present liked those odds. It had 'trap' or 'ambush' written all over it.

'And you've found nothing along the valley?' the general asked, not for the first time.

'The valley appears to be clear, Consul,' Galronus replied wearily, now approaching his second day without sleep. 'Though it should be noted that the sides are steep, there are woodlands, scree slopes and rocky outcroppings – places where cavalry simply cannot go. We cannot say for certain that nothing awaits you, just that nothing waits where the cavalry can see.'

Caesar nodded. They had also sent out native scouts on foot, men from Deiotarus' army, and nothing had been spotted, but then it had been night-time, after all.

'Then, all being well, our path is clear. We move at speed through the valley and fortify our position once we face the enemy.'

'And if the enemy *do* have traps and ambushes in place along that valley?' Cassius asked.

'We are in the hands of the gods, Cassius.'

The general waved over the man in the white robe. 'What have you seen, Meno,' he asked the man.

The augur stretched his hands wide, theatrically. 'Mighty Caesar, the omens are good. I have seen in the first strains of dawn light this morning four eagles, which, being the number of legions' eagles with this army, shows the favour of Jove, Minerva and Mars. The largest eagle soared north into that same valley, and within moments put up a flock of lesser birds, returning with one of them in its talons. The gods are with us.'

Caesar straightened. He looked down from the tribunal rock on which they stood with its unparalleled view of city, plain and mountain pass ahead, moonlight still giving the world a silvery glow with dawn yet an hour or two away. The better part of ten thousand soldiers stood in ordered columns below, waiting for the signal, cavalry off to the side – those who were not still out scouting – and the slaves drawn from the baggage train gathered in clusters, weighed down with the kit they bore. Everyone waited, silent and tense, including the officers.

Caesar stepped to the edge of the rise, reached up with his left hand and pulled his white cloak up over his head so that the folds hung like a hood, the usual crimson cloak bundled ready on his horse close by. Suitably attired, he waited as four men brought a heavy altar before him, grunting under the weight, while others set a brazier nearby, producing a white towel and a bowl of water.

Once everything was in position, Caesar raised his hand. A flautist began to play an oddly haunting melody nearby. The consul then washed his hands in the bowl, drying them on the towel before drawing the ornate silver-hilted pugio at his side. Hirtius poured a little wine into the brazier, to which Cassius added incense, the heady smoke that rose with a loud hiss strange and otherworldly.

'Jupiter, greatest and best,' Caesar intoned loudly, 'accept this sacrifice and grant your sons swift victory this day, that we might restore to Rome that which has been taken, and chastise the thief-king and his horde.'

As he finished, two slaves appeared, dressed in pristine white and carrying a lamb draped with red ribbons and gold phalerae. Caesar held out his free hand, and the small jug of wine was handed over. As the lamb, which seemed oddly calm, dazed even, was laid on the altar, Caesar anointed it with a few drops of wine on the head.

Cassius stepped forwards and swiftly removed the ribbons and medals, leaving a quiet, still, white lamb. Fronto watched as the knife plunged down, and the lamb briefly cried out and struggled, too late to do much else. The two slaves came to hold it still as Caesar went to work, blood running up his arms to the elbows and coating his ornate blade as he continued to intone his prayers, removing the meat for the god and pushing it onto the stick held up by Hirtius. This was then placed in the brazier, an offering for Jupiter. The rest of the animal, the god appeased, was divided up and plated for meals.

There would be no sacrificial banquet, of course – there rarely was with Caesar's rituals, for there was always a battle to fight – so the remains of the lamb would go to worthies in the city, helping tie them to Rome once more. As everything was taken away, Caesar handed his knife to a slave to clean, and washed his hands once more, drying them.

The crowds below remained silent. The auguries were good, and Caesar had invoked the greatest god of Rome, sacrificing to him, and nothing had gone amiss. No one could now doubt their success.

Dry and clean once more, Caesar removed the white cloak, lowering his makeshift hood, and a slave brought forth his red cloak and fastened it about him. Fronto couldn't help but notice the symbolism of pure white to blood red. The consul held his hands up to the waiting legions.

'Men of Rome, the gods are with us. Beyond the valley lies a man who has stolen land from the republic and tortured and murdered our people with impunity. We go now with divine blessings to teach him a lesson. Are you with me?'

The answer came in a roar that rose like a wave, dipped and crested at least three times as the legions of Rome assembled before them gave their approval to their general and the cause. Even Cassius, usually dour in the consul's company, seemed to be caught up in the fervour. Fronto smiled. Days like this were why a man knotted a general's belt around his middle, or drew his sword at all.

'Give the order,' Caesar said finally to the men around him. 'Everyone knows their deployment and order of march, the cavalry have scouted the terrain at the far end of the valley, and all is in place. There are only three miles to cover. The men can move at double time, with support to follow, lightest kit possible. Have the slaves got everything?'

Hirtius nodded. 'An entire camp on the backs of men, sir. Remarkable.'

Brutus turned a furrowed brow on the general. 'Sir, at double speed and with light kit, the men will be easy targets. We might have scouted as much as possible, but if Pharnaces *does* have traps and ambushes waiting for us in the valley, then this battle might be over before it's begun. We should move steadily and alert, clearing out each woodland as we pass, and checking every outcrop.'

Caesar nodded. 'That is most certainly what a general would usually do, and Pharnaces knows that. He therefore must know that any small ambushes he has left will come to naught. No, the valley is clear. The gods have confirmed it for us. And Pharnaces will be expecting a slow and careful approach. But just as we force-marched here and took him by surprise, so we shall do the same once more. We shall emerge before his forces long before he anticipates us, and at dawn, when he will only just be expecting us to break camp.'

'Sir?'

'Pharnaces is an impulsive man. He may have men of moderation in his army, but unlike the forces of Rome, his army is that of one man alone, a sole ruler with absolute power. It is my belief that when confronted with something so unexpected, he will react instinctively, without thought for strategy and care. *That*, Brutus, is where our advantage lies, and why the disparity in numbers will make no difference today. We've come this far and we can all but see the enemy waiting. I will be damned if we do not defeat them this day. Onward.'

As Caesar turned and marched towards his horse, the signals went up in the valley, whistles and cornua blaring and shrieking. The legions began to move towards that narrow defile in the pre-dawn gloom.

Fronto's hand went to the figurine of Fortuna at his neck. Prayers to Jupiter notwithstanding, he felt that in the circumstances *luck* was what they needed.

Let that valley be clear.

* * *

Fronto rode Bucephalus along the last stretch of the valley. They had traversed two miles in minimal time, marching at impressive speed. Despite the fears of a number of the officers, no traps or ambushes had been sprung along the snaking, narrow valley. Now, the army was moving with officer-driven restraint, the men straining at the leash and wanting to be out into the plain and finally at the enemy. The gods were truly with them, and every man was sure of it.

As the mackerel streaks of dawn began to lace themselves through the high, dark, indigo cloud, they reached their destination. The lead elements of the army, consisting of Calvinus' Thirty Sixth Legion, rounded the last corner of the valley, scouts ahead waving the all clear, and Fronto, along with several of the other senior officers, emerged into the new valley with them.

The defile they had left had been tight and winding, spacious enough only for a column twelve men wide much of the time, and switching this way and that, following a dry seasonal river bed. What that defile opened into was impressive in its dimensions. A wide vale, almost a mile across and some four miles long, filled with good arable land and dotted with native farmsteads, lay hemmed in by moors and peaks. Pharnaces' army was visible the moment they rounded the last turn, sitting on a rise at the far side of the valley. The huge, sprawling fortress that awaited them was instantly daunting, powerful ramparts atop high slopes, filled with fervent warriors.

Fronto was reminded unpleasantly of Gergovia, one of few occasions during the Gaulish campaign when the legions had been roundly battered and defeated by the tribes. The slope and the situation was reminiscent. He prayed that Caesar's divine entreaty had been enough, and that his own dear lady of luck would shelter them through the day.

The riders, including the figure of Galronus, who had scouted ahead, were now sitting upon the slope to the left of the valley's entrance, of a height with the enemy camp, and facing it over a distance of perhaps three quarters of a mile.

In response to their signals, the legions began to move into position. Along with the staff officers, Fronto climbed the slope to meet with Galronus and watch the army settle around them. The camp they were creating upon this slope was not intended as a massive defence from which to hold off an aggressive enemy. Caesar had avowed his intent to see this fight finished today, and would countenance no delay; certainly no siege. But, despite that, Pharnaces was an unknown quantity, and the legions' approach would place them in instant danger. Thus they would deploy immediately into a makeshift fortification, while the next move was considered.

The problem had been that they could hardly afford the time to construct a camp. A fortification large enough to hold this number of men would take at least two hours, during which time they would be at risk of attack from a clever enemy. Moreover, digging ditches and raising ramparts would tire legionaries who were clearly expected to win a battle today against overwhelming odds, and that they could scant risk.

Fronto watched Caesar's innovative solution at work.

The men of the Thirty Sixth, weighed down with only shields and armour, filed to the left hand, western, end of the rise, and formed up ready for a fight. Behind them, Deiotarus' native legion followed suit, so perfectly a reflection of the Thirty Sixth that they might as well have been Roman themselves, with Calvinus' other forces falling in next, and the Sixth bringing up the rear on the eastern flank. It was all perfectly organised, and would even now be causing urgent discussion in the enemy camp. Indeed, Fronto could see sudden and widespread movement behind Pharnaces' ramparts. They would be coming soon, if Pharnaces was half as impulsive as they had been led to believe. While they were still undefended, the rebel king would see his opportunity. Was that what was happening? The entire enemy force preparing to sally forth?

As they stood, watching, the camp began to form around them. The slaves, usually shuffling along as part of the lengthy baggage train under the watchful eye of a few veteran centuries, had instead moved forwards behind the legions, each man carrying a burden equal to the weight of the legionaries' own gear.

They hurried into position immediately. Every two paces along the northern edge, facing the enemy, a slave arrived with a mattock, another with a basket of detritus and a third with three sudis stakes over their shoulder. Between them they also carried mallets, nails, lengths of rope and more. Everything required.

Each slave, under the instruction of the legionaries behind them, went to work. One hacked at the ground for a short while, breaking up the gritty soil to allow for extra traction, then stepped back and produced more equipment. The second slave then tipped their basket out beyond the broken soil, comprising a collection of broken pot sherds, jagged stones, thorny brambles and more. Every naturally occurring obstacle that threatened the feet and legs of an attacker, all of which had easily been gathered en route. They too stepped back, the trio now working together as the three sudis stakes were put into position, criss-crossed like a giant wooden caltrop, presenting sharpened points to all sides. They then used the rope lengths to tie them all together. In mere moments there was an impenetrable fence of sharp timber, fronted by a patch of troublesome ground, all along the edge of the slope, such that the legions awaited attack on the hill behind them.

It was so swiftly done that it impressed even those who'd been involved in its planning. All this and without more than a few words of advice and command from the legionaries, who would usually be doing the labouring. Instead they waited, resting. They would not be exhausted from their labours in the coming hours, while still having put the defences in place. Similar lines were now being drawn around the flanks, too.

A series of loud horn blasts echoed out across the valley from the fortress at the far side. Fronto's gaze shot to the north once more, away from their works. The gates of Pharnaces' fortress were open and his men were filtering out through them in droves.

'Is this it?' asked a man close by, and Fronto turned to see that he was now at the edge of the Sixth's First Cohort, and Decimus Carfulenus stood implacable, vine cane drumming slowly on his greave.

Fronto shrugged. 'If King Deiotarus' summary of the man is correct. Caesar seems to think so. Personally, in my opinion, only a fool would abandon a place like that and come at us.'

'A fool or a man who knows he can win,' Carfulenus pointed out.

Fronto nodded absently. It was true. An attack would be foolish in most ways, but that depended upon more than one factor, many of which were out of the Romans' hands. The enemy outnumbered them two to one and were in good spirits. That they could fight was evidenced by the sound beating they had given Calvinus' army last year, and the simple fact that they had so easily carved out a kingdom in such a short space of time.

Fronto began to worry. Perhaps they *were* good enough. If they were strong enough, brave enough, numerous enough and disciplined enough, then the sudis fence and the broken pottery awaiting them on the slope could be wholly inadequate.

His hand went up once more to the figurine of the luck goddess at his neck. *Please, Divine Fortuna, don't let us have come through all those months of shit in Aegyptus just to fall now.*

He watched, tense. Across the wide valley, the army of the would-be king of Pontus was lining up in formation before their walls. What was he up to? The army was huge. And disciplined. He could see that from the efficiency with which they moved from garrison positions to an army on a war footing, spread across the slope. That did not bode over-well.

Somewhere along the line, a Roman officer gave the legions the order to fortify. Immediately, the front lines of legionaries began to go to work, taking mattocks from the slaves nearby and starting to dig turfs to create an additional rampart behind the stake fence. Fronto watched his own men begin to do the same and contemplated telling them to stand to again, but decided against it. Everything right now was a judgement call until they were committed, and Pharnaces might just be flexing his muscles. Certainly he *seemed* to be doing so, lining his forces up in direct sight, so heavily outnumbering the Romans and with such clear discipline.

Fronto chewed his lip, not really sure whether he wanted Pharnaces to attack or not. If he did so now, with things the way they stood, it suggested that he was confident of victory. In moments, the entire Bosporan force was in position, watching them from across the valley.

A weird silence descended, broken only by the crack and thud of mattocks and shovels as the men of four legions worked feverishly to improve their defences, somewhat negating the entire point of keeping the men fresh. At least they'd not had to lug the gear here because of the slaves. Fronto wondered who had ordered the works, and turned to look back at Caesar, who sat astride his horse at the high point with Deiotarus and a few others. What he saw did not fill him with confidence. Caesar was gesturing wildly at the enemy and was involved in what appeared to be an argument with the king. In that moment, Fronto suspected that it was Deiotarus of Galatia who had given the order for further fortification, which had then been picked up by Caesar's legions, and that the general was arguing against it. That the two commanders of this army could not agree did not improve matters. Indeed, even Caesar looked uncertain, going by his movements and general manner. After one last fevered discussion Caesar issued further orders, and riders hurtled from there all around the army. Fronto waited, tense, until the courier reached him.

'Sir, the consul orders work to start on general fortification. Deploy the front line beyond the defences and have the legion work on a rampart and ditch.'

The king had won out, then. Fronto looked back across the valley. The enemy still were not moving, just standing in ordered lines. What were they up to? Their inscrutability was playing havoc with decision making in the Roman command. With a nervous shake of the head, Fronto relayed the orders to Carfulenus and immediately the front rows of legionaries began to shuffle carefully through gaps that were hastily made in the sudis fence. Once they were there and lined up, the Sixth went to work on a full defensive system.

Caesar would be irritated, he knew. The general had been determined to end this today, but now that was looking unlikely. The enemy did not seem to have taken the bait the way Caesar had expected, but were instead posturing and showing their strength. In response, Deiotarus, who had already lost one battle to the invader, had advocated preparing for the worst.

And that was what they were doing.

Fronto twitched, his fingers drumming a tattoo on his belt. He didn't like this one bit. Not just the not knowing what was going to happen, but also the not being sure what he even *wanted* to happen.

If Pharnaces suddenly broke into the attack, it meant he was prepared and believed he could win. And worse, now that the legions were at work digging, and not lined up for the fight, the army was less prepared than ever to deal with an attack. An assault by the enemy, despite being what Caesar had hoped for, might now be the very last thing they needed.

On the other hand, a lengthy face off and siege across the valley, with both sides entrenched, sounded like a hell none of them could wish for, a repeat of Alexandria but without the comforts. Neither force had the supply chain in place for something like that. It would be dreadful, have an uncertain outcome, and every day of delay would make things worse for the consul elsewhere in the republic.

So that left just one other option. If the enemy were not going to charge the Roman line, which was what they had hoped for yet feared at the same time, and no one was prepared for a long-term siege, then that meant the only option was for the legions of Rome to march across the valley, and attempt to storm an extremely well defended fortress manned by an army twice their size. Hardly a move to be welcomed.

The gods had sanctioned this, hadn't they? What were the silly divine bastards playing at? Briefly, he wondered whether actually the white lamb had been corrupt and riddled with disease, displaying divine warnings, and the general had hidden it and pronounced it clean. He wondered whether Caesar had primed the priest in white with what he needed men to hear. Roman generals had done as much before, Fronto knew, and he would hardly put such a thing past Caesar, for whom appearance was a weapon. Were the gods truly actually against them, and Caesar was hiding it all?

He fretted.

'What the fuck are they?' said a soldier somewhere nearby, earning himself a smack across the shoulders from a centurion's vine stick.

But his sentiments were being echoed along the line. Fronto peered off across the valley, following many pointing digits. Something else was happening there. He watched in fascination as chariots filed out of the gates of the fortress and arced around the periphery of the gathered Bosporan King's force.

As the vehicles were brought in front of the enemy infantry, they settled into a single line in wide-spaced formation. Fronto peered at them. At this distance, perhaps three quarters of a mile, he could make out much about the chariots even with his eyesight. They were quadrigas of sorts, the traces fitted Greek-style, with a single line of four horses. On the platform stood two figures, one burdened with a spear, the other seemingly unarmed. A warrior and a driver, then.

'I hate chariots,' he muttered.

'Especially this sort,' said another horseman coming to a halt next to him. Fronto turned to see one of the Galatian officers beside him.

'Why?'

'Scythed chariots,' the man said quietly.

Fronto's lip twitched. Rome had faced Pontic scythed chariots three times during the Mithridatic wars. The first time had been a disaster. A complete slaughter and routing of the Roman forces. Tales had abounded for years thereafter of men watching their friends literally sliced in half by the long, heavy scythe blades jutting from the axles. Men who were still screaming in agony while their top halves lay ten feet from the bottom, the ground in between a mess of blood, churned turf and ground-under intestines.

Of course, Rome was nothing if not adaptable. When the Pontics had tried to repeat their victory, the Roman commander had been prepared. They had leapt aside and let the chariots pass through the lines, where they were taken down with javelins. And the third time they had lured the chariots into charging where a line of sharpened stakes awaited them.

This would be different. The Romans did not have the space on the hilltop to open up and let the vehicles through. The enemy had watched them put the stake fence in position and so would not allow themselves to die upon it. That meant that they had some other tactic in mind.

'What will they do?'

The Galatian officer shrugged. 'Given their capabilities, the width of four horses, and their knowledge of what awaits them, I know what *I* would do. Charge at the front ranks, then issue a sharp turn at the last moment, and race along the line.'

'Wouldn't that put them at a rather heavy risk? They'd be open to attack.'

The Galatian's face soured. 'Wait 'til you see the speed they move and the length of that scythe blade. By the time a rider gets taken down, he'll have cut a hundred men in two. They know what they're doing, and if their chariots are used right, then they are a true nightmare in the field. Fortunately, few commanders ever really use them to their best advantage. Best pray Pharnaces' master of chariots has not learned from history.'

Fronto tried to picture the effect of a chariot with scythed wheels turning just right so that it ran along the front ranks of legionaries, its blade at waist height, strong enough and moving fast enough to shear straight through both a shield and the man holding it. The moment he managed to picture it, he wished he hadn't, and that he could unsee the mental image.

Bringing the men back inside the line might be the answer, but then they would just find another tactic, he felt certain. No, if the chariots reached them, there would be trouble. The best solution would be to stop them getting this far. If only they could spread caltrops out down there, they might be able to do so, but there wasn't time.

He frowned, and turned to the man beside him. 'What are you doing over here anyway?' he muttered to the Galatian.

The man smiled. 'My king has ordered our officer corps to join yours during the battle. Anything new we might learn from the lions of Rome is of value to the army of the king.'

Fronto nodded. 'At the moment you'll just be learning how screwed we are,' he grunted, peering at the distant chariots once more. Slowly, though, he began to smile. 'No. Perhaps not.'

As he watched, there was a distant tumultuous roar of raised voices, blarting horns and thundering swords and spears, and the army of Pharnaces surged forth down the slope.

They were coming. For better or for worse, the army of Pharnaces was moving to attack, chariots at the fore. Fronto turned and waved to one of the message riders. The horseman trotted over, and he bowed.

Fronto pointed at the man. 'Take these orders to every commander above the rank of centurion, and do it quickly...'

CHAPTER TWENTY SIX

T he units were moving into position, as the constant echo of calls and whistles attested. A Syrian officer in his bronze armour, long white robe beneath, bow over his shoulder and crowned with a decorative conical helmet, attended Fronto with a curt bow.

Fronto gestured to the legionary he had ready, unarmoured and breathing deeply, carrying only a white stick. 'Four hundred paces. Go.'

The man burst into a quick jog, trying to measure the paces of his journey but at the quickest speed possible, pushing between the men and out through a temporary gap in the sudis fence. As he ran down the slope, Fronto returned to watching the enemy. He had marked out in his mind one of the region's interminable dry stream beds some way across the valley, and a small stand of juniper somewhat closer. *Two hundred paces* closer, he was confident. One thing about having faced an army across open ground more times than most people bought new boots, was that a man became a fairly shrewd judge of speeds and distances.

Two hundred paces.

Two hundred paces was the maximum range of a trained archer with any level of constancy and accuracy. And the archers that were now falling in all along the Roman lines, behind the first ranks of legionaries, were all trained units and good, solid veterans. Cretans, Hamians, Carians and Galatians. All with strong, compact composite bows of wood, horn and sinew.

The legionary was now at four hundred paces from Fronto, which also meant from the lines of archers. He peered through the gap between legionaries, opened up specifically for his sighting. Tense, he waited for the oncoming chariots. The legionary hammered in his white stick, eyes darting nervously to the flood of vehicles now at the base of the far slope and racing across the flat valley bottom with deadly speed, the blades on their wheels now visible and gleaming in the dawn light.

This would be Rome's fourth encounter with the deadly vehicles in this region. Only the first battle had been lost, and Fronto was determined not to be the man commanding the second.

The lead chariot reached the dry river bed. Fronto started counting, rhythmically.

One hundred and fifty paces.

One hundred paces.

Fifty paces.

The chariot passed the juniper. They had traversed the two hundred paces between the two landmarks to Fronto's count of twenty two. He took a steady breath, and looked back and forth along the Roman line. Archers were falling in in blocks, nocking arrows, just one each – the rest remained in their quivers. This had to be perfectly timed, and that could only be done with one shot.

Twenty Two. He chewed his lip. But there would be a count of one or two while they drew and released – he had to take that into account. He knew from the experience of a score of battles that it took roughly a count of three for the arrow to travel two hundred paces, but he'd almost forgotten to factor in the draw and release time.

Twenty four, then.

Oh, and a count of two for the order to be relayed. Nearly forgot that.

Twenty six.

He became aware that the legionary down the slope was still standing by his white stick, waiting for the order to return. Fronto waved him back frantically, and the soldier hurtled up the slope towards the legion, where a mate waited with his gear in the fifth line. Behind the man, at the bottom of the valley, the chariots were closing, the racing infantry of Pharnaces' army surprisingly close behind, the momentum of charging down the slope still with them.

Momentum. Slope.

Damn it. He hadn't factored in the slope. Uphill riding instead of down. How much would that slow a chariot? Fretting like mad, and wishing he could ask someone, he plucked a number from the air, the one that for some reason was hovering on the tip of his tongue. Three. Oh, how he hoped that was the work of Fortuna.

Three it was, then. Subtract three for the change in gradient.

Twenty three, then.

Minus the three seconds of flight time, of course.

Twenty in all.

Gods, but he hoped he was right.

And then there was no more time to plan. The chariots had crossed the wide flat area and were beginning to climb the slope. The enemy foot were now further behind and lagging more and more, the chariots still moving at horse speed, while the infantry were no longer boosted by advantageous terrain.

Fronto drew a deep breath. The chariots had spread out into a line as long as the Roman front, plenty of room between each to allow time and space for manoeuvring. There was little doubt now in Fronto's mind that the Galatian officer had been absolutely on the nose with his theory. They intended to turn at the last moment and ravage the front line. If not, then they were going to plough through the line of men and impale themselves on the sudis fence, and no enemy was that stupid.

Three.

Two

One.

The chariots passed the white stick marker. Fronto began to count.

Twenty...

He couldn't help himself, so tense was he, and his fingers began to tick off the numbers as they dropped in his head. He became aware of other men gathering around him and made sure not to lose count or change speed as he glanced back. Caesar and the king had come forward, along with several senior officers, having been informed that the archers had moved on legate Fronto's orders. The legions had stopped digging and building now, and had readied themselves for a fight once more. The brave lad who'd run with the white stick was armoured again at last and being helped on with his baldric as a friend tied the fastenings on his helmet's cheek pieces.

Three.

Two.

One.

It was a horrifying sight. The chariots were terribly close now, having covered almost half the distance from the white marker, and they were moving at an incredible pace, given the slope.

If this failed there were going to be a lot of bisected legionaries screaming on that hillside.

Fronto's hand dropped.

'Now.'

Whistles gave two short blasts. He counted two before the bows began to rise. Strings were drawn back. He counted another two until with a sound like a whisper of death, a thousand bow strings snapped tight, sending their arrows into the air.

Fronto prayed.

The arrows arced up over the heads of the legionaries who, almost to a man, were cringing back in panic, bending away from the enemy menace and gripping their shields in white-knuckled hands.

The missiles fell.

Fortuna had been with him.

All along the Roman lines, the charging chariots reached the two hundred pace mark just as the arrows plunged down. One or two struck a driver or a spear man. Many went wild, thudding into turf or skittering off scree, or simply snapping in the tangle of wheels and wooden vehicles. But enough hit the mark just as Fronto had planned. Enough to change it all.

The horses were the key. Any chariot driver would tell you that a biga or a quadriga was only as effective as the horses pulling it. Oddly, Fronto had never given it much thought. He preferred bouts in the arena to chariot racing, but over the years Galronus had been with him, the Remi noble had become something of an afficionado of the races, and like all enthusiasts felt the need to barrage Fronto with facts and titbits with monotonous regularity.

Now, perhaps it was paying off. If it hadn't been for Galronus' little notes, he'd probably have had them aim for the drivers. Most would have missed and it wouldn't have made much difference.

The horses were the key.

Arrows thudded into the beasts that raced forwards, pulling the chariots. Each vehicle was drawn by four horses, and at best two, or occasionally three were hit, which was enough. *One* would be enough. The moment a horse in one of those traces felt the arrow plunge into its muscly hide, it screamed in agonised panic, and it did what all panicked beasts did. It stopped, or it reared, or it slewed and fell. No matter what it did, though, the fact was that it was not doing what the other horses in the trace were.

Every vehicle was suddenly a chaotic mess of contradictory forces, pulling this way and that. Many immediately fell, the horses suddenly coming to a halt. One chariot even pitched impressively up into the air with the momentum, over the top of the beasts pulling it, slamming down to the ground and mangling the men beneath it. Others scraped to a halt in the dirt as the traces broke, wounded animals racing away in panic as the others milled in confusion. A little to the left, two chariots collided and the result was like one of the more horrific accidents in the circus, a massive explosion of kindling, a cacophony of snapping limbs from both men and horses, and then just a shuddering pile of timber and animal parts. A screaming heap of death, and the nearby legionaries lightly misted with a spray of blood and dust.

At least one chariot got through. He could hear desperate cries in Latin way off to his left, probably in Calvinus' legion, and screams and carnage. But even as the chariot tried to pull away from its line of victims and leave the fray, the driver realised there was no hope. The chaos of ruined chariots in the way prevented his flight, and before he could leave, he was struck by a dozen shafts from enterprising archers along to the west.

Fronto watched the result of his action with grisly satisfaction.

There had been maybe sixty chariots fielded along the line. He could see six racing away for home, at the periphery of the field, around the rest of the enemy force, which stomped resolutely towards them. Another five or six chariots were milling around, their drivers either dead or desperately trying to coax panicked or wounded horses into action.

The enemy's charge had been meant to break the Roman lines.

They had failed.

Caesar's tones cut through the general din.

'Impressive.'

It was all he said, but it was enough. They had a moment to breathe. The enemy infantry were now trudging up the slope, filtering between ruined chariots to form up on the near side once more. Fronto couldn't see their faces yet, but he could only imagine the look on them. The utter destruction of their shock weapons would have shaken them, and then having to walk through the carnage would not have improved matters.

It spoke of their discipline and spirit that they were still coming at all, let alone at such speed and in such tight formation. Pharnaces might be impulsive, but he was no fool. He had sent out a dreadful attack to break and demoralise his enemy, and then followed it up with a superior force of strong and determined veterans. It could hardly be said to be Pharnaces' fault that his attack had failed. It might so easily have succeeded.

Caesar's voice once more, though apparently speaking to someone else. 'See how poor a commander Pharnaces is? If this is the quality of enemies we have left to face, then thank the gods I must soon face Scipio for a challenge.'

Someone laughed.

Not Fronto.

He turned and glared at Caesar, though the look he caught momentarily on the general's face was not the one of derision he expected, but one of uncertainty. The comment had been bravado, aimed at a doubter. Politics again. Fronto's lip curled as he turned back to the enemy who, as far as he was concerned, were presenting a perfectly adequate challenge, thank you very much.

'Front line, back step. Behind the sudis,' called a voice. Fronto glanced off to his left to see Cassius giving orders. Caesar shot the officer a look born of surprise and irritation, yet he nodded. Fronto had thought to do as much before the initial contact but, with that unpleasant decision officers sometimes had to make, he had left the line of men in deadly danger in front of the stakes. Had he not, the chariots might not have been induced to charge into the killing zone of the arrows. He had used them as bait to kill off the enemy's main strike. It was a horrible decision to make, but it had worked.

Now, however, Cassius was quite right. It was time to pull the men back. In response to the officer's command, centurions all along the front issued orders. Every few paces along the line, men shuffled aside to leave gaps, and the soldiers who had stood out front and faced down the chariot charge filtered through and to the rear lines, where they could recover and where, Fronto hoped as some of them passed close by, the more nervous ones might have a chance to change their underwear. A chariot charge was a terrifying thing, after all.

In a matter of heartbeats the front line had changed. The men – those who had survived – from the front were safe at the rear now, and the gaps that had opened to let them through closed once more. Those grimly-determined looking foot soldiers stomping up the slope would have watched their enemy filter back and then been faced instead with a fence of sharpened points, behind which fresh legionaries waited.

He still couldn't see their faces clearly, but he'd be willing to bet that the change had shaken them further. Fronto smiled coldly. Every tiny thing now would be another nail hammering into the crucifix of their morale. They were still strong, numerically superior, and disciplined. But the one thing they had been, which would be starting to slide, was certain. They had to now be questioning their ability to win the day. And as their morale slid, it would begin to take with it the discipline.

That was how it worked. Those moments when a battle's outcome hung in the balance and an army teetered on the edge of a rout. It always began with faltering confidence. Then that ate away at discipline, eroded the chain of command until it rusted and broke. Then went their strength. All that remained was numbers, and numbers meant nothing if they were running the other way.

He had to break them. That had begun with the chariots, then the stake fence and the fresh lines of men. Now, he thought, let's try the old fashioned way.

'Carfulenus.'

'Sir?'

'Have the men give them the old war drums.'

The centurion grinned and saluted.

'To my rhythm, lads,' he called out, then began to pound his *vitus* vine cane against the bronze greave encasing his right shin. In moments the rhythm was picked up all across the legion. Men were rapping their swords against their shield edges in time, signifers were slapping the silver discs on their standards with their free hands, centurions smacking their greaves and optios hammering their staves on the stony ground. The rhythmic banging was impressive.

The enemy did not falter, but they were coming close and now Fronto could see their faces. There was uncertainty. Their officers were keeping them in line and in order, but were it not for such rigid control, Fronto doubted they would be marching so keenly.

They were going to break.

He knew it at that moment. The enemy would break. It was just a matter of pushing until it happened, and making sure his own men did not break first.

Before he realised he was doing it, his voice cut out across the general hubbub, just about audible over the crash of swords on shields.

'Ro – ma – vic – trix... Ro – ma – vic – trix...'

By the third iteration, the chant was spreading, first through the centurions and signifers, then throughout the legions. There was an odd lull as the Galatian army of King Deiotarus faltered, uncertain whether or not to join in this foreign chant. After all, they were not Romans, yet as the army of Pharnaces closed on the Roman line, they began to pick up the rhythm.

The din was such, as four legions crashed and chanted, that it was all but impossible to hear anything else across the field. The enemy tried to respond with their own war cries, some Bosporan song of battle backed by the booing of horns, but it was as ineffective in the face of the Roman effort as a man shouting in a howling gale.

'Fourth line: pila,' shouted Carfulenus, an order that echoed across the Roman line from centurion to centurion. The front line of the enemy had reached missile range. The first three rows of legionaries remained locked in their shield wall behind the sudis fence, second and third lending their strength to the first, helping brace them. The fourth and fifth lines, however, were spaced out, three paces between they and the men in front. At the command, every legionary in the fourth line brought down the heavy javelin that they had held upright and positioned it, gripping underneath the shaft behind the weighted section, angled up and ready to throw.

'Release.'

Even as they did so, drawing their blades immediately and stepping forwards to join the first three lines in tight formation, and even as the shafts flew out over the heads of the Romans, the centurions were repeating themselves.

'Fifth line: pila.'

Again, the next line lowered their javelins, shifting their grip and angling ready.

Such was the speed of the command and its obeying, that the second volley was ready to launch just as the first fell.

Fronto watched the pila plunging down out of the air in a long narrow cloud. He had no idea how well the other younger, or foreign, legions did, but the Sixth were veterans and only the best throwers had been placed in the fourth and fifth lines. The pila slammed into shields and bodies, eliciting screams and bellows all along the enemy line.

Men fell with their limbs, torsos, shields and more pierced, one man before where Fronto stood had the misfortune for a pilum to plunge into his foot, pinning it to the ground hard. He stopped in his tracks with a shriek, but there was no hope of halting, for the entire army of the invading king were behind him, still pressing forwards. The man screamed again as he was pushed forward and his foot pulled up from the turf while the pilum remained lodged, tearing its way out between the toes.

He disappeared beneath the feet of his comrades, howling in agony. The enemy's war song seemed to have stopped. They were still coming, though. The number of dead from the pilum volley was comparatively small, after all. The second volley hit even as Fronto was wondering how close they were to breaking. More men fell, injured, transfixed, issuing bloodcurdling howls, lost amid the tramping feet of their fellows.

Fronto turned. The Hamian archery officer was still close by.

'Can your men drop arrows among them safely without hitting our lads in between?' he yelled.

The man bowed his head sharply, pointed helmet almost putting Fronto's eye out, and replied loudly in a thick Syrian accent.

'Yes, Legatoos. For certainment.

'Do it. Pepper the bastards at will.'

'Quid, Legatoos?'

'Shoot them,' he said simply and with exaggerated clarity.

'Yes, Legatoos. Happyness.'

He hurried back to his unit, who had clearly been waiting for such an order. The front line of the enemy were almost at the barrier. Fronto leaned across to Carfulenus and bellowed in his ear over the crashing noises.

'We're going to break the shitbags, Carfulenus.'

'That we are, sir.'

Fronto grinned. 'I don't mean the army as a whole, Carfulenus. I mean us. The Sixth. We're going to break them and push them back. Then we're going to flank them. They're only confident now because of the numbers. They think they can swamp us, and little can disabuse them of that notion, but if we can flank them, then they'll realise that their numbers no longer mean anything. If we do that, we win. We break the flank and use that to panic the rest. Got it?'

Carfulenus nodded. 'How though, Sir?'

Fronto snorted. 'No special trick. Just sheer brutality. The Sixth are the strongest unit in this whole valley. They fought at Alesia, for Jove's sake. At Pharsalus. They are undefeated lunatics. And you are the man who broke the king of Aegyptus. The man who took a fortress of ten thousand with a hundred men and frightened them into surrender. And me? Well I'm just a cantankerous, unkillable old bastard.'

Carfulenus laughed.

'Let's break them, then, sir.'

'Yes, let's.'

The enemy engaged at that moment. The sudis stake fence was a serious impediment, and the detritus beyond it was effective. Fronto watched between men as the enemy reached the fence and attempted to pull the triple-stake contraptions aside and out of the way. Some found that the loose earth, brambles, broken pots and the like were simply too treacherous on the slope for good footing, and the moment they began to heave at the stakes, they slipped and fell. One man not far away felt his feet disappear out from under him on a loose pot sherd and pitched forwards, ending his days impaled on the sharpened stake, gurgling, dark blood pouring from his mouth as he twitched, while his friends attempted to shift the sudis contraption with him still stuck on it.

Gradually, the sudis fence was dismantled, pulled away and separated by the enemy, the ropes binding them together hacked apart and the whole thing dismantled, leaving the enemy with a clear run at the waiting legionaries. Of course, that achievement came at a high price. They might have managed to clear away the obstacle, but for every single stake that was shifted a man died, stabbed at any given opportunity by the legionaries in the front row. Additionally, of course, the Hamian archers at the rear were dropping clouds of arrows with constant accuracy amid the approaching block of men, causing havoc. The carnage was horrifying. Bosporan soldiers were now standing two feet taller than the waiting Romans due to the sheer volume of bodies carpeting the ground beneath them.

Fronto could feel it in the air. He looked up. Black shapes were circling in the gold-azure dawn light high above. The carrion birds could feel it too. The battle was close to the moment of decision. Close to an end.

He caught sight then of Carfulenus to his right beginning to move. The centurion had spotted a small gap opening and had ripped his sword free, marching in that direction. The legate turned and looked around. The knot of senior officers who had been hovering nearby at the start had moved away. No senior commander placed themselves in the thick of it, after all. Well, *almost* no senior commander.

Fronto felt a moment of guilt. Somewhere way off west, Lucilia and the boys were sitting in a villa, safe from the world of civil war, but probably worrying about him, wondering where he was, what he was doing, and when he was coming home. Lucilia would smack him repeatedly around the head if she knew the danger in which he kept placing himself.

He had vowed now that he was a little older to take more of a back seat. To actually act like an officer and direct battles. He'd begun the winter by doing precisely that in Alexandria, but as the season had turned, he'd found himself slipping more and more into old habits, beginning with that stupid jump from the ship to Pharos' shore, where he'd almost ended his days drowned in the harbour, then finding himself trapped on the Heptastadion fortress wall and having to belly flop gracelessly into the water.

He felt that guilt.

But he also felt it overridden by his very nature. With a feral growl, he ripped his sword from its sheath and raced after the centurion.

* * *

Decimus Carfulenus had seen the gap opening up. A small knot of enemy warriors more heavily armoured and richly dressed than the rest had managed to force a breach, and were now trying to exploit it, pushing their way in among the Romans. One of them had dropped his shield and drawn a dagger, using it and a short sword in the press to horrifying effect, knifing legionary after legionary. The others were laying about them with longer swords and axes, those with shields using them to punch the iron or bronze boss out at the Romans, breaking limbs and faces.

Their helmets were bronze and archaic-looking, their cheek pieces designed so that when pulled together and tied they almost completely covered the face, embossed with a fierce demonic visage themselves.

They were clearly some sort of elite force. Perhaps part of a royal guard or something. What was certain was that while most of the enemy were already faltering, they remained fierce and intent on battle. They also represented the most danger, having forced a breach.

Carfulenus yelled to his men, exhorting them to close the breach, but he was there anyway, for a centurion had to be in the thick of it. He had to be the man leading by example, and right now he was wading into those elite soldiers like a champion gladiator. He may not have the bulk of many of his peers, but he knew he was faster than most. His sword lanced out left, having spotted an opening and seeking a gap in the bronze, where the tip found its way through black leather pteruges and into flesh. Even as the blade bit home, his vine stick, a formidable enough weapon in its own right, came down in an angled overhand blow, smashing into the decorative bronze helmet of another warrior, sending a puff of horsehair plume up into the air as the helmet cracked to the side, dazing, mashing and deafening the head within. He felt something pressing into his midriff and instinctively spun right, the blade that had only failed to impale him due to being blunted by chain shirt skittering off to the side.

'Oh no you don't you Bosporan turd,' he snapped, bringing the stick back round for another blow across that man's face. Even as the man ducked back away, Carfulenus' rising knee caught him between the legs. The man cried out in agony and staggered backwards, dropping his weapons to clutch in horror at his ruined privates. Leg greaves of bronze that came up over the knee had so many uses...

As he stuck his blade in another target of opportunity, he was thrown to the side when a warrior punched out with his shield, the bronze boss slamming into the centurion's ribs. Winded, he staggered for a moment. As he recovered and righted himself, ready to return the favour, the shape of the warrior with the smug, victorious grin and the dented shield boss was replaced with a familiar one.

'Sir?'

Fronto ignored him, his blade lancing out and back, out and back, out and back like some sort of automated butchery machine, face smeared with blood that clearly wasn't his, free hand grabbing shields and ripping them to the side so that elbows, knees and even teeth could be employed to their best effect.

Carfulenus stared for only a moment, and then fell in beside his commander, the two of them working at hacking and slashing, stabbing, kicking and maiming. He gradually became aware that they had healed the breach and were now on the front line of their men. The legionaries were beside and behind them, desperately calling the legate to retreat, the shock of watching their senior officer at the front too much.

But Fronto wasn't stopping. They had healed the breach and had killed that small knot of elite guardsmen, but that wasn't enough. Fronto had kept going. Having reformed the Roman front line, he had stepped forwards and begun to carve his own breach into the enemy in return.

Carfulenus stared and boggled only for a moment before he began to laugh maniacally. It was impossible to not be impressed. The centurion threw himself in alongside his commander, dragging the men of the First Cohort with him into their freshly-formed breach, and desperately hoping that someone would warn the Hamian archers at the rear to stop their barrage.

'We're going to break the shitbags, sir,' he snarled as he carved Rome's displeasure into a terrified, howling warrior. But the legate was   too   busy   to   reply.

CHAPTER TWENTY SEVEN

F ronto's blade bit out and slashed with crazed speed and strength, each blow powered by frustration long pent up and now released.

Months of watching the political tension ebbing and flowing around Caesar, Cleopatra and Cassius, of worrying about the future of Caesar, of Fronto's service to the consul, and even of the future of the republic. A Bosporan swordsman deep in the press, where they had driven their breach, reacted to suddenly being faced with the snarling, feral legate by raising his shield and cowering behind it. Fronto's free hand grasped the bronze rim and ripped it to one side, his sword slamming point-first into that narrow V' between the man's collar bones, where it ripped deep into flesh, muscle and windpipe. Bastards and their politics.

Months of being forced to live in a besieged city with the atmosphere of a warm, damp sock, where sweat and burned skin were the norm, and water was a more prized commodity than gold, all because of some damned succession crisis in a state too important for Rome to leave alone, where no claimant to the throne seemed to be worthwhile anyway. Bloody Aegyptus. A warrior's eyes widened as Fronto dropped to a near crouch, ducking a stabbing spear and slamming the sharp edge of his blade into the hamstrings of the man. As he fell, Fronto nearly followed him, rising slowly and with difficulty on his weak knee.

Another damned irritation: this getting old. Fronto knew well that his hair was now more shot with grey than ever, and had become aware that when he shaved, the whiskers were now white and brittle, that he had acquired odd hairs in his eyebrows that were steely coloured and with a similar consistency, like wire. He was aware that the wrinkles of his face had become craggy. The problem was that inside he still felt twenty. Still felt he should be able to do everything he used to. But it was being driven home every passing month that he was becoming physically a shadow of the man who had marched into Gaul. Muscles ached, joints hurt and stiffened, breathing was more laboured when he ran, his eyesight seemed to be declining, and there was ever the trouble with the damned knee. Gritting his teeth, he slammed his sword into a man's side and huffed at the effort it took, even as he pushed the man aside and waded on.

It did little to improve that latter that young Carfulenus – far too young really for a senior centurion – was hacking and stabbing away next to him with easy violence, displaying not one sign of trouble. Stab. Hack. Slash. Push.

Then there was the ongoing war. He'd finally decided after Massilia and Ilerda that it was time to give this up and retire. Even without debts Caesar still owed him, there was the wine trade. When he'd last left it, Catháin had already surpassed mere profitability and moved into lucrative areas. From what he understood, he would soon be rich, if he wasn't already. Of course, it wasn't done for a man of patrician blood to dabble in trade. Land and finance were the stock of the senatorial class, and trade and mercantilism was below them, the province of the equites. But Fronto also knew damn well just how many senators with ancient names had factors who dealt with just such businesses for them, some of them simply letting their wives deal with the finance and enjoying the benefits. Fronto had just taken one step further in initiating the whole thing himself.

He'd intended to be back in Puteoli by now, the war over, and his family back in their ancestral home. Or if the war insisted on dragging out, he would at least have been in that villa near Tarraco that he'd inherited from Longinus, still with his family, watching the death throes of the republic from a safe distance.

Family. It was time to spend the rest of his days with his lovely Lucilia. It was time to watch his boys grow into men. To steer them away from becoming what he'd become. To break the chain of sour militarism and alcohol. To make them productive and bright stars of Rome. But Caesar had managed to drag him east and to Dyrrachium, then to Pharsalus, then Alexandria, and now to Zela. Next, though, there would be Rome, and Fronto would insist that it end for him there. That he finally go home to his family.

A howling warrior brought a blade down in a strong two-handed blow and Fronto reached up, gripping his own sword in both hands and slamming it in the way, deflecting the strike so that it slid harmlessly off to his left, a hand's breadth from his shoulder. As the man lurched forwards, sword dropping, Fronto angled his own blade and brought it back down, smashing it across the man's forearms, breaking the bones in both and chopping deep into the flesh. As his victim dropped away, screaming, Fronto snarled at the next man and pushed forwards once more.

This had to be it. The last battle. He would win Caesar his victory over Pharnaces. A victory over an army twice their size, fought on the enemy's chosen ground and won with strength and speed. And then it would be over. Caesar wouldn't need him in the senate. What use was Fronto in debates, after all? He would return to his family and friends, and urge Galronus to join him. He would grow old disgracefully, living that same lavish lifestyle he had shunned as a younger man. He'd damn well *earned* it. The republic – Caesar in particular – had had his youth. Every hour of his strength and will, he'd poured into these campaigns. Now he was owed. And if Caesar insisted on going to Africa to put Cato down, which he might not need to do if Cassius was right, then Fronto would not be going with him this time.

He was suddenly well aware of his own words to Cassius on the subject, though. That there could never be a peaceful solution with Cato's party, at least as long as Labienus was there. And that brought back an image of Titus Labienus. A man Fronto had looked up to. A philanthropist and humanitarian, despite his military genius. A man who could be everything the republic needed. In many ways, an anti-Caesar, Fronto was forced to admit.

Somewhere deep inside, Fronto had the feeling that this could never be over until he'd looked deep into Labienus' eyes and seen if he could be turned from his destructive path.

That meant the war would go on, and Fronto with it. That meant that this *wouldn't* be the last battle. And that unpleasant thought was perhaps the worst of all.

Fronto bellowed with rage and threw himself at the next knot of men, slamming into them like a wrestler, sending them staggering back into each other, where they fell in a graceless heap. Fronto stared. How was there enough room for them to fall over in this press?

Something touched his shoulder and he spun, alert, sword coming up, and only just pulled it back in time as he realised that it was the hand of Decimus Carfulenus on his shoulder. His own wild eyes settled on the younger officer and he realised that through the spray of blood and filth on the man's face, he was grinning, perfect white teeth shining through the muck.

'What?'

'They're on the run, sir. Look. The flank is broken.'

Fronto turned. Space was opening up everywhere now. Men were falling over one another to get away from the bellowing, ferocious legionaries of the Sixth. The entire eastern flank of the army of King Pharnaces was on the run, perhaps two thousand men fleeing the field, racing back down the slope, along and across the valley.

It suddenly occurred to Fronto that he was no longer standing on a steep incline as he had been when they'd started, and he hadn't the trouble keeping his footing that he'd had. He was perhaps two thirds of the way down the slope from the Roman camp…

He turned in shock. He'd realised, of course, that they'd begun to take the fight to the enemy. The moment they had healed the breach in their own lines, Fronto had begun to push forwards, bowing the line once more but this time outwards, into the enemy. He'd formed a breach in their forces in turn, Carfulenus by his side and staunch warriors of the Sixth all around and behind him. But he hadn't realised just how long he'd been hacking, slashing and pushing, nor quite how far they'd gone.

He turned, still surprised. The sun was up above the hills now, baking the land with its August heat, making bronze and iron glow, making the blood, mud and piss of the battlefield steam. The front lines of Pharnaces' force were still way back up the hill behind him, but the professional centurions of the Sixth had been on it. Even as they had descended the slope, the officers had manoeuvred the blocks and lines of the Sixth so that while they continued to push the flanking units down the slope, they had also begun to reform, presenting a solid front along the enemy's flanks as their peripheral units crumbled. Now, the entire Roman force had become an 'L' shape, half boxing in the remaining formed enemy units.

Even as Fronto watched, he could see the fight now going out of the remaining forces under Pharnaces' command. With the collapse of their left flank, the centre of the enemy force had come under pressure from the Sixth, who were as wolves now, their blood up and the taste of victory already on their lips.

A Bosporan soldier ran past and Fronto lanced out with his blade, almost negligently, delivering a deep cut to the man's thigh as he ran. The fleeing warrior stumbled and fell. Before he hit the ground two legionaries were on him, stabbing and hacking.

There were no calls for retreat. Pharnaces either still thought he could win, or was so blindly deluded in his avarice that he could not countenance retreat. No horns called for his men to fall back. It was a mistake. Fronto could feel the atmosphere emanating from the Bosporan force. They were on the cusp. He'd made a similar mistake at the Heptastadion. When he'd known the Roman force was in trouble, he should have sounded the retreat earlier, and he'd have saved more lives. As it was, he had avoided utter catastrophe by sounding the call in time to save many. Pharnaces was not quite so astute, apparently. Had he the nous to sound the retreat now, the rest of his army could pull back in good order across the plain and to his fortress. There, he could regroup and prepare to defend against Caesar. He would still outnumber Rome considerably, and there would be time for his army to recover its spirit.

Still no call came. It would be too late to form an orderly withdrawal any moment now.

Fronto felt that change in the air. He could almost reach out and grasp the moment that Pharnaces lost the battle. There was a cry from somewhere in the army's centre. The source couldn't possibly be identified, for it was just the voice of one man raised in panic as he realised that, while two of his comrades remained between he and the Roman force up the slope, more Roman shapes were visible through the crowd off to his left. They had been flanked, and that knowledge had begun to filter through the huge army.

It started slowly. Fronto had once watched a building fall down in Rome. Some builder doing a little work on a two-storey street-front structure down the road from his own townhouse had demolished something he'd not been meant to. Turned out that the supporting wall he had broken into had not been the one at the edge of the building upon which they worked, but the main support of the building next door.

Fronto had watched with fascination. The builder had known what he'd done the moment he did it, for he backed hurriedly along the street away from the wall, shouting to his mates to get out. They did so, abandoning the site like rats leaving a ship. As they'd done that, they had called warnings to the owners and occupants of the next building. Fortunately for them, the family were out and only slaves and servants were in residence, all of whom fled immediately as the entire structure started to tremble like a cold animal, making the same groaning sounds as a very hungry belly.

They had gathered to watch from a safe distance, residents, builders and onlookers all, as the thing had gone. It had begun slowly. The groaning and the trembling. Then a shudder had run through the entire structure, like a man shivering. Dust and mortar started to puff out from the walls, dropping to the cobbles. A slate fell. Then another. The damaged wall leaned out. Further and further, looking untenable even at the start.

The groaning had become louder and louder, the wall bowing and changing in shape as pressures from above increased. Slowly, ever so slowly, it had started to fall. Fronto had almost been dying with the anticipation. And then it fell. After a long period of slowly changing and leaning, discarding bits and pieces, the entire building collapsed in on itself. It had come straight down, fortunately, not damaging any of the surrounding buildings, but the blast wave of dust and detritus had engulfed two streets and every figure watching.

Fronto's mother had bollocked him for an hour for the state he was in when he'd got home.

This army went the same way as that building. The groaning of the tortured masonry here was the din of shouting from the men of the centre and the right flank, as they howled their dismay at the collapse of their own supporting wall to the hammer of the Sixth Legion. And then the structure began to change shape. The central mass started to curve inwards under pressure from the Sixth. Fronto couldn't see the far side of the field, but he'd be willing to bet that in response to all the pressure, Pharnaces' right flank would now be leaning outwards, away from the fight.

Dust, mortar and slates started to come away. Now standing in clear ground where the enemy's flank had fled, Fronto had an excellent view. Wherever the Roman forces had yet to press the enemy, men were dropping out of the lines and following in the wake of their fleeing fellows. At the rear, the block was beginning to disintegrate, small units of men departing in clusters, safe at the back and running for the security of their fortifications.

The detritus falling from Pharnaces' house became bulkier and bulkier, the rear now coming away in clumps as they ran. The groaning of the doomed army became louder and more pronounced. Someone, possibly Pharnaces himself, had finally decided that retreat was called for, but it was pointless. The call was just too late to make any difference now. The horn calls were all but lost amid the cries of pain and terror.

The army of Pharnaces shuddered en masse, just as the damaged house in Rome had done. Fronto watched it, and knew what was coming next.

The enemy broke. The entire force suddenly tried to run for safety. Those still caught in the press only fought on as much as they needed to in order to get away. Whole units, hundreds strong, were running now with no thought to order and unit cohesion. In moments the enemy force went from a strong, solid block to a mass flight, every man concerned with his own survival and sparing not a thought for his countrymen.

Fronto watched as the house collapsed. Pharnaces' warriors were killing each other in desperate attempts to be past their own. Panic reigned. Worst of all the front of the fighting had still been high up the slope before the Roman camp. As men turned and tried to run, they lost their footing and fell, tumbling over one another and rolling down the hill, picking up wounds, bruises and broken bones, some smashing into the remains of chariots and horses where they still lay amid the press of their own fleeing force. As the Romans stomped slowly down the slope in formation, discipline intact, they constantly passed heaps of panicked enemies, still trying to disentangle themselves, to rise and to flee. As they reached fallen warriors they casually dispatched them with sword blows before stomping on them in hobnailed boots, and pressing on down the slope in the pursuit of the routing force.

The battle was already won, but the enemy still had high numbers. What they could not now afford to do was allow Pharnaces time and opportunity to regroup. If he could manage to reinstil discipline into the army, they would still be a threat to Caesar. They had to be pressed and utterly broken, such that the force disbanded, enough dead or enslaved to remove any future threat, the rest encouraged to flee across the countryside far and wide, too spread out to possibly regroup.

Somewhere back in the camp, Fronto could hear a new call. The call for melee. Caesar had removed the leash from his dogs. In response, the legions' centurions put out their own calls, releasing their men to chase down and kill the enemy with impunity.

Fronto paused, something nagging at him. He saw Carfulenus nearby. The Sixth were not yet falling upon the fleeing rabble in the melee, for Carfulenus and his subordinates had more of a job doing so. The Sixth was spread out down the hill in a line where they had flanked the enemy

Fronto waved to him as he put the whistle to his lips, and Carfulenus paused.

'Don't let them loose just yet.'

His gaze went up past the melee and the panicked, fleeing force of Pharnaces.

He saw them a moment later: the royal banners among a small party of horsemen, beyond the broken army and fleeing up the slope, back towards their fortress. Pharnaces had managed to get the bulk of his army between Rome, and himself and was racing for safety. Fronto's gaze rose further, realising what it had been that had nagged at him.

Men still lined the ramparts of the enemy fortress. Pharnaces had left perhaps two or three cohorts' worth of men defending his camp while he advanced. Now he was racing for the safety of those men. Fronto chewed his lip. There were not enough men there to hold it against Caesar's army, and the fleeing men were too demoralised to be of use in that respect, but it still posed a problem.

Pharnaces was escaping. If he got to that fortress unmolested, he would be able to gather those cohorts and flee the field. The rest of the army was bogged down chasing the routing force, killing with glee, and would take far too long to rein in, but the Sixth were still in formation. There was almost no chance of reaching the fortress on foot before the king, who was closer and on horseback, but they would take time to gather the cohorts and depart. Maybe, just maybe, Fronto could catch them before they left.

'Carfulenus, have the entire Sixth break off and make for the enemy fortress at double time. The king is escaping.'

Carfulenus took a precious moment to glance away at the riders on the slope, then nodded and began shouting orders to his signallers, waving and blowing his whistle. Moments later the Sixth were on the move, racing for the slope and the fortress atop it.

Fronto took a deep breath. Whether the future held a return to the bosom of his family or another season of stomping through the grain fields of Africa in search of Titus Labienus, for now he had to finish this.

Once more he found himself grumbling about his age and the youth of the men around him, legionaries beginning to pass by, as they crossed the flat ground and began to climb the slope. Few of the fleeing men of the flank remained before them. Those who had run for the safety of the defences would already be there, and many had fled the field, running for the edges of the fight and the open ground, seeking a way to depart this dreadful valley entirely. While Galronus and his scouts had found no mountain paths suitable to bring an army over, a small unit of fleeing soldiers could take any one of a number of such routes, as could Pharnaces, of course.

Fronto stomped on up the slope. Briefly, he caught sight of Carfulenus up ahead with a century of men, almost at the ramparts of the enemy camp. Fronto paused for breath, the slope here surprisingly steep, and looked around. The main fleeing enemy force had started to change direction. With the Sixth now pressing up the slope for the fortress, the bulk of the escaping army had turned away from this fresh threat and were racing away to the west. Many had discarded their arms and shields to allow for greater speed in flight. Others had stopped, and were surrendering. Despite the legions' battle fury, they were being well restrained by their centurions and optios, and were allowing the enemy to surrender without too many needless killings. Small groups of legionaries here and there were already guarding units of prisoners.

That left only the few reserve cohorts atop the fortress, along with the fleeing king and his horse guard, and a few of the panicked routing flankers, who were largely unarmed. The quality of those men now facing them was clear from the fact that Carfulenus did not seem to be having too much trouble climbing the walls with his men.

Fronto swallowed a little bile from the climb, took another deep breath that smelled of blood and sizzling dust, and began to ascend once more. Slowly, the ground began to even out, the slope less pronounced, and finally he reached the defences. Legionaries from the Sixth were still arriving, for they had been strung out along the flank. The walls had once been quite strong, and had been rebuilt with speed and efficiency, but not with skill. Legionaries had reached the defences and had pulled out whole handfuls of mortar from between the stone blocks to make handholds, climbing it with every bit of the ease they had displayed at the mudbrick walls of the Pharos fort. The south gate had been blocked up with rubble, the side and rear gates left open for the king's force to use, but the rubble here had already been cleared down to almost head height by the legionaries.

Fronto made for the gate. Soldiers were already fighting the defending cohorts for control of the wall tops, and Carfulenus and the First Century were visible up there. They would soon seize the defences, Fronto was sure, but there was an element of time involved here. He needed to get to Pharnaces before the man could escape.

Briefly, he considered running to the fortress's west gate, which would be where the king himself had entered the defences, but apart from the additional distance and the time taken to get there, he could be sure of a specially warm welcome there from the defenders. They would certainly have concentrated there if that was where the king was.

Settling upon his path, he raced for the blocked south gate, facing the valley and the battlefield. The legionaries of the Sixth were fighting hard for ingress there, some of the men tussling with the defenders, swords and shields clattering and clanging as they fought hard. Others were trying to clear the blockage further, to make it more accessible, while their comrades held shields above them, holding off the enemy's desperate blows.

Fronto closed on the gate, watching as men continually pulled away huge stones, crumbling mortar puffing up in clouds into the dry heat. The enemy were warriors, not engineers. A Roman force would be horrified at the poor mix of the dry, weak mortar. He watched, tense, as the blockage shrank constantly. Finally, as he was starting to think about another access point, a legionary cried out in triumph and began to push his way through the gate, clambering up over the ruined stones. His mates tried to shield him. He fell to the defenders, two blades jammed into his sides, and the first man over the wall tumbled away out of sight. But the damage had been done.

The two men who had dispatched the legionary followed him into oblivion a moment later at the hands of angry Romans. Another legionary pulled his way up and over the destroyed blockage, this time finding better luck. An enemy warrior came for him but was quickly put down by the other attackers from the Sixth. He was in, and behind him two more legionaries pulled themselves up with one hand, sword in the other and shield discarded for the climb. The third man in took a spear thrust from somewhere and tumbled back down the slope, falling at Fronto's feet, but the access had been made, and men were now determined. Others pulled more stones out of the way, widening the aperture.

Fronto, acutely aware of the time slipping by, pushed his way forwards.

'Sir?' one of the legionaries said, surprised at the legate's presence.

'The king is escaping. With me.'

Ignoring the surprised stares of the legionaries, who hadn't realised their commander was present, he pushed past the man and grasped the stones in the gateway with his left hand, pulling himself up. As he tried to clamber up to the cleared opening, he cursed his weak knee and bit down on the pain as it sent him urgent messages that it was not happy with the climb. He forced the pain into the back of his mind, determined not to show weakness in front of the men, and hauled and pushed, trying not to pant and blow like an old man.

He pulled his way through into the fortress in the wake of another legionary and was suddenly in the thick of it once more. The men Pharnaces had left in charge of the camp did not seem to have succumbed to panic like their friends on the plain below. They had seen it all happening and had clearly been waiting in defence of their fortress and their king's banner.

Fronto fought to stand. A Bosporan swordsman in one of those bronze helms with the pointed peak and the embossed cheek plates came for him, blade chopping. Fronto ducked out of the way, ignoring the screaming pain in his knee, and responded with a blow of his own. The soldier caught and turned his strike, and in moments the two were locked in one-on-one combat.

For just a moment, Fronto wondered why the man's eyes kept flicking away to the camp's interior and, risking death for just a heartbeat, he glanced that way himself. In that instant, he saw the king and his horsemen at the banner and the large tent on the hill's summit, and he knew exactly what was happening. The king was about to leave. He'd gathered a sizeable force about him now, and the defenders at the walls were thinning out.

That was what was planned. The cohorts left to defend were dismounted cavalry, and were only expected to hold long enough for the king to get away. That was why the soldier kept looking that way. Any moment now the king would be gone, and every man in this fortress would abandon the defences, run for his horse and race for freedom.

Fronto fretted.

Galronus and the cavalry could have intercepted them, but they were back at the Roman camp, beyond the battle. They had not been fielded as no horse unit could fight effectively on a steep slope. They would never get this far in time to stop the king's horsemen, and would be entirely unaware of the whole thing, since it was taking place in the enemy camp, and they were undoubtedly planning to leave by the north gate, unseen by the main force below. Worst of all, Fronto's men were on foot and tired, while the king and his men would be on fresh, rested horses.

Fronto clenched his teeth. Hundreds of horsemen had gathered around the king. Fronto had hundreds of legionaries, but their chances were small. Still, they had to try.

With a grunt, he deflected another blow from the warrior with whom he had been locked in combat, and struck with speed, seeing a single opening. It was not a killing blow, and his sword struck armour, but it stunned and winded the man, and he had no time to recover before Fronto's shoulder hit him in the chest and he sailed from the top of the gate, falling into the murk below. Fronto looked this way and that, and spotted the green feathered crest of Carfulenus some way along the wall, already atop the parapet and guiding his men with gestures from his vine cane. Fronto cupped his hands around his mouth.

'Carfulenus!'

The centurion's head snapped towards him, and Fronto pointed at the crest of the hill.

'The king. We have to get the king.'

Carfulenus shook his head. Fronto stared in surprise. How dare the centurion refuse?

The man was also pointing towards that tent, though, and Fronto turned.

The king's banner was no longer visible, and even as he watched, the horsemen were moving. The entire force, probably nearing a thousand now, was racing for the north gate and freedom. The king had gone. And as Fronto felt the hope of finishing this draining away from him, he realised that every remaining defender had pulled back and was running for the horse he had tethered somewhere nearby.

Carfulenus had realised in an instant that they had no chance of catching the king. Indeed, they would be lucky to take down more than a few dozen of those remaining defenders fleeing the camp. Fronto straightened and lowered his blade, favouring the centurion with a nod of understanding and acceptance.

Pharnaces had escaped.

Still, Fronto reminded himself, they had won the battle. Against heavy odds, they had crushed the force of Pharnaces. Facing two to one odds, fighting on the enemy's home ground and having raced unexpected into battle, they had won. It was a victory to make even Pharsalus look laboured. Pharnaces might have got away with perhaps a thousand horse, but with the defeat of his army, that would see the end of the king's dreams of conquest and a new empire. He might yet be a thorn in Rome's side, but the threat he posed had now diminished almost to naught.

Fronto sighed and looked down.

Gods, but he needed a bath.

And a foot stool.

And a cup of wine.

EPILOGUE

Tarsus, Ides of September 47 BC

'Pharnaces could still cause further trouble, of course,' Hirtius noted, drumming his fingers on his folded arms.

Caesar shook his head. 'Pharnaces may have fled with a force of a thousand cavalry, but he lost control of near twenty thousand men at Zela. Most of those were allies or clients who had thrown the dice and joined him. Having lost the game, they will be unwilling to take part again and risk worse. Pharnaces no longer has sufficient military power to launch any kind of campaign, and Calvinus will pursue him now until the last power he has is destroyed. If he lives beyond the winter it will be as a petty king back in his Bosporian land, and even there his time is coming.'

The others nodded their agreement. Calvinus may have lost to Pharnaces once, but he would not let that happen again. After the astounding victory at Zela, Calvinus had been given command of all the forces barring the Sixth, with the veteran legate Caelius Vinicianus as his aide, and sent off to chase down the fleeing king. The last intelligence received suggested that the beleaguered Pharnaces had been trapped by Calvinus at Sinope on the north coast. There, he could not hold out for long. The would-be King of Pontus was done.

'This land is settled, I think, thanks in no small part to our courageous allies.'

Caesar gestured to the two men standing to his left, each surrounded by slaves and attendants.

'Deiotarus, friend of Rome and King of Galatia, will administer Pontus, and also Cappadocia until the senate agrees the appointment of client kings there in due course. New ties between Galatia and the republic should see trade flourish in the region.'

The king bowed his head. For his troubles, he had been given a transitory control of lands, but the benefits Galatia could reap in that time would be great. The king was more than satisfied.

'Mithridates, victor of the Nilus, I charge you with seizing control of Bosporus, leaving Pharnaces nowhere to flee.'

The prince of Pergamon nodded solemnly. He had been told to declare war, but the benefits of control of the Bosporus would grant him similar benefits to Deiotarus in Cappadocia. With Rome's backing, he would double his territory and more. He would be pleased.

'Thus,' Caesar smiled, 'is the region settled. Friends of Rome in control of every land. And between these two great kings and Calvinus in Syria, there will be nowhere for Pharnaces to run.'

'Then the east truly *is* at peace,' Nero said with an air of satisfaction.

'I believe so. The Sixth should by now be closing on Italia to recover and rest through the winter.'

Fronto smiled for a moment, remembering Carfulenus' face at the news. After three major campaigns in a row, in Greece, Aegyptus and Cappadocia, every man in the Sixth dreamt of warm food, a warm bed and a warm girl. And having been given, along with the other victorious legions, the pick of the loot from Pharnaces' camp, every last man had gone home with a stuffed purse to see him through the winter and beyond.

Fronto winced at that, though, and the smile slid from his face. It *seemed* like grand largesse to give the soldiers such loot, but he worried about the other legions back home. The knowledge that they had already had their noses put out of joint by Caesar's lavish triumph on the Nilus without them made him nervous. What would those legions say when the Sixth joined them with purses overflowing with gold from the latest campaign?

Caesar had deftly sidestepped his troubles with the senate, largely because of his ongoing popularity with both the people and the army. If the army started to take offence at him, though, then things could change.

'And, of course, Aegyptus is secure,' Brutus put in, earning a bitter look from Cassius.

'With the queen now in full control,' Caesar agreed, 'the land remains a bastion of strength in the east. Indeed, the legions there could now safely be withdrawn, I think. And that leads me to tidings that I feel I should share with you all before they become public and reach Rome.'

The officers gathered a touch closer. News was almost uniformly unpleasant these days, but Caesar's face was calm, suggesting good tidings for a change.

'Caesar?' Hirtius prompted.

The general leaned back, arms folded. 'A missive from the palace in Alexandria reached me this morning, sealed with the royal seal. The queen of Aegyptus has given birth to an heir.'

Fronto felt his teeth clench. The room underwent an odd change in atmosphere at this news. Some of the gathered dignitaries, in particular the two kings and Brutus, broke into smiles of genuine pleasure. Many officers seemed to struggle with how to accept the news, though, and Fronto watched smiles riveted over uncertainty. The tidings seemed, in particular, to sit badly with Cassius, whose face slipped into an expression of discontent.

'It will, I am sure, come as no surprise to any present to learn that the boy is a scion of our great line. The house of Ptolemy and the house of the Julii are joined by blood. The boy is to be named Ptolemy Philopator Philometor Caesar.'

Cassius could not prevent the disgusted curl of a lip. Caesar glanced in his direction and pretended not to notice, refusing to allow the sour expression to ruin his moment of triumph. Fronto plastered a smile across his face with the rest, while his mind raced. What Caesar saw as a boon could well turn into a millstone around his neck. The Roman people might not take well to their consul fathering a child with a foreign queen, tying himself to a royal house outside the republic. Moreover, the man had been slowly and steadily bringing his great nephew Octavian under his wing, treating the precocious young man as something of an heir and son. Fronto wondered what the extremely clever, and almost certainly ambitious, Octavian would make of being ousted in favour of a half-Aegyptian child.

And then there was Caesar's wife, of course. Calpurnia was unlikely to be thrilled by the news, despite her clear acceptance that the consul would always be a man for the ladies.

He shivered. The civil wars of the past few years, and the political turmoil that had underpinned them, might seem like children squabbling compared with what could begin to brew in the coming days.

'Tell me that you intend to return to Rome, Caesar.'

All eyes shifted from the consul to Cassius, who stood like some defiant stormcrow in the corner of the room. The shadow of a column fell in such a disconcerting way that it cast the man in gloom in an otherwise bright room, and that simple effect made Fronto shudder all over again.

'Cassius?' the consul said, an edge to his tone.

'Tell me, Caesar, that you do not intend to return to Aegyptus for the winter. That you will make for Rome with all haste and attempt to right the problems of the republic.'

Caesar frowned. 'Of course. This is not the season for war, but…'

Cassius shook his head and cut the general off. 'I am not talking about *war*, Caesar. The republic has had enough of war. Our enemies are crushed, and those men who remain opposed to you are Romans. Cato and his companions can be reasoned with. I *mean* that you need to return to Rome. Calm the legions. Restore the senate to order. Make overtures of peace and begin the healing process. You were made dictator in order to save the republic, not go to war with it, or to marry it to foreign queens.'

This last was dangerously close to the knife edge, and Fronto saw Caesar tense.

'You walk near to insult, Cassius.'

'I speak the plain truth, Caesar, without dissembling. Will you return to Rome and save the republic?'

The consul nodded. 'Rome is my priority, Cassius, but I will say without hesitation that no overture of peace to Africa will heal that rift. I will make an attempt, but I can guarantee that the coming year will see war with Cato's army.'

Cassius shook his head. 'Then that is not a war in which I will fight, Caesar. I will return to Rome with you and help in any way I can to heal the state, but I will no longer lead citizen against citizen.'

'That is your prerogative,' Caesar said, coldly, all traces of the good mood his tidings had brought now gone. The room felt suddenly awkward and cold.

'To Rome, then,' Fronto said with enforced brightness, trying to dispel the new icy aura of the meeting.

Aulus Hirtius cleared his throat, nodding at Fronto and picking up the thread, trying to lighten the mood once more. 'I have almost completed my chronicle of the campaign to be published back home, Consul, but Amantius begs for news already; for tidings he can give the senate and the people. Word of Zela and Pharnaces' defeat have not yet been announced at home, after all.'

Caesar turned slowly, having to tear his cold gaze from Cassius, and straightened to address Hirtius.

'Send Amantius a dispatch, then, ahead of our own arrival.' He reached down, drawing his pugio from his belt and slammed it into the map on the table, the point driving down through the campaign map there, pinning the location of his great victory as it stuck in the wood, reverberating as the consul let go.

They all stared at the knife vibrating over Zela.

'Tell him I came, I saw, and I conquered,' Caesar said.

The end.

HISTORICAL NOTE

I will first hold up my hands and say "Mea Culpa" over the first couple of chapters of this book. The detailed history of these events is relayed to us only primarily in Caesar's Civil War and the Alexandrian War, likely written by Aulus Hirtius. Hirtius is not my favourite writer. Caesar managed to convey in his earlier books a great vivid view of events that was nicely clear and workable. Hirtius takes ten times as many words to say half as much, and his detail is too cluttered to be very clear. Similarly, Caesar concentrates on certain events at the end of his Civil War and glosses over others with little detail.

At the end of book 11, I had the enemy fleet sailing back towards Alexandria and the army inbound. The entire first chapter here is my own invention. The harbour needs to have a fleet in it to be burned in chapter 3, and yet we are told that Caesar's fleet survives intact and that it is Egyptian ships that burn. Given that there was no real reason for that fleet to be in Alexandria previously, I'd had it out and sailing around. Consequently, I started this book with the issue of having to put the Egyptian fleet back in the harbour so it could be burned. That's what I did.

Similarly, we are told in Caesar's diary that "Achillas [...] was trying to occupy Alexandria except that part [...] Caesar held with his troops, though at the first assault he had endeavoured to burst into his house; but Caesar, placing cohorts about the streets, held his attack in check. And at the same time a battle was fought at the port, and this affair produced by far the most serious fighting."

399

Consequently I knew that the fighting in Alexandria's streets had to be bad, it had to be with appallingly unbalanced numbers, and it needed to fail, leaving them in control of only the small redoubt around the palace, another fight going on at the harbour. Given the inventiveness of Romans in siege situations, what I've portrayed is extrapolating from what has happened in similar situations throughout history but with a Caesarian slant. The pits into sewers etc was inspired by the events later in the story when Ganymedes cuts off and poisons the water. I think it worked, and I could only show a small slice of the action through Salvius' eyes, but I enjoyed it. Hope you did too.

As the war goes on, we are told by Caesar "These defences he increased on subsequent days so that they might take the place of a wall as a barrier against the foe" and by Hirtius "Meanwhile he daily strengthened his fortifications by new works; and such parts of the town as appeared less tenable were strengthened with testudos and mantelets". In truth, it is of Achillas' army that Hirtius is speaking when he says "They shut up all the avenues and passes by a triple wall built of square stones". I moved this to Caesar, justifying it quite reasonably with Hirtius' further comment "they so well copied what they saw done by us" to have Achillas building his own triple wall in a subsequent chapter. Mea Culpa once again.

There may be students of ancient Egypt reading who will bridle at where I have placed the Canopus Canal, passing the palace region and emptying into the Great Harbour nearby. Most maps you search will show the canal skirting the entire city and emptying into the western harbour. I found only one map showing it where I placed it, and used that as it suited my story. I will justify myself in two ways: firstly, the actual geography of the ancient city is scantily recorded and largely theoretical, and secondly the line of the canal shown on most maps is actually that of the Mahmoudiyah Canal constructed in 1817, and if this was the line of the ancient canal, it seems unlikely they would have to completely dig anew. Thus, the ancient canal likely vanished and is yet to be identified under Alexandria's streets. I am unrepentant therefore in my placing of it.

With Caesar's maritime expedition for water and to gather his relief legion, accounts are vague. How the legion actually reaches the city is never explained. Caesar learns the legion is kept away by the winds, sails his ships out to get water with no men on board, then battles those same winds to get back, and at some point thereafter the 37th is in the city. I have combined the two events following a suggestion by Luciano Canfora in his book on Caesar (this is also the book from which I have drawn my dates.) Hirtius' writing says that Caesar gets his water at a part of the coast called Chersonesus. The nearest part of the coast that bears a name of that derivation is near Benghazi in Libya, some 400 miles away and more than a third of the way back to Rome. As such, I suggest this is utter rubbish. Likely Hirtius is referring to some minor location much closer of which no other record survives. Caesar wouldn't sail his entire fleet 400 miles away in search of water. As such I have had these events happen around El-Alamein, 60 miles away and on the very edge of the farmable area of Egyptian coastline. Anything further is madness.

For the record, in case purists are standing there with a copy of Canfora's book open to the timeline for Caesar, I have shuffled and conflated the events of the naval battle and the attack on Pharos. In the timeline they are much more spread out over time. I have shuffled them together for the sake of tension and immediacy. This is one of those moments with the emphasis on the second word in 'Historical fiction'. Mind you, the events follow the text, just not quite the timing.

The battle of the Heptastadion mole is one of the most complex sequences of action in any of Caesarian history. As such, I have cut through the narrative, marked where people were and when, taken the main actions and portrayed them in the clearest manner I could, attempting to give better reasoning to the decisions made. As such, for instance, the disaster on the ships that led to sinkings and Caesar's swim I turned from them attacking Egyptians on the Heptastadion, and driving off ships, to dealing with land units in the harbour. The result is the same, and the sequence for the reader makes a lot more sense. In some ways what I have done with the main fighting in this battle is to make the disaster an Aegyptian achievement rather than a Roman mistake.

As to the changes in Egyptian command, I have somewhat chosen my own path for this book. What is generally agreed upon is that the king had initially commanded with Achillas. He had gone to the palace and become Caesar's hostage. Achillas then prosecuted the war in his name. Later, Arsinoë sneaks out of the palace with Ganymedes and takes control of the army, executing Achillas. There is then a complete change in the way the war goes. So far, so good. This I have replicated from the sources.

The real question is what happens when the king is then released. In Hirtius' Alexandrian War he has Ptolemy beg not to send him back. There is no mention of what happens to Ganymedes or Arsinoë, though they both appear to be with the enemy until the end, when Ptolemy dies, for Hirtius says they are captured and taken away from Egypt. Though the king is named as commanding throughout this time, clearly Ganymedes and Arsinoë were still present.

Florus, writing a century and a half later, has Ganymedes die in the chaotic flight after the battle in the delta. His only mention of Arsinoë is that she is paraded in Caesar's triumph. Cassius Dio has Ganymedes being the one deciding to execute Achillas. Dio also has Ganymedes' subordinates being the ones asking for the king's return as they are sick of Ganymedes and Arsinoë. I decided against this, trusting less to this much later source than to the contemporary Hirtius despite his difficulties. It also seems unlikely that after the huge success Ganymedes had brought them in his time, they would turn on him so easily. Dio also does not note the fate of the pair after the king's return, and is of little use in that.

Thus I have filled in the gaps in Hirtius and satisfied the best I could from the sources by having Ganymedes still enjoying success, turning on the princess as they had previously done on Achillas, and then leading the army alongside the returned king to defeat in the delta. Having the general becoming strong and using Ptolemy as a figurehead while Arsinoë sulks in a tent works logically and for the plot, given the fact that Achillas had clearly done much the same.

In the texts we are told that Caesar is informed of Mithridates' approach and his victory at Pelusium and runs to join him. Ptolemy then sets off to race him. I have set these motivations the other way around, for Caesar is far too wily a creature to abandon his position of power in Alexandria and run off to an uncertain fate in the delta when he could remain where he was and wait for Mithridates to come to him, then be easily strong enough to wipe out his enemy. Only the relief army being threatened would likely drag Caesar from Alexandria. After all, he is more or less besieged there, and Alexandria remains of political import. The only reason to abandon it is if it is no longer under threat and the greater threat is elsewhere.

In the Marius' Mules series I have made every effort where possible to stay true to the sequence of events in Caesar's text, using outside sources like Florus or Plutarch or (in this book) Josephus only to add or clarify on events too important (or juicy) to ignore. This is the first book where significant parts of the action have been tweaked in ways, and I am content to pass the blame for that on to Aulus Hirtius. The complexity and often contradictory action in Hirtius's account makes it difficult to draw into a narrative. As examples of this I will cite two passages that deal with the war moving on to Pontus. Firstly, that Hirtius says (in the Loeb edition): "He then summoned all the states of this latter province to forgather at Tarsus [...] There he settled all the affairs of the province its neighbouring states" and then goes on to note that "his eagerness to set out and prosecute the war admitted no further delay". These two events side by side in the text do not seem to fit. Moreover, in the McDevitte and Bohn translation, we are told in even more contradictory terms: "Having thus settled the kingdom, he marched by land into Syria" and then later "sailed himself for Cilicia, with the fleet he had brought from Egypt." Barring the world's largest portage operation, someone had their wires crossed at the time of writing. This only goes to show how big a pinch of salt we must take with Hirtius' writings. Oh woe is me, Caesar, that you farmed out your latter works to a poor second.

Add to this that Hirtius is clearly trying to 'big up' his boss in a way that even Caesar didn't do, and you discover that Hirtius concentrates at times too heavily on motive and blame than on the actual events, so the reader ends up with gaping holes, missing information and hurried accounts punctuated by long passages of very little use for the reworker of the tale.

So I have, as you now know, taken the events, the people and the sequence and made them work as a timeline, squeezing and pushing events into place where they need to be and cutting to the chase in order to nail my particular sequence down. It is the only way the Alexandrian War makes common sense. Upon completion of this book, I now understand why almost all academic works on Caesar devote as little time, space and effort as possible to these few crucial months.

Another point upon which I diverged from the sources is the death of Ptolemy. Upon fleeing the fortress, we are told by Hirtius "It is ascertained that the king escaped from the camp, and was received on board a ship; but by the crowd that followed him, the ship in which he fled was overloaded and sunk." This suggests that this was only a report. As such I chose to give him a slightly different end, partially because I feel he deserved it, but also because by now in this tale I was getting sick of ships sinking under the weight of survivors. It had already happened to Caesar. And in a recent book I wrote with Gordon Doherty an emperor died when a bridge collapsed under the weight of men, something that happens in yet another book I am working on. So quite simply I saved you from repetitive endings. And fed a crocodile.

Decimus Carfulenus is mentioned only peripherally in the tale. He leads the attack on the south wall, as I have reported. He must have been from a plebeian family, for he is later appointed a tribune of the plebs. His family are attested in Aquileia. That made it ever so nice to tie together. A poor soldier from the swampy regions of Veneto leading an attack through a swamp? Perfect.

Finally, I have conflated the events leading up to the battle of Zela. The original texts diverge for some time telling us what is happening of import all over the Roman world and then take up with Caesar again as he reaches Syria. We are then treated to an odd stop-start journey through the east where Caesar alternately spends time doing local administration and waiting, then rushing off at speed because he has somewhere to be, until finally he hooks up with Deiotarus and then meets Pharnaces to end the tale with one of those Caesarian phrases that has come down through the centuries as a classic quote. I have cut through the bulk of this and taken us almost straight from reaching Syria, through a few brief scenes, into Zela. In the grand scheme of things, the events of the east after Alexandria are peripheral to my main story, and I might have skipped them entirely were it not for the Veni Vidi Vici element. That, and the fact that I love Deiotarus. His personal army was so closely modelled on the Roman system that when he died without issue in the time of Augustus and willed his entire kingdom to Rome as a province, the army was immediately incorporated into Rome's forces as the legion XXII Deiotariana. Thus their last king's name lived on in glory. I have a soft spot for he and his people.

For the record, my favourite part of the research for this book was working out how long it took the chariots to move one hundred paces at Zela. Assuming somewhere around the 25km/h speed for a charging chariot, working that into miles and then paces, then using the paces/hr measurement to work out how long it took to move 200 paces, then converting that from hours to heartbeats. Fascinating stuff, if a little 'mathsy' for me.

One thing that will probably not have escaped the astute Roman historians among you, and I hope this comes as no spoiler to any of you, is the sense in this book that we are building to a certain conclusion. It has been my stated goal since the early days of the series to conclude the entire arc on book 15, which will detail the events of 44BC. We are therefore but three years (and three books) from the end. If anyone has no idea what happens of import in 44BC, best stop reading here.

Certain names begin to crop up now of import. Names that have come down to us through history partially through the efforts of Mr Shakespeare. Cassius. Brutus. Galba. Casca. Trebonius. The end times are coming, and things are beginning to change. And with my, I think, less than flattering portrayal of Cleopatra, I hope you feel, like me, that there is a little something of the Yoko Ono effect with Cleopatra and Caesar. He may have had his enemies before Alexandria, but that particular woman's influence (even if accidentally) seems to trigger the slide from Caesar's high point into that dreadful chasm that ends it all on the steps of Pompey's theatre.

For now, I'll leave it here. The civil war is finally almost over. A few of Caesar's detractors continue to defy him in the west, and that tale will come next.

Fronto will be back next year, leading the war in Africa.

Veni, Vidi, Scripsi

Simon Turney, June 2019

If you enjoyed Marius' Mules XII, please do leave a review online, and also checkout other books by the same author and others in the genre:

Praetorian: The Great Game

By S.J.A. Turney

Promoted to the elite Praetorian Guard in the thick of battle, a young legionary is thrust into a seedy world of imperial politics and corruption. Tasked with uncovering a plot against the newly-crowned emperor Commodus, his mission takes him from the cold Danubian border all the way to the heart of Rome, the villa of the emperor's scheming sister, and the great Colosseum.

What seems a straightforward, if terrifying, assignment soon descends into Machiavellian treachery and peril as everything in which young Rufinus trusts and believes is called into question and he faces warring commanders, Sarmatian cannibals, vicious dogs, mercenary killers and even a clandestine Imperial agent. In a race against time to save the Emperor, Rufinus will be introduced, willing or not, to the great game.

"Entertaining, exciting and beautifully researched" - Douglas Jackson

"From the Legion to the Guard, from battles to the deep intrigue of court, Praetorian: The Great Game is packed with great characters, wonderfully researched locations and a powerful plot." - Robin Carter

The Damned Emperors: Caligula

By Simon Turney

'An engrossing new spin on a well-known tale' Antonia Senior, *The Times*

'Caligula as you've never seen him before! A powerfully moving read from one of the best ancient world authors in the business' Kate Quinn, author of *The Alice Network*

Everyone knows his name.
Everyone *thinks* they know his story.

Rome 37AD. The emperor is dying. No-one knows how long he has left. The power struggle has begun.

When the ailing Tiberius thrusts Caligula's family into the imperial succession in a bid to restore order, he will change the fate of the empire and create one of history's most infamous tyrants, Caligula.
But was he *really* a monster?

Forget everything you think you know. Let Livilla, Caligula's youngest sister and confidante, tell you what really happened. How her quiet, caring brother became the most powerful man on earth. And how, with lies, murder and betrayal, Rome was changed for ever . . .

'**A truly different take on one of history's villains** . . . All through this **I am seeing Al Pacino in *The Godfather***, slowly stained darker and darker by power and blood' Robert Low, author of The Oathsworn series

'**Enthralling and original, brutal and lyrical by turns.** With powerful imagery and carefully considered history Simon Turney provides a credible alternative to the Caligula myth that **will have the reader questioning everything they believe they know about the period**' Anthony Riches, author of the Empire series

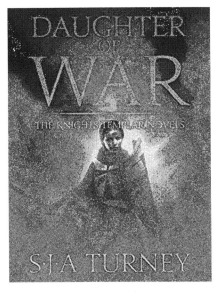

Templar: Daughter of War

By S.J.A. Turney

Europe is aflame. On the Iberian Peninsula the wars of the Reconquista rage across Aragon and Castile. Once again, the Moors are gaining the upper hand. Christendom is divided.

Amidst the chaos is a young knight: **Arnau of Vallbona**. After his Lord is killed in an act of treachery, Arnau pledges to look after his daughter, whose life is now at risk. But in protecting her Arnau will face terrible challenges, and enter a world of Templars, steely knights and visceral combat he could never have imagined.

She in turn will find a new destiny with the Knights as a daughter of war… Can she survive? And can Arnau find his destiny?

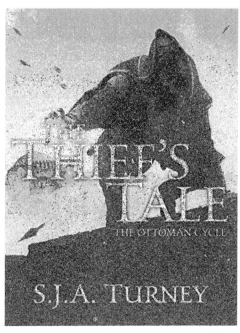

The Thief's Tale

By S.J.A. Turney

Istanbul, 1481: The once great city of Constantine, a strange mix of Christians, Turks and Jews, now forms the heart of the Ottoman empire. The conquest, still a recent memory, means emotions run high; danger is never far away.

Skiouros and **Lykaion**, sons of a Greek farmer, are conscripted into the infamous Janissary guards and taken to Istanbul. As Skiouros escapes into the Greek quarter, Lykaion remains with the slave chain, becomes an Islamic convert and guards the Imperial palace.

But one fateful day Skiouros picks the wrong pocket and begins to unravel a plot reaching to the highest peaks of Imperial power. He and his brother are left with the most difficult decision faced by a conquered Greek: is the rule of the Ottoman Sultan is worth saving?

Empires of Bronze:

Son of Ishtar

By Gordon Doherty

Four sons. One throne. A world on the precipice.

1315 BC: Tensions soar between the great powers of the Late Bronze Age. The Hittites stand toe-to-toe with Egypt, Assyria and Mycenaean Ahhiyawa, and war seems inevitable. More, the fierce Kaskan tribes – age-old enemies of the Hittites – amass at the northern borders.

When Prince Hattu is born, it should be a rare joyous moment for all the Hittite people. But when the Goddess Ishtar comes to King Mursili in a dream, she warns that the boy is no blessing, telling of a dark future where he will stain Mursili's throne with blood and bring destruction upon the world.

Thus, Hattu endures a solitary boyhood in the shadow of his siblings, spurned by his father and shunned by the Hittite people. But when the Kaskans invade, Hattu is drawn into the fray. It is a savage journey in which he strives to show his worth and valour. Yet with his every step, the shadow of Ishtar's prophecy darkens…

The New Achilles

By Christian Cameron

Alexanor is a man who has seen too much blood. He has left the sword behind him to become a healer in the greatest sanctuary in Greece, turning his back on war.

But war has followed him to his refuge at Epidauros, and now a battle to end the freedom of Greece is all around him. The Mediterranean superpowers of Rome, Egypt and Macedon are waging their proxy wars on Hellenic soil, turning Greek farmers into slaves and mercenaries.

When wounded soldier Philopoemen is carried into his temple, Alexanor believes the man's wounds are mortal but that he is not destined to die. Because he knows Philopoemen will become Greece's champion. Its last hero. The new Achilles.

In Christian Cameron's latest historical novel the old orders of the world begin to fall apart as Rome rises to supremacy - and Greece struggles to survive. Perfect for readers of Conn Iggulden, Ben Kane, Harry Sidebottom and Simon Turney.

Printed in Great Britain
by Amazon

57171365R00255